WITCHES,
STITCHES &
BITCHES

Published by Evil Girlfriend Media, P.O. BOX 3856, Federal Way, WA 98063
Copyright © 2013

Cover photo by Igorigorevich, courtesy of Dreamstime.
Photo manipulation by Mark Ferrari. Cover design by Matt Youngmark.

ISBN: 978-1-940154-01-5

Dedicated to all who've been called

a bitch for being assertive,

a witch for being weird,

and for those who still keep it stitched together

in the end

TABLE OF CONTENTS

INTRODUCTION

A witch, a stitch, and a bitch: three simple words, conveying a world of meanings. All of them, as it happens, so very *female*.

Witches are scary, warty old women in league with the Devil, bent cackling over their cauldrons as they brew up some terrible poison from toads' blood... or they are pagan lovers of Mother Earth, seeking to counter the excesses of the modern industrial world... or they are seductresses, forever young, forever casting their spells on unwary men... or perhaps they are confused teenage girls just experimenting with their own power. Sometimes a witch doesn't know she is one until magic comes tumbling out of her at a time of need; sometimes she has carefully studied and practiced her art.

Stitches are women's work: sewing, knitting, embroidering. Stitches create something new out of disparate pieces; stitches draw together what has been torn asunder, whether fabric or flesh. They heal, they repair. Stitching is small work, precise work, delicate. Even beautiful, at times.

And bitches? The very epitome of female. She's a sharp-tongued, cruel woman; she's your ex-wife; or that mean girl who called you fat in the seventh grade; or your boss at that awful job; or any woman exerting a bit of power that a man (and it's usually a man) doesn't like. Or, of course, a female dog. It's an insult to call a woman a bitch, unless she calls herself one, owning it. Even so, it's an uncomfortable term, prickly and a bit shocking. Not polite.

ᙡ

The sixteen stories collected here range from light to dark, fun to disturbingly spooky, and everything in between. We have retellings of fairy tales, modern edgy fantasies, stories of delicious revenge. We have romance, and some broken hearts. We even have a few tales by male authors, just to be inclusive.

I hope you enjoy reading them as much as I enjoyed collecting and editing them.

Shannon Page, Editor
Portland, Oregon
June 25, 2013

Blood Magic

by Gabrielle Harbowy

The night held its breath; all was still in the castle, and particularly in the little room in Aya's narrow tower.

Only after the footsteps had faded away down the stone steps and, a five-count later, the tower door opened and whumped quietly shut—more a shift of air than a real sound—did the night breathe again. It was a slow, tentative exhale, like a flock of birds gradually testing their voices again after a troop of horsemen thunder past. And only after that did Aya let out her own sore sigh.

Breathing hurt. It always did, one way or another, after Master Merrin was through with her. He had been distracted tonight, and accidentally gentle because of it; his mind, she suspected, still full of the meeting of her father's council. But still he had held her firmly, bracing his muscles against her body's wish to flee. Her throat hurt and her jaw ached, as if her teeth had forgotten quite how to fit against each other. Her lips were sore and cracked, but it was a lesser hurt, as these things went, than the hurt when he turned her over and made as if to split her up the middle.

Unlike that ache, this one would pass somewhere in the hours between now and morning. It was only the essence of him on her tongue that would still be lingering when the songbirds greeted the new day; it would take more than the flavor of strong tea and summer stonefruits to chase it away.

Aya sat up carefully, dangling one foot off the edge of the bed, then both, and then took a careful hop to the ground that bypassed the thickly woven rug. The stone floor should have felt cold under her bare feet, she was almost hopeful that it would, but in truth she felt very little these days. She lived in the numb place, where the things that happened to her body did not affect her so much as they otherwise might. As a result, the chill of the floor was muted, distant. She recalled a ghost of the memory of what cold felt like, as if it were a thing she could imagine only because someone had described it to her. Her toes tingled in some strange sort of body-sympathy for the telling.

Across the chamber, a second set of stairs curved upwards to the sitting room at the top of Aya's tower. It was here that her numb and halting feet now carried her. Several of the steps had false tops, stone lids that she had painstakingly chiseled to fit perfectly over hollow-carved centers, and in these she hid the most prized of her belongings—the things that were not for the eyes of the chambermaids or the governesses or the other young ladies of the court who were invited often, but never by Aya herself, to bring their needlecrafts to the little round chamber where she sought only solitude.

Slowly, as if through water, her distant-feeling hands prised the lid from the fifth step and set it carefully upturned on the sixth. Wrapped in torn cheesecloth, a slender bundle lay where she had wedged it the night before.

One by one, Aya drew the items from their careful wrappings: the stone, the brooch with the thick, sharp pin on its backing, the wicked-looking scalpel she had palmed from the chirurgeon, should the pin not prove sharp enough. She inspected them in the silvery moonlight that now peeked through the high, narrow window and spilled thinly across her hands. The moon had averted its eyes while Merrin was in the chamber, had cast his acts into darkness; now it drifted back, seeing if it was indeed safe to shine into the room again.

The pin was sufficient. In the moonlight, Aya's blood beaded black and slick at her fingertip. She squeezed the pad of her thumb to enlarge the quivering sphere, and when it was of a size that she knew would soon break and spill, she pressed it to the dimple in the smooth, sandy stone.

The stone soaked up her blood—evidence enough of magic. But it remained unchanged for the sacrifice she gave it. Nothing happened.

Nor had it the previous night, or the night before. Her virgin blood, the spellcrone had been quite particular, was to be applied to this stone. It would, the crone swore with her hands full of the jewels of a princess's birthright, unlock a rebirth that would be the end to Aya's torment.

Oh, for certain, she could leave the tower anytime, and none would stop her longer than to ask if she wanted her maidservants burdened with a basket for her lunch or dinner, or whether she would rather the saddle or the carriage. But the whole kingdom was her father's, and Master Merrin served at her father's whim, utterly faithfully, too faithfully for his loyalty to be questioned... save in one detail where the spirit of the law was more appealing to him than the letter—namely, Aya. His responsibility for Aya's learning, and her suitability for marriage.

Unfelt chill was beginning to seep in through the bare soles of her feet and the thinness of her nightshirt. Aya shivered. She was still not cold, but the ghost of cold had walked through her. She pressed her thumb harder to the thumb-shaped dimple. The blood was gone, into the stone, but she felt unchanged. Would it prevent a visit the next night? It had not worked yet, but perhaps she had not bled enough. She could do nothing but believe that the fault lay with her and not with the inert rock. The spellcrone had taken a lock of her hair the week before, and Aya had the crone's word that the stone had been enchanted. That it took the blood was proof of its magic.

Virgin blood, the crone had insisted. Merrin was still mindful of keeping her intact for the eventual marriage for which he was supposed to be safeguarding her. But she suspected his power of will would not outlast her youth. Already he seemed to be growing bored with the same few diversions, finding new and terrible and closer ways to skirt her ruin, and his own. She needed that virtue unspoiled in order to come of age a proper lady and gain her seat on the council. Royal women never used that privilege, but Aya would. She would break the silence expected of women and make her father understand the failings of his rule, the sufferings of his people. She would do all these things once she was betrothed and had a voice his ear could hear.

But only if her blood was still virgin. Only if Master Merrin remained satisfied with lesser torments. If he took her, if he spoiled her, then the enchantment wouldn't work at all. The stone would probably reject her blood then, possibly even mock it, or sting the pad of her thumb, and there would never be a council seat, or a voice.

It would work. It had to work. Perhaps... perhaps, somehow, it just hadn't had enough yet. Perhaps it needed filling until the lacy beige stone turned red with her; until she had poured so much of herself into the stone that she *became* it, hard and impervious, and left her own weak and yielding softness behind.

It would work, and soon.

But for now, the stone remained stone and Aya remained flesh. Visits continued, and between them the empty days, during which she tried to pour some measure of care for minor wastework like embroidery into the used and vacant, unfeeling husk of her body. She put finger after finger to the stone while her blood was still innocent, praying for it to catch somehow in the little pebble's depths and trigger some inclusion of crystal that would release her. It did not happen. Or at least, it had not happened yet. But knowing that it might be soon now, so very soon, gave her strength to endure him, and bleed, and shuffle dazed through another day, barely touching the world around her.

Miss Finch had been Aya's governess as far back as Aya could remember. She had been governess to Aya's aunts before her, and that difficult quintet had trained her to develop an eagle's eye and a sparrow's sensitivity to the slightest detail out of place.

When Aya's father had come along, finally a male to secure the succession, he had received his own tutors and caregivers. But then the sisters had only become more dangerous, bitter and vengeful and each brewing her own schemes to exterminate the pest who ate away with steady nibbles at the attention and power that had first been theirs. Such experience herding the acidic princesses had likely also been responsible for the way Miss Finch spoke the titles of her masters and mistresses with a slightly hard edge that always sounded brushed with sarcasm. Yet, knowing her aunts, Aya could not blame the woman for it, either. It had always sounded to Aya, since she was very young, as though the governess used honorifics as a cruelly-hooked instrument to suggest she found the bearers too tedious or dull-witted to be worthy of their titles. Aya was always surprised when others seemed not to notice.

Thus, when Miss Finch came round behind Aya while she was practicing her calligraphy and said, "Suddenly clumsy at needlework, Highness?" it was not completely unexpected. Her fingers were in an obvious state from all the pricking, and a lack of appetite meant a paling of her complexion, from its usual ruddy olive to something more ashen.

"There is a draft in the top tower room," Aya answered woodenly, though a damp, anxious tingle squirmed along her spine. Miss Finch answered directly to Master Merrin. "I have always been clumsy at needlework, but with the chill, I cannot feel the needle until it has pierced me." She tucked her thumbs in self-consciously, on both the hand holding the parchment steady and the hand with the fine-tipped brush.

Etiquette demanded that a lady did not snort; what Miss Finch made, therefore, was rather a hawk-like *kik* of skeptical disapproval in her sinuses. And rightly so. Such slender jabs would not bring such bruising, nor such scabs, nor on so many fingers. Aya had worked at squeezing out her blood, and she knew that it showed.

Miss Finch paced two more precise circuits around Aya and the small table, hands folded into her sleeves. "We must protect my lady's health," she decided when she was once again behind her. "Your needles will be dulled."

Dulled needles were what little girls used, with safe, rounded points that were unable to prick the skin—or the canvas. It would make pushing the thin slivers through cloth that much more painful on her wounded fingertips, but Aya found herself almost looking forward to the pain. It would be nice to feel something through her numbness. Even that.

Master Merrin seemed more gaunt tonight, his scything shoulders more prominent. He had a dry cough and a grating sneer, and he handled Aya more roughly, as though he were using her to vent his frustrations with another member of the council. Or perhaps he knew. Bleeding into the stone was the key to a rebirth, the spellcrone had said. Perhaps his rebirth had begun.

She hoped he would be born into something that could not harm her. Otherwise, she thought, she would be forced to regret the whole exercise: the bleeding, the lying about her fingers and the painful needlework, the frivolous squandering of her jewels. But she trusted the spellcrone at least this far. There was no sense in turning a predator into something even *more* predatory, was there? If the crone had meant him to be able to do Aya harm, she could have spared herself the work and the enchantment, and just pocketed Aya's jewels and left things all alone.

Yes, she would just have to trust that he was turning into something less harmful. Yet, clearly there were intermediate stages. Perhaps he'd somehow connected his incremental changes to her, and was punishing her for her feeble attempt at revenge.

He pushed her over onto her belly with a growl. Had he always made such noises, or was some beast of the enchantment's devising breaking through his skin? She was paranoid now, so concerned with trying to recall the minute differences in something she preferred to block out entirely, that she only returned to the moment when she felt a new kind of white-hot lance of pain stab up her spine.

He knew her virtue had to be preserved; he knew it as well as she. But no, he held her fast, snarling angry words she rarely gave him cause to say to her, and made clear his intent to visit himself upon that place—that secret, sacred seat of maidenhood. And above knowing that it was forbidden and improper and would strangle any chance she had in royal society; above all that, she knew that if he did this, committed this final insult upon her body, that her chances with the enchantment in the stone lay as ruined as she herself would be. It was that knowledge, that fear, which fueled her struggles, against his gruff and angry admonishments for her to be good and lay still and how she dare not summon anyone from the hallway lest her fate be far worse than simple pain and mess.

Still she panicked, so he struck. He hit the back of her head with something harder than his palm—an elbow, perhaps, she thought through the sudden sluggishness of rattled wits, or a book from her bedstand, or her candleholder. She was uncertain, but could only reflect, with an odd sort of clarity, on the fact that she had brought the blow upon herself.

And she could also see now that the rebirth was already working. That was what had started this whole thing, tonight, wasn't it? He could feel himself changing and wanted to complete his betrayal while he still could.

She slumped beneath him, wetting the pillow with her tears and using the sodden down to smother her cries. Oh, but it did hurt. It was like a spreading, burning that stabbed in the deepest part of her, in places she'd not have thought it possible to reach, made worse in distinct blooms of searing pain with each of Master Merrin's agitations. But she could let him have this, now, because she accepted that the stone had worked. She could return to the numb place where she felt no pain. She could let him do this to her body, and wait complacently for it to be over.

Aya shifted onto her side and cupped her hand to the pain, feeling its loud echoes through her body the same way the loud echoes of angry footfalls and the closing door still whumped in her ears. The moon peeked back in from around the windowsill with such a slowness, seeming to offer an apology for hiding away from the thing Master Merrin had done. She accepted its silver glow over her body. It was all right, she told the moon. She had hidden away, too.

It hurt to wriggle off the high bed, but the numbing cool of the stone floor seeped up through her legs, replenishing her own numbness in a way that was almost refreshing. Her fingers were clumsy on the lid to the fifth stair, and on the wrappings that housed her little stone and her sharp things. She already had the stone clutched in her hand before she noticed the mess on the cloth. It was smeared with dark sticky streaks that hadn't been there when she had put it away the night before, and her stomach—so recently jostled out of true—lurched again. Had someone else been here and found this?

But when she turned her hands over in the moonlight, she saw that same sticky darkness clinging to her. It was only her own blood. She knew that he had hurt her, but she felt a distant ripple of something like surprise to realize she had actually bled from him.

Aya set the cloth aside and let the stone spill into her palm. It sparked inside, with little inclusions of golden light like the citrines of her father's chain of office when he turned them for her in the sunlight. Surprised, Aya dropped it with a clatter that made her stomach lurch toward her throat. But if no one had heard Master Merrin's growls, surely no one heard the faint tink of a pebble rattling onto stone.

Curiously, it retained its light, where it lay.

Was it shining because it knew his transformation had begun?

Aya reached for the stone, but hesitated and looked to her hands again. Blood was blood, wasn't it? Perhaps not when it came to magic. Slowly, eyes fixed on the faint glow lest it fade away without warning, she slipped careful fingers beneath her nightshirt and brought them out from between her thighs, slippery and dark. She transferred the pebble into her slick hand and curled her fingers around it. It flared to light like a bright little beacon at her touch. The light was her blood, sinking into the stone as before, but now leaving glowing trails in its path.

She laughed aloud. The spellcrone had spoken truth. Not her virgin blood; her *virgin blood*. All the while she had been racing to feed the stone, to fill it while she still had her purity, she had been guarding herself against the very thing that it required.

She clasped the little rock to her, curled up, and pressed her cheek to the stair. It was cool, so cool, filling her not with numbness but with starlight and potential, soothing the aches of her sore bottom and womanhood where she sat. She slept there, savoring the cold, her slender, bloodied hands clutching her glowing stone over her heart through the thin nightdress.

When the moon finally slumbered and the sun peeked over the window ledge in its turn, it shone upon a little songbird, with feathers deep bronze in the new light and wingtips gilded red, beak sheltered cozily in her wingfeathers and body puffed gently in sleep. She greeted the dawn with a curious cant of her head and working of her little beak, stretching her wings and loosening them with a couple of graceful flaps. Then, clutching a glowing golden stone in the curve of one talon, she fluttered out the window without a glance back.

URGENT CARE

BY CHRISTINE MORGAN

Once upon a time, there was a little girl whose dumbass big brother got mixed up in an occult gang war.

The details, she'd pieced together over the years. Not that those details mattered much, not to her. Her memories of that other life, that early life, were vague... glimpses, flickers and impressions... half-remembered voices to go along with half-remembered faces and places.

They'd had a dog. Her room was yellow, so yellow and cheery and bright. Their house was big. It had a green yard lined with trees. Daddy wore a blue uniform and built things in the garage. Mommy read lots of books. The new baby cried a lot and was stinky.

And there was Mr. Deadface.

Except, there wasn't Mr. Deadface. There had only been her dumbass big brother, who thought it would be funny to hide in little Laura's closet, wearing the new gang mask he was so proud of, and creep out and scare her so bad that she almost wet the bed.

Their parents had been furious.

A few nights later, it hadn't mattered anymore, because their parents were dead.

So was her dumbass big brother, and so was the stinky baby who cried a lot.

So was the family dog.

As far as the rest of the world knew, little Laura died right there with them.

The spell-wards woke her the instant someone opened the gate. She sat up, fully alert, reaching to brush her fingertips across the top of the clock on her bedside table. A soft voice from it informed her that it was 1:07 AM.

Lovely. Another middle-of-the-night emergency.

She threw back the quilt and swung her legs out. Since she slept in simple cotton scrubs, all she had to do was tuck her feet into the slippers waiting on the rug. As soon as she rose from the mattress, Grimalkin moved to curl up in the just-vacated warm spot, rumbling a loud, smug purr.

Her second-floor living area consisted of a sitting room, a kitchenette, the bedroom and a tiny bathroom. Needing no light, she made her way by familiarity of long habit to the door on the landing at the top of the stairs.

As quaint and cottage-cozy as her private quarters were furnished, the ground floor was all business. She padded down the steps, avoiding the creaks, hearing someone outside.

A heavy, burdened tread clumped on the porch. A male voice spoke, the words too muffled to make out, but the tone one of worry and concern masquerading beneath reassurance… a "hang in there, just a few more minutes, you're going to be fine" hearty encouragement kind of tone.

The first knock had no sooner fallen than she turned the deadbolt and opened the door. Her initial assumption—sick kid, panicky parents, urgent care, couldn't wait until proper civilized hours—vanished as she inhaled the thick smell of blood tinged with gunpowder.

"Need some help, he's hurt," the male voice said.

A second voice groaned, then wheezed in a way that threatened to turn into a gurgling cough. The sound of it told her this was a bad one, and time would not be on her side. Slow, fat drips splatted on the mat.

"In here," she said. "This way."

"It's pitch dark; I can't see a damn thing."

She slapped at wall-switches as she led them through the lobby and into the home surgery. The drips splatted onto industrial linoleum now, the clumping boot-steps and labored wheezes of breath seeming to echo in the more confined and enclosed space, where the scent of antiseptic predominated.

"Put him on the table," she said as she made for the sink.

"You're Larrah?" the man asked, once he'd done as she instructed. "The doctor?"

"I'm Larrah, the closest you're going to get to a doctor." Scrubbed up and gloved up, she turned around.

As usual, this elicited a startled pause. She could almost feel the man's gaze sweeping over her—chalky complexion, black hair liberally salted with premature white, slight stature and slim frame—but always returning with unease to her face.

"You're blind?"

"What gave it away?"

Without waiting for a reply, she went to the table.

It was her eyes, of course. Or her lack thereof; the discolored lids sunken and perpetually sealed shut, skin grown together over hollowed sockets. That was what gave it away.

She could, and sometimes did, conceal them behind dark glasses when she needed to go out of town. The only reason to do it here at home would be to spare others the awkwardness and unease of having to see her disfigurement.

To which she reasoned, screw them, that was their problem, not hers. If they felt guilty or uncomfortable, too bad.

A word and a gesture brought the witch-sight to her so that she could examine her patient.

Then it was her turn to pause.

Not for long. She didn't have time to. She quickly worked a stabilizing spell, then an incantation of anesthesia.

A gunshot wound was what she'd expected.

She was no stranger to gunshot wounds, of course. Even here, far from a big city. Some patients preferred the discretion of her less orthodox care, and a real doctor or hospital would be obligated to report such injuries to the authorities.

Devil's Cape—come for the quaint coastal New England charm, stay for the seemingly random rashes of madness and violence.

This was no gunshot wound.

But it was nonetheless obvious why they'd come to her.

Couldn't very well call for an ambulance or take someone into an emergency room with a giant damn claw sticking out of his chest.

Curses, hexes, inexplicable illnesses, magical mishaps, hauntings, possessions, attacks by supernatural creatures... 'questions better left unanswered' and things that people were reluctant to take to the authorities made up a large part of her practice.

Giant damn claws definitely fell into that category.

"Wait in the lobby if you want," she said, as she cut rapidly through the patient's shirt with surgical snips.

"I'll stay," the other man said.

"Gonna be messy."

"I'll stay!" he repeated. "Will he make it?"

"Maybe."

Not the response he'd been wanting, but, he could do the reassuring-and-encouraging tone all he liked. Larrah didn't mollycoddle or spew false hope. Even neighborhood regulars who'd been visiting the clinic for years remarked that she was... well, 'brusque,' to say the least. Bedside manner of a coroner, others said.

Or, according to the local children, so mean she didn't even give them a lollipop or sticker after they got a shot.

Tough. They could go see their pediatricians for that. If it gave her a bitchy reputation, so what? Better a bitch than a sow or a cow.

As for this guy, he was all the way under and couldn't hear her anyway. Why sugar-coat it?

She snipped open his plaid flannel shirt. He wore a Kevlar-type vest and undershirt beneath it, which hadn't done him much good. Snip-snip. Neither had the charm-bracelet cluster of protective amulets on a silver chain around his neck. That, she didn't snip but slipped over his head and set aside.

Traumatic impalement. The giant damn claw had gone in between two lower ribs, angled up. Pierced a lung. The only reason the man was still alive was because his friend had the presence of mind not to try and pull it out. If he'd done that, she wouldn't have a patient on her hands. She'd have a bled-out corpse.

Instead, the claw itself acted as a stopper, a cork in a bottle, the bung in a keg. Imperfectly, though. That slow drip came from where the blood welled up, overflowed, oozed and drizzled. Moving him, however necessary, however carefully done, had still resulted in some bumping and jostling.

More blood, on his lips and chin, was what he'd coughed from the punctured, collapsed lung. Each struggling breath, each of those wheezing gurgles and wet gasps, had made it worse.

The claw itself...

... wasn't quite a claw after all, but more of a blade. A blade of greyish, chitinous, hornlike stuff. It was tapered and slightly curved, like the digging scoop of a very long, very thin garden trowel.

The tip had almost gone through, stopping lodged against the man's shoulderblade from the inside. By some fluke of luck, miracle or fate, it hadn't severed any major blood vessels—again, if it had, she wouldn't have a patient on her hands, but a corpse.

The grey blade's other end, jutting out of his torso, sported the stump of some sort of... limb. An ugly knob of knucklebone and ragged gristle, trailing mangled connective tissue and tatters of scaly-looking slate-colored leather... covered with dark clots of coagulated ichor... the strange flesh scorched in places, as if it had been not severed but blown off at point-blank range...

"He got a name?" she asked as she laid out her tray of medical and magical tools.

"Steve. He works for me. Kind of an idiot sometimes, but, he's loyal."

"And you are?"

"Theo March."

"Ah," Larrah said. "The Conclave's troubleshooter. Your reputation precedes you."

"Independent contractor. I'm not officially with the Conclave. I have some friends there, connections, sources. That's how I heard about you."

"What do they say about me?"

"That you're a witch and a doctor, but not a witch-doctor."

She snorted and picked up a ridged forceps. "Close enough, I guess. You might want to stand back."

"I told you, I'm staying."

"Okay, but I warned you. When I yank this son of a bitch out, your buddy Steve is probably, in oil-driller parlance, gonna go a gusher."

Theo swallowed uneasily. Larrah heard his throat click. He cleared it, and took a step back. "Right. Ready. Tell me if there's anything I can do."

"What's your blood type?"

"Uh…"

"Don't worry about it. I have fresh bloodwort out back. Here goes."

Gripping the claw in the forceps, augmenting her strength with an adrenaline-boost cantrip, she drew it out of Steve's chest with one fast, smooth pull.

Little Laura.

The world thought she must have died that night, her remains too thoroughly consumed in the fire to be identified.

They even hoped so. For her sake. For pity's sake. The alternatives… abducted for vile and nefarious purposes, perhaps… yes, it was better to believe she'd died along with the rest of them, died as quickly as the rest of them.

In a way, she *had*. A life ended. A life of home and family, innocence and sight.

Ended. Over. Done.

Slashed and burned.

Murders. Arson. Tragedy.

Nine gang members were also found dead in the charred wreckage… bodies impossibly contorted, limbs twisted, faces locked in expressions of unbearable suffering and agony...

The authorities never figured out what had killed them.

Or who.

But she knew. She remembered. She wasn't about to forget the very last things she'd seen with her own two eyes.

Steve had indeed gone a gusher, but Larrah had thrust her hand into the wound to cleanse and heal it, to knit the torn muscle and mend the veins. The blood-geyser slowed to a burble, then ceased. Where the grisly hole had been was a lump of pinkish, pulpy meat seeping with crimson beads; she washed it, applied an herbal poultice, and affixed a gauze pad with strips of tape.

Theo remained tensely silent, watching her every move but not interrupting. Only when Larrah stepped back from the table, took a deep breath, and stretched until her spine crackled did he stir from his spot.

"Well?" he asked.

"So far, so good. It'd help to know if some pissed-off monster is going to bust in here, waving a stump and wanting to finish the job."

"Not likely," said Theo. "I got the bastard."

"Even for here, it's not every night I get someone showing up with a giant claw through his chest. Yeah, yeah, questions better left unanswered and all that... but if I'm going to treat him, I need to know what I'm dealing with."

After that, her job was easy, if time-consuming. A collapsed lung to reinflate, an infusion of bloodwort to replace what he'd lost, monitoring and stabilizing spells, some other minor injuries to tend to—scrapes, cuts and bruises. While she tended to these more mundane tasks, Theo talked.

He told her about what had started as a routine investigation into a break-in at an antiquities shop. Stolen items, suspected cult activity, a proprietor who'd been making illicit deals on the side and didn't want the Conclave to find out, bribes, threats, lies, misdirections, false leads, dead ends. The usual.

The trail eventually brought them to Devil's Cape, which got its name from the rugged and rocky headland jutting out into the Atlantic… site of countless wrecked boats over the years, fishing vessels and pleasure craft alike… where untold lives had been lost to the wicked tides and cold, black water.

A summoning gone wrong, a ritual interrupted, the cult's leader transforming into a big grey scaly demon-thing. Again, as was all too often the case in these situations, the usual.

In the course of the ensuing battle, Steve dodged the wrong way at the wrong time and got jabbed like a butterfly on a pin. Theo managed to put some bullets in the demon-thing's head, dropping it. Then he'd shot off the creature's limb rather than attempt to pull out the claw.

"Fortunately for him," Larrah said, shucking off her gloves.

With her witch-sight fixed on her patient, she hadn't been able to spare a glance at his companion, but had put together a general impression of Theo March based on his voice and actions. Young, strong, fit and healthy… he had to be, given the way he'd lugged Steve's impaled body all the way here from wherever. Likely good-looking, as well, since that trait tended to follow those others.

Now she did turn the witch-sight upon him, and found out she'd been right. The Conclave's troubleshooter was one handsome hunk, his skin ruddy, his hair long and dark and tied back in a ponytail. Cargo pants tucked into steel-toed boots. The hilt of a knife rose from each boot-top. He'd taken off a many-pocketed fatigue jacket, and his armored vest hung open over a form-fitting black T-shirt emblazoned with one of the Greater Sigils in gold. A tactical gunbelt hooked around his waist. Larrah suspected he had other weapons secreted about his person, not to mention a few magic tricks of his own up his figurative sleeve.

"What about this thing?" He leaned over the stainless steel pan where she'd deposited the greyish chitinous claw-blade. Steve's blood had oozed from it to puddle on the pan's bottom.

"Need a souvenir?"

He grimaced. "Not a hobby of mine."

"I can dispose of it, biohazard," she said. "Or sell it, there's people into that."

"No… I better hang onto it."

"Evidence?"

"Something like that. How is he? What can I do?"

"You can help me get him cleaned up the rest of the way, and moved to one of the beds," she said, indicating a gurney in the corner.

Working together, they did just that—got the unconscious Steve out of what was left of his clothes, sponged off, and heaved onto the gurney.

In addition to the lobby and the home surgery, the clinic had two exam rooms, a four-bed general ward, a storeroom, a bathroom, an even smaller kitchenette than the one in her living quarters upstairs, and a cluttered combination pharmacist/alchemist lab.

They rolled Steve into the ward, shifted him to one of the four beds, put a cotton hospital-style gown on him, and arranged him comfortably. Larrah rinsed the silver chain with its cluster of protective amulets, though instead of putting it back around his neck she looped it over the rail near his hand.

Once she was satisfied with his condition, she turned to Theo. "Okay, your turn."

"My what?"

She led him into one of the exam rooms and pointed at the table. "Did you not notice that you're bleeding?"

He craned his neck to peer down at his side, at the blood-caked rip in his T-shirt between the bottom edge of his vest and the top edge of his belt. "Just a scratch—"

"If you're such a great doctor, then," Larrah said, "what brought you to my door at one in the morning?"

"Right, right, right," he said, sighing. He shrugged out of the vest, peeled the torn T-shirt over his head, and made to boost himself onto the table.

"Pants, too."

"Uh…"

"Don't worry," she said. "Nothing I haven't seen before."

He considered that, then gave a resigned chuckle and continued undressing. She tossed him a towel he could hold strategically placed for modesty, and rummaged through the supply cabinets.

"On your side, facing the wall."

Theo clambered onto the table as instructed. Paper crinkled. He grumbled dourly under his breath.

"I heard that," said Larrah. "Remember, we blind people tend to have pretty good ears. And, for the record, I wouldn't have to be a damn pushy woman if you weren't being a damn stubborn man."

A damn stubborn man with, she did have to admit, a damn finely sculpted torso, especially when he propped himself up on one elbow and half-turned to watch what she was doing. And one hell of a nice backside.

"Not quite just a scratch," she said as she inspected the wound. "Even if it was, consider the source. I'll want to disinfect this, and put in some charm-stitches. Three should do it."

"C'mon, I don't really need stitches, do I?"

"The more you keep twisting around like that, the more you'll open it up and need more than three. Hold still. Or do I have to zap you with a paralysis hex?"

He held still, but he grumbled again, so she didn't warn him before swabbing the gash with a cleansing elixir. Theo sucked in air through clenched teeth as it bubbled and foamed.

"Oh yeah," she said. "This might sting a little."

"It was cold," he replied, teeth still clenched.

"Uh-huh." She lit a squat indigo candle in a shallow dish. Runes glimmered, embedded deep in the wax.

"You think I'm one of those stoic action-movie guys who goes through the whole fight feeling no pain, then yelps like a baby when he's getting patched up?"

"Better not be, because I don't hand out lollipops and stickers."

"Do you at least use Snoopy band-aids?"

Larrah threaded three needles from three different spools. "Nope."

"I bet you're unpopular with the kiddies."

"Pretty much." She passed the point of the first needle thrice through the candle flame.

"What are you—ow!"

"I thought you weren't going to yelp." Her deft fingers on the needle drew the stitch shut, tied off the ends of white thread and snipped the excess. "White for purification."

"This part of the proceedings must be more witch than doctor," Theo said. "Does the AMA know?"

"That would require having a license." She picked up the next needle, trailing its tail of thread, and ran it through the flame as well before poking it into his skin. "Green for healing."

He winced but did not yelp this time. "No license?"

"No license, no medical degree, no formal schooling at all."

"No medical degree, and you just went ahead and had me get naked?"

"Hey, this job has few enough perks as it is." She took up the third needle. "Silver for protection."

When she was done with the stitches, Theo cast a dubious look at the neat row of intricate knots holding his side together. Larrah dabbed the line with an ointment of marigold and elderberry, then covered it with a pad of light gauze.

"There you go," she said. "All done. Wash up. There's a sink right there, or a bathroom down the hall with a shower."

"Can I put my clothes back on?"

"If you want. No need on my account; maintaining a witch-sight spell too long gives me a headache." She traced her thumbs over her brow, and the familiar blindness descended. With it came the weary crash as her adrenaline boost wore off, letting the past few hours catch up with her. "I'm going to change into fresh scrubs, go check on your friend, then make some tea. It's so late, it's early."

Steve would be out for a few more hours at least, while the magically-accelerated healing process did its job. In the meantime, she'd continue monitoring his vitals, both corporeal and ethereal, to make sure no infections or lingering curses took hold.

Theo joined her in the clinic's kitchenette, which was less a room in its own right and more a closet with mini-fridge, microwave and coffee pot. Now that she no longer had medical emergencies on her hands, her senses detected something like a faint but pervasive hum. Enchantments; bound to the weapons, she surmised.

"He's stable," she said, dancing her fingertips along the row of jar lids to select the blends she wanted. "Tea?"

"Sure." His pause had a tone of amusement—pauses and silences could have tones every bit as eloquent as facial expressions were said to. "Loose leaf?"

"There's teabags in the cabinet, if you prefer stale leaf-dust and grass clippings."

"Appetizing. I'll have what you're having."

"Wise choice."

Then he laughed. "Loose leaf, but microwaved hot water?"

"I keep the real teapot and service upstairs. Most of my patients aren't picky."

They took the cups out into the lobby seating area. She sensed his curious glance at the staircase on the way by.

"So… what *is* your story?" he asked.

"Once upon a time," said Larrah, "there was a little girl whose dumbass big brother got mixed up in an occult gang war."

He waited. She didn't go on. He said, "Is that it? The end?"

"What, didn't your snitches in the Conclave give you the juicy details?"

"Sources. Not snitches." He blew on the tea, then added, "Okay, some of them are snitches. But, like I said, just the witch/doctor thing. Doesn't sound like you're a big fan of the Conclave, though."

"Doesn't it? I wonder why. Oh, yeah. Because, fuck the Conclave, that's why."

This time, his pause was of surprise, though whether at the language or the sentiment, she couldn't be sure.

"Now I really want to know," he said.

"Remember that occult gang war I mentioned?"

"Yeah?"

"The dumbass big brother joined the Ghouls. Part of his initiation involved some ritual murders of the enemy faction, but he was sloppy. The Reapers found out who did it. They came for revenge."

"Scorched earth? Bones and ashes?"

Larrah nodded. "Except for me."

Mr. Deadface in her closet had scared her so bad she almost wet the bed.

Mr. Skullface was worse.

There were lots of skullfaces. Most of them wore jeans and black jackets. They had knives. They whooped and hooted and laughed as they went through the house, breaking stuff, knocking stuff over.

She tried to hide. Hide under her bed, in her yellow room, safe. But the skullfaces found her. They pulled her out. They brought her downstairs.

Where they were hurting people.

Her mommy. Her daddy. The noisy, stinky baby. Their doggy.

Making them scream and cry. Making them bleed. And die.

Scream and cry, bleed and die.

While her brother had to watch. Not Mr. Deadface now. Just Tommy, stupid Tommy blubbering and begging, saying how he was sorry, he didn't mean it, he took it back. His mask, his stupid grey-green rubber deadface mask, was all cut to pieces on the floor.

And Mr. Skullface was there, the leader, the one who had on a black robe with a hood, who had skull-hand gloves too, and instead of a knife a long stick with a sharp curve of rusty metal on the end.

"Now the girl," said Mr. Skullface to her big brother. "Now the girl, and then you, because this is what you get when you mess with the Reapers."

Only, as the skullfaces came toward her, with the knives, something happened.

It happened in her head and the middle of her chest. A tickle that became a rush that became an explosion like a sneeze.

Dark light burst from her eyes. She saw the skullfaces and *they* were scared now, they were scared as the dark light swallowed them up, scared and screaming… and Tommy was scared too, Tommy was scared and screaming and it was his fault all *his* fault so she let the dark light have Tommy, too.

"That was the night little Laura discovered she was a witch." Larrah folded her hands around the teacup, absorbing its warmth. "I killed them. And my brother. I killed my brother."

For a few moments, they were both silent, a silence of the pensive and troubled variety.

"I'm sorry," Theo said.

She shrugged, lips twitching in a wan smile.

"I read about that case," he went on. "Something like a dozen Reapers died—"

"Only nine," she said quietly.

"—and it became one of those unsolved mysteries, no one ever really knew all the facts."

"The leader survived. Grim, he called himself. Original, yeah?"

"Grim, the Reaper." Theo groaned. "Yeah. Real original."

"He had enough magic of his own to ward off that initial blast. It injured him, though. Damn near crippled him. As for me…" Larrah brushed the closed and sunken lids of her eyes. "It blinded me. Probably almost killed me, too. I was exhausted, helpless, confused. Barely remembered my own name."

"Traumatized, and no damn wonder."

"Grim figured I'd be worth more alive than dead. That he might be able to profit from using my power. He took me with him."

"Bastard."

"Yeah. But he was right. I hadn't burned out. I could still *do* things. I could hurt people. I could cause them pain, or make them sick."

"Or, on the flip side," he said, "you could heal… which is a hell of a lot more valuable."

"Turns out Grim wasn't the only one who thought that way. Everybody wanted control of the little witch-girl. I spent the next fifteen or so years bouncing around from one group to the next. Traded, sold, stolen, swapped, a prize, a trophy, a bargaining chip, you name it."

"What? That's outrageous! I did some time getting shunted from one foster home to the next when I was a teenager, but what you're talking about, that's just wrong, that's child-trafficking."

"Gangs like the Reapers," said Larrah. "Covens. Occult societies. Mystic cults. All in all, they treated me pretty well, because nobody wanted to damage the goods."

"Or piss off the girl with the healing touch," Theo said, though his voice held an angry glower. "Still…"

"Wherever I ended up, I'd study, I'd learn, I'd pick up bits of whatever was available. When I was about nineteen, I realized they couldn't force me to work for them. What did they have on me? No family, nothing to hold over me as a threat."

"The Conclave should have done something. If they'd known—"

"Oh, they knew. They didn't interfere. They didn't think one kid was worth upsetting the applecart or ruffling the feathers or pick your metaphor. Then that kid grew up, grew into her abilities, and told the Conclave where they could stick it."

"They went along with that?"

"We reached an understanding."

"In other words, they don't hassle you, and you remain available for the occasional on-call favor like tonight."

"Basically."

W

Their parents had been furious. Not only about Tommy scaring his sister, though that was what set it off.

All of it.

Furious, worried, concerned.

The Mr. Deadface mask, looking like a Halloween monster, a starved and hungry ghoul, was only part of it.

Like his new friends, and his attitude. And the late nights. The tattoos. The clothes. The music and movies. All parts of it.

Mostly, though, it was the books.

"Oh, like you're any different?" her brother yelled at Mommy. "I know what you do. I know what you are, with your library and your languages! What Grandpa was, and how the Conclave—"

Mommy slapped him.

Late had become early. Early gave way to normal morning, birds warming up for choir practice in the hedge outside, Grimalkin wandering downstairs to demand breakfast.

The first patients of the day began to arrive, some bringing goodwill gifts of coffee and baked goods since Larrah did a lot of her business on a basis of barter and trade. Others came bearing neighborhood gossip, and wild rumors of suspicious mischief that had gone on in the old cemetery last night.

Theo napped until noon in the bed beside Steve's, waking each time Larrah came in to check on them. They were both mending nicely. She judged it was safe for Steve to be moved, if it was carefully done, so Theo called one of his other employees to come pick them up in a hired medical transport van.

"You should get some sleep, too," he said to Larrah as they were preparing to leave.

She stifled a yawn. "I will. Canceled this afternoon's office hours and appointments."

"What do we owe you?"

"Just Steve's life, no big deal. Cheating death, I do it all the time."

"Heh. But, seriously."

"I could bill you," she said, "or you could do what you can to help keep the Conclave off my back."

"I'll talk to my snitches. I mean sources."

Larrah smiled. "Thanks."

"No, thank *you*." He startled her by leaning in to place a quick kiss on her cheek. His lips were very warm, and softer than she might have expected. "Steve thanks you too, or, he will once he's through the full course of that elixir you prescribed. He says he never wants to know what's in it."

"That's probably best," she said. "He'll be happier that way."

They walked down the flagstone path to the front gate. She could hear the van's engine idling, a low rumble against the backdrop of daily life.

"So... hey," Theo said. "Are you, uh..." He broke off and she heard the fleshy smack of the heel of his hand on his forehead. "Damn it. I can't believe I almost said that."

"What?"

"Seeing anyone," he said in an I-could-kick-myself tone.

She laughed, then stopped as his meaning sank in. "As it happens, I'm not, in either the literal or the figurative sense. Most people seem to find my charming personality and bedside manner off-putting. Why?"

"Because I'm not most people. I was thinking that, if you didn't mind, I could stop by again some time. Only, not show up bleeding on your doorstep in the middle of the night."

"But then how would I get you out of your clothes?"

It was his turn to laugh. "Oh, knowing you, I expect you'll find a way."

THE KNITTED MAN

BY BO BALDER

When Sylke turned twenty, the aunties decided to knit her a man. In all these years, the men from the village had never come to woo her, fearing the witchy women from the house under the dunes. The aunties themselves had never married, either.

Sylke was offended. Were the aunties disparaging her charms? Her skin was smooth, her light blonde hair without a trace of red. She could fish, spin, milk sheep and make soup. What more could a man want?

"It isn't your fault," Aunt Charm said. Sylke was never sure if she meant things or not.

"We love you," said Aunt Song, and Aunt Whisper nodded.

It had to take place within one day, preferably at full moon, as magic wills. The aunts dragged Sylke to the beach.

When it stormed, Old Taeke lit the lighthouse fires to lure passing ships into the bay. If a drowned man washed up, wearing a sailor's gold ring in his ear, he was buried in the village, otherwise the aunties used the bones to strengthen their roof. Few trees grew on the windswept island, and they never got high or strong. So every broken spar or thighbone was welcome.

But even without a shipwreck, the beach was littered with driftwood and seaweed.

Aunt Song stirred a heap of seaweed with her cane. A smell of salt and decay drifted out. "What color hair do you want for him, honey?" she asked. "Red, green or purple?"

Sylke scooped up a wet hank of kelp. "Just brown."

Aunt Charm rummaged through the shells. "Linen for the hands, shells for the ears, caterpillars for eyebrows. Blue or brown eyes?"

In Sylke's mirror shard (also washed-up), she daily encountered blue eyes, and the aunts had brown ones. "Green!" she said.

"Hairy or smooth?" asked Aunt Song.

Sylke had dreamed about what she'd find beneath a fisherman's sweater, but hadn't been able to imagine beyond the elbow. She liked the fisher boys' tanned, muscled forearms, and their bare calves when they dragged for shrimp in the surf. Old fishermen got hairy, she was fairly sure. "Smooth," she whispered.

The aunties cackled with laughter. "We know the rest!" they cried. "Red lips, a straight nose, firm muscles. We were young once."

Aunt Whisper held up a handful of red burnet roses. "For the heart," she said softly. Aunt Whisper was the sweetest, the one who silently tucked a hot water bottle under her blankets on cold nights.

"Go knit a sweater for him," Aunt Charm said. "Someone has to stay with the sheep." Aunt Charm was boss.

Sylke started to think she liked the idea of a husband. She picked the softest sheep and shaved off its fleece. She washed the wool, dried and carded it, and then started spinning. She spun on her stool until her head ached. Full moon was a week away and she had to knit a whole sweater by then.

Occasionally an aunt hurried past, cheeks red with exertion or excitement, and gave advice. "Remember to put in the Tree of Life." Or, "A good heart is important."

Sylke got up, tucked spindle and wool under her arm, and walked to the village. She needed examples. What did she want in a man?

Young Taeke had beautiful silver blond hair, but otherwise he resembled grumpy Old Taeke far too much. Lieuwe had broad shoulders, but drank too much and hit his wife. Pier had the biggest boat in the whole village, but sported a potato nose and had not a tooth left in his mouth. The vicar knew Latin, but every Sunday he preached half the village to sleep in three minutes flat.

Sylke walked around the village three times, and saw that sweet little boys became boring men. What was that one special thing that would make someone her perfect husband? She loved to dream in the dune valleys, she loved to stare into the fire. She loved listening to the storm while she lay in bed.

Her feet carried her to the cemetery. There were a few fancy tombstones, from the times when the island had been rich. And newer, wooden crosses. Those she didn't dare to touch because the aunties didn't allow a cross into the long house, not even in the kindling.

She slid her bare foot over the inscriptions in the largest stone. She couldn't read them, but the regularity of the letters impressed her. And suddenly she knew. A poet. Her husband must have the heart of a poet. She looked around to check whether anybody could see her. She pushed the tuft of wool hanging from her spindle into the carved words, muttering a spell.

Satisfied, she walked back to the sheep. The sweater flew from her needles and the day before the full moon, it was ten-elevenths done.

When the full moon rose, they built a driftwood fire on the beach and lit it. Sylke was made to undress and dance naked around the fire. It was only April, so it was cold and she did it reluctantly. The aunts blew on their numb hands and stamped their feet. They sang unintelligible spells, softly so Sylke couldn't hear.

"Now dance three times counterclockwise," said Aunt Song.

Aunt Whisper nodded and boiled water on a corner of the fire.

Sylke's teeth chattered and her feet had gone numb. "Can I have my clothes back now?"

"Wait a minute. This is important. Here are my sewing scissors. If things go wrong, you can still undo the spell."

Sylke stared at the scissors. They fit into her palm and they'd been used for cutting off the ends of embroidery silks for twenty-five years. "What do you mean go wrong? What could go wrong?"

Aunt Song was suddenly busy rearranging the seaweed hair. "If no human soul, but a monstrous soul enters. Or a soulless animal. This almost never happens, but just in case…"

What? Until now, the aunts had pretended the spell was about as complicated as making soup. She wasn't prepared for soulless animals or monsters.

Aunt Whisper helped her into her socks, skirts and dress. She put a warm shawl around Sylke's shoulders and offered her a cup of herbal tea.

"A sip for you, spit one on your husband," Aunt Charm commanded.

Sylke's stockings were twisted and her petticoat inside-out, but she didn't care. Her knitted man with his poet's heart would look past things like that.

The moon shone on the piles of seaweed, old sailors' bones and bobbins of linen and wool, while the aunts knitted and knitted and stitched. In a blur of flashing needles, the fingers took shape on Aunt Song's thin needles, while Aunt Whisper's coarser needles magically made the legs appear and Aunt Charm did complicated things with flaxen hair and ear shells. Sylke knitted the last rows of her fisherman sweater, without looking. She couldn't take her eyes off the limp form lying on the shore, occasionally moving as the aunts turned their work. Aunt Song stuffed the sausage fingers with twigs and bones and wool, then the forearms, the upper arms. Aunt Charm had reached the hips, and did a complicated job with her back to Sylke. Aunt Song polished black stones on her sleeve so that the eyes would shine. Didn't the nose look a bit big? Could those cranberry lips even open, and what was behind them? She hadn't seen a tongue go in.

Sylke's fingers continued to work and attached the neck trim to the sweater. She bit the thread and wove the ends in. Done.

The eastern sky was graying by the time the aunts put the finishing touches to the knitted man while they knelt in the sand. Aunt Song attached the right arm to the shoulder with big stabbing strokes. Aunt Charm did the same with the left leg, the right leg already done. Aunt Whisper fixed curls of wool to the chest. A wave of irritation rose inside Sylke. Hadn't she said she wanted a smooth man?

For the final touch, Sylke put the little silk bag with burnet rose petals into the heart.

The first rays of the sun glinted on the knitted man. His legs twitched.

The aunts pulled Sylke away. "Wait," whispered Aunt Charm.

A shiver went through the body of the knitted man. He jerked upright. He opened his eyes and looked at Sylke. Eyes black as coal and as dull. He was very big.

Sylke felt like crying from disappointment. His hair was flaxen, his nose looked like a potato and he had hands like shovels. She could have found a dozen like him in the fishing village. Couldn't the aunts do anything right? Her list had specified brown hair, green eyes and a smooth chest, and everything was exactly the opposite.

Sylke threw the sweater at him. "Here's your sweater, but don't think I'm going to marry you. I wanted a poet."

"Honey, what's wrong? Isn't he a pretty one?" Aunt Charm asked.

Sylke sniffed. "You call that pretty? He has the same nose as Piet and I wanted a smooth chest and green eyes."

The aunts pursed their lips. "This is what the sea washed up for you, and you're going to have to settle for it."

The man rose up and stretched out his knitted hands to her. They were like sausages. He was so tall. He rose above her, smelling like seaweed and decaying shark. He opened his red lips and the roaring of the sea came out. Sylke took a step back. Instead of following her, he grew bigger and bigger so his arms became longer. He could still reach her.

"Charm, what did you do?" Aunt Song whispered.

Charm laughed. Sylke had never liked her laugh.

The man's moon shadow grew even faster than he himself did. When the shadow touched the heap of seaweed to the left, it let out a puff of foul air. It started moving. The heap slithered slowly closer to Sylke.

Sylke shook her head. "I'm not marrying that!"

She took the scissors and raked at the sausage finger. A bit of stuffing fell out. The knitted man lifted his dull eyes to her. How dare he look at her! She stuck the scissors in his knitted breast, where the rose heart resided. There. That would teach him.

The stabbing made a small, sucking sound.

Blood ran out. Red, human blood.

The knitted man gasped. His black eyebrows drew together and he pushed her hand away. He was shrinking and fell over. He held his hand out again, but now Sylke felt no fear. The hand was warm. Sylke put her palm on his chest to feel if the skin was warm there as well. The chest rose and fell. Smooth taut skin, a beating heart underneath.

His shadow was normal size, the heap of seaweed just a heap of seaweed.

His eyes were dark brown, almost black.

"Why did you do that?" he asked. "What's your name?"

His teeth were a bit crooked, but white. And the potato nose was exactly right in his face, it was a tough nose. His hair curled.

Blood still oozed from the wound she'd made. She tore a strip off her petticoats.

"Here," she said. She smoothed the cotton onto his broad chest. She wanted to be sure it would stay put. To be on the safe side, she ran her hands over the warm skin one more time.

He smiled. "Is that sweater for me?"

"Yes."

"What's your name?"

"Sylke."

"A name like a kiss."

Sylke sighed. He'd turned out to be a poet after all.

SPARE PARTS

BY STEPHANIE BISSETTE-ROARK

The arms. The arms were the problem. It wasn't the shirt's fault its sleeves fell just an inch above my wrists. I tugged at them in annoyance, trying to close the gap between blouse and gloves, but all the yanking in the world wouldn't grant me that extra bit of coverage. Maybe if I hadn't confiscated these limbs from what I was now certain must have been a female hairless gorilla, I wouldn't have had this problem. Damned replacement parts.

It shouldn't have bothered me, but it did. Even in the dim light that filtered into the back seat of the SUV, I could clearly make out the maggot-white stitches which bound my wrists to my hands. Maybe I could look into bangles or something. The drawback to bracelets, though, was that they caused too much of a racket. And I was all about the sneaking.

Keys rattled in the driver's side door and I froze. I forced myself to relax, to not give myself away underneath the cheap army blanket I was using as concealment. The scratchy olive green wool was covered in short, white dog hairs. It looked like either a small fluffy critter had been done to death on this thing, or a large dog routinely used it as an unwilling sexual partner. Lucky for me, I didn't have to breathe and risk choking on eau de canine. Otherwise this might have turned into a very unpleasant operation.

As it was, it was already later than I'd have liked. My target had been in the store for hours. The inactivity made the planes of my borrowed skin itch; the still-original expanse beneath my porcelain mask all but begged for a good scratch. I could feel the rise of the full moon like an impossibly long tether, pulling me taut. If we didn't get this show on the road soon, I'd run the risk of someone finding the body before I'd even finished with it. And I couldn't have that.

The car dipped slightly as the woman got into the vehicle. I peered from beneath the blanket and watched as her pert ponytail bloomed into a golden coruscate against the grey of the driver's headrest. The staticky crinkle of plastic announced the landing of some bags into the passenger seat. Whatever else might be said about her, this woman couldn't half shop.

The engine roared to life, purring like only a V-8 could. We left the parking lot and listed right, bound for the highway. Streetlights blipped a strobe effect into the back seat of the car as we rushed beneath them. When we hit open road, the car picked up speed and the lights grew infrequent. It wouldn't be long now.

She drove for about fifteen minutes in blissful ignorance. I knew because I had to suffer through her butchering the same Adele song half a dozen times. If for no other reason than that exquisite torture, I'd have killed her. Not that I needed more reasons, but it did help to get the hate-machine churning. I was ready.

I forced myself to concentrate on her rhythms. The rested beat of her heart, the long pull of air as she drew breath, the xylophone-like way she clicked her acrylic fingernails across the seams on her leather steering wheel. But the effort was trying.

The restless shades that hung about her pressed against me for solace, smothering me in their icy chill. Even in my grave-cold body I had to fight not to shiver. The pair of tiny souls demanded retribution. I was eager to give it to them.

She reached over to push the repeat button on her player one more time. For me, and Adele, it was now or never.

I sat up slowly. The straight razor was already in my hand; a shining silver reassurance of purpose. I situated myself behind her, one arm quickly snaking around her shoulder, the other poising the blade just outside the casing of her artery. She screamed and grabbed at my arm.

"Calm down and take the wheel," I ordered, my voice muffled beneath the cool armor of my white ceramic mask. I could feel her heartbeat as it pounded into the cool flesh of my arm like a field mouse flailing against the coils of a constrictor.

She continued to scream as the car drifted off the road. I pressed the razor a little into her flesh; just enough for the sharp edge to get a nip, just enough for her to catch sight in the rearview mirror of the tiny line of crimson that ruined the perfect pale of her neck.

I waited. She'd get the hint. More times than not my tools spoke for me.

When she noticed the blood, she shut up. Quickly she returned shaking hands to the steering wheel. We swerved back into the center lane from our adventure on the shoulder, pinging gravel bits behind us in our wake.

Her shudders threatened my steady hold and I scolded her by tightening my grip, suppressing the heaves of her bosom. Though her tremors didn't cease, they at least grew more subdued. I'd always found that fear was a great motivator.

"What do you want?" she asked, her blood-drained lips quivering on the question.

I glanced behind us to make certain there were no authorities. All I needed right now was for the police to pull us over for unlawful lane changes.

I returned my gaze to her. "I want you to take me somewhere."

She looked at me through the mirror, her eyes wide as they focused on the expressionless planes of my mask; the two round holes for my eyes, the painted orange triangle for my nose, the simple dash of black that demarcated my mouth. "Why?"

"Because I need a lift."

"Why me?"

I resisted the urge to shrug and risk truncating this conversation with a faulty slip of my blade.

"You were an easy target," I answered blithely.

She began to blubber again. I didn't want to risk damaging more of her neck by forcing her to shut up. That would come later. So I let her sob, the thick mascara of her tarantula-legged lashes creating streaks of smeared jet across her skin. I resisted the urge to chuckle. She looked more like a clown than I did.

"Please!" she begged. Stygian tears slipped down her cheeks to pool on the surface of the razor. "Please just let me go. I'll give you anything! Anything! Take the car. Take whatever you want."

I smiled, though she couldn't see the expression.

"Everything I want is right here," I stated coolly.

She shook her head as if to contradict me, and then thought better of the motion. "Why are you doing this to me?" she sobbed.

I leaned forward so that my whisper would reach her.

"You know why."

That got her tears flowing harder, but this time I didn't shush her. It was all currency for me. If there weren't tears, I'd be doing my job wrong, and I took a lot of pride in my work.

We drove for about an hour towards the mountain. It was a special kind of gloom in the depths of the forest, like the black at the end of the world. The heavy canopy of evergreens obscured much of the moon's glow and lent our journey little in the form of light. A perfect night.

Just when I thought we must have missed it, a short wooden spike marked with a bit of electrical tape flashed silver beneath the blue-white glow of the headlights.

"Turn here," I ordered.

The woman complied, a little wounded-animal sound escaping from her mouth. It was telling, that whimper. I doubted she'd even known she done it. The soul knows what the mind doesn't want to consider.

We took the turnout. It ended a few hundred yards later, at the beginning of a makeshift walking trail. From our view we couldn't see the nearby river, but we could hear it.

"Turn off the engine."

She complied woodenly; the motion slow, almost weary.

With the power off, it felt oddly intimate in the hushed dark of the cab. The only sounds to punctuate the false sensory deprivation were the woman's frightened pantings and the occasional ping of the engine as it cooled against the chill outside. In the heavy dark, she couldn't see my face, but I could feel her eyes on me all the same.

I let go of her and held out my left hand, the razor still an unspoken threat against her throat.

"Give me the keys," I demanded.

She moved with a tired resignation, dropping the keys in my hand, careful not to risk her fingers touching mine. I curled my gloved digits possessively around the shards of metal, and withdrew my arm to tuck the keys into my pocket.

I eased back away from her slowly, the razor held limply at my side. Her shoulders relaxed and then tensed. I watched the cues idly; her body giving away its intent. I waited for a few seconds, drawing the moment out.

"Get out of the car."

The woman opened the door. A sallow glow from the dome lights overhead flooded the space, killing my night vision. When fresh air met her, she reacted instinctively, nearly choking herself on her seatbelt as she lunged for the gap. Her panicked hands fumbled over the belt buckle, and then she was free, bolting towards the shadowy woods. I blearily watched her form until it was swallowed by the night.

I eased myself out of my crouch and crawled out of the car. The going was stiff and slow, the old knees not up to the penitent task of kneeling for long periods of time. I stretched and heard my back pop; the awkward shift of vertebrae, cartilage, and muscle as they readjusted, accordion-like, to my new verticality. With gloved hands I tucked the razor in the pocket of my white vinyl apron, and withdrew the duct tape, slipping it onto my wrist like some kind of industrial decoration.

She had a head start, but I was faster. Not to mention smarter. Running headlong into dark woods was never a wise move. Sure, she had a lot riding on escape, but with the way she was going, it wouldn't be long before something tripped her or speared her or took her down. I only hoped I'd get to her before she managed to do herself a real mischief. Couldn't have her killing herself before I did.

I took off into the woods after her, my steps sure as I surged over the familiar ground. This was my favorite part. The hunt. The primal symphony of life to which even my undead form could sing along.

Despite my lack of an active circulatory system, I could almost feel the cold pink tissue of my adrenal glands working, filling my useless heart with liquid speed. My muscles sang. The incredible strength even these outdated limbs could offer allowed me to quickly eat up the distance between us. It was over all too quickly, but then again, it always was.

I could hear her crashing through the brush somewhere ahead, like a hart that'd been spooked from her hiding. I lagged behind, wanting her to think she'd gotten away, wanting her to experience those first flickers of hope before I dashed them.

I caught up to her at the river. Pale light filtered down onto the surface of the water through the gap in the tree line overhead, gilding the surrounds in ghostly silver. She was waist-deep in the icy current, pushing forward; the bob of her blond hair catching my eye like the ass-end of a white-tailed deer.

I approached slowly. A hunk of granite shone dully in the damp of the riverbank. I toed the rock loose from the mud and swiped it up with my left hand. With just a second's aim, I lobbed it at her.

The rock met her head with enough force to take her off her feet. She crumbled face-first into the water like a doll suddenly devoid of stuffing. I had to rush forward to grab her before she was carried downriver.

When she finally came to, I already had her bound, gagged, and hung upside down in the clearing I'd prepared earlier that day. A little camping lantern illuminated the area, lending an almost romantic air to the sur-roundings.

"Do you know where you are?" I asked her.

Her eyes were ringed in white as she looked up at me. She mumbled something against her tape.

"You are about twenty miles from the campsite where you took your children," I prompted. "You remember, don't you?"

I bent over and worked my plastic-gloved fingers beneath a corner of the tape across her mouth. When I yanked the tape off, she yelped.

"Please!" she begged. "I didn't do anything! You've got the wrong person."

"Really?" I knelt down next to her and angled my neck so that one of my ears was pointed up. If I listened hard enough, I imagined I could almost hear the bullshit piling up. "Hmm… for some reason, I don't believe you," I confessed, running a hand through my fire-engine red hair. The short mass was like the wires of a Brillo Pad, and in the cool, wet night, they stuck out wildly in all directions. I must have looked a fright.

She was blubbering again, sobbing; choking on her own snot and slobber. I sighed, though I didn't have to. Old habits die hard, and all that.

I flicked open my razor and sliced it across her midriff where her gathered shirt exposed the tender flesh. The pale, pink skin drew apart slightly and began to seep red. It wasn't a deep cut, but it must have stung like hell.

She started to wail when the warm slickness trickled from the cut down her neck and across her face. Nothing like seeing one's own blood to get the heart pounding. But at least it got her focused again.

"Let me ask you straight. Did you murder your two children?"

She shook her head, eyes pinched tightly closed; denial mode. I had to finger her fresh cut to convince her to talk.

"Please!" she wailed at the pain. "Please, I'll give you money! Anything you want. Just let me go. I won't tell anyone, I swear!"

"Now why don't I believe you?" Careful to miss my black army boots, I shoved her so that the blood that dripped off her scalp trickled a thin line of crimson in the dirt.

I stepped away from her, disgusted.

"You must have thought you'd gotten away with the perfect murders," I told her, watching her swing like a pendulum. "Telling the police they'd drowned when playing too near the river. But they didn't drown, did they?" I continued. "Well… not without help. You held them under the water, first the brother, then the little sister. You sat on his chest as he fought to get air and watched him die. And then you went and got the little one. She was too young to know what was going on, and she clung to you as you picked her up. Even as she struggled for breath, she clung to you."

I grabbed her legs to kill her momentum. They were firm beneath my hold, yet supple. I squeezed gently, like testing a melon for ripeness in the produce aisle.

"Do you work out?" I asked, eying the smooth, unblemished stretch of her limbs appreciatively.

She'd stilled her sobbing enough to look up at me, confused. "What?"

I'd bet she was a runner; probably one of those weekend marathon people. Though, I amended silently, not fast enough today. I shook my head. I was getting off track.

"Never mind."

"How do you know these things?" she asked, voice thick from all the bawling.

It was all the admission I needed. I grabbed the large plastic bucket from my kit, and went over to the river to fill it up.

"And the truth will out," I proclaimed as I lugged the full pail back to the clearing. I placed it beneath the woman and watched as the water grew a bit cloudy and pink from the blood still dripping off the top of her head.

"I admitted what you wanted," she shrieked, glaring up at me; false bravado making her bold. "Are you happy now? Is this what you do to get off, you sick bitch!?"

I ignored her clawless jab. But I needed to know.

"Why did you do it?"

She scoffed, glancing away.

"What does it matter to you?"

"Lady, I am the one with the razor," I said, patting my pocket. "It matters to me."

She was silent so long I thought she might've required a bit more encouragement, but then she started to talk. It was as if a stopper had been pulled, letting all the ichor ooze out from the festering wound that was her soul.

"I wanted to hurt him." The way she said it, I knew she didn't mean her son. "When he left me for that other woman, my world ended. I gave him everything I had and he just used me up like a sponge." She glanced up at me briefly as if expecting a fellow utero-American to sympathize, but I remained silent, giving her nothing. These weren't my sins to confess.

"And then he was gone," she continued, "and all I had left was his brood. They both looked so much like him; nothing of me in them at all. And he loved them so... damned... much. I had to hurt him, had to cut out his heart like he'd done to me. They were the only ammunition I had left."

She glanced up at me, suddenly calm. I waited for the proposition I knew was sure to come.

"You know, you don't have to kill me," she pleaded, her words soft like one might use to talk down a tantrum-throwing child. Or a mad dog. "If it's a confession you want I'll go to the police tonight, recant my original statement. I'll admit to everything. They'll send me to prison for the rest of my life. I'll never breathe free air again. Isn't that what you want? Justice?"

The option hung in the air a moment, pregnant with possibility.

"Sorry," I said, though I wasn't. "No can do."

"Why then!? Why are you doing this to me?!"

I shrugged, eyeing the luminous way her exposed legs shimmered in the lamplight.

"I need the parts."

I loosened the slack of the rope that suspended her from the tree limb and lowered her head into the bucket. Her muddy, matted crown of hair disappeared into the blackness. She began to struggle, wasting precious air to scream into the cold, unforgiving water.

She held on for a long time, taking greedy lungfuls of breath every time I lifted her out of the water. Eventually, I grew tired of the game. I began to hammer into her flesh with my fists, cracking ribs, busting veins. I railed against her like the rocks of the nearby river must have savaged the unprotected flesh of her children as they were carried downstream.

I watched her die by inches, helping her along when she stalled. It was what my creator had raised me to do. What I'd been trained to do. I was a blood-soaked cog in a horrible, if necessary, machine with no credence given to concepts like salvation or mercy.

In the end, we didn't do it for justice. We did it for the pain. Because sometimes everyone deserved their pound of flesh.

The tiny red stitches were a false garter across my upper thigh. I stood, balancing on one foot, so Marcella could get the donor leg in place before I affixed the last little bit of threading in the back. I could have done it myself, but I found having more hands made the job easier. As well as a lot straighter. I couldn't bear the thought of crooked seams.

"Did she at least die well?" Marcella asked from her squatted perch below me. I shifted beneath her careful hold, the cold meat of my new leg like a friendly, but still foreign, thing. The leg wouldn't become fully integrated until after I'd applied the unguent and the words, and only then after it'd been broken in a bit. Sorta like a pair of new boots.

"Define *well*," I murmured, the U-shaped needle I gripped in my mouth making it hard to speak clearly.

Marcella sighed and brushed her dark curls away from her eyes with the back of her hand. She looked up at me. "Was there begging or bribery?"

I finished the last few stitches in my leg, pulled the thick red cord taut, and tied it off into a knot. Before I could ask, Marcella was up, searching the work tabletop for a pair of shears to cut the thread.

"Isn't that always the way of it?" I couldn't remember a single target I'd dispatched who hadn't resorted to some form of blubbering. If I wasn't such a naturally optimistic person, I'd have said it was a sign of how the human race was so messed up that in their last minutes, they showed themselves to be total gutless douches.

Marcella cursed in her native Italian; just a bunch of swear words and not the real thing. The air always tingled a bit and got cold when she did it for real.

"Where is integrity?" she cried, the silver flash of blades punctuating her exasperation as she waved the scissors about wildly. "Where is a person's sense of honor? Why, in those last moments, do they always fall so short of something worthy of life?"

I shrugged, the motion hampered by my awkward hunch. "If you're looking for a philosophical debate, you've come to the wrong freak. I've got too much on my plate as it is to worry about how someone chooses to go out. I just do the endings; I'm not about emotionalizing a fitting epilogue."

"Annie..." Marcella implored, the mother-tongue accent she'd struggled her adult life to mute making the plea lilt prettily at the end. She was the one who'd chosen the name Annie for me when she'd crafted me. I was the one who silently added the word "raggedy" just before it. "What you do is so much more than just killing. You must realize that. How a person faces the end says so much more about who they are than anything else." With a precise snip, Marcella cut the extra bit of thread from my thigh.

I stretched and admired my new legs. "I thought we were more concerned with deeds, not statements. What do I care how somebody receives that final cut? They've dug their graves; I'm just kicking them in." The long, slender limbs glowed warmly beneath me, not a tan line or stretch mark in sight. I'd lucked out. They really were a delicious pair.

Marcella busied herself by tossing the leftovers in the pig bin, but I could tell by the stiff set of her petite shoulders that the conversation wasn't over yet. When she was done cleaning up, she sighed and turned to me.

"We don't do what we do because we are animals, Annie. We do what we do because it is right. And part of that sacred path is being a living memory for those souls we've condemned to die. Even in the end there is the chance for grace."

I dropped my gaze so she wouldn't see me roll my eyes. Damned Catholic brainwashing. Arguing with Marcella was like scaring Mormons off the front porch. Sure, they'd leave then, but they'd eventually come back with rhetorical reinforcement. Guess you could cast the black witch out of the church, but you couldn't cast the church out of the black witch.

We'd had this little chat before, and frankly I was sick of it.

"Grace or not, we're murderers; let's not mince words here. Our self-appointed job is to kill, plain and simple. Not to save. Not to hope. We stay busy, up to our nipples in the sins of others, because we choose to be the ones covered in someone else's gore. Because the dead deserve whatever peace we can give them, no matter what the cost."

"Spoken like a true convert," she sassed at me. I frowned and tested my new gait by walking over towards her. Her moral high ground was eroding, and I wanted to be there to pick her up once she'd slid on her ass down that slippery slope.

"Yeah," I said, nodding. "I drank the Kool-Aid; bought in on this scheme. But let's not forget it was *you* who talked me into this gig. Just because I don't share your religiosity, doesn't mean I'm not in it for the long haul. I shouldn't need to remind you, the one who made me, what we're all about."

"But don't you see?" she implored. "There is more to our blessed work than just dispatching flesh. We are talking about eternal life here!"

"No we're not! We're talking about principles versus application. Maybe I'd think differently if I wasn't the one doing the killing, if I didn't have to stand there spearing holes into so much meat. Maybe I'd think of their souls if I wasn't so convinced they'd gotten at the end of my knife because they didn't have one." I forced myself to take a calming breath. "You made me to be your tool, your dark justice. I'd be buried and forgotten if not for your magics. Spreading judicious hate around to those who deserve it is just a perk of my un-life. What else am I supposed to do with the gifts given to me? Ignore them?" I shook my head. "It's better that you aren't the one in the field, so you can remain the moral compass of our dynamic duo."

"But what about God's salvation?" she asked, breathing the question to me in a soft, child-like appeal. "Where is the room in your cold equations for that?"

I couldn't stay mad at her when she looked at me that way; brown eyes large, imploring.

"Maybe we're already a part of your god's end game. Ever think of that?" I conceded.

She smiled, though the motion never reached her eyes. "All the time."

I placed a hand against her soft cheek. "Then let's leave the salvation part to the big guy in the sky. We'll handle the flesh; let Him deal with the rest."

Her warm hand came up to cup mine, her lips tantalizingly close. "How did you get to be so prudent and practical?"

I grinned, eating up the distance between us until her body was pressed flush against mine. "I don't know. Must have been re-born that way."

Our mouths found each other in greedy abandon. I kissed her breathless, hungrily taking in all the life and love and hope she had to give. My fingers were fumbling over the tiny pearl buttons of her blouse when her hands stilled mine.

"We can't right now, Annie," she said, pulling away. "We've got work to do."

"Uh… come on," I wheedled. I managed to get the top button undone before moving on to the next. "Can't the dead wait for a while?"

She arched an eyebrow at me. "I don't know, can you?"

"Low blow, meanie." I stepped away from her. Devoid of her warm touch, my skin chilled quickly. "Fine. Who do we have on our dance cards today?"

"A John Doe. Walked into a local Quik-E-Save sometime late yesterday evening and did himself in with a shotgun in the men's bathroom."

"Ah man," I shuddered. "I hate suicides."

Marcella nodded her silent agreement. "He must have sat there all night too, because I only got the call this morning."

"Damnit. That brain matter he plastered on those walls will have hardened to cement by now. There'll be no scrubbing that mortar off once it's had this much time to set."

"Come on, then," she said, walking away from me. "No rest for the wicked."

"Or the saintly," I murmured, staring at her pointedly.

We loaded the van with our cleaning gear and headed out. In my blue hazmat suit and filtered respirator, none of my stitches showed. It was the only perk to an otherwise shitty job. Well, that and the pay.

The store manager met us at the employee entrance in the back. In his ruffled off-the-rack business casual, he looked like he hadn't slept all night.

"Thank you for coming on such short notice," he said in way of greeting. He eyed my get-up warily and then offered his hand to the still unsuited Marcella.

"Mr. Pimbly?" she asked as she took his hand. Her warm, comforting smile lit up her entire face. I watched as Mr. Pimbly relaxed his wire-taut stance a hair. Marcella just had that effect on people.

"Yes. Of course," he answered apologetically. "So sorry to call you folks out on a Saturday morning."

"It's no bother," she supplied humbly.

"Terrible thing, this business." The way he said it, I didn't know if he meant our choice in occupation or the remains of the corpse inside the store. He looked at Marcella as if waiting for validation.

She nodded. "Not to worry. When my co-worker and I are finished, the place will be as good as new."

"You're sure?" he asked. He reached trembling fingers up to adjust the wayward grey hairs across his balding pate. "Not a trace?"

"Not to worry, Mr. Pimbly. When we're done, it will be as if nothing ever happened."

He showed us into the store and down a long, dim hallway. The over-waxed vinyl squeaked plaintively beneath our industrial yellow booties. In this get-up, we couldn't have snuck up on a corpse. Luckily, we didn't have to.

The police and coroners had already been by to retrieve the body, but in cases like this there were bound to be large chunks of matter left over.

Mr. Pimbly stopped about twenty feet from the bathrooms.

"It's just there," he explained, gesturing in the direction of the men's room.

"Thank you, Mr. Pimbly," Marcella said, quick to release the man from his unwanted charge. "We can take it from here."

"Oh, all right then." Relief poured off of him in waves. "If you need anything, I will be around."

There was always this place of silence before the big reveal of the scene. A moment where the imagination generates the worst horrors it can conceive while the soul shores itself up for what's to come. I walked into the bathroom first to give Marcella a chance to finish arranging her gear.

From my viewpoint at the doorway, it looked like a pressure cooker of chili had exploded in one of the stalls. My brain scrambled for a mundane excuse. There weren't many things messier than a shotgun suicide. Give me a fatal stabbing any day.

Marcella walked in and stopped just behind me. I could almost hear her mind totting up the damages; the amount of cleansers we'd need, the tile we'd have to remove and replace, the hours it'd take to see this room right again. She always fell back to logistics; it was the safe, calculating place she compartmentalized down into to continue functioning.

The silence drew out like an old man's death rattle.

"Another day, another D.O.A," I quipped.

"My. Aren't we witty?"

"Just trying to break the tension." My eyes landed on a large hunk of meat on the floor. From the funny curlicue of still-perfect flesh, I knew it was a slice of face with a side of ear. I couldn't say where the eye was, but I knew we'd come across it sooner or later.

We went to work. The trick to being in the crime and trauma scene decontamination business, or CTS Decon, was a sympathetic nature and a very strong stomach. That was also how Marcella and I tended to split the chores. I was better at the scrubbing and she was better at the humanizing.

I was on the top shelf of a stepladder working at a particularly stubborn bit of embedded skull fragment when Marcella spoke up, breaking our usual solemn no-chatting work rule.

"I found him, Annie." Her words were muffled by her mask.

"Yeah, I found him too. Right here…" I said, gesturing to the chunk of grey matter I was busy chiseling off, "and here…" I pointed at a clump of hair plastered, upside down, to one of the ceiling tiles. "And over there," I finished, motioning towards the congealed, Jell-O-like blood on the ground.

"No," she explained. "I mean *him*."

A cold chill speared up my spine. Obviously, she wasn't talking about the suicide. I stopped scrubbing to look down at her. She avoided my eyes, intent instead on bagging up some of the larger chunks of pulverized flesh into sterilized red sacks.

"Where?"

"Not far from here, actually. Apparently, after he'd—" Her voice broke, and I watched mutely as she struggled to finish the thought. "He didn't go far," she concluded.

My mind raced. She'd finally found him, my ex-husband. After all this time I might actually be able to put to rest my own unsolved murder.

"When can I go see him?"

She stood and stared up at me. "Do you think you're ready?" Over the rim of her filtered respirator, I could see the worry in her eyes.

"Guess I'll find out."

The Ex was surprisingly easy to find. He'd moved about thirty miles south of where Marcella said we'd lived together; not all that far, really, for a man with a guilty conscience. It was curious, but not curious enough for me to really give a damn.

I caught up to him on his boat, a forty-foot penis extension that must have set him back at least a quarter million. Strapped awkwardly to the hull, I waited until we were a ways out to sea before I let him draw me in like a mackerel. When he saw what was on the other end of his line, he panicked and dropped the fishing pole into the water.

I hauled myself onboard with some difficulty. The sea water had run havoc with my undead flesh, making it all waterlogged and squishy. It'd take a few hours before I'd dry out enough to get the lot back into shape again. Marcella had warned me; something about saltwater being bad for her spells, but I hadn't listened. Sure, it was a royal pain, but I was a sucker for a dramatic entrance.

Bloated, I collapsed onto the deck, my legs needing time before they'd be able to hold me up properly. The Ex was screaming and backing away. Chants of "What the fuck, dude! What the fuck?" rang dully in my fluid-filled ears.

I eased myself up onto all fours and regurgitated the water I'd swallowed during the trip. It was touch-and-go to get the massive fishing hook out of my shoulder without ripping chunks of my flesh off, but I managed.

Just as I was about to chance standing, I was struck over the head. A sickening crunch sounded in the dome of my skull and I felt it cave inward. I collapsed with a startled oomph, my water-slickened mask sent skittering across the deck.

I raised a hand to stop the downfall of another blow. When the Ex saw my uncovered face, he started. Slowly, he lowered the first-aid kit he'd just bludgeoned me with to his side.

"Gloria?" he asked, the question preposterously gentle considering the dent he'd just given me.

I didn't remember his name. I'd been so worked up to deal with him that I hadn't even asked Marcella what it was. Why hadn't I bothered? Somehow it seemed ridiculous that I didn't know my own ex-husband's name, especially considering I was here to kill him.

I stood slowly, using the railing as support. He watched me rise; an odd mix of horror, disgust, and curiosity warring across his features. Eventually, disgust won out, and he eased away like a man who'd just been served road-kill for lunch.

He grimaced, the perfect ridge of his lips ruined by the motion. "What happened to you?"

I stared for a moment, taking him in. His face was smooth and clear, his cheeks sun-touched, like a baby who'd had its bottom exposed too long at the beach. Heavily tinted Ray-Bans obscured his eyes, but instinct told me they'd be blue and startling. His short, yellow-gold hair had been carefully gelled to look like he'd just gotten out of bed, a style no female could hope to pull off. Khakis and a polo shirt with a little croc on it finished off the yacht-yuppie look.

For some reason, looking at him made me want to diversify my portfolio or screw my secretary. I felt my skin crawl with something other than drying salt crystals. Had I really once fallen for this slippery-as-an-oil-slick package?

"Gloria? Is that really you?" he asked again.

The name was just on this side of familiar. However, if he'd yelled it at me in a crowd, I wouldn't have turned my head. But there it was, between us. What could I do but nod?

He grimaced at my silent admission. "Jesus, what happened to you?"

I opened my mouth to speak. The last of the fluid in my stomach burbled up to stifle my reply. Cold sea water drooled down my apron front to join the expanding puddle beneath me. The tail end of a bit of kelp slipped partway out of my mouth and dangled across my chin like a second tongue.

I slowly pulled the yard of slippery green seaweed out of my mouth and flung it onto the deck between us. It landed wetly near his sandaled feet and he backed away quickly. It took a good chest-shuddering cough before I could reply.

"I died," I said simply.

He stared at me, mouth open in shock, knuckles milky-white as he brought up the metal box of bandages in front of him like a shield. With the bold, sanguine cross emblazoned on the front, he could have been Saint George. Guess that made me the dragon.

"But if you're dead how can you… how can you—"

"Be up and walking around?" I supplied. "Let's just call it magic."

I could feel his gaze skip across the piecemeal segments of my body. Finally, his eyes settled on the still-original expanse of my face. I fought an almost childish desire to reach a hand up and check to make sure my nose wasn't crooked or something. Did I really look that different from how I used to be?

"Magic?" He said it like he didn't believe it, even though I was the squelchy, shambling proof right in front of him. "But that's impossible."

I shrugged. "It doesn't matter *how* I got here. What matters is that I *am* here."

"Damn, girl!" he exclaimed, shaking his head. Despite the motion, his well-gelled hair refused to shift a millimeter. "Who did this to you?"

"Funny you should ask…" I let the suggestion drag out until a little imaginary light-bulb seemed to appear above his head.

He raised his hands, and the first-aid kit, defensively. "You don't think that I did that to you, do you?"

"Do you think I should pin my death on someone other than my murderer?"

My legs were still unsteady as I shuffled a step towards him. He retreated in kind. If the rail at the other side of the boat hadn't brought him up short, I felt sure he'd have backpedaled into the drink.

"I swear…" he said, shaking his head emphatically. "I swear I didn't know you'd end up like this."

"Swear?" I asked incredulously. "Swear on what? On your honor? Your conscience?"

"But I'm telling the truth!" he proclaimed. "You've got to believe me!"

"No," I said coldly. "I don't."

I surged forward. He let out a shriek of surprise as I grabbed his shirtfront and hefted him off his feet. He flailed above me, hands clutched at the vise that was my fingers, feet kicking vainly against the unforgiving flesh of my brand new shins.

"What are you going to do?" he garbled.

I watched him struggle for a bit, surprised when I didn't feel any thrill of satisfaction from the effort. For all the lead-up, I could have been taking the garbage out to the curb for how much the motions meant to me.

"I'm going to enact vengeance against the one who killed me," I explained. Even to my ears, the words felt flat.

"No, wait!" he pleaded, red-faced. I eased up on my grip so that he could move his hands over mine; give himself more slack for air. "It wasn't me! I didn't kill you! It was her! She was the one who cooked up the whole scheme! I didn't have my hand in any of it."

I gave him a shake. "Her? Her who?"

"My girlfriend. Marcella."

For the second time that day, he clocked me upside the head. Only this time it wasn't with a blunt object. I'd never even considered the possibility. Marcella. He couldn't mean my Marcella, could he?

"Explain!" I demanded. I had to consciously relax my hold or risk snapping that pretty little neck of his.

"I didn't mean to cheat on you, baby, it just happened. You were my little stay-at-home wifey. But I had urges! I needed more affection than you were ready to give. When I met Marcella, it was like kismet. She said she'd handle everything; get you to leave us alone so we could be together."

"Keep talking," I all but growled.

"I didn't know she meant to kill you, I just thought she'd get you to agree to a divorce, sign some papers or something."

"How did you know I was dead?"

"I didn't at first. She told me how it'd gone down. Said you took it well enough."

"And you believed her?"

"Why wouldn't I? I had no clue she'd actually killed you. What kind of woman does that? She must have forged that email describing how you wanted to go far away, start over somewhere. There was no body, no sign of foul play. Your bags were packed. You'd signed the divorce papers. It was all so believable."

"What about the police?"

"What police? They were never called. You'd simply vanished. Off to start your new life."

It was all so clean, so horribly simple. I'd been swept under the rug with almost no effort. I felt betrayed by the notion. Not because the man who should have loved me obviously didn't, but because no one else had seemed to either. Hadn't there been neighbors, book-club pals, yoga buddies? Anyone who would have missed me? How could I have lived nearly thirty years in another life and not mattered to anyone but this one man?

They were treacherous thoughts, threatening weakness. I had to stay focused.

"But you didn't really believe those lies, did you?" I asked him. "If anyone should have known better, it was my husband; the man who was supposed to love, honor and protect me."

"I think… maybe I let myself believe at first that you'd just gone. But I didn't know for sure you were dead."

"When did you catch on?"

"It wasn't till after I'd called it off with Marcella that she told me what she'd really done to you. By then it was too late."

I scowled. "Too late? Too late for what? For my murderer to be brought to justice? For my husband to retrieve my remains and give me a proper buri-al?" I shook him, dislodging the perch of his sunglasses to reveal his eyes be-neath. They weren't brilliant sapphire at all, but something closer to a cloudy sky; insipid and dull.

"She said she still had your… body," he choked out, "and if I ratted on her she'd see that the murder was pinned on me; that she'd just been an un-willing accomplice. What could I do?"

I tightened my grip. "I don't know, grow a pair? Be a man and do the right thing?"

"You don't understand," he garbled, the effort turning his face a funny shade of purple. "I couldn't go to prison. Do you know what they do to pretty white men in there?" He shook his head emphatically as if I were a dunce to even have brought it up. "And you were an orphan," he continued, racking up the oh-so-perfect logic leaps he'd taken to write me off like he was proud of them. "There was no family that would be looking for you except me. No job, no coworkers; you just stayed home, cooking and clean-ing all day."

I finished the thought for him. "It was like I hadn't existed at all."

"Yeah… I mean, no," he backpedaled. "We'd had something good, you and me." He glanced down at me, the whites of his eyes now red and blood-shot. Whatever else he might have been trying to express, all that came through was revulsion. He couldn't see me without seeing my present form. I was wholly and truly dead to him.

"Just not good enough," I finished his thought for him.

He shook his head, or at least gave the motion a good try consider-ing his awkward position. "You know that I never intended to marry that woman!"

"Just use her like a cat's-paw to off your wife."

"I'm not a killer!"

"Just a man who'd leave his wife's fate to his mistress' whims."

"That doesn't make me a murderer."

"No, but it does make you a bad husband."

"I was good to you, Gloria. You had everything you could have asked for: the big house, the cars, all that money. You loved your pampered life. So don't tell me differently. I pulled you up from obscurity when I married you and introduced you to good society. Maybe you had to turn a blind eye to a few indiscretions, but you always seemed willing to pay that price."

"Are you really wasting breath trying to blame my own murder on me?"

"No, of course not, honey. What happened to you was horrible. But I didn't kill you! I never raised a hand to you in my entire life. You know that!"

The sad part was I didn't. I didn't know if the guy was speaking truth or just telling me what I wanted to hear. Everything from my life before was a blank.

He could have claimed we'd been square-dancing geologists and I wouldn't have known any different. It was sloppy of me to have come out here when I hadn't done my usual level of homework, hadn't put in the necessary planning for a clean kill. I couldn't tell the truth from the lies. My moral compass was broken.

Still, he was scum; there was no doubt about that. No matter how blue his blood might be, he was white trash through and through. I wanted to think that once I'd loved him, had been happy to prop him up from beneath his shadow. That cooking and cleaning and caring had been enough to make me supremely happy, because frankly the alternative was too damned horrible to contemplate.

Sure, it'd be sweet to think he'd been a classic Lifetime series bad guy, but somehow I doubted it. Things were never that clear-cut. What felt more likely was that I had used him too. Let him buy me a new life with all his money and purchased that comfort with a judicious amount of carefully ap-plied ignorance. Did that mean then, in some way, I had deserved my fate? I couldn't say for sure, and that thought bothered me.

I let go of my strangle-hold about his neck. He collapsed onto the deck, coughing and hacking for breath. I stepped away and then sat down heavily on the nearby plush bench.

He sputtered and coughed until some white began to seep back into the purpley-red blob that was his face. I watched him silently as he struggled for breath. What the hell was I going to do now?

We stayed like that for some time. Finally, he spoke.

"I've missed you, you know."

I wanted to laugh, but something stopped me. "Somehow I doubt that," I murmured.

"No, really. Only after you had gone away did I realize just what an amazing person I had let slip out of my life."

I leaned back against the cherry-red cushions of the bench. "Was that before or after you got tired of diddling Marcella?"

He looked away. "You were the best part of my life," he stated simply. "I was stupid to think I needed anything more than you."

I eyed the golden crown of his head for a time, letting the weight of my stare linger on his heavy brow. "Rather critical time to come to that determination, don't you think?"

At that, he looked up at me. "I never forgot you, Gloria. Not ever. And for all that happened between us, well… I'm sorry."

I didn't say anything. I didn't have anything to say.

"So what do we do now?" he asked.

"I don't know," I admitted. Everything on this run had gone tits-up and I didn't have the exit strategy to see me cleanly out of it.

"Listen…" he implored, easing slowly to his feet. "It's been a long time, and a lot has… changed. Neither one of us knows where to go from here, and that's okay. Why don't we just take some time, soak up some rays, and have some bubbly. We can discuss what comes next after the champagne."

I arched an eyebrow at him. "Strange to share a drink with the person who tried to kill you." Even as I said it, I didn't know if I meant him writing me off for Marcella or me coming here today to make him pay for what he'd done.

He smiled, a dazzling, if practiced, maneuver that showcased his perfect, bleached teeth. "I can't curse whatever it was that brought us back together again. So instead I choose to celebrate. Just wait here for a mo…" he ordered, pointing at me, "and I'll fetch the drinks."

I watched him scurry below deck and listened quietly to the clink and clatter of wine glasses jarring together.

"I've changed," I admitted aloud. Not only was I a bit on the dead side, I also had a rather questionable hobby.

"Honey, I've changed too." His voice was muffled by the distance separating us. "Besides, how important are natural looks anyway?" he continued gaily. "With the right funds, a discreet plastic surgeon, I bet we could get you looking almost as good as new in no time."

"What for?" I asked him.

"To have a normal life, of course," he answered blithely. The idea caught me unawares. I guess I'd never put much thought into a *normal* life, whatever that meant. "You don't want to spend the rest of your days looking like that, do you?" He asked the question like he already knew the answer. "You want to be able to walk around like a real woman. Start a new life where you don't have to hide all the time. I can help you with that."

He was offering to take me back into his life, doll me up; upgrade my breasts and buns and lips; turn me into a pretty, plastic girl. I'd have said it was sort of sweet if it wasn't being done in a blatant attempt to buy off his guilt over what he'd done, or more precisely, what he hadn't done. But at the moment I couldn't put much thought into it. All I could think about was Marcella.

She'd killed me. Gouged her way into my life by sleeping with my idiot husband and then spear-headed the plan to get rid of me. The notion sounded so ridiculous, like the plot to a trashy, bargain-bin murder mystery. And yet, she had been the one to bring me back from the dead. How big of a leap was it for her to also be the one who had done the ending? How else could she have gotten hold of my body?

But Marcella… my Marcella. Why hadn't she ever told me? She must have known my coming out here today could lead me to the truth. Why had she chanced it?

Ultimately, it didn't matter. She'd murdered me, lied about it, and let me love her with a pure and unfettered passion. To call it a betrayal wasn't quite right, but it was the closest thing that came to mind. For all those moments, all those tears and tenderness… she had to answer.

The knowledge caused a cold lump of caustic bile to settle in my stomach, but there was no helping that. She'd made me the way I was. There was no going back from what I'd have to do to make this right.

The Ex reappeared on deck, ripping me out of my malaise. He carried a tray draped with a long, white linen cloth jauntily before him. Upon it stood two tall, if emaciated-looking, pieces of stemware. A pale golden fluid effervesced from each glass making me think of antacid tablets.

I stood, not because I wanted to appear respectful, but because I couldn't bear the thought of him having a position of power over me. Been there. Done that. Didn't want the T-shirt.

He took up a glass. "To fateful reunions… and happy endings," he intoned dramatically.

I reached over automatically. I didn't have the heart to tell him liquor was wasted on the dead. Literally, didn't have one. I'd had it removed months ago after an unfortunate, if ironic, javelin mishap while dispatching a P.E. teacher.

The second my hand encircled the glass, the serving tray fell away to reveal a large, comically-yellow flare gun gripped in his hand.

I watched, frozen, as he pulled the trigger. The slug slammed into my chest, taking me off my feet. The white-hot phosphorescent projectile burrowed into my now-shattered ribcage, eating me up from inside.

I slid across the slickened deck until the side brought me up short. Blood-red smoke billowed out of my broiling carcass like a daemon released from its bottle. I could hear the layers of my borrowed skin crackling away like fried pork rinds. It was the most interesting of sensations, like being tickled on the inside by an over-eager wire brush.

A smear of retina-burning brilliance seared into my senses, blinding me. I remained unmoving on the floor. Through the deck, I could feel the Ex's self-assured strut as he stepped evenly, and without hurry, towards where I had fallen. What he didn't know would kill him. When it came to playing dead, I was the best.

"What a sad, unfortunate soul you are, Gloria," he mocked. His voice came to me from within the obscuring veil of smoke, like something out of a dream. "And such a waste!" he continued. "To think, I used to fantasize about fucking you one more time." He laughed, the kind of laugh that make me think of enormous black spiders scurrying for cover. "But look!" he said with false wonder. "I guess I had it in me for one more husbandly screw after all."

He approached within arm's reach; such a rookie move. I wrapped a hand behind his nearest ankle. With a yank, I pulled him off his feet. He landed hard, crashing onto the deck with a loud thud.

I crawled up his body like a kid on a big toy, not wanting to waste the time it'd take to stand. Out of what was now my gaping chest cavity, the flare continued to issue smoke. I ripped the projectile out of my chest, twisting it past the clinging shards of breastbone that hampered the way.

I held the searing brand up to his face and let him fully appreciate the view of its white-hot tip. "This is going to hurt you more than it hurt me," I promised.

The Ex was wearing shorts, but the legs were wide enough to allow the cylindrical object an unobstructed pathway upwards. When the incendiary met his unprotected, delicate flesh, he began to scream.

It was like being woken up from a bad dream. Here was my chorus; the throaty melody to which I set my life's rhythms. The exquisitely pure note of total abandonment of faith, of the trappings of hope, of the thoughtless lie that was salvation.

My tainted soul thrilled to the chorus of my righteous symphony, my entire body humming with the purity of that sound. I closed my eyes for a moment and savored its haunting gospel as I continued to apply pressure on the projectile, ensuring a steady, constant contact.

When the cries died down, I knew that shock had set in. I scrambled to my feet, dragging his thrashing form behind me. Though I'd never piloted a boat before, the keys hung in the ignition just like in any other vehicle, and Hollywood had taught me that the flat-handled bar was the throttle. I turned one, pushed the other, and off we surged.

Waves bucked against the hull of the boat as it tore further out to sea. In which direction, I didn't care. Just as long as we had strong engines and the setting sun to sail her by.

My charge was curled up into himself as if that primitive maneuver could somehow dull his intimate pain. I hauled him to the rear of the boat. He was nearly insensate, more focused on his seared manhood than where he was being dragged.

Whatever kept him occupied was fine by me. I lifted him to his feet; no easy task considering his legs didn't seem to want to support him. With deliberate care, I intertwined my right arm around the rear railing for support.

"I really want to thank you," I supplied cheerily, giving him a bit of a shake. I eyed the white, foamy current that ripped across the surface of the sea from the boat's large steel propellers.

He stammered and struggled, garbled oaths and prayers dripping from those two perfect rosebud lips of his. If any gods heard him, they were silent.

"You've given me the greatest gift I could ask for," I shouted over the roar of the outboard motors. "Renewed purpose."

I palmed his face with my left hand and leaned all the way down, pushing his head into the water. Too late, his hands shot out, struggling against my grip. Desperate fingernails dug into my flesh, raking long grey riverbeds into the cold wastelands of my arms. His eyes locked with mine between my fingers, desperate and wide.

A moment later his head hit the water, then the back of his skull met the spinning propeller blades with a satisfying dull crunch. I could feel his entire skeleton rattle as it jarred against the flesh-hungry metal. Sea foam turned a frothy pink as his head was pulped like a nut in a blender. And still I kept pushing, shoving whatever was still left of his face into the spinning blades, until even my own hand became a sacrifice.

The rest of the body slipped away from me and into the drink. I watched it float like a buoy upon the waves until it passed out of sight. But already I was thinking of something else; someone else. Already I was planning my next deeds, my next mission, my next call. It was time to show Marcella just how forgiving a person I could be.

𝖂

Our home was dark when I arrived, the lights conspicuously absent given the lateness of the hour. I found Marcella in bed, our bed, her eyes closed in the fullness of sleep. When she heard me come in, she awoke. The ready smile she reserved for me faltered when I neared.

"Annie?" she asked, voice still froggy with sleep. "What's happened to you?"

I grinned humorlessly. "I've had a bad day."

She nodded, the motion shifting the dark curls that splayed across the pillow. "I know," she stated with a hushed, sympathetic voice.

We were silent for some time, the sound of the bedside clock a passionless, mechanical heartbeat measuring the distance between us. I wanted to ask her about before, about why she'd killed me for the love of that man, but it didn't matter anymore. Only one thing was important. I almost couldn't form the question.

"Why? Why did you set me on this path?" I finally asked. We could have lived a lifetime together without me ever knowing, without it having to end like this. Hadn't we been worth that inconvenience? Wasn't I worth the pain of that little falsehood?

She smiled, a beauteous creature that tugged at the strings of my heart. Even now I couldn't deny that she was enchanting.

"I had to," she said in way of explanation. "I couldn't live a lie any longer. You had to know."

I walked towards her until only a handful of inches, and my unwillingness to trespass across that space, separated us. "Was *everything* a lie?" I demanded. It was a struggle to keep the plea out of my voice.

"Oh my dear Annie," she said, smiling. "No matter what other evils I may have committed in my life, pretending to love you was not one of them."

I looked away. "Do you know why I'm here?"

Marcella took a deep breath before responding. "I do," she said evenly. "But I will not force you to make that choice. Consider it my final gift."

"What do you mean?" I asked, glancing back at her.

She gestured to the empty wineglass on the bedside table. The cut-glass goblet held the remains of a murky, dark residue which lingered ominously in its recesses.

"You see… I have already done it for you. It shouldn't be long now. I am so happy I got to see you before I had to leave."

I shook my head as if that motion could somehow dislodge the absurd idea, but the truth of her deeds was reflected in her resigned gaze. "Why are you doing this?" I asked her.

"So you won't have to. Oh, Annie… you imagine yourself so filled with sins, I couldn't add this one to you as well." Marcella placed her hand over her heart, her delicate fingers splayed protectively over the fragile organ. "It is my price to pay; a life for a life."

I fell to my knees and took up her hand in my own, the self-imposed division separating us forgotten. "This isn't how it should be."

Marcella clenched my hand with a feeble resolve. "But it is just."

"No. I won't let you do this!"

"It is done," she explained by way of a shrug. "If nothing else can be said about me, I know how to make a decent poison."

I knelt beside her for some time, not wanting the moment to expire, not willing to release the hurt that would see this whole thing ended.

Slowly, I drew my fingers away from where they'd intertwined with hers. As I stood, I felt the cold from within wash over me like a protective, insulating blanket.

"No," I said, letting the detached place from which I now dwelled chill my words. "You're not going out that way."

Marcella stared up at me, eyes large with a quiet acceptance. "My sweet Annie… ruthless to the last."

Wordlessly, I crouched over her and positioned my one good forearm across her neck. With my full weight on her throat, I pressed down. She relented at first, but then that part of her brain not governed by rational thought took over and she began to struggle.

She fought against me as the seconds ticked into minutes. Flailing, she kicked off the covers, ripping apart our bed, until exertion took its toll. In the end, I didn't know whether it was my efforts that did her in, or the poison-tinged blood that coursed through her body with the surge of adrenaline. I chose to believe the former. All I could say was that she died in my arms, free of the sin of suicide. As far as salvation went, it was all I could think to give her.

I held her for some time afterwards, surprisingly calm, intent. With her death, the cycle of retribution was over. The slate had been cleaned. I had been given a new life, one no longer shadowed by my tragic history and Marcella's unfortunate part in it.

But was it a life I actually wanted?

The answer was clear, like a church bell ringing across my mind. What good was a tool without someone to direct it? What good was the dark if it wasn't showcased by the light? I stared down at Marcella's sleeping form, the cold touch of death still yet to rob her of her warm glow.

This didn't have to be the end for us.

We could start over.

Sure, her memories might be muddled from the ritual, but that was a risk I was willing to take. I knew how to say the words, was familiar with the herbs and rites required for the transference. If it was fated for us to be together, I wasn't going to let a thing as simple as death keep us apart.

Marcella may have killed me, but she'd also saved me. She'd shown me what true love was and I wasn't willing to give up on that promise. Not now, not ever. If it was meant to be, her heart would find its way back to me. And in the meantime, we still had a lot of work to do.

THE SECRET LIFE OF DREAMS

BY TOM HOWARD

I slip into the dream right where I always do. I'm following an old man, with his hat in his hand, around a sidewalk to a small cottage. Ahead of him is his wife, a short, thin woman wearing a hat constructed to look like a giant magnolia flower. It might even be a real magnolia blossom. The couple doesn't notice me, and I wonder why I am not a participant in my own dream.

I don't know the old man's name at this point. I know it will come to me later and even then it won't be important. His suit and tie are as gray as the fringe of hair around his bald pate, but the hat he's holding is a wonderful chocolate brown. Its unexpected richness somehow makes the surrounding greenery more saturated and alive.

His wife is Mavis, but from the thrust of her bony shoulders and the omniscience of a dreamer, I know she is only addressed as Mrs. Briarwood.

Mrs. Briarwood is in a mood. She's late for her appointment and somehow it's her husband's fault. It's always her poor husband's fault, and somehow, by association, I am also to blame.

I watch her march around the corner of the house, but I am too distracted by my colorful surroundings to pay attention to her. Rows of large houses—half dilapidated and blanketed with ivy—cover the hillside. Trees grow up through ulcerated asphalt and crowd together in overgrown lawns.

"I told you she was gone," says Mrs. Briarwood. "She took the money and left." She glares at her husband and ignores me.

Poor Mr. Briarwood turns his hat endlessly in his hands and silently absorbs his wife's contemptuous gaze.

The front door of the cottage is open, and the sun pours in from everywhere. A single chair sits in the middle of the abode's only room. The planks forming the walls of the cottage are so ancient that their edges have worn down, letting air and sunlight into the room through wide slots in the walls.

Time shifts into slow gear and dust motes sparkle in the rays of sunlight. They drift by me in mesmerizing eddies and currents. The cottage is a golden oasis in the forest of green.

Mrs. Briarwood stamps her foot, and the floorboards echo with the sound. "She is supposed to do my hair. I have an appointment."

Startled, I realize she is looking directly at me for the first time, and I duck my head and see my middle-aged paunch covered by a pink golf shirt. Beige slacks and brown loafers stretch beneath my belly. I refrain from apologizing automatically. I am scolded enough at my job at the bank every day. I don't need a little old woman giving me crap about a wash and set. Her silver beehive looks fine under its giant magnolia blossom.

Why can't I at least look younger and thinner in my own damn dream?

"Perhaps there's another beautician in town," I tell her, surprised. I haven't talked to Mrs. Briarwood in previous dreams. Usually she disappears by this time.

Mr. Briarwood looks at his wife hopefully at my suggestion, but her scowl deepens and her eyes narrow.

The small room darkens, and a cold wind whips though the latticework walls. I try to make myself wake up, but I am having trouble breathing. While I watch, ivy grows up over the cottage windows, and the room grows darker still.

Mr. Briarwood steps back, his eyes wide with fear. His wife's face elongates, and her eyes darken into ebon pools. I cringe when I see the fangs in her mouth and the thin, red ribbon of her tongue.

Just as Mrs. Briarwood's face fills my field of vision and the sound of thunder buffets my ears, the door flies open and a small woman, owl-shaped handbag in hand, steps into the room. I am pinching myself, desperately trying to wake up, when she appears like a welcome summer breeze. I don't realize that the cottage door was closed until it slams open. The thunder disappears, and the room brightens.

"I'm so sorry," says the woman I don't recognize. I'd have remembered those apple cheeks and long, chestnut curls. She smiles at all of us. "I was almost out of town when I remembered our appointment, Mrs. Briarwood. I couldn't leave without making sure you were taken care of."

An old woman once more, Mrs. Briarwood gives me a hungry look and steps back.

"Please, take a seat," says the beautician. "This won't take long." She winks at me, and I see her eyes are deep purple.

"Take a seat, Mrs. Briarwood," repeats the woman, her voice firm.

"I don't want to," says the old woman, sounding like a small child, but she marches forward with steps so mechanical I expect to see a windup key protruding from her back. She sits in the chair.

Mr. Briarwood rotates his chocolate-colored hat and watches.

"Are you just going to stand there?" the hairdresser asks me, but her tone is light and she smiles as she carefully removes Mrs. Briarwood's magnolia hat.

"What can I do?" I ask, hoping I'm not going to have to shampoo that beehive. I watch with suspended disbelief as the summer woman takes two knitting needles from her now goldfish-shaped bag and sticks them into the top of Mrs. Briarwood's head.

I flinch, sure I am sliding into the granddaddy of all nightmares. I expect to see blood and gore erupt from the top of her head like lava from a volcano. Instead, the beautician works the needles as if she is knitting, and a gray string runs from the top of Mrs. Briarwood's head to the knitting needles. "If you want to make yourself useful," says the woman, "wrap this yarn around your hands."

I hold out my hands and stare at the top of Mrs. Briarwood's head as it slowly unravels onto the woman's needles. The yarn, now flesh colored, snakes from the needles and wraps around my waiting hands. The inside of

Mrs. Briarwood's head isn't gray matter and brain fluid. It is totally empty. I watch the old woman breathe as her face disappears, followed by her neck and her blue suit.

The amount of yarn I hold grows larger as more and more of Mrs. Briarwood vanishes. I look at Mr. Briarwood; afraid he is as shocked by what is happening as I am, but he is slowly fading away.

"I'm Ginger Rose," says the beautician as she works. "Not your typical dream, I imagine."

"I'm Clinton," I say. "I don't know what's going on." Mrs. Briarwood's legs are disappearing.

"What if this has nothing to do with you?" asks Ginger Rose. "What if a friendly witch decides to leave town and forgets a nasty spell she left behind? One that survives by attracting floaters like you and gobbling them up? To us, you are simply visitors that drift in while you sleep. This isn't the first time you've been here, is it?"

"No," I say, "but I've never gotten this far into the cottage before." I watch the sunlight gather around as she finishes. "Was Mrs. Briarwood doing something to me?"

She sighs, putting her needles back in her bag. "You floaters think the universe revolves around you. What if you're the figment and we are the reality?"

I look for Mr. Briarwood. With the sound of a popped bubble, he and his hat disappear.

She continues, "Next time you feel drawn repeatedly to a dream, Clinton, remember what happens to a moth near a flame." She picks up her bag and looks around the little cottage. "Again, I apologize for Mrs. Briarwood. I should have known she was becoming too powerful when she created herself a husband." She takes the yarn from my hands, shapes it into a ball, and drops it into her purse. "I'll be more cautious with her next time. And I will keep her away from nice, juicy floaters like you."

She takes me by the arm and leads me to the door. "Do you remember your dreams when you wake up, Clinton?"

"Not usually," I reply.

"Good," she says, and closes the door behind us.

FROGSONG

BY KATE BRANDT

O n the TV it's Boston versus Chicago. 4-0 lead White Sox in the fifth with one out when Lou Marson is up at bat. Marson hits and Buehrlie, the pitcher, tries to stop the ground ball with his left foot when it ricochets and rolls up his shin. He races after the ball, grabs it with his glove, then—unbelievable!—throws it backhand between his legs to Konerko, the first baseman, who makes the out. An impossible play. The crowd roars. I want to roar with it. I start to. I rise and my head pokes out of the water. Then I remember.

I'm a frog.

That's right, an amphibian. It still surprises me. I look down expecting the old body and my heart always stops when I see what I've got. The little green drumsticks, the white belly, the webs. My new digs—a twenty-four-inch tank with a water filter, a little duckweed floating in it and some pebbles on the bottom. I kind of hang here, my arms and legs floating, my head just clearing the surface. There's a small plastic hut that looks like a coconut shell. Sometimes, when I can't take it anymore, I climb inside. It's just big enough for me to crouch there, my legs packed against my chest, my webs firmly planted on the glass below me. I like the feeling—the safety, the darkness. An instinct, I guess.

A frog for the time being, that's what I tell myself. I haven't always been. For the first twenty-three years and seven months of my life I was Frank Farms of Dobbs, New York, and I still would be if I hadn't had the bad luck to run into Daphne. She's a witch. A gorgeous witch, yes, with that curly brown hair down her back, those dancing eyes, that truculent mouth. A body to die for—hips swinging back and forth when she walks; breasts like mangos. But, apparently, possessed of supernatural powers.

I'm not her only victim. My tank is in Daphne's living room, but over on the other side, near the kitchen, are the other cages. There's Nestor the milk snake curled around a fake branch asleep most of the time; Carlyle the ferret in his pen of newspaper shavings; Mo and Chippy the hermit crabs. A motley assortment of animals—I've often wondered about that. Not the sort of grouping that implies *purpose*. There's a kind of manic randomness to it, as if someone went into a PetSmart with $200 to spend and ten minutes to do it, and came out with us.

According to Daphne, she doesn't have control over it. The magic comes *through* her, she says. She doesn't control the form we take. Something makes her angry and then—and here her eyes get all big like some four-year-old telling you *it wasn't my fault, the glass broke itself*—it just happens. The magic just comes.

A big talker, Daphne. She's here most of the time, playing online chess, fussing over our food or our cages, skating around the floor in her stockinged feet. There are no bubbling cauldrons, no eye of newt or anything, and not much witch-talk. It's all about the weather and what she's making for dinner. Sometimes she talks about the friends she makes over the internet playing online games—Phil with the doomed marriage who she worries has fallen in love with her; Warren who has a sickness that won't allow him to leave the house.

Sometimes she talks about the future. She takes me out of the tank, sets me on the countertop while she chops up onions or something and her face gets all earnest. "You can change back," she says. She sweeps her hand in the air, indicating the other side of the kitchen. "You and the others," she says. "You lost sight of yourself, got a little out of control, but you can do it. The spell's reversible. You just have to figure it out; take back your humanity again," she says. "That's all it takes."

Which is a little frustrating, a little vague. Nevertheless I take it seriously. Here in my tank, I've had a lot of time to think about things. What my priorities should be. What life as a man is really all about.

$$\mathbb{V}$$

As brown-haired, six-foot-one Frank Farms of Dobbs, N.Y., I was pretty much average. I had a middle management job—building manager for an apartment complex in town called Hathaway Gardens. I went to bars a lot. I tried to keep a certain look going—dark pants, suede ankle boots, hip-length leather coat.

There was my brother Kyle, who'd moved to the City and become a photographer. I was a little jealous of him, with the money he made doing freelance, and the models he dated. There were my parents, Bev and Raymond, big TV watchers. And then there was Nellie, my girlfriend. Beautiful girl: long brown hair, somber eyes, delicate breasts the shape of margarita glasses. Bit of a problem child, though: a habit of dressing in clothes she thought were Bohemian—thrift store skirts and tennis shoes; sweatshirts worn inside out with silk scarves to dress them up. Sexy in the sense that it was something a college student would wear, but also kind of dowdy. Lately I'd been trying to get her to change her look. "You have a great body," I urged. "Go to the Gap or something—buy clothes that fit you." Which was apparently insensitive.

"Why are you always trying to change me?" she wailed. "Why can't you like me the way I am?

A theme with her: *like me the way I am.* Nellie was not from Dobbs: she was from Gloucester, Massachusetts. A real New England blue blood, she grew up reading Stendhal and Proust, hearing her father recite Milton as he paced around the living room. Evidently his was a big name at the university town they lived in and Nellie was his protégé, the daughter who was so talented he had her apply for a Fulbright when she was eighteen. She didn't get it, and that was when the arguments started. Her father told her that if she wanted to make something of herself, be like him, she'd have to work a lot harder. Nellie told him she just wanted to be herself.

It ended badly, I guess. After one argument he told her to "live elsewhere." Elsewhere turned out to be Dobbs.

In her mind *not trying to change me* meant not saying anything about the fact that once we moved in together, she never left the apartment. She had a job four days a week at the farmer's market selling baked goods. Aside from that, she never left the house. I'd come home from work and there she'd be in some shapeless thrift store dress, writing in her journal. It wasn't just her presence; it was the *atmosphere.*

"We're in our *twenties,*" I said once to her, urgently. "The *party* decade."

She looked up at me all starry-eyed. "I just read the most beautiful sonnet," she said. "Listen to this: *Yourself the sun and I the melting frost.* It's so… *ardent.*"

I looked at her. There were times making love—the cries she made, her dark, wet eyes in the darkness—that I thought how lucky I was. But that night I had to ask myself how I ended up with Emily Dickinson. Why couldn't I have some model in my bed like my brother Kyle?

"Sonnet," I said. "What's that, some kind of douche?" Her face fell. I felt guilty, but I also felt like I wouldn't mind punching a wall.

♥

This whole thing happened in a bar. Girls Night Out at Seelie's and I wasn't even supposed to be there. Nellie and I had had an argument about that back at the apartment. I'd been pushing her to make friends and she'd met some people, but she was self-conscious.

"Just drop me off," said Nellie. "I don't want you in there."

"You won't notice me," I'd said. "I just want one beer."

"No, Frank." Her voice rose one octave. "This is *my* night. With *my* friends. This is for *me.*"

I didn't want to fight with her; we'd been doing too much of that lately. "All right, I won't go in," I said. "Don't worry about it. I'll go to Foley's instead."

"Really?" said Nellie. Her face softened.

"No big deal," I said.

"Thank you, Frank," said Nellie. She came and rubbed her face against my chest and I laughed a little. *See, Frank?* I said to myself. *It isn't difficult. It really isn't that hard to be a nice guy.*

And I was planning to keep my promise to her, I really was. Nellie came out in her fitted bell-bottom jeans and a black button-down sweater and I told her how nice she looked. We got into the car and drove the two miles to Seelie's.

At Seelie's, I pulled the Toyota over to the curb to let her off. Nellie opened the door, put her foot out. That's when I saw Daphne.

That curly brown hair down to her shoulders. That mouth with the permanent smirk to it. That night she was in jeans and a brilliant turquoise button-down shirt that must have been silk or something the way it fluttered around her hips. She came sashaying up the street. As she did, her leather coat swung open and I stared.

"Listen, Nellie," I leaned out the open car door. "I don't have money for the meters. I'm just going to run in and get change."

"It's seven." Nellie furrowed her brow. "You can park on the street at Foley's for free by now."

"I don't think so." I shook my head. "I think they changed the rules."

She made a face. "All right. Whatever." Later I could always say that I ran into someone I knew from high school. It happened all the time.

In Seelie's they know me. Jake Carr, who I went to kindergarten with, is the bartender. It's a nice place—dark wood everywhere and one long bar with a ten-foot mirror behind it, all silvery. That night I angled myself so I could see the room behind me. I swiveled to the left and saw Nellie with two girls I didn't recognize. Then I swiveled to the right, looking for that turquoise shirt I'd seen. I found her at the pool table. She wasn't alone—she was playing some guy in a Who T-shirt. *Lose,* I thought. *Lose. Lose.* It worked. As soon as he put down his cue, I was there.

"Up for another game?" I asked. She had just put her cue down. Her brown hair cascaded around her. She looked at me lazily.

"Sure, I'll play again." She had crouched down to the slit in the table where you reach your arm in to get the balls out, and I crouched down beside her. That's when I felt it—the longing. It reached out like a giant fist and grabbed me, pulled me close. For a minute I thought I was going to tip over, fall right into her.

That was the first sign, I guess, that Daphne wasn't ordinary... but who questions pleasure? People go toward what feels good, and that night I did too.

"It looked like you were beating the pants off that guy," I said, with both our arms sunk inside the table. Her eyes flicked over at me.

"I was."

"Was he bad or are you just really good?"

She smiled. "I tend to win a lot."

"A real pool shark, huh," I said.

"Not just pool," she said. "I play everything. Scrabble, backgammon, chess, croquet..."

"And do you always win?" I asked.

She dipped her head, hiding another smile.

"You're scaring me," I said. "I feel like I should ask for a handicap or something." I darted her a look but she didn't return it.

"Let's see how you do on your own. I'll let you break, how's that... What's your name?"

"Frank. What's yours?"

"Daphne. You break, Frank."

"Great," I said. I took my shot and the balls scattered.

Then it was Daphne's turn. "Solids," she said. "I'll pocket over there," she pointed. One quick thrust of the cue and the green and the red disappeared.

"Jeez," I said. "What, do you personally command each ball?"

She laughed, happily. "They like me."

"What is it, your perfume?"

"Energy. They like my energy."

"Goddess energy," I said. "You're the game goddess." I caught her eye. I let my glance drop, taking in the landscape, the slope of the breasts. I remember what I thought in that moment: *in the hole.*

Of course there was Nellie. Most of the time I was able to keep my back to her, but sometimes I had to go to the side of the table that faced her. I just kept my head down, swiveled my eyes around.

"Your shot," said Daphne. I eyed the table. There was a well-placed stripe at the far corner.

Concentrate, Frank, I told myself. *Focus.*

"You're not from Dobbs, are you?" I said as I bent over the table. "I haven't seen you."

"I moved recently. I live down at Bridgewood Condos."

"Oh yeah? How is that place?" I tried to picture it. I'd driven by—a big white sign at the bottom of a hill.

"It's fine. The parking isn't great."

"Yeah, that's always an issue." My ball headed towards the pocket but ricocheted at the last minute and I winced.

"You live alone?" I tried to make it sound casual. I was already imagining her there, walking around in underpants and that silk shirt of hers. She'd come toward me, swaying those hips. A stitch would come loose—one stitch. A button would pop and then I'd see those glorious mangos.

"Yeah." She raised her eyebrows. "Why are you asking, Frank? Are you getting ideas about me?"

I blushed with pleasure. "Maybe."

"I wouldn't," she said. "I can be dangerous."

I smiled down at the pool table as I aimed. "You know that's exactly the kind of thing that turns a man on, don't you?" I said.

"Seriously, Frank."

I looked up. Her face was all earnest.

"Okay," I smirked. "Whatever you say."

W

By then we were nearing the end of the game, and Daphne was winning, but there was still hope left for me. I had four striped balls still on the table and I was hoping for a combination shot. I had to win; I knew that. Daphne was a game girl—she lived for the excitement of it. If I lost I would be just another opponent who hadn't made the cut.

Daphne interrupted. "Someone's staring at you."

I turned around, just for a second. Nellie's face had a glazed look. I could see the pain and for a moment I even thought of giving up the game, just leaving. But then I thought there was going to be hell to pay anyway. I might as well enjoy myself in the time I had left.

"Who is that?" asked Daphne.

"That's Nellie," I said. "My girlfriend."

"She looks pretty upset."

"She would be. I'm not really supposed to be here." I smiled conspiratorially at Daphne. "I told her I'd leave."

Daphne didn't smile back.

"And you didn't?"

"Hey, it's just a pool game," I said. "One game." She frowned. I gave her a jaunty look. Daphne looked down at the table. There were two balls lined up with the eight ball behind them. She was going to get it, I knew. She did. All three of them—right into the pocket she called.

"Well, it's my game now," she said, putting down her cue.

"Almost your game." I smiled.

"No, my game. No more eight ball."

"It's a foul," I said. "You can't send the eight ball down with object balls."

"A foul," said Daphne incredulously. "You're kidding, right?"

"That's how you play," I said gently.

"In what universe?" She had a hand on one hip.

"Every universe," I said. "Everywhere. Really. Ask anyone. Go to the bar. Ask Jake over there."

"I don't need to ask other people how to play pool, Frank," she said. "I know how to play pool."

That's when I started to lose it. I hate cheating. My brother Kyle used to cheat and my father used to pretend he didn't notice. "Well, obviously you don't know how to play," I said acidly. "Because you don't know the rules."

"Listen, Frank." Daphne put her cue down. "I'm sorry we have a dis-agreement about how to play the game of billiards, but I won the game. I see you have something going on with your girlfriend over there, and I think I'm leaving. I've had my two games and I'm satisfied and I'm going to go."

"What a fucking bitch," I said incredulously.

"Watch it, Frank." Daphne turned around, bent over to reach for her coat.

"Bitch," I said again.

"I'm leaving, Frank," said Daphne calmly. "Goodbye."

$$\mathbb{W}$$

I've asked myself a gazillion times why. I've gone down in my little co-conut shell hut and asked myself *what was I thinking for crissake*. But I've always known the answer. I was tired of it. Tired of being Mr. Average, Mr. Second Best.

With her back to me, Daphne bent down to pick her coat up, and stuck her arms through the sleeves. Once it was on, she started to turn around again. I picked up the pool cue from the side of the table and jabbed her with it, right above her left clavicle. Lightly—more like a poke. Just to get her attention.

"Don't do that, Frank," she said. She turned around and looked at me.

"Don't do what?" I asked with mock innocence. "Break the rules?"

She held my eyes. "Don't be an asshole. Don't get me mad."

"You don't have to get mad," I said lightly. "You can just leave. Weren't you leaving anyway?"

"You're acting like a four-year-old, Frank."

"And you're not?" I scoffed. "Leaving because you might lose a pool game?"

Daphne turned around to pick up her bag, then looked at me earnestly. "Please don't get me mad, Frank. Bad things happen when I get mad."

"Oh yeah," I laughed. "Like what? What are you, She-Hulk?" I mocked. "She-Hulk mad. She-Hulk smash pool table."

"I have powers. There's a spell I cast. I can't help it."

I gave a loud ha-ha at that one. I raised my voice. "Witch here, everyone," I said. "Watch out. Witch." A few heads turned for a second, then looked away. "What, am I supposed to be afraid of you now?" I poked her again, right on the spine, which probably hurt.

"Frank, don't," she said firmly. "Stop it."

But I wouldn't. I kept poking—her back, her shoulders, her arms, even her head.

That's when it happened.

I remember this: things got dark suddenly. Not jet black, more of a graying, like someone hit a dimmer switch. The sounds of the bar faded, too. I was still looking at Daphne but it was more the blue of her shirt that I saw. Then her eyes, burning. They wouldn't let go of me. She was mumbling something but I couldn't hear.

Then I got thirsty. So thirsty. It was like I'd been eating sand for a year and all I wanted was water, and there was no water in sight.

Let me tell you what runs through a man's mind when he wakes up and discovers he has frog legs. There's a phrase for it, I believe: *a state of fugue*. I'd look down at myself—those horrible springy legs, that spongy skin. I knew it wasn't possible. But each time I opened my eyes again, there I was.

My first thought was *run*. That first month, I must have tried escaping ten times a day—swimming up to the top of my tank, pushing off the edge of it, then five mad hops toward the front door. I never got very far. Daphne would come after me and scoop me up, drop me back into my tank again. "This is who you are now, Frank," she'd say to me. "Face it. You're a frog."

Sometimes she'd put me on the kitchen counter, deliver little lectures. How escaping wasn't the point here. How the point was becoming human again, *changing*. Her voice would get all high and defensive and that's when I realized it wasn't just me she was talking to. Mo, Chippy and Carlyle were all guys who had pissed her off too. Once I knew that, all I wanted to do was talk to them, find out what had happened. But you can't talk, obviously. You've got your animal sound, you can hop around, make gestures, right leg out, left leg bent, but that's about it.

According to Daphne, that's the point. Being human isn't about words, she says. Being human is about being *connected*. You're not getting it, guys, she'd say to us. Connecting. Opening your heart. *Love*.

Once I was sitting on the counter and this documentary about frogs came on the television. Daphne got all excited. "Look, Frankie, look," she said. "Frogs!" I couldn't help being interested. It turns out my species is *Lithobates Catesbeiana*, American Bullfrog.

"Listen, Frank," said Daphne breathlessly. "He's going to sing."

Then it came—the sound of another bullfrog. A sound like no other— just that *chump*, like a bite taken out of the air.

"He's singing," Daphne whispered. "Sing back to him."

And I did. I pulled a big lungful of air in and pushed it back out. Some- how I knew how to do it, where to send it. A sac of skin inflated just below my chin and then the sound came out, loud and low. I felt kind of happy—a thing I couldn't put into words. Daphne smiled at me, and if I hadn't had this frog face, I would have smiled back.

◊

On the TV, Boston has just scored its tenth home run. It's the seventh inning and they're so far ahead I know they're going to win. They'll be going to the playoffs now. There will be at least five more games.

Outside, it's getting dark. When I look at the computer, I see Daphne's not there anymore. I hear her upstairs in the bedroom moving around, back and forth, like she's going through the closet, trying things on. I realize she's going out. That doesn't happen often and it gets us all excited. I can hear Mo and Chippy banging their shells against the plastic cage. Carlyle starts gnawing on the wooden slats of the gate to his enclosure. By the time Daphne comes down, it's pretty tense in here.

Tonight, she's wearing her heeled boots, and a silk shirt like the one she wore the night of our fatal meeting at Seelie's, although it's a different color—flame orange instead of blue. She clip-clops into the kitchen, opening drawers and closing them again.

She makes the rounds, dropping in a snack for each of us: coconut bits for Mo and Chippy, a piece of steak for Carlyle, frog pellets for me. The door swings shut behind her.

Then, silence. The kind of silence you hear; the kind that actually has infinitesimal sounds in it. Carlyle pawing his newspaper strips. The clock ticking. I already miss her—Daphne, I mean. It's hard when it's just us animals. *The female presence*, I think. I think of Nellie, how she used to tell me I looked like Leonardo DiCaprio—*handsome*. Once when we were in bed together in the afternoon she told me how love was when the other person saved you. How I'd saved her.

I knew what she wanted me to say—she wanted me to say that she'd saved me too. I wanted to. I started. But in the end, all I said was that I was glad she was happy.

It must be 3 a.m. when the lights come on—I can hear the clock chiming. There are voices—human voices, which means *there's more than one person in the apartment.* Scared, I crouch down low in the safety of my hut.

Both female, I realize. I want to see so I push off from the bottom of my tank and glide up, the water sluicing past my legs, till I can poke my head out. The sofa is at a right angle to my tank. I watch Daphne plump down on the couch, her hair thrown against the back of it in a fan shape. The other woman is turned away from me, draping her coat over the armchair, but when she turns around I see.

Nellie.

There are a bunch of hormones frogs have that humans don't—Daphne's told me about them. But frogs do have adrenaline, and that kicks in now. I start pushing the air out of my lungs so I sink back to the bottom. I'm half-way down when it occurs to me that I won't be abl e to hear or see anything if I go back into my hut. That's how I end up backed into a corner, shaking a little, while the two of them talk.

♥

They're both slouched against the back seat of the couch, looking up at the ceiling.

"It was so great playing pool with you," says Nellie. "You're such a great teacher. I was never into games, y'know? I never was interested. But now I think I could really do it. I could really play."

"I play *too much* pool," says Daphne. "Games," she says in a disgusted voice. "It's like all I do. I want to *help* someone, y'know?" She looks urgently at Nellie. "Do something good."

Nellie's taken aback—I can see that. She nods her head.

From my tank I have a good view of her. She's wearing those same fitted bell-bottom jeans she wore the night she went to Seelie's, but over them a multi-colored top that really suits her, loose in the sleeves, but hugging her top part, so you can see the shape of her breasts. Terrific, actually. *She's different*, I think. My legs jerk up like I'm on a Nautilus machine.

"What time is it?" says Nellie, still gazing at the ceiling. Daphne looks at the clock on the wall.

"Around three."

"Three. Jesus. Are you tired?"

"No."

"Me neither," Nellie sighs. "I don't really sleep anymore."

"Too much coffee?"

"I guess thinking too much."

"About what?"

"Frank. My old boyfriend." *My old boyfriend.* My legs contract. Daphne starts to blush. "He left me," says Nellie. "About a month ago. It's still kind of raw."

"Where did he go?" says Daphne, red-faced.

"I don't know," says Nellie. "I actually don't know. One minute we were in this bar; he was playing pool with some girl and then… he was gone."

Silence.

"Wow," says Daphne finally.

"Wow," says Daphne again—this time there's a hush in her voice. I guess I feel the same way. It suddenly comes to me that I never really thought about what it was like for Nellie in all this. She already kind of hated herself, then her boyfriend starts flirting with some hot chick at the pool table, and disappears.

"Did you report it?" asks Daphne.

Nellie sighs. "I thought about it," she says. "But then I realized it was just…" Her voice breaks. "He wanted to be gone."

"Mmm," says Daphne, embarrassed. "Well, at least you're out there again. Going to bars… it looked like that guy you were sitting with was really into you."

"Actually, he was getting obnoxious," says Nellie. "I'm glad you were there. You, like, rescued me."

Daphne laughs. "Yeah, you looked kind of cornered."

"I was."

Daphne clears her throat. "Listen, I'm suddenly exhausted, aren't you? Do you want to sleep over? I have an extra bed in the other room. It's made up and everything." Daphne's eyes are pleading and I find myself feeling the same way, leaning forward in my tank. *Stay,* I think. *Stay.*

Nellie thinks for a minute. "Sure," she says. "Sure, that would be great."

It's a long night. In my tank I'm suddenly cold—I can't stop shaking. With her being close, it's all so real again; what I am. What I used to be.

I must have slept some, because when I wake up morning light streams in through the kitchen window. Daphne's coffee maker churns away and the two of them are sitting there at the kitchen table.

"Did you sleep okay?" asks Daphne.

"Yeah, I slept great," says Nellie.

"Listen, I've got bagels. What would you like, sesame, poppy?"

"Poppy, I guess. You don't have to feed me…" she falters.

"Of course I'm going to feed you," says Daphne. "Sit. Eat." The toaster pops and Nellie sits crunching her bagel. Behind her Carlyle gnaws at the foundation of his pen.

"What is that?" says Nellie.

"The scratching? That's Carlyle, my ferret. See?" Daphne walks over, picks him up by the scruff of his neck. In her arms, Carlyle's head moves back and forth, sniffing. For a minute I wonder what he was before Daphne changed him—a crack addict? a Wall Street trader? Daphne smiles over at Nellie. "Do you want to pet him?"

"No thanks," says Nellie. I watch her move back a little in her seat; Nellie isn't an animal person.

"These are the crabbies," says Daphne, dumping Carlyle back in his pen and walking over to the crab tank. "Mo. Chippy."

"Quite a menagerie here," says Nellie.

Daphne laughs gaily—a little *too* gaily, I think. "I'm just weird." She crosses to my side of the kitchen. "And finally…" she walks over to my tank… "there's Frank."

Oh no you don't I think. I dive down deep but Daphne is too quick for me. She reaches her hand in and her fingers close around me. She carries me into the kitchen. Her palm opens and there I am, two feet from Nellie's face. It's as big as the moon and just as familiar. The somber eyes; the knobs of the cheekbones; the mauve half circles that I used to trace with my finger when she lay under me. She looks back at me in wonderment. My legs start to shake.

"Frankie is an American Bullfrog." Daphne talks in a sing-song, as if I'm some sort of museum exhibit. "He eats frog pellets. He needs to stay in the water to keep his skin moist… and he sings."

"He sings?" says Nellie doubtfully.

"Well, frog-sings. It's a mating thing, y'know?" She giggles.

"Does he sing in here?"

"I don't think so. He has to be outside," says Daphne. "In the wild. In the presence of his mate."

I look at Nellie. Her eyes are so sad. I think of how she used to tell me I rescued her. She'd look at me all wet-eyed and it scared me. It seemed to me she saw something in me that wasn't really there.

I inhale. My throat feels hot. The sound startles us all.

When I'm over, it's quiet.

Nellie's giant face puffs up and gets kind of pinkish. Her eyes crinkle. Her lashes are wet.

"Are you okay?" says Daphne.

Nellie nods, tightly, but her voice is all choked. "It's the name, I guess. I actually loved him, y'know?" Her voice breaks. "And I thought he loved me back." She gives Daphne a watery smile.

"Jesus, I'm sorry," says Daphne. She looks sorry. She looks like she feels like an asshole, actually.

More than anything, I want to throw myself at Nellie. I want to feel her tears on my skin and roll in them. I want to touch that white skin, get close to those wet-dark eyes.

That's when I take the leap, right up at her. Nellie's hand flies up, warding me off, and I ricochet. For the first time in my frog life I'm falling. Fast. My body tenses. At the last minute I hit hard with a smacking sound. Daphne's stuck her hand out, caught me just like a baseball.

"I'm sorry," says Nellie. "I don't like things jumping at me. I'm sorry. Is he okay?"

"Yeah, I think so," says Daphne. I'm in the palm of her hand and she holds it up to the light, turning me around, gazing at me. I stare at her deep-set eyes, her smirky mouth. "Wow, Frankie really likes you," she says. "I've never seen him do that. That was very sweet of you, Frankie," she says, lowering me down to eye level. "A very human thing to do."

Silence. I look at Nellie. Nellie looks at Daphne. Then Nellie steps back.

"So I really should go," says Nellie.

"Don't do that!" Daphne cries.

"Really," says Nellie. My heart's pumping again—my legs jerk up and down like marionettes. I know she can't do that. She can't leave me here. Not after this.

I see her moving toward the coat closet and I jump down onto the top of Daphne's desk, then on to the floor. I hop in front of Nellie's giant feet, zig-zagging.

"No, Frank!" Daphne calls after me. I hear her behind me, scrambling over furniture. "You can't do that, Frank," she says urgently. "You're gonna get killed." I ignore her and keep going. I jump on top of Nellie's shoe, which is just lifting. I feel Daphne's hand above me. She grabs me and lifts me up.

"Oh my God," says Daphne. "Oh my GOD, Nellie, look at this."

"What?"

"Look." She holds up her hand, thrusts me in Nellie's face. "Look! His skin is changing."

"It is?" Nellie looks terrified.

"It's white! It looks white!" Nellie leans forward, furrows her brow.

"Is he sick or something?"

"It looks human."

"WHAT?"

"Look." More than anything I want to jump over to a mirror and look at myself, but I force myself to stay. I look at Nellie's face. There's a look coming over it—half horror, half disbelief.

"Jesus Christ."

"What is it?"

"No. That's Frank."

"I know it is."

"No, *Frank*. My old boyfriend. Frank?" she says tentatively. I open my mouth. I croak.

Nellie sits. None of us moves or says anything. For a moment I think how long it's been with my skin out of the water, what will happen if I don't go back. Daphne stays where she is, standing. She puts me on the coffee table, then stands again. She watches Nellie's face anxiously.

"I'm just wondering," says Nellie finally. "How the face of my old boyfriend would appear on the face of a frog who lives in your house."

"It's just a power I have," Daphne says apologetically.

"*You* did this?" Daphne's fingers twist.

"An accident." Daphne looks pleadingly at her.

"What about your other… pets?" Nellie points with her chin to Carlyle's pen.

"It's when they get me angry," Daphne says guiltily. "Mo and Chippy were date rape… attempted date rape. Carlyle was… well, Carlyle tried to run me over with a car."

"Jesus," Nellie breathes.

"I *really* regret it," Daphne says earnestly. "And between me and Frank? I want you to know—there was nothing between us. We were playing pool and he started poking me with his cue and…" Her voice trails off.

"So it was *you* that night."

"I'm so sorry." Daphne's eyes are as big as saucers.

"He *poked* you?"

"I won and he wasn't liking it."

"Jesus, what an asshole."

"Well…" says Daphne. Her eyes are all big, resting on Nellie. "I think he's changing back," says Daphne hopefully. "Are you going to take him home with you?"

I look at Nellie's face and I see the answer. I can't even picture how grotesque I must be, a frog body, a tiny Frank face. Maybe it's the frog pellets, but I want to throw up.

It makes sense, I tell myself. I left her. Now she's leaving me. Nellie's eyes flick over me. I open my mouth. I push the air through. Something comes out but it sounds like a human burp.

"I don't know," she says. "Me and Frank… I don't know, maybe it's over. It actually made sense to me that he left. We were… we were really different, y'know?"

My limbs are numb. My whole body is heavy.

"He must have liked something about you," says Daphne. "He chose you."

"Yeah," says Nellie. "I guess. I don't know why."

"How did you two meet?"

"I was working at the Farm Stand, living at the Y." Her face clears. "I guess he kind of rescued me."

"So—he chose you."

"Yeah," says Nellie sadly. "Yeah, I guess he did."

"So now it's your turn," says Daphne, her eyes on Nellie's face. "*You* can choose." *F you witch-friend,* I think. I open my mouth again. *Words,* I command my body. *Poetry. Something. Talk to her—let her know.*

And they come. Not from my Frank-mind, but from my frog belly, so I don't know what I'm going to say until it comes out. Then I don't recognize myself.

Yourself the sun, and I the melting frost.

I'm hopping as I say it; I can't help myself.

Myself the flax and you the kindling fire.

I wonder what I look like; a tiny jumping Frank reciting poetry.

Yourself the maze wherein myself is lost.

I don't think I'll ever forget Nellie's face, though: part terrorist attack, part day-at-the-ballet.

I stop. There's silence.

"Wow," says Daphne.

Nellie is smiling. "Wow, Frank," she says. "I didn't know you had it in you. A *sonnet.*"

"Yeah," I say in a daze. "A sonnet."

"So it's done!" says Daphne joyfully. Which I don't think is what Nellie means, but then she looks over at Daphne and her face clears and I know she's going to go along with it. And I have a chance.

It's a tough spell to break, though, because it's been a long metamorphosis. Two months now and I've gotten a lot bigger but I'm still half green. Nellie's the breadwinner now—I can't really work with an arm and a leg covered with frog skin. I've been watching the playoffs with a wet towel over that half of my body, and there have been some real highlights. Marson catching a pop fly and ending the seventh inning. Buehrlie sliding into home at the bottom of the eighth.

Daphne comes over sometimes. She can't stay away—she's fascinated. I'm her only success story—well, half success story, and she can't get over it, lifting the towel, inspecting my frog arm. I'd be happier if I never had to see her again, but Nellie adores her, and lately, after all this, that's all I want. I want to watch the game, and I want Nellie to be happy.

So I don't forget the poetry. I keep *Oxford's Book of English Sonnets* beside me on the coffee table and when commercials come I flip through it, deciding what to memorize. Between poems, I do a little thinking. I think what it means to be human and how in the end, it isn't all that different from being a frog or a marten or a hermit crab. The powers of our hearts call to us, and generally we follow the song.

No Substitute

By Caren Gussoff

Jonquil died the day they found Kate's purse in the roadhouse dumpster. The Delanor sheriff combed the woods with a tangle of angry-eyed mastiffs who snorted the grass and dirt until they found a jawbone.

Kate's braces were still attached.

Poppy had liked Kate. She'd almost been best friends with Kate when they were little, only Ber didn't like how the Gatsonises made Poppy go to church with them the morning after a sleepover. Poppy remembered how Kate's lips were always chapped, a layer of papery skin peeling that Poppy wanted to reach out and tug off.

At Jonquil's funeral, the townspeople whispered about the jawbone through the whole service. Worse, Arden Harrus slipped her arm through Ber's, a gesture that suggested more than just comfort to a widower.

Poppy wanted to punch Arden right in the face. Instead, she tried to focus on the glossy mahogany box that held the ravaged remains of her mother. She watched it lower into the ground. She tried to say goodbye.

But, she couldn't. It felt like her mother was one of the missing girls, and until she was found, there was still hope.

And at least the town wasn't talking about Aunt Wisteria any more.

W

Like a tumor inexpertly excised from the body of the family, remnants of Aunt Wisteria rooted and multiplied, in the forms of stories and warnings.

Stories came from Jonquil, Wisteria's sister and Poppy's mother, wistful and vague, and always starting with "When we lost your aunt," like Wisteria was a sweater left on the bus and whose substitute was never as good. Then Jonquil would trail off at the end, as she caught herself speaking of Aunt Wisteria.

Warnings, which came more regularly, were issued from Poppy's father about wantonness and wildness and also trailed off at the end, but for very different reasons.

Aunt Wisteria had been expunged, erased from the family history before Poppy could remember much about her. It was the same year there had been a number of teenage girls disappeared, and somehow Aunt Wisteria's departure inextricably linked her to the disappearances in the minds of the thousand residents of Montbridge.

They started again when Poppy turned sixteen. At the same time, Jonquil was dying of cancer. The disappearances were almost a welcome relief; they distracted the whole town away from visiting the Breyan family night and day with hot dishes and prayer cards and endless cups of coffee.

Renna Osterud never made it home after a Thursday night rendezvous, drinking cooking Madeira in the library parking lot with Tanner Vegh. Aside from a hickey, Tanner was completely clean and free from all suspicion, and even broke down crying at the town meeting about it.

Poppy felt bad that Tanner's tears only made her want to punch him in his face. Poppy had known Tanner—and Renna—her whole life, and, she thought, could know him for all the rest and do without seeing Tanner cry.

Poppy was growing up to be more like her father than she realized or wanted. Ber Breyan was fast to anger and slow to cool down. He reviled weakness, which he picked apart in others at the dinner table. Once he made up his mind about someone, just like he had with Aunt Wisteria, a person was more likely to wake up with a pineapple for a head than change his mind. But he was big and strong, and doted on his daughter and his wife.

He never came home without something for both of them, even if it was just a candy bar from the vending machines at work or a small figurine he twisted from paperclips.

No one mentioned Aunt Wisteria at the meeting though you could feel they wanted to. Aunt Wisteria couldn't be tied to Renna. She was a hundred miles away. Maybe more. She only visited the town in stories and warnings.

They found pieces of Renna throughout the woods alongside the highway that linked Montbridge with Delanor the same day Kate Gatsonis's mother reported her missing. The townspeople were convinced now it was some sort of a nocturnal animal. A mountain lioness, perhaps, aggressively protecting new cubs from wandering teenagers. Or maybe a wolf or coyote, mad and rabid.

Jonquil lay in bed, dying through all of it. She made Poppy give her an extra kiss goodbye in the morning before school, then rush up there as soon as she returned. She told Poppy she was terrified about the disappearances, but Poppy knew it was because Jonquil was afraid she'd die during the day. Poppy wasn't in danger; Ber would have insisted on driving her to and from school if she was, but both girls disappeared at night after visiting with a boy.

Poppy didn't go out with boys at all, much less at night. All the boys, like Tanner, she'd known since birth and all at some point disappointed her. She was saving herself for college.

After Kate was gone twenty-four hours, most adults took or borrowed rifles and walked off trails at twilight. Someone found a deer, a five-point buck, but nothing of suitable size or temperament to rip apart a teenage girl.

Meanwhile, the only one who came regularly anymore was Arden Harrus, and Arden came as often to sit with Jonquil as she did with Ber. Arden timed her visits after Poppy had gone upstairs for the night to watch movies or play videogames or read before bed. But Poppy knew when Arden came—each time Arden moved, she shook loose a brume of lemons, lavender, and patchouli.

Barely a month after Jonquil's funeral, Poppy's hope ran out. Arden moved in completely. She wasn't even unpacked the first time she ran Poppy out.

"You should go to the library to study," Arden said.

"I'm done with my homework," Poppy said. "Where's Dad?"

"He'll be home soon," Arden said. "And I didn't say homework, I said study." She looked at Poppy like she was really first seeing her. "Your mother really spoiled you. You think you're special. Like you're going to get out of this town on your grace and wits. You need to work hard to get into college. Go study." She shook Poppy's jacket like she was a bullfighter. "Now."

"It's dark," Poppy said.

"Take your bike and stay on the roads," Arden said. "I don't want to see you back before nine."

Poppy grabbed her jacket from Arden fiercely, but something in Arden's face told Poppy to leave it at that.

She pedaled hard and stuck to the roads both ways. She came home fifteen minutes early, but stood outside, in the wet-smelling dark of the backyard oak tree, watching the lights in her house go off, one by one, until only the porch light and the one in her parents' bedroom burned. She let herself in quietly.

Her parents' bedroom door was already closed. She heard muffled voices and the rustle of bed sheets. She thought she even heard giggling.

Poppy made a lot of noise as she heaped some leftover spaghetti, cold from the fridge, onto a paper towel and ate it with her fingers. She willed Ber to come down and check out the racket. She imagined him coming down, and seeing his only daughter eating cold spaghetti off a paper towel, and thought how she'd tell him Arden forced her off to the library in the dark, without so much as a granola bar for dinner.

But Ber didn't come down. Poppy left the dirty paper towel on the kitchen counter, and tossed her backpack on the stairs. She wished Arden would trip over it in the night.

Even with her bedroom door closed and her head underneath the covers, Poppy could still hear the giggles from the next room, and smell Arden's perfume. Filtered through the walls and her father, it smelled like cleaning products.

It took her a few hours to fall asleep.

Things continued on in this manner for some time. In the morning, Arden barely acknowledged her, and Ber seemed to take a cue from her. He talked to her very little, and almost never left Poppy a treat, since Arden regularly chased Poppy out of the house before Ber came home.

Poppy wasn't sure where her father went after work. He went someplace, since he wasn't home right at five like he always had been. Arden would feed Poppy dinner, or sometimes not, then send her to the library, or to classes Arden signed her up for at the community center. Even though Poppy actually enjoyed some of them—she loved pottery and the Spanish-for-travelers classes, and didn't mind the cooking classes—each evening she fought Arden about having to go at all, and always Arden got her out the front door.

Sometimes, Arden said the classes would look good on Poppy's college applications, and repeated that studying at the library would be great proof of Poppy's curiosity and aptitude for those same applications. But other times, she would get a cruel look and tell her how sick she was of having to look at Poppy, deal with Poppy, talk to Poppy. Arden said Poppy'd been spoiled too much and for too long, and she really needed to learn to keep her head down and her mouth shut. One evening, she told Poppy, "You're lucky I don't have you shipped off to a boarding school. Or send you off to live with your Aunt Wisteria." She smiled when she said that. "You want to live with your aunt?"

Poppy shook her head and silently rode off to the library. But once Arden made the comment about Aunt Wisteria, she repeated it nightly. She even tried to command Poppy to go. "You should go live with your Aunt Wisteria," she said. "It'd be better for all of us." And as if to prove her point, she started leaving an envelope of cash, marked "for a bus ticket," around for Poppy to find.

Poppy opened the envelope from time to time. There was at least $200 in it. She told herself one day she'd take it and bike to the Delanor Galleria and spend it. But she could never do more than open the envelope, peek inside, and then put it back like she'd never touched it.

One day in March, Poppy decided if her father wasn't going to come to her, she'd go to him. She hid in the bushes until he left for work. Then, she sprung out as he backed up the car and blocked the driveway until he unlocked the passenger side door.

"Spring's coming," Ber said.

Poppy didn't answer. Ber opened his fingers, palm still on the steering wheel, gesturing at the window, as if Poppy may not have understood. "Daffodils are coming up."

Poppy stared at her father like he'd made a swear. Her father never commented on the weather. He'd always said it was the comfortable fallback of weak-minded individuals afraid of silence. Ber noticed his daughter's face in his peripheral vision, and coughed. "There's something I've been meaning to talk to you about."

Poppy shifted around in her seat. Her father also never cushioned his speech with introductions.

"I've asked Arden to marry me and she has said yes," Ber said. "We're having a spring wedding." He glanced at her. "What do you think?"

Poppy's back broke out in nausea sweats. Her mouth started to water like it did right before she vomited. She paled and clutched her middle.

"Whoa," Ber said. "You need me to pull over?" He slowed the car and came to a stop. They were two blocks from school. "Sweetheart?"

Poppy leaned forward and rested her forehead on the dashboard. Her father laid his hand across the back of her neck. The coolness of it helped, and the nausea passed.

"Dad," she said, sitting up. "Please don't marry Arden."

"Sweetheart…" he said. He didn't seem like he knew what he wanted to say next, also something Poppy had never seen.

"She's horrible," Poppy said. It didn't quite cover it all, but it was the best she could do.

That was all it took. Ber slammed down on the steering wheel hard. "Arden is a wonderful woman," he said. "She has done nothing but help this family since your mother died. You will not call her horrible."

Poppy could see her father's mind was made up. He hadn't been asking her what she thought. He was telling her what would happen. She opened the car door and slipped out of the seat.

"Get back in the damn car, Poppy Ann Breyan. So help me."

Poppy slammed the door. Her father rolled down the passenger side window. His face was so red it made his beard look orange. He was yelling things at her, but she yelled over them. "You don't know her, Dad."

Ber stopped, mid-yell. He gave his daughter a cold stare. As he drove away—her backpack still in the back seat, as she would realize a second later—he said, "Neither do you."

She was lucky, that day, although her luck at not needing her books came at the expense of others. As soon as Poppy made it to school, she was ushered into the auditorium where the principal announced that the sheriff had found the remains of Kate Gatsonis. Then, he announced that another schoolmate was missing—Annika Poncaire—and that if any of them had any information about Annika's whereabouts for the last twenty-four hours, they should step forward immediately.

Then, he dismissed school for the rest of the day, so everyone could go home, and "be with their families."

Poppy almost cried when the principal said that. Then she wanted to punish herself for her weakness. She ran home, as hard as she could. Without her backpack, she was faster than usual, but she was no runner, and by the time she reached her street, she was flushed and panting and a little sick.

She didn't want to go home, but there was no place for her to go, except the library or the community center, and she spent enough time at both of those. She caught her breath and thought about the envelope of money. She'd sneak in the house, take it, and really go to the mall.

Poppy stuck close to the bushes by the Williams's house, but across their yard, she could see her house was empty.

Poppy let herself in. She kept her shoes on instead of taking them off by the front door in case Arden came home, she could slip out, with the cash, to the mall.

The envelope was neither on the counter or the hallway divan where Arden usually left it. Obviously, she didn't keep it out all the time. So, for the first time since Jonquil died, Poppy went into her parents' bedroom.

The room used to have a comforting smell. Her mother's lotion, some vanilla potpourri Jonquil would buy from Mrs. Williams's Avon catalog, and a yeasty smell that came off her father when he needed to shower. Now the room smelled like Arden. Her bottles and beads were spread across Poppy's mother's vanity. But no envelope.

Poppy opened the vanity drawer. Her mother used to keep her important papers in there: her and Ber's marriage license, Poppy's birth certificate and report cards, clippings she wanted to save, and the only photo of Aunt Wisteria Poppy knew of. Wisteria and Jonquil wore matching lace dresses. Wisteria had a rag doll, obviously given to her as a prop, because she held it in front of herself like it was a bag of garbage. Jonquil held up her arm like she wanted to ask a question.

All the papers were still there, covered now by a layer of scarves, a pair of formal looking white gloves, and some extra bottles of Arden's musky citrus perfume.

Everything smelled of that perfume.

Poppy closed the drawer, and went to the dresser. The top drawer still held her mother's underthings, some pantyhose, a few camisoles, only now topped with some big lace underwires and a few see-through things Poppy didn't want to examine closely. No envelope. The second drawer held socks and more stockings, and a cigar-style box locked by a flimsy metal latch. Poppy squatted down and picked off the latch with a fingernail.

Inside the box was the envelope of money.

There were also some strange items tucked underneath. A dirty red ribbon. A little plastic tiara keychain. A rolled-up daisy chain of folded gum wrappers. A lip gloss with the brand name worn off. And a thin gold chain with a nearly weightless gold cross pendant, as insubstantial as the latch of the box.

Poppy knew that cross.

Kate Gatsonis got a cross like that for her confirmation. Everyone else had to take off their jewelry for PE, but Ms. Satzman let Kate wear her cross, and let Susan Grossman wear her Star of David.

Poppy held up the cross. A single hair was caught in the minute little links, dark and long, like Kate's. Poppy fell back hard from the squat onto her tailbone, but the pain barely registered. She dropped the cross back into the box. She shook as she tucked the envelope under her arm and replaced the box into the drawer. She covered the box with socks. She couldn't do anything about the foil latch, but she'd be long gone by the time Arden saw it, she hoped.

She counted the money in the bathroom. There was $300, and a sticky note with a name and address. Wisteria McLellend in Chicago, Illinois.

Ber still had her backpack in his car, so she filled her old gym bag with whatever she could.

It wasn't until she was already on the Greyhound bus heading northwest to Chicago that she realized she'd done exactly what Arden wanted her to do. Arden knew where she was going and how to reach her. Maybe she'd even been set up. Maybe Wisteria was in on it, and she'd add a little twisted paper clip figurine into Arden's souvenir box. Poppy balanced her duffle bag on her knees and squeezed the web handles until she could barely feel her hands.

◥

The woman stood on the stoop with Jonquil's face, Jonquil's hair, even Jonquil's stance. Poppy walked into her aunt's arms before she knew what she was doing. Then she pulled back with a start.

No substitute was as good.

Her mother's face was softer, prettier. And Aunt Wisteria's split ends badly needed trimming.

"Come upstairs," Wisteria said. "I bought ice cream."

"I'm not a kid," Poppy said.

Wisteria looked at Poppy a few seconds longer than most people did before speaking. Then she said, "It's as much for me as it is for you."

Wisteria's apartment was small but light. All of her furniture seemed to either be on or close to the ground. She took Poppy into her room, which had a futon and a bunch of small, fragrant yellow flowers. "They're jonquils," Wisteria explained, and closed the bedroom door.

Poppy was thankful for the door. She could block herself in at night. At the very least.

Wisteria ate all the ice cream herself. Poppy noticed the empty pint in the trash when Wisteria called her for dinner.

Neither of them spoke. Wisteria passed Poppy salad and baked tofu, and brown rice with some sort of mushy lentils. The only thing that tasted familiar was the iced tea. Poppy waited for the poison in the tofu to take effect, then for Wisteria to attack her in the shower after dinner, but neither happened.

When Poppy came out to the living room in her one pair of pajama pants, Wisteria was sitting cross-legged in front of a low table. A candle burned at each corner of the table, and in the center were some of the jonquils and a shiny bright dagger.

Poppy waited for Wisteria to stab her. To ritually slit her throat and carve her up and seize her heart from her chest.

These didn't happen either. Her aunt sat quietly in front of the table with her eyes closed and lips moving. Poppy coughed, but Wisteria didn't look at her. She asked, "Do you want to join me?"

"What are you doing?" Poppy sat down on the low living room futon facing her aunt. Her knees blocked her vision.

"I guess you'd call it praying," Wisteria said.

"What are you praying for?" Poppy asked. She didn't want to ask, wasn't sure she wanted to know the answer, but it just came out. Her parents had considered praying a personal matter, done behind closed doors like number two, which is why Ber had been so outraged and forbade her from sleeping over at Kate Gatsonis' house, even though she'd liked Kate, they had satellite TV with no parental controls, and Poppy didn't mind church.

"I'm praying for—" Wisteria scooted around to look at Poppy. The candles lit her hair from behind. Like Jonquil, Wisteria's hair was red in the light. "I'm praying for you," she said.

As far as Poppy knew, no one had ever prayed for her before. It didn't seem like the sort of thing someone did before they killed someone else. "You ate all the ice cream," Poppy said.

Wisteria turned back to her table, and blew out the candles, one at a time. Then she said, "There's another container in the freezer, for you."

A person definitely didn't buy extra ice cream and pray for someone they were going to kill. "I want to go home," Poppy said.

Wisteria pushed herself up, brushed off her skirt, and started for her own bedroom. On the way, she looked like she wanted to touch Poppy, maybe put a hand on her shoulder or hug her. But she didn't. "I know," she said to Poppy. "Good night."

There wasn't much to do, at first, at Wisteria's. School was out for the summer, and Wisteria didn't make her go to summer school or day camp or take classes. Most of the time, she stayed around the apartment. Aunt and niece were good at occupying the same place without interacting, sometimes for hours.

Sometimes Poppy helped Wisteria garden in her giant containers and tubs on the balcony. Wisteria grew all kinds of herbs and plants, a lot of which she cooked with or turned into terrible tasting teas and juices, which she offered to Poppy, "for your health." Wisteria also gave Poppy a small beaded bag filled with the now-dried jonquil, and some sage and slices of burdock, "for protection."

Poppy wore the bag around her neck because she thought the beads were pretty, though she was sure a sock full of change would be better protection.

Other times, Poppy went to the library a few times of her own volition. The library was air conditioned, unlike Wisteria's, and filled with other people who didn't have any place to be: hobos, the unemployed, and musty-smelling gutter-punk kids. She'd sit at a computer station, sometimes she'd read magazines, and always she looked at the *Montbridge-Delanor Times* which still came out on paper.

Right after Poppy left—she caught up, reading back—the *Times* ran a story about Kelsie Dorfman, who'd been feared missing but had just run away with her Delanor boyfriend until they ran out of money.

Then, Poppy herself was declared missing. The paper ran her yearbook pho-to, and Poppy colored her fingertips black tracing the outline of her own face.

Poppy looked at her photo for a long time, and then carefully folded it in half, tucked it under her arm, and sat down on a reading chair until any-one that might have been looking at her stopped looking. Then, she walked out of the library with the paper. When she got back to Wisteria's, she slid the paper underneath a stack of papers on the bookshelf in her room.

Poppy called home. When Arden picked up, Poppy hung up. She dialed her father's cell phone. Again, Arden picked up. On the cell, Arden could see it was Wisteria's number. "Don't call here," Arden said. "Don't call or come back. You are dead to us."

Poppy held the receiver in her hand long after Arden hung up and the signal went from a buzz to a honk, then nothing.

Her father remembered to check his email once or twice a month, but even that was better than never. Poppy wrote to him, first just "I'm OK. I am at Aunt Wisteria's," but then she typed out how Arden had sent her away and that he needed to be careful of her. She finished off by asking him to come and get her the minute he read it.

Weeks passed. He never came. He never replied.

When it became apparent that he wouldn't, probably because Arden herself intercepted the email, Poppy pulled out the paper and brought it to Wisteria. She dropped it on Wisteria's lap. "I need to go home," she said, then let Wisteria read.

"Why didn't you tell me girls were disappearing?" Wisteria asked.

"I thought you knew," Poppy said.

"Why would I know?"

"You are involved somehow." Now that she said it, it sounded stupid.

"Why would you think that?"

Wisteria was here. She had been here when Poppy arrived. She hadn't gone anywhere. "My father said…"

"Your father said." Wisteria smacked the paper onto the table. "Your father."

"I thought…" Poppy tried to think what she'd thought. "I don't know. You left and there was talk. And my father…" If Wisteria wasn't involved, then it was Arden herself. "He married her," she said.

"Married who?"

"He married the killer," Poppy said.

"He married the killer? What do you mean?"

"Why do you think I came here?"

"After Jonquil died, I just thought…" Wisteria looked at Poppy. "That you'd want to get to know me." She shook her head. "I always thought you'd come. I always thought your mother would too."

Poppy shook her head. "He married her." She whispered then, afraid to say it loud. "Arden."

"Arden Harrus? I saw her at the funeral. I thought…" Wisteria trailed off again.

"You were at the funeral?"

"Of course. In the back," Wisteria said. "She was my sister."

"Didn't you see them holding hands? They were carrying on. It was gross." She whispered again. "She's horrible."

"I thought she was just comforting your father. She knows him well. She knows all of us well," Wisteria said. "Your mother, Arden and I were very close growing up. She's how I knew Jonquil had passed. She's how I knew you were coming here."

"I have to go home," Poppy said.

"You can't." Wisteria sat there, head in her hands. "This is on me. I thought it was over. I thought…"

"I want to go home," Poppy repeated. Her father must be crazy with worry. Arden was a complete monster. A killer, and a torturer; the only thing worse than losing someone is not knowing what happened to them.

"You can never go home," Wisteria said. "It's my fault. I am so sorry."

"I'm going to go home. Whether you help me or not." Poppy left her aunt and the paper and went into her bedroom. Everything she owned, even with the clothes and books Wisteria bought her, still fit into the gym bag. She had the other half of the money.

It took her five minutes to pack, but it was already dark. She couldn't leave in the dark; girls disappeared in the dark. She flung herself onto the bed, as if punishing it. She wanted to cry, knew a cry would do her good. But she couldn't. She flung her arm over her face and waited.

Wisteria shook her awake. She didn't know how long she'd slept. Wisteria sat on the edge of the bed. "You really want to go home?"

"More than anything."

"I can make it so you can go home. But it won't be the same. Not ever. You can go back, but not in time." She touched Poppy's leg lightly. "You may not like it."

"I don't like it now."

Poppy didn't know anyone who knit, aside from the Montbridge church ladies who turned out cozy after cozy for bazaar fundraisers, and certainly no one who spun their yarn. Wisteria explained it was critical, for the magic to work, that the materials were hers, from sheep to end.

Poppy didn't go with her to the farm to shear the sheep. She'd seen enough sheep between Montbridge and Delanor. When Wisteria returned, though, Poppy helped her aunt wash the smelly wool and pull it into roving. She crushed and chopped madder roots and birch bark, goldenrod flowers and butternuts to turn into saucepans of dye. She stirred the puffs of roving into the dyes, and stained her hands red and brown, yellow and grey squeezing out the excess and laying them to dry on the balcony.

And she just winced as Wisteria pricked all of Poppy's fingers and let the blood droplets swirl into a bucket of clean water; that bucket dyed the last puff balls a beautiful carnation pink.

Poppy had a hard time with the spinning, keeping the draft all the same thickness, so Wisteria took over most of it. But Poppy twisted the hanks into skeins, and learned to knit and purl. The basics were enough: all they needed were big rectangles, stuffed and tucked, then sewn into place.

Summer arrived, and they knitted through it. They sweated on the scratchy wool, and the plant dyes rubbed off onto their hands and faces. But soon, they had it.

Wisteria took care with the face. She embroidered the pink lips with the blood yarn, and pinched and stitched at the nose so it was the same shape as Poppy's. For eyes, Wisteria had Poppy pull two buttons from her favorite green and brown plaid shirt. Wisteria looked at Poppy's face long and hard, deciding their placement, then sewed them on with thick thread.

Wisteria took the newspaper, folded it around Poppy's picture, and wrote some symbols on it with red grease pencil. They looked like Elvish, or code, or the outdated shorthand she would have been made to learn in Montbridge Senior High's business skills seminar. Wisteria shoved the paper into the open seam between knitted breasts, moved it around so it was in the center, then whip-stitched the chest seam closed. She bit the end of the yarn off with her teeth.

They dressed it in Poppy's favorite jeans, and used safety pins to secure around the missing buttons of the flannel shirt. They tied Poppy's boots on its feet, and styled the yarn hair into a ponytail.

Wisteria and Poppy sat it on the couch and stood back, taking in their month of work. If Poppy were a little girl again, she decided, she would have loved to have a life-size doll of herself.

But she was not a little girl, and something about the knitted Poppy frightened her.

"Poppy," Wisteria said. "Meet Poppy."

Poppy took knitted Poppy's hand awkwardly. If she looked too closely or for too long, Poppy could see her chest rise and fall—just a little. Poppy thought she saw her button eyes blink, but not only was that impossible, Poppy couldn't catch her doing it.

"Now," Poppy asked, turning her back on knitted Poppy. "Will you tell me what we are going to do with her?"

"We're going to take her home."

⩔

They buckled knitted Poppy into the back seat of Wisteria's Camry.

Wisteria let Poppy drive on long stretches of straight road south to Montbridge. Once when Poppy looked back in the rear-view mirror at the knitted Poppy, knitted Poppy turned her chin slightly to look from the window to Poppy's reflected eyes. The second time she looked back, she could swear knitted Poppy had dozed off, though her button eyes stared sightlessly ahead.

The three arrived in town just after dark. Wisteria had both Poppys scoot down in their seats so no one would see them.

Poppy wanted desperately to look around. She could smell home, all grass and animal and mud and clean, after three months in Chicago. She'd already almost forgot how much darker the night could be, and how many stars there actually were in a clear sky. Knitted Poppy slid around on the seat as if she wanted to look too.

Poppy could tell by the turns and the bump and the brush of the low oak branches that they were at their corner. Wisteria placed her hand on Poppy's head as she slowed, as if to hold Poppy down. Then she let both Poppys out.

Knitted Poppy did move on her own. She moved slowly, like she had bad knees and a bad back. But she moved. And she seemed amused, at first, at Poppy's disbelief. But then she was annoyed. She looked at Poppy like she wanted to punch her.

Wisteria joined their hands, then guided Poppy to sit on the ground while knitted Poppy walked to the Breyans' front door.

"Close your eyes," Wisteria said. "Then open them while they are closed."

Poppy closed her eyes, about to ask what Wisteria meant by opening when closed, but within a second she knew. Behind her eyes, there was all the instant movement and lights like anyone sees when they close their eyes. But then it coalesced into sight. She was shambling to the door. The lights were off, but she reached out and knocked.

Ber answered the door. He looked at her, and instant joy and relief spread across his face. He held out his arms, and Poppy started to step into them, but he held her so he could step outside onto the stoop with her.

His mouth moved, but Poppy couldn't hear him, only see him. She could read his mouth saying her name, and then holding a finger up, saying "Quiet." He closed the door carefully behind him.

Then, he took her in his arms and squeezed her hard. He swung her off the stoop and onto the front walkway. When he placed her down, he looked back at the dark house. "We have to go," his lips formed, and took her hand.

"I can't hear anything," Poppy whispered to Wisteria. She opened her eyes, out of knitted Poppy's head.

"I'm not strong enough for that," Wisteria said. "But you can see?"

"I can see," Poppy said. "He thinks she's me."

Wisteria squeezed her shoulder in answer. "She is you."

Ber took knitted Poppy's hand and led her down the road.

Poppy looked after them, then closed her eyes.

Ber moved fast, talking the whole way, and she had trouble keeping up with his words and pace. He kept looking behind them. When she tripped, Ber picked her up beneath her armpits, like she was a doll—she *was* a doll—and carried her.

He headed away from the Williams's house and away from the street-lights and into the woods. It was hard to see more than outlines. Trees and Ber.

"Where is he taking me?" Poppy asked, and felt light through her eye-lids. She opened her eyes again.

The lights came from inside the house. Arden pulled aside the curtains, looked out into the night. She opened the front door, called out into the night. She stood on the stoop in her nightgown and flip-flops, squinting down the street.

She called again, then went inside, reappearing holding Poppy's alumi-num softball bat. She held the bat like a sword and headed down the street.

"She has a bat," Poppy said. "We need to stop her."

Wisteria clamped down on Poppy, keeping her down. Her palms were warm and a little wet on Poppy's shoulder. "Close your eyes," she said. "Look."

Ber carried her deeper into the woods. Poppy realized she'd lost a boot somewhere as she limped over sharp rocks and sticks.

She couldn't tell where they were, only that they were west of the street and far enough that she could no longer see houses or streetlights.

Ber looked over his shoulder. She could feel his panic rising, and he put her down. He said something before grabbing her hand again. He pulled her behind him in a run.

"He's trying to get us away from her," Poppy said.

Poppy stumbled on her stiff legs and uneven feet, and Ber lost his grip on her. She crashed through saplings into a clearing. But before she hit the ground, her father was there. He caught her. He propped her against a tree trunk at the edge, and he bent over to catch his breath.

There was a little starlight that filtered down into the open circle of sky. Ber stood up, listening for Arden. Poppy could tell by his expression he was afraid.

Poppy tried say something, but nothing came through her stitched lips. Still, Ber clamped his hand over her mouth. "Quiet," his lips shaped.

There was so much she wanted to say to her father. Part of her hoped Arden would find them, and that her father could end this, once and for all. He'd see her for what she was.

But Poppy stood still, with her father's hand over her mouth. She bent her stiff arm and placed her own hand over his on her mouth.

They hid until Ber seemed satisfied it was safe. He brushed some thorns from his shirt, and smiled. His mouth made some words. She could recognize "Baby."

The soft light reflected off Ber's white teeth. Poppy smiled back at her father under their hands.

She was home.

Then, Ber spread his palm to cover her nose too, and clamped his other hand over hers. He shoved her against the tree. Now, the light also glinted on tears in his eyes.

His mouth formed "I'm sorry," and "Baby," and "I cannot help myself." Poppy couldn't breathe under her father's hand. It tasted like salt and dirt.

She was choking. She was drowning. She tried to scream, but couldn't. Ber moved his second hand and pushed on her neck. "Forgive me," she read from his mouth.

"He's killing me," she said, or tried to. She didn't know if she did, but then Wisteria shook her and yelled, "Open your eyes!"

Poppy could just hear her, as if her ears were stuffed with cotton.

"Open your eyes!"

Poppy didn't open her eyes. She watched her father's face as he killed her. As he killed all those other girls.

The starlight started to fade.

But then, a shadow. Dim, then a body in the clearing. Arden, swinging the baseball bat. Her father leaned hard one last time onto Poppy, then dropped her against the tree.

Poppy understood now. She understood why Wisteria left and why Arden drove her away. Poppy saw her for what she really was.

Arden was protecting her.

Arden was saving her. She carried Jonquil's secret. She offered herself to Ber as a substitute, but the substitute was never as good.

Now, Arden was there. Poppy saw with her own button eyes. She saw everything. She saw Arden swing, wildly. She saw Arden swing at Ber's head. Arden swung the bat.

And then, she made contact.

FORGETTING TOMORROW

BY BOB BROWN

Drucilla pushed the cloth across the worn ridges of the washboard. The delicate fabric required special care and the Mistress demanded her clothes be clean. The soap, even the soft white French soap, burned into the deep cracks that marked Drucilla's chafed hands. Her back ached from bending over the washboard.

Thin wisps of once-golden hair clung to the edges of her face and caught in the corners of her mouth.

With controlled deliberateness she watched, and then felt, her hand slip across the washboard. The wooden frame tore loose and sharp serrated metal sliced into her flesh, turning the water red as blood poured from the cut. With horror, she watched red drops roll down her arm and drip from her elbow onto the freshly cleaned clothing. Bright red rivulets spread across the clothing with chest-tightening speed, the fabric ruined.

Fear, cold clinging fear, drenched her. Drucilla clutched her hand, trying to stem the flow. The cloth of her skirts did nothing. The blood saturated the flimsy rags in an instant. Over her shoulder she heard an opening door.

The Mistress.

Drucilla woke in a cold sweat. The fear still gripped her. The sharp burning pain of the cut, the cold grit of the stone floors grinding into her knees. They were real. Too real for a dream. But it was. It had to be. She was here. She clenched her fists around the soft microfiber comforter and pushed her head into the crisp pillowcase. This was her room. Her apartment. She would forget the dream.

The clock's numbers glowed a dim blue. Still an hour before she had to get up, but lingering disquiet made sleep futile. She made her way to the shower. Hot water washed down her back as she lathered her hair. It hung from her scalp like silk, falling to her elbows. A curtained backdrop for a slender neck. It was her vanity.

The feel of her clean soapy hair in her hands drove the dream into distant memory.

Normally if she got up early she would push on to the office. Not today. She needed a slower morning, a buffer between the dream and her life. Breakfast, with a newspaper.

Dru ate breakfast at the diner almost every Sunday morning but virtually never on working days. The pace was different. The sharp busy sounds of forks and coffee cups replaced the conversations of families and couples. The harried pace of the servers matched the sullen crowd as patrons steeled themselves, looking past their eggs and toast to the work day with distant unfocused stares.

A boy with longish hair and a baggy Seahawks jersey watched her from across the diner. She wasn't bothered at first. She was used to being looked at. She knew she was attractive, and this was the city. Men looked, but the boy was different. The intensity was more than a simple pre-masturbation fantasy. Those, she could laugh off. The kid penetrated her, challenging her to notice him. She chose not to.

The paper was a waste. The news had no spark.

When she lifted her eyes, he was still there. Invading her thoughts, knowing her when she didn't know him. Being familiar from across the room. Her chest tightened. With clenched teeth, Drucilla forced herself to stare back. He turned away slowly, but not before she found his eyes. Green, green like a forest, a deep sea. Green with malevolent intent. He smiled.

"No," Drucilla whispered to herself. She would shake this off. If she forgot him, he would disappear.

She rifled through the newspaper, looking for the comics. She needed

Dilbert.

The damned dream was going to mess her whole day up. Already her breakfast was ruined, the eggs cold, the toast dried-out bread with vestiges of congealed margarine.

She felt the boy leave. She knew he wouldn't be there when she looked up. She was right. The servers were dumping the dishes from his table into a large gray pan.

"Dru?" The shout echoed across the diner. Nobody even looked up in response to the clarion call. This was the city.

"Drucilla Bradbury!" The nasal whine of the woman's voice forced the words past Drucilla's offended eardrums. The source of the voice was closer now.

Dru peered over her paper at the woman now standing over her table. A harbinger of a further deteriorating day.

"Do I know you?" Dru asked flatly. Breakfast had been a bad idea. The waitress refilled her cup and, with a subtle gesture with the coffee pot, looked at the newcomer. A large woman. Stiff blond hair, a Hollywood tan, clothing tailored to hide the fullness of her frame.

The newcomer flashed a dismissive look at Dru and nodded to the waitress who promptly filled her cup.

"I asked you if I know you," Dru demanded. Assertiveness was the only defendable ground she could find. This strange woman with her brazen familiarity was already slipping into Dru's booth and, Drucilla feared, her life.

Drucilla paused for a second. A client. Must have been a client. She laughed silently at her own paranoia.

"It's been a long time…"

"Oh no dearie, you were right the first time. You don't know me from Adam. You and I have some business, and I'm here to do it."

Drucilla groped in her purse for money. She wanted to drop a twenty on the table and run, but all she had was a credit card.

"Shit." She didn't care who heard it. She pulled the card from her purse and waved for the waitress. Her unwelcome guest sipped her coffee and smiled at Dru; she didn't look like someone to fear. A fifty-year-old woman with forty extra pounds, good clothes, decent makeup; well, the makeup was a bit overdone, but it matched the hair.

"Look, it's nice you want to do some business, but you'll have to catch me at the office. In fact, don't. I don't know you; I don't want to know you. I'm sorry, but it's just not a good day. Now, if you'll excuse me, I've got to go to work." Dru scooted out of the booth. She would meet the waitress at the check stand.

"Oh Dru," said the stranger. "You don't have to be at work for thirty minutes, and it's only three blocks."

Dru stopped in her tracks. The dream, the boy in the Seahawks jersey, this whoever she was. All of it gathered into a boiling ball in her stomach.

"What the hell do you want?" She leaned over the woman. "Let me guess, you're my Fairy Fucking Godmother."

"Heavens no, girl." She snorted an approximation of a laugh. "Not yours, anyway." A slight smell of brimstone filled the air. An after-tint of sulphur answered any further questions.

"Oh my God." The world wavered like air on a hot day and then suddenly crystallized into clarity. "I'm not giving them back. You can't make me." She ran in staggering steps through the front door, throwing a mumbled apology at the waitress as she went.

She never saw the bicycle messenger until it was too late. His helmeted head caught her in the jaw. The last thing she saw before losing consciousness was the strange woman and the boy with the oversized Seahawks jersey standing together on the sidewalk looking at her, hungrily.

Drucilla looked down at her hands. They were red and chapped, the knuckles raw. Her nails were little more than bleeding stubs. She could feel the weariness in her shoulders; it hung like a weight from her gaunt frame. She looked up from the sink she was cleaning. She only startled for a moment at the sunken face that looked back from the mirror. It was her scream that woke her.

Consciousness wasn't an improvement. Even with the abruptness of her wakening she realized she was in a hospital room. Naked except for the gown, an IV unit connected to the needle in the back of her hand.

Her jaw hurt. She ran her fingers down her cheek. The bandage was not large, but the pulling sensation when she rotated her jaw told her she had stitches. She thought, but only for a second, about the scar it would leave, and with a determined grit of her teeth slid the IV unit free. That hurt was minor next to the agonizing streaking pain in her head when she stood. She ignored it. Her clothes were in the closet. They were dirty and smelled of the gutter. Blood spatters marked her blouse.

How long had she been here? It didn't matter. She had to leave. She wasn't safe anymore. They had found her. She dressed in frantic silence. The memories flooded into her mind. The knowledge of what awaited her gave her resolve. If she was to remain free, she had to go home first.

The door to her apartment was open. Pushing past, she scanned the room. Everything was intact. With gut-wrenching panic, she went to the bedroom. The closet was open. Her ears roared in a maelstrom of panic. The pain of loss was an anticlimax when she opened the small wooden box that she kept, without remembering, buried in the back corner, under the Christmas wrap. They were gone.

"Are you looking for these?" She could see the shape of the slippers in the plastic bag.

The boy from the diner spoke from the hallway. She remembered him now. The coachman. He seemed younger than she remembered. Must be the hair.

"She found me," she said in soft defeat. "Why can't she just leave me alone?"

"She might have." He stepped into the bedroom. "But you took the slippers." He raised the bag.

"I had to. They were the only way out."

"You hid good. Really good. How'd you do it?" He leaned forward with an almost feral intensity.

"I just forgot."

"Do you remember now?"

There was no kindness or concern driving the questions. He was cruel. He wanted to hear the pain in her voice as she remembered. Drucilla remembered him putting the whip to the horses on that first fateful night. She had watched the frantic cruelty from the palace balcony.

"Yes," she answered. "I remember." Whoever she had become, that person was being washed away by returning memories. She had buried the past so deep she had forgotten it.

"My mother? And sister?"

"Don't worry, they're waiting for you."

"Let me go," she begged. "Take the slippers and go."

"And what? She would turn me back." He winced. "I like being human. And besides, I want to be there when you go back. I want to see." He stepped close and reached out, tilting Dru's head up in an almost tender motion. "Your stepsister," he said, "she hasn't forgiven you yet. And after this, I don't think she ever will."

"Please," Drucilla begged. "Please. I'll do anything."

"I know." His answer brought a new wave of horror-bearing memories. Her face tightened up as the terror of what was about to happen overwhelmed her. Tears welled up as sobs engulfed her.

"That was so long ago, we were too young to know. Please. Take the cursed things and go. You don't need me. Tell her I'm dead." Dru clenched her fists against the memories of what awaited her.

"I'm afraid it isn't that simple, honey." The woman from the restaurant stepped through the door. "You screwed this up a long time ago." She turned to the long-haired boy.

"If I thought for a minute you were going to let her stay, I would turn you back into a rat."

And with no further discussion she took the bag from the boy and pulled out the glass slippers. They glistened like diamonds. "These aren't yours. I gave them to your stepsister."

"And she gave us to you," said Dru. "To punish." She dropped onto the bed and with a defeated sigh added, "I remember."

"Good," said the woman. "I'll fix it so you never forget. I want you to remember this too." She gestured towards the neat apartment. "I want you to remember how it could have been. I want you to remember forever." She smiled. "Now, I believe you still have laundry to do. Your mother and sister can't do it all by themselves."

It was something other than stardust that she scattered around the room as together they faded away.

THE BITCHY WITCH QUEEN AND THE UNDONE STITCHES

BY GARTH UPSHAW

A high-pitched scream pierced the air, ending with a snapping, crashing, skidding crunch behind the house. I woke up, wings flapping, dreams fragmenting away, and fell off my bed. A lantern flared and dimmed in the hall, casting a sliver of burnt yellow light under the door.

I wriggled into a dress, scratchy but welcome for its warmth, and then reached behind my back to tug each wing through its slit in the material. My wings are small and asymmetrical. Embarrassing. I'm skinny, light even for a girl, but they wouldn't lift a mouse. The left one is a mottled brown that matches my eyes, while the right is the gray of old dishwater. Pigeon—not eagle.

"Lianne?" Mitroan's voice sounded like boulders rubbing together. The door opened and my father's huge body filled the frame. He held the lantern towards my face.

"What's going on?" I blinked in the harsh light, worried and frightened by the terrible noises that had woken me.

"Stay here." Mitroan's bullheaded, but he had the horns trimmed before I was born, after the war officially ended.

"What was that noise?"

Mitroan shrugged. "Sounded like an artillery shell, but if it'd been live, we wouldn't be talking now." He waved me back. "I'll check it out."

I listened to him thump down the stairs. Mitroan seemed even tenser than usual lately. I didn't want to set him off. A breeze stirred the window shade, and I'd just crept over to look outside when a finger tapped my shoulder. My heart tried to leap out my throat. "Who—? What—?"

"Put a sock in it," hissed a familiar voice.

"Feldsken. Queen's tits, you scared the living blood right out of my body. How'd you get in?"

"Ssst." He put a finger to his lips. "I didn't know Mitroan was back." Feldsken's triangular rat face ended with a chin sharp enough to cut cheese. "I climbed the trellis." He gestured to the window. "Peel an eyeball."

Nobody liked Feldsken much. He skulked around dressed in an ankle-length, seam-popped army jacket, scrounging trash, eavesdropping, finishing off abandoned beers at outside cafes. He was my best friend.

"What's out there?" I bent to look, curiosity overwhelming any caution. Mitroan's lantern bobbed straight towards our largest patch of golden yellow timber bamboo.

"Frickin' big flying fish." Feldsken's voice tripped all over itself with excitement. "Courier grade."

"An FF-236?"

"Big." Feldsken shrugged. "And look what clever, clever me found." He lifted his coat. Slung over his shoulder, a dispatch case gleamed, tooled leather worn smooth from long years of handling.

My eyes popped. "Queen's hemorrhoids, Feldsken."

"The pilots take bennies to stay awake. Long flights. I read all about it in the free press."

"Exaggerations." I hated when Feldsken tried crazy shit just to cop a buzz.

"There'll be a high for me here. I have no doubt." Feldsken's nimble fingers plucked at the buckle.

"You're dead." Most of the time, I loved the thrill of hanging with Feldsken, but tonight I was pissed. "You'll get us all killed."

Feldsken didn't even look up. "Keep watch. I'll find a pillbox, and then

I'll toss the case in the bushes. No one the wiser." He looked at me and winked.

"Fuck you," I snapped. "We'll be wrapped in chains and singing for the Queen's question men." A thought occurred to me. "What were you doing around here anyway?"

Feldsken's face turned bright red under his thin, soft cheek fur. I prepared myself for a wise-ass comment, but he mumbled something incomprehensible and kept fiddling with the case.

"You pervert." I scowled. "I hope you got an eyeful." I stomped to the other side of the window, clenching my fists, a hair's breadth from pushing him out and laughing as he tumbled to the ground.

I smelled smoke. Flames licked the edge of the grove. More lights trickled our way from the neighbors' houses. Sirens from downtown grew louder and louder.

The catch opened with a click. "I've got it." Feldsken riffled through the case, grabbing handfuls of papers and tossing them to the floor. "Nothing, nothing, nothing. An enormous fucking zero." He turned the case upside down, shook it, and when nothing came out, tossed it to the floor on top of the papers. "A huge, fat, gigantic, fucking zip. Queen's balls."

"What'd you expect? A gift-wrapped box stuffed with bennies?" I was furious. "The Queen doesn't have balls."

Feldsken scratched his nose. "Listen. You never saw me. Right?"

"I wish."

He thrust a leg over the windowsill and slipped outside. "She does so. Cantaloupes, baby." He cocked an eyebrow, and then slid into the night.

The sirens' shriek rattled my bones. I put my hands to my ears. One long squad cart pulled up, horses glowing red from quickspells, and then another. A knock shivered the house frame. As I stuffed the papers back in the case my fingernail caught on a line of tiny black stitches. I tore the threads, curiosity winning out over good sense, to expose a thick envelope. The pounding at the front door intensified. "Coming, coming." I slipped the envelope into my shirt drawer and threw the case out the window as far as I could towards the bamboo.

"Yes?" I opened the door to two Queen's men standing on the stoop as if they owned the whole neighborhood.

"Report of a crash. Flying fish." The larger of the two leered at me, piggy eyes as black and shiny as chips of mica.

"In the bamboo. My father went to see." I felt too young for the eyes that looked at me.

"Righto. You have a coffee maker?" The smaller man stepped forward and blew a cloud of cigar smoke to the side. "I'm Denab, Queen's chief." He looked past me. "Nice place. What does your father do?" His neck bulged over a green collar, stiff black hairs sticking out like brush bristles.

"He's a bamboo farmer and salesman. We lease from Lord Zorahn." I'd hoped the mention of the leader of the Queen's inner circle would generate some respect, but Denab just wrinkled his snout and pushed into the living room.

Buttery yellow flooring offset a warmer-toned wall panel and end table. Lord Zorahn's sales force showed this part of the house to important customers. Mitroan and I lived in an addition out back. I didn't say anything about how hard Mitroan worked, or how much he went without to send me to school.

"Huh." Denab scraped a thumbnail across the paneling and squinted at the scratch. "Well, hop to it. More crimes are solved with coffee than clues." He turned and spoke to the other Queen's man. "Put up a perimeter. Send teams to the neighbors. You know the drill."

By the time dawn tinted the sky, I'd fixed half a dozen pots of coffee and fended off as many groping pinches. Their fat fingers made my skin crawl. I was angry and upset with Mitroan for staying outside fighting the fire the whole time, leaving me on my own. Every minute, I felt sure they'd find Feldsken, or search my room. My stomach churned with terror. I wished Mitroan could be here with me.

The Queen's men dragged a Shamus inside, a frail, toad-headed old man who smelled like last week's seaweed. Denab gave him a strip of leather and told him it was the courier's belt.

The Shamus lit candles in the study and mumbled harsh-sounding words in a liquidy foreign language, running the leather through the flames and stroking the metal collar around his neck. The Queen's men lounged against the walls smoking, or sat in chairs telling dirty jokes. I tried to fade into the shadows, fascinated by watching real magic, but not wanting anyone to notice me. After almost an hour, the Shamus spat a glop of greenish mucus into a basket of office supplies.

A stapler hunched up all by itself, clacking like a pair of castanets. It scooted off the desk onto the floor. I gasped with surprise. Denab frowned at me but didn't say anything. The Shamus opened the back door. The stapler lurched outside, scrunching and stretching like a manic inchworm.

The Queen's men followed the stapler to a rotting stack of bamboo culms. I trailed behind Denab, compelled to see even though part of me wanted to run away and hide. The stapler clacked once more, and then fell sideways, inert. The men ripped the culms apart, scattering dirt and dead leaves over the path. One man extracted the case and hoisted it high above his head.

Back inside, Denab grinned past a misshapen cigar and spoke to me. "There now. You see? We always get what we want." The other Queen's men laughed. They slouched towards the door, pocketing candlesticks and ashtrays as they left.

I locked up and ran towards the crash, relieved that the Queen's men were gone. Ash dotted the ground like tiny scraps of black paper. In the distance, the Queen's Spire stabbed the sky. A wounded icicle the color of rotten buttermilk, old scaffolding clinging to its side like desiccated ivy.

I sprinted past a trio of neighbors towards my father. "Mitroan!" He towered over the others, bare shoulders covered with soot, hair wild and tangled as a briar patch. I wanted to throw myself in his arms like a toddler but stopped and stood panting.

"The fire's out. We're cleaning up." He sounded angry.

I looked past Mitroan's bulk. The flying fish lay sideways on a rucked-up patch of earth, its metal and bone body twisted beyond repair. One filmed-over eye the size of a dinner plate stared at the sky. A line of snapped bamboo pointed from the crash towards the launch pads south of the Spire.

I wrinkled my nose at the reek of jet fuel, burned bamboo, red-hot metal, and a wet, salty odor I couldn't identify. Small popping sounds emanated from underneath the fish. Blood and pus oozed from terrible gashes. I tried to make out the model markings on the tail, but tears blurred my vision.

Two days later, Feldsken met me on my walk home from school. I hadn't touched the envelope. I was scared. Terrified, really, and wished I had left it alone. The nights since the crash I'd lain awake picturing the Queen's dungeons, the torture I was sure was coming for me any minute, but at the same time I was curious.

I shook my head. Enough. Here was Feldsken. Nothing would happen. I took a deep breath and steadied my nerves. If Feldsken didn't meet me, no one else would keep me company on the way home. I hated the other students, rich, spoiled brats who never accepted me, but Mitroan said it was important for us to meet that sort of people. That we'd learn necessary information. Feldsken didn't go to school himself, of course, but I let him read my textbooks, and he helped with the assignments.

"Hey, Lianne." Feldsken dropped into place beside me, whiskers twitching.

"Hey, yourself." Relief that he hadn't gone for good gave my voice a friendlier tone than I meant.

"I saw a Queen's man eating a cruller outside school." Feldsken smiled.

"They're like corpse maggots." I'd seen them on the way to school, their creepy, piggy eyes staring at me like I was a butterfly they wanted to pin to a board.

"Word is, they're looking for something. Something missing." Feldsken took an extra-big step to keep up.

I shot him a glance. "You didn't take anything else, did you?"

"Me?" He put a hand to his chest. Innocence radiated from his features.

"Yeah. You." I stopped at a sidewalk vendor. An ancient Tamaskan immigrant stood behind a hot grill built into the side of a tiny cart. She worked five days a span, all year round. I cocked my head at Feldsken. "Want a rollup?" Hot grease sputtered amid the scrape of an iron spatula.

"Sure." Feldsken never turned down free food. "Extra hot. Side of grasshoppers."

"Make that two." I ordered in simple Tamaskan. I was born there, but when my mother got sick, Mitroan had moved our family here. He never spoke our native tongue anymore, but I still had bits and pieces I liked to use whenever I could.

The vendor slid hot flatbread off the grill and wrapped it around meat and spices. "Two rollups." She spoke in flawless Queen's tongue.

The Queen had technically beat the Tamaskans two decades ago, reducing our cities to rubble before declaring victory, but she still maintained a heavy garrison. Ten years ago, on my sixth birthday, Believers had bombed the Spire, killing hundreds. The Queen left the repairs half-finished to remind us of the enemy's disregard for innocent lives.

"Did Mitroan see anything?" Feldsken held the rollup in one hand and poured grasshoppers into his mouth with the other.

"Mitroan's out of town." I shrugged. "He's visiting the farmers." I nibbled the end of my rollup, talking while we walked along the sidewalk.

Feldsken waggled his eyebrows. "You're all alone?"

I stopped in my tracks, wings flaring, irritated that Feldsken had started with the stupid boy-girl jokes. "Did you have fun spying on me the night of the crash?" I waited. I don't weigh much, but I can give a hard stare like nobody else.

Feldsken backpedaled. "Bad joke." He swallowed. "I didn't mean to spy. I'd hoped you'd sneak out with me, and then the crash happened." He took a breath. "There you were. I couldn't take my eyes off you." He swallowed the last grasshopper.

I felt like punching him. I wanted the old Feldsken back. The wisecracking, scheming buddy I'd known since we were kids.

"You're beautiful." He leaned forward.

"What does that matter?" I had no idea what to do with the new Feldsken.

I opened my mouth, but couldn't think what else to say. I stood there like a fool.

"Gorgeous." His face loomed closer.

I stomped my foot. "Race you. Loser does the math homework." I didn't wait, but leapt forward, legs pumping, elbowing Feldsken against a wall.

I ran flat out, head down, giving the contest everything I had. Feldsken's fast, and I didn't trust my lead. Rounding the last corner, I glanced back, and then slammed into a thick body, green cloth filling my vision. Reeling backwards, I tried to catch my breath.

Denab grabbed my shoulder. "Can you fly with these?" He stroked my left wing with his free hand. I felt violated, dirtied. His fingers disturbed the careful overlapping of my feathers, making me twitch. A rank, ashy odor wafted from his open mouth.

I shook myself loose. I'd always had a fantasy of getting my wings altered. But I couldn't let Denab know that. "Can you root for truffles?"

He narrowed his eyes, and then threw his head back with laughter. "You have spirit, girl." He wiped his face with a rumpled handkerchief and leaned close. "Keep your eyes open. You see anything unusual, get in touch." He stuffed a business card in the front pocket of my jeans. "Rub the card and say my name. We can talk." He paused. "We think it was sabotage."

"Sabotage?" I frowned, confused. Why would Denab tell me this?

"Fish don't fall out of the sky for no reason." He seemed to wait for my reaction, but got nothing. He snorted. "Go home."

I trudged to my front door and mumbled the combination. Feldsken had disappeared. Exhaustion leeched my bones of strength, but I felt twitchy and hyper-alert. Wide awake from anxiety at night and school all day. I slogged up the stairs. I half expected Feldsken to be there, but the only thing that greeted me was the stale smell of dirty laundry.

A fly buzzed in my room, banging into the mirror and ricocheting from the screen. I opened the window to let it out and rested my arms on the sill. The Spire glinted in the sun, cold and beautiful. Everyone said the Queen lived there, but I'd never seen her.

I lifted a shirt off a pile of books and sniffed it, checking to see if I could wear it tomorrow. Nope. I opened my dresser drawer. The envelope seemed to call to me. My hand moved the pile of folded shirts out of the way. I stared at the creamy white paper and jet black ink of the words scrawled across the front: Lord Zorahn.

A hero of our times. That's what my civics teacher said. Mitroan thought the situation was more complicated. I agreed. Lord Zorahn's soldiers had rounded Tamaskans up for no reason. People had disappeared in the middle of night, and their families had been slaughtered in their sleep. My civics teacher called Lord Zorahn a brilliant general.

I turned the envelope over, rubbing the soft, expensive paper with my fingers. A blob of wine-red wax sealed the back. Pressed into the wax, the likeness of the Queen stared back at me, haughty eyes and bee-stung lips condemning me to insignificance.

"That's the Queen's mark," whispered Feldsken from the window.

I shrieked, stomach falling through the floor. "Queen's teeth," I stammered. "Don't do that."

"They're watching your house." Feldsken nodded towards the front. "For good reason, it seems." He stared at the envelope, whiskers twitching, and then climbed through the window.

I narrowed my eyes at Feldsken, pissed that he'd scampered when Denab buttonholed me, and then unfolded my pocketknife and slid the blade under the flap. I cut upwards, and the fibers of the envelope parted like tissue.

"Careful." Feldsken grabbed my arm and the envelope twisted away from me.

The wax seal screamed, "Insufficient identification," and an arc of sparking blackness erupted from the seal's mouth, singeing my fingers and making Feldsken leap backwards. Magic slammed into the mirror with a tingly ozone smell, warped our images, and melted the glass into slag. My ears buzzed, and my hand burned.

"Oh, fuck me. That hurts." I put my fingers in my mouth and sucked. I tasted hot iron and salt before my tongue went numb.

Feldsken gripped my wrist. "Let's see." He gently pulled my hand. "No worries." He dragged me to the bathroom and rummaged through the medicine cabinet. He squeezed a generous dollop of aloe gel on my fingers, tore a length of cotton from the end of his shirt, and wrapped the cloth around my hand.

I blinked away the spots in front of my eyes. "We're damn lucky." My mouth felt like it had been stuffed with old socks. My fingers throbbed in time with my heart.

"The mirror confused it." Feldsken laughed and reached for the envelope. "Can I see that?"

"I can do it." I turned my shoulder and emptied the contents of the envelope onto the counter. A letter written on stiff, bone-white paper unfolded to reveal a sheaf of crisp, new bills, higher denominations than I'd ever seen before.

"I'm gobsmacked," Feldsken breathed. He rubbed his fingers together.

"Not so fast." I raised the letter to my face, holding the money behind the paper. "My dear Zorahn," it began. "How are you and your darling imp mistress? And the little guttersnipes? How many do you have now? Six? Seven? You all breed with such amazing fecundity. I hope nothing untoward happens to any of them.

"I have a small request. Another Spire bombing seems due. Make it nefarious, blatant. Anything to shut up the naysayers. These funds are untraceable—consider them a down payment."

The signature was an illegible extravagance, but I recognized the writing: it graced each of the bills in my hand. My bones felt rubbery. I collapsed onto the toilet. The cool seat pressed against the backs of my thighs. "Is this…"

Feldsken sank to the tile floor, crossing his legs underneath his body. "Gobsmacked squared." His gaze never left the money.

"We are neck deep, and the bottom is dropping." My hand tingled. Pain crept up my forearm.

"I could hold that for you." Feldsken's nose twitched as if he smelled a breakfast feast.

"Uh…" I hesitated. A cold distrust settled over me. I tucked the bills in the envelope, but one fluttered free, drifting into Feldsken's lap.

He narrowed his eyes and folded the bill into a long rectangle before tucking it in his shirt pocket. "It should all be mine, you know."

The next day at school, I tried to pretend everything was normal, but without much success. Ms. Kenali, my civics instructor, called on me, but I couldn't remember what year the Queen was born. My whole arm ached with steady insistence. Other students laughed behind their hands and stole my homework when I wasn't looking. I felt half-baked, off kilter. Even worse than normal.

At lunch, I pictured taking the envelope out of my pocket and paying with the Queen's money, riffling through the bills like flash. The same way I sometimes thought about leaping off a cliff, or stepping between a water elephant and the river.

I skipped my afternoon classes, hanging out on the roof, my knees tucked to my chin, wings flat against my back. I peeled away the cloth wrapped around my fingers. Dead, gray skin met my eyes. My hand smelled like meat left too long in the sun.

I shuddered and wrapped the bandage tighter, turning my gaze outward. Maybe it would get better. The school buildings rambled below me. Bits and pieces had been tacked on over the last five hundred years. Its hallways and classrooms formed a rabbit's warren of twisty passages, a maze that took students years to master. Feldsken sometimes met me up here, but today he stayed away.

Beyond the school, houses and shops lined streets that all pointed south, downtown, towards the Queen's Spire. Factory smoke threaded through the air and left a metallic taste in the back of my throat. I turned north, looking instead at the lumpy earthen towers of Goblintown.

A flying fish roared high above me, an FF-216 or 215. Wind tugged at my hair. Other flyers, people born with wings like mine but magically altered, dropped from roofs and soared low over the city. I had the money now. I could be like them. I wanted to simply sit here with Feldsken.

On the way home, I kicked a pebble along the sidewalk, raising spurts of gritty dust. I wished I could ask Mitroan about boys, about Feldsken, but he never had time to talk. Feet thumped behind me. I walked faster. A large, meaty hand clapped my shoulder, whirling me around. Denab nodded. "Ah, Lianne. Care to chat?"

He proffered his arm in porcine mockery of a gentleman, but I ignored it. "Sure." Every step crumpled the letter in my pocket, a sound I felt positive Queen's men were trained to hear.

"I'd be delighted to speak with a young man you might know. A Feldspar, or Fieldkin, or something."

"Feldsken."

"That's it." His tongue lolled from his mouth. His eyes glittered. "Mitroan still out of town?"

I nodded, sweat trickling down my side. Guilt surrounded me like an odious cloud.

"You know he's on a list?"

"Feldsken?" Part of me wanted to tell Denab everything, but I bit my tongue.

"Mitroan." Denab put his arm around my shoulder and squeezed. "How'd you hurt your hand?"

I shrugged. "Making pancakes. I, uh, burned my fingers."

Denab frowned. "You'll be wanting to put butter on it then." He pushed me forward. "Remember, tell Feldsken we'd like a word."

When I got home, I didn't go inside. Instead, I walked to our ancestor shrine. The stone path wound through pots of flowering jasmine, dropping lower until a stand of aspens blocked sight of the house. Their silvery leaves fluttered light-dark, light-dark in the breeze, making a soothing whisper.

I rested on the low bench in front of the shrine and folded my hands. Lichen dotted the stones. A cool dampness rose from the trickling water by my side. My mother's teacup perched on a wooden coaster. I loved my mother, but Mitroan said it was better to let go, accept her death. He never visited the shrine.

I touched the cup with my uninjured fingers, rubbing the smooth sides. "Hello, Mother." I picked the cup up and rested the cool porcelain in my palm.

The whisper of aspen leaves grew louder. Particles of ash stirred by my feet. "Lianne." My mother's voice spoke to me from over my left shoulder. "It's been so long."

Tears pressed against my eyelids, but I blinked them away. Ghosts were always lonely. "I came right from school."

"Are you doing your homework?" The leaves rustled.

"Yes," I lied.

"And eating right? Breakfast is the most important meal of the day."

"What if your friend was in trouble?" I hunched closer. "What if you had a fortune? What would you do?"

"Are you brushing your teeth?"

I felt let down. No one could help me. Ghosts were sketchy things, prone to flightiness. To Mother I'd always be a child. She continued talking, but the answers I searched for remained elusive. When she paused, I set the cup on the coaster. "Time to go."

"Wait. Not yet." The creek burbled.

"Love you." I stood up, breaking contact. Tears burst from their hiding places. I leaned against a tree, wishing that Mitroan were here, that the FF-236 hadn't crashed, that Feldsken had never found the dispatch case.

I rubbed my sleeve across my eyes and trudged back to the house. The sun glowed red behind the Spire, gilding the noxious clouds of smoke that poured night and day from the Queen's factories. The front door opened at my touch. Light glowed from within. "Mitroan? You're home early." I stepped into the kitchen.

Feldsken turned from the stove holding an enormous pan of bubbling sauce. "Hey, you. I'm making us dinner. A veritable banquet." Purple feathers sprouted from a sequined hat.

I stuttered to a halt. "Feldsken?"

A fancy three-piece suit of iridescent silk gleamed on his body, accenting his shoulders. He grinned sheepishly, and then gestured towards the nook where a pair of candles burned. A bottle of red wine breathed on the counter. "I got takeout, but the chef insisted I learn how to do the sauce. Sit down." His eyes sparkled.

I felt sucker-punched. "We don't use this kitchen. Where did—? Why are you dressed like that?" He looked great. Sexy. Older.

Feldsken preened. "Money, money, money. Cash makes the world go 'round, baby." He snapped his fingers, and the sauce burst into flames. "Flashspell. Cool, huh?"

"Stop."

Feldsken poured the flaming sauce over a platter of stuffed hens. "Dinner's ready." He took me by the elbow and tried to guide me towards a chair.

"Feldsken." I set my feet. "Have your brains leaked out your ears? Did you think all this flash and glitter would go unnoticed? The Queen's chief asked about you today."

As if on cue, a sharp knock sounded at the door. The smell of a cheap cigar drifted through the open window. The knock sounded again. Shave-and-a-haircut-two-bits. Loud.

All trace of glam dropped from Feldsken's demeanor. "Your window. There's space behind the trellis." He turned and sped up the stairs.

I followed. The thought of Denab's nicotine-stained fingers touching my wings spurred me faster. I rounded the corner into my room. Feldsken crouched by the window. Piggy shapes moved in the semi-darkness of the yard.

Feldsken slipped over the sill, smooth as water. I eased behind him, placing my sandals on the wooden crossbars. My injured arm slipped, and dry twigs cracked under my feet.

A lantern, light focused by mirrors into a cone of brightness, swept across the trellis, isolating Feldsken. "Run, Lianne." He jumped out of hiding and sprinted towards the nearest Queen's man, snapping his fingers. Hair and bristles burst into flames.

Roars of anger pursued him into the bamboo. I crept along the path to the shrine, heart pounding like a wild animal was trapped in my chest.

"Where's the girl?" The end of a lit cigar bobbed in the darkness behind me.

I hurried towards the water, pausing only to scoop up my mother's cup with my good hand.

"Lianne?" The trees rustled. "What are Queen's men doing in the shrine?" She sounded indignant.

"Not now." I tucked the cup in my pack and slunk into the trees on the far bank. My sandals squelched, so I kicked them off and tucked them under my arm. Mud stained my shirt.

Cursing under my breath, I crawled through narrow shortcuts too small for anyone but a kid to navigate. Every bump made my injured fingers flare with agony. Branches plucked at my wings. Feathers ripped out with sharp pinches.

At last, dirty and bedraggled, I stepped onto a sidewalk free of Queen's men. My hand throbbed. Jolts of pain stabbed up my forearm. Red lights blinked on the Spire like a hundred malevolent eyes. I turned my back and faced north, out of town. I had to find my father.

I spent the last of my lunch money on a fry-up and coffee at an all-night diner, huddled in a corner booth, starting to my feet whenever the door slammed open. The food helped but couldn't fill the hole my stomach had become. I felt lost, adrift. In free-fall.

I'd visited the out-of-town bamboo farmers as a kid, but to find them now I needed a map, supplies, and a driver. Where would I find a doctor for my hand? My wrist was going gray and stiff and my arm hurt all the way to the elbow. Problems grew faster than I could think of them.

I visited the bathroom, a narrow, smelly structure that looked like it had never seen a scrub brush. I read the Queen's letter again before wrapping it in an old layer of wax paper and slipping it in my underwear. Plumbing gurgled. I secreted portions of the money in my shoes, my pockets, and my school books. I was afraid to look under the bandage. I splashed my face and returned to the diner.

The waitress, a tall woman with a long, horse face, slipped me a day-old sandwich as I paid. "You look like you'll need lunch any minute. Get some flesh on your bones."

I goggled at the free food, unnerved by her generosity. "Thanks."

She cocked her head, pulling fleshy lips back from flat, white teeth. "We could use a dishwasher. Life's hard in the city for a runaway. You know about the Queen's press gangs?"

"Yes. I'm not—I'm trying to find my father."

"Of course." She smiled, but her eyes stayed sad. "Remember us if you need a job."

I slipped out the door and crammed the sandwich in my pack. My fingers brushed Mother's cup, and a breeze tickled my calves, sending a bit of litter skittering past my feet. "Mom?" An idea simmered in the back of my brain.

"Humm. That grease will clog your arteries. You should have a glass of milk, dry toast, and scrambled eggs."

"Where's that bookstore Mitroan goes to? I need a map." I kept my hand in my pack, fingers laced through the handle of the cup.

"The Bookworm? We used to take you there."

"Where is it?"

"What happened to your arm?" Warm air caressed my fingers.

I gripped the cup tighter. "Mom. I need to know."

"Know what, honey?"

"Where. Is. The. Bookworm?" My cheeks hurt from clenching my teeth.

"Where are we now?"

"Near River Street. North of Goblintown."

The air went still. "It looks so different."

"Well, of course." I didn't spell it out.

A sign creaked. Mom told me the directions using obsolete landmarks, stopping and starting over half a dozen times, but I followed well enough.

"Thanks." I shifted the pack to my back and broke into a jog. Early workers trickled into the streets in carts, on bicycles, and on foot. A lounging knot of unemployed veterans filled a bombed-out street corner, their missing limbs or eye patches accusing me of the crime of wholeness. I hurried past, ignoring hands outstretched for spare coins.

Sick worry for Feldsken filled my belly. I hoped he'd escaped, but feared he hadn't. Mitroan would know what to do, but I felt like I was flying blind. Down the hill, a hawk dived, swooping over a scrabbly vacant lot before landing on a stump. I had enough money to get my wings altered, to buy spells that tamed the wind. Learn to fly. The hawk glared at me, and then took off, soaring over houses and trees. I put my head down and kept marching.

A boy selling broadsheets waved the cheaply-made papers in my direction. "Queen's Men Capture Believer Spy. More Spies on the Loose."

I stopped. "Can I see?" I had to know.

"A Queen's head a page." He kept one eye aimed my way while scanning the crowd with the other. "Believer Spies Loose in Town," he yelled.

I'd spent all my normal money. "A quick peek?"

"Stop wasting my time." He frowned and thrust the papers in front of a man hurrying by. "Sabotage!"

I tried to read the broadsheets as he waved them around, but he straight-armed me so hard in the chest my lungs felt like they'd never get air again. I gasped and staggered onwards.

The Bookworm occupied a long, low building that looked embarrassed to still be standing. Grime covered the windows, and stacks of mouldering books and papers blocked my view inside. A round, old man with bug eyes and wild gray hair pushed a heavy cart through the front door. A wheel jammed.

"Can I help?" I extended my arm across the tottering top row of books. "I'm Lianne."

"Ogile." The man nodded. "We're having a sidewalk sale."

"And how much do sidewalks cost around here?" I forced my mouth into a smile.

"Oh, a joker?" Ogile pushed the cart fully outside, and then forced it against the wall. He paused. "Lianne. I should recognize that name." The facets of his eyes glittered in the light.

"My folks used to bring me here when I was a kid."

"No, I have it." He waddled inside and reached behind the counter, extracting a familiar broadsheet from a listing pile. He read the paper, finger moving back and forth across the sheet. His face fell. "Here." He handed the broadsheet to me.

"Queen's Men Capture Spy!" read the big black headline. The article continued in breathless, edge-of-seat style, regaling me with the detective prowess of the Queen's men and their brave determination to keep our city safe from Believers. The last paragraph mentioned further uncaught spies and said they were interested in talking to Lianne Helstrom, a winged young woman.

My mouth went dry. The air in the room seemed too thin to breathe. "That's not my name."

Ogile wiped nonexistent dust off the counter. "Of course not." He stopped moving the cloth. "I'm no friend of the Queen. The bully boys come through every few spans searching for contraband. I leave some cash folded in a book, and when they discover the money, they go away."

I didn't know what to say. My stomach growled. "Do you have any food?"

Ogile opened a small box and removed a sandwich and a fruit shake. "Have the sandwich."

I took the proffered food. "What do you mean you're no friend to the Queen?"

Ogile's smile seemed kind. "The extremely wealthy luxuriate in unimaginable decadence while grandmothers starve in the gutters. Children fight and die in a generation-long war." He lifted his shake and unrolled a long, thin tongue into the frothy liquid. "I believe in change." Ogile slurped his drink in one enormous swallow.

"You're a Believer." I couldn't keep incredulity from my voice.

"So are you."

"What?"

"You might as well be." Ogile shrugged. "There's no losing the designation."

"I don't understand."

"The Queen's men want to talk to you. They won't ask nicely. If they have to, uh, augment their questions, you won't be the same afterwards." He spoke slowly, as if to a simpleton. "There's no percentage for them to admit you're not a Believer." Ogile sighed. "It's a difficult world. One less young woman won't be missed."

Tears threatened as I thought of Feldsken taking the question. "What should I do?"

"Finish your sandwich." Ogile cocked an eyebrow. "And then impart to me the complete narrative."

Relief suffused my body. Through mouthfuls of pastry, I told Ogile about the flying fish crash, Feldsken appearing with the dispatch case, and making the Queen's men coffee the rest of the night.

Ogile nodded, eyes alight. "Continue."

I opened my mouth to tell him about the letter, but a knot of caution settled in my belly. I needed something to hold in reserve, a secret of my own, still. "Feldsken found some money." I showed Ogile the wad of bills from my left pocket, about a tenth of the total. "And I got zapped." I unrolled the edge of the bandage. A sweet, rotten odor tickled my nostrils.

Ogile frowned and touched my palm. "You caught the edge of one of the Queen's death magics. You're lucky." I didn't feel especially lucky, but I nodded as if I agreed, and then finished the story of my escape.

Ogile helped me change the dressing on my hand, washing until the water stayed clear. The skin had gone gray and rubbery. Black lines radiated up my arm. I winced, but when he wrapped clean cloth around my fingers the pain diminished to a dull ache.

The rest of the day, I unpacked boxes of books one-handed and cleaned dusty corners of the store. Ogile stayed ensconced behind his counter, a massive table of dark ironwood, directing my tasks with utmost courtesy. When potential customers drifted in, Ogile waved me out of sight.

I peeked at the browsers, spying while curled above the topmost shelf. I didn't let myself worry, trusting Ogile to do the thinking for me. Most customers seemed to be ordinary people looking for distraction or information, but occasionally a lone person would murmur something in Ogile's ear and Ogile would lean beneath his counter and hand over a folded broadsheet.

During a lull, Ogile waddled up the aisle towards me, holding a plate of sliced apples and cheese. "I have closed early, Lianne. Would you care for a late-afternoon repast?"

I uncurled and lowered myself one-handed to the floor. "You sell a free press, don't you?" I felt calm, like I belonged here. I knew Ogile's secrets.

Ogile stopped in front of me, sweat beading his temples. "Why, yes." He touched my good elbow. "Your intelligence does you credit."

"Do you write the articles yourself? Who does your woodcuts? Why you don't get caught?"

Ogile paused and thought for a minute. "Come. I will illuminate the issue." He led me to the main counter and groped under the smooth wood. A latch clicked.

"What are you doing?"

"Observe, my dear." Ogile pushed the ironwood counter, and the whole table rolled away from us, exposing a ring set flush in the floor.

I saw the round metal, but then found myself looking out the window, considering the purchase of a new shirt. My thoughts drifted and floated like ribbons set loose in a river. I shook my head to clear the unnatural fogginess. "What are you doing to me?"

Ogile lifted the ring and slid a door open. "Magic. It's harmless, but I need to hide what's below." A narrow, steep set of stairs plunged downward into darkness. "With practice, you'll learn to keep your focus."

I stared, trying not to blink, curiosity burning at my brain.

Ogile mumbled a short spell. Lights flared. I followed him down the stairs, feeling like I was leaving the normal world far behind. Ogile pulled a rope at the bottom, and the door slid shut above us. My head cleared, ears popping. An enormous metal contraption hulked in the basement, a black hole in its side open like a giant maw. Paper hung from lines strung wall to wall.

"A printing press." The sharp smell of solvents made my eyes water.

Ogile nodded. "We're doing well. Keeping a body count. Publishing memorials. It's called the Gadfly." He pointed to a newly printed sheet. A woodcut of a bug-eyed man buzzing the Spire framed the top right corner. "Have you seen it?"

"Of course." People passed old copies hand-to-hand until the paper shredded. "You shouldn't be showing me this. You could be thrown in jail."

Ogile smiled. "You trusted me. I'll help you find Feldsken and Mitroan. Get you maps and a driver." He got very still. "That money could buy an enormous quantity of supplies. Paper is quite expensive. Shortages. Supply and demand."

"You think you're making a difference?"

Ogile nodded. "Absolutely, my dear. We have contacts in the Queen's inner circle. Guild leaders, wealthy merchants. Powerful people who want the war to end. The Queen lives in the past. Perhaps this issue will tip the balance."

We sat in the basement among the hanging broadsheets, using buckets of ink as stools, and ate a cold dinner.

Ogile wrote a story about Feldsken and the injustice of the Queen's men. We worked till early morning, rolling ink over metal type and feeding page after page under a heavy cylinder that pulled the paper from my hand like a hungry beast. His fat, nimble fingers plucked fresh-printed pages from the press and hung them until all the space on the lines had vanished.

I fell asleep, head nodding forward, waking the next instant when the machine grabbed my hair and jerked me off balance. Ogile flicked a switch, stopping the press. "Unforgivable. I should have ascertained how tired you were." He pried the rollers apart and led me upstairs to a small room off the back of the store.

I collapsed face down onto a cot, feeling the exhausted satisfaction of work well done, and fell asleep to the sound of Ogile puttering. My hand throbbed. I dreamed of Feldsken, smashed flat and staring skyward with eyes as big as dinner plates, while Denab blew green cigar smoke in my face and demanded the whereabouts of the letter.

I woke in pitch darkness, sure I'd dived off a cliff, feeling my wings catch the air. My left arm beat pain in time with my heart, but my hand was numb.

I poked at my fingers, feeling nothing but cold, dead skin.

Light flared in the main room, and I heard Ogile whispering. Tap-tap-tap on my door. "Lianne? Wake up." Ogile peered around the jamb. "I've brought a doctor." Behind Ogile, a tall man with six thin arms hoisted a black medicine bag.

"How long since the incident?" The doctor snipped the bandages away, prodding the flesh of my palm with a blunt metal tool. "Does this hurt?"

"Two and a half days?" It seemed either much shorter or longer. "No. Nothing."

"The necrosis has progressed here and here." He poked the inside of my arm just short of the elbow. "It'll have to come off." He addressed Ogile.

Ogile's cheeks seemed tinged with green. He darted his gaze back and forth from the doctor to my hand. "Do what needs to be done."

"Hey, wait a sec." I snatched my arm from the doctor's grasp and sat up. "Don't be in such an all-fired hurry to lop."

The doctor leaned back, insectile hands opening and shutting. "There's no choice."

Ogile patted my shoulder. "Listen to him, dear."

I looked at my hand. My hand. The fingers had curled into dark gray claws. The skin had cracked and oozed a thin, clear pus. The nails had sloughed off. Bone poked from the ends of my fingers. I tried to make a fist, straighten my hand, anything. My thumb jerked. Anger at my helplessness, at the doctor, at Mitroan made me want to smash plates, throw rocks through windows. "Help me find Feldsken," I hissed at Ogile.

He nodded and looked away. The doctor rummaged in his bag, extracting a flat, silver bracelet. Tiny runes glowed in the dimness. He slipped the bracelet over my hand and slid it to my elbow. It dangled loosely around my arm, but he stroked the metal and mumbled a few words. After a minute, the bracelet tightened, pinching painfully. "Drink this." The doctor pressed a flask into my hand.

I unscrewed the cap. Sharp, alcoholic fumes made me wrinkle my nose.

"Every drop." He stared at me.

I stared back. My anger had drained away, replaced by a sick sense of loss. My mother. Mitroan. Feldsken. My hand. I tipped my head back. Whiskey burned like hot lava down my throat. I tasted a musty, organic flavor under the alcohol, and then my bones turned to jelly. The world went black.

𝗩

I woke to a painful pressure in my bladder. My head felt woozy. I reached for the wall. I missed. I stared at my left arm. What was left. I snorted at the pun, finding gallows humor comforting. My arm ended in a shiny pink stub at the elbow. If I looked away, I could still feel the forearm and hand. I stood upright, swaying. "Ogile?"

"Lianne." Ogile bustled into the room carrying a glass of water and a plate of toast. "How do you feel?"

"Fine." Nausea threatened to overwhelm me. My mind skittered away from thoughts of life as a cripple. "Where's Feldsken? I need to pee."

Ogile followed me to the bathroom, chattering on about my recovery until I shut the door in his face. I pulled my pants down and the letter fell to the floor with a damp thump. I'd been planning to tell Ogile, but now I felt resentful. I wanted to keep something back. I checked my other pockets. All the money was still there.

I finished peeing and stood up. Every tiny action felt different. Harder. I couldn't button my pants or open the door while clutching my jeans to keep them from falling around my ankles. I had to call Ogile. I stood, embarrassed and angry, while he buttoned my pants for me.

Ogile patted my shoulder, and then led me to the front of the store. He flipped the "Open" sign "Closed" and taped a message to the door. "Back in an hour." He hurried me into a waiting carriage and pulled the curtains shut.

"Where are we going?" The warped floorboards gaped open, giving me a view of the street moving beneath us.

Ogile whispered in my ear. "I can't cash the bills you have. They're much too large. The doctor needs remuneration. I have friends who can assist us."

"More Rebels?" I sounded grumpy, unsure that anything we did could rescue Feldsken. "Do they blow things up?"

Ogile frowned. "We call ourselves 'Believers' because we believe a better life is possible for all citizens. 'Rebels' sounds so... reactive. My friends may have different methods than mine. More, uh, violent. But they'll have smaller bills. Untraceable money. And I have other reasons to visit them."

I pressed Ogile for details, but he refused to answer, sinking into himself and cutting off further attempts at conversation. Sunlight filtered through the frayed curtains. The horse clopped forward. I lost track of the twists and turns but could smell the salty, dead-fish odor of the docks.

We stopped. Ogile helped me step into a cramped dirt alley. I flexed my wings, stretching from the ride, while Ogile paid the driver. The cart departed, rattling over the hard ground. Ogile looked left and right as if a squad of Queen's men might appear any second.

Unpainted wooden walls, devoid of any windows, blocked all but a thin slice of gray sky. Garbage spilled from a rusting metal container at the mouth of the alley. A ragged, whiny voice sang an off-key lullaby somewhere out of sight.

Ogile knocked at a low window and hissed a reply to a gravelly query from within. A door opened. A rough, hairy hand motioned us inside. I entered and blinked my eyes against the sooty darkness. A stumpy man who stood no taller than my chest lifted a lantern. He shined it in my face. "Who's she?"

"One of us." Ogile gave a short bow.

The man grunted. His body looked as thick and solid as a barrel of cement. His hands could have crushed my skull. He pulled a dirty handkerchief from a back pocket. "She can't be seeing the route."

Ogile nodded. I stood, shaking with fear, and let myself be blindfolded. Ogile gripped my good elbow. We started walking. Water trickled off the walls. The smell of damp rot permeated the passageway. Puddles of oily liquid soaked my feet.

Every cell in my body screamed at me to run back to open air. I pulled my wings as close as they'd go, but the feathers still brushed wet stone. I could feel the weight of the earth above me. Every step downward felt like being buried alive.

The stumpy man stopped. "Here you be." He pulled the blindfold free. We stood in front of a wooden door that shone black with ship's tar.

Ogile thanked him and knocked. The door cracked open. Bright yellow light from a suntorch cut through the darkness. I squinted. Hard-faced men sat reading broadsheets or cleaning weapons at a square table held up at one corner by a broken chair. Takeout wrappers littered the floor. The air stank of stale sweat.

I stepped into the room behind Ogile, mouth dry and stomach clenching. A broad-shouldered man at the far side of the room turned towards me. I goggled in disbelief. "Mitroan!"

"What are you doing here?" Mitoran strode forward and swept me up, holding me at arm's length. "How did you find me?" He frowned. "What happened to your arm?"

"I wasn't looking for you," I stammered. "I mean, I was, and Ogile was going to give me maps, but he needed some money for ink—" words bubbled out of me. I stopped and began over again with the night of the crash, skipping the letter because I didn't want Ogile to think I'd lied to him.

When I got to the part with the Queen's men chasing Feldsken into the bamboo, my voice hitched. "They caught him. They said they got a spy."

"Feldsken?" Mitroan exchanged glances with the other men at the table.

A lumpy-faced man with doggish ears scratched under his arm. "At least the kid don't know any names. Could be worse."

Mitroan frowned and motioned for me to continue. I swallowed and kept going. When I ended my story, I pulled out the wad of bills I'd showed Ogile earlier.

Every pair of eyes fixed on the money. A faucet dripped from another room. Mitroan took my hand and unfolded my fingers, slipping the bills one by one into his palm. "That's a fortune, girl." He turned to Ogile. "This'd buy enough ink to drown the city."

"I wasn't going to use it all for ink." Ogile looked from me to Mitroan. "The press needs maintenance. Paper is anything but cheap."

"I'll make sure you get your ink. Thanks for returning Lianne." Mitroan tucked the money into his front pocket. "We can use more weapons, better spells." His laughter rumbled like thunder. "It'll be fun to use Her Majesty's own dosh against her, won't it now, boys?"

"What about Feldsken?" I thrust my chin forward.

Mitroan frowned. "We'll keep our eyes open. Put the word out." He looked uncomfortable.

Everyone else turned away. The faucet dripped louder. I thought my head would explode. Mitroan stared at my feet. "Let me introduce you around." He gestured at a ferrety-faced man slouching at the end of the table. "Gorm. Next is Ravel. And Pink. Nicknames, obviously." Pink's lumpy face and bulldog jaw twisted into an expression that perhaps was meant to be a smile.

Mitroan leaned over the table. "Pink, move your gear."

Pink growled, ears lying flat on his shaved head, but after a minute he slid his chair back and clomped into a tiny room off the kitchen. He returned holding a worn duffel bag and a wicked-looking crossbow.

Mitroan turned to me. "We'll set you up in your own room. You'll live here now."

Ogile spoke to Mitroan. "I must return to the store."

Mitroan unfolded a thick leather wallet. He counted out a tall stack of crumpled bills into Ogile's hand. Worth a tenth of what he'd taken from me.

Ogile bowed. "I will arrange for the press repair. Good day, Lianne." He backed out the door. I felt bad for Ogile, like he'd been cheated.

Mitroan turned a sharp knife over and over in his hands. "We have a job to do." The blade glinted in the light. "Time to spend this money." He glanced at the other men, and then at me. "You should take a nap. You look knackered." He rubbed an earring.

At Mitroan's words, a wave of tiredness overwhelmed me. I knew he'd spelled me, but I was too tired to care. Mitroan took my shoulder and led me to the room Pink had cleared. He stood outside while I folded a Murphy bed down from the wall, leaving just enough space to edge around. Mitroan closed the door.

My heart beat faster as my eyes adjusted to the dark. A thin line of light outlined the door frame. Inky blackness concealed the rest of the room. Pink said something about sabotage, but I couldn't make out the details.

I lay face down, trying to sleep, wings pulled close to my back, feeling guilty about not telling Mitroan the whole story, but also mad at him for lying to me and short-changing Ogile. I wondered how many of his "business trips" had been to places like this, cells of grim men making resonator bombs.

The spell's influence faded. I groped under the bed for my pack, extracting Mother's teacup and setting it on the floor in a circle of my fingers. I breathed and rubbed the smooth sides, trying to reach a calm center.

A mouse skittered through the walls. A wisp of fresh air touched my arm hairs. "Lianne."

"Mother." I adjusted the scratchy blanket. "Tell me about Father."

"Mitroan?" The smell of cinnamon filled the room. "He's big and strong. And he laughs all the time. When we dance, he swings me up, and the world spins around."

"What happened?" My voice hitched as I pictured the fierce, grim man in the other room.

"I got sick." The air felt clammy.

"How?" I'd never heard the full story.

"Operation Toddler Bait." My mother's voice took on a steel edge. "Lord Zorahn had toys dropped all through our village during the night. The next morning I went outside and saw a doll beside the path. A beautiful girl with long hair and soft wings. It reminded me of you." Water dripped from the other room.

I waited. "Then what?"

"Oh. Well, the toys were poisoned, of course. Evil magic that twisted my insides. Mitroan brought us to the capital hoping to find someone to cure me, but magic is expensive. They chopped his horns off." The darkness pressed close.

"Why?" I tried to take it all in. "I didn't know."

"Know what, honey?" Tiny claws scrabbled against stone. "Where's my shrine? What happened to the aspens?"

I tried to get more details, but my mother never got back on track. Ghosts fray away. Tears dripped off my face as I returned the cup to my pack. I lay down and tried to fall asleep.

I thought about my mother and father, and the horrible story she'd told me. Why'd Zorahn have to poison toys? I kept turning the scenes over in my mind, picturing my father's laughing face, the doll, the wasting sickness.

I wanted to tell someone, to talk about my mother, but the idea of bringing it up with Mitroan seemed ludicrous. Feldsken. Where was Feldsken? I had to believe that he still lived, that Ogile could help me find him. I fell into a restless sleep considering and discarding crazy rescue schemes.

When I woke up, Pink's conversation clicked into place in my brain, and at breakfast I confronted Mitroan. "You sabotaged the flying fish, didn't you?"

Mitroan looked startled. Gorm leapt to his feet. "How does she know? Does her boyfriend know? They'll have it out in no time." Gorm bared his teeth, fear oozing off him like a cloud.

I stared into Gorm's twitchy face. "You did. What were you thinking? The crash could have taken out a whole block, killed hundreds of people."

Mitroan stepped forward. "We weighed the risks." He smelled of gunpowder and tingly defensive magic.

Pink spoke up. "The bamboo farm is the only open area after launch. We figured the pilot'd try to put her down there." He shrugged off a backpack, placing it on top of a stack of crates that hadn't been there last night.

"We knew the courier had something big." Mitroan frowned. "We'd hoped for more. The money is good, but…"

I pictured the giant fish eye staring at the sky and the swath of crushed bamboo. "That was your plan?"

Mitroan's eyes got stormy. "We take what we get, girl. What do you want?"

"Fresh air," I snapped. "And Feldsken back."

"Once someone's taken, you never forget," Mitroan snarled. "You get your revenge. But they might as well be dead." The stumps of his horns reflected the light.

"Revenge? You kill more people. Workers. Ordinary folks."

"They die for a cause," Mitroan thundered.

"Mother told me about, about how she got sick." Words seemed to stick in my throat. "I want people to live."

"They're monsters. We have no choice."

I stormed into the kitchen, trapped by the weight of earth above me. Had I ever really known my father? I agreed that Lord Zorahn was a monster, but the Rebels bombed train stations, markets. And the Queen cracked down even harder every time.

They finished breakfast and made their way to their small bedrooms. Pink unrolled a mat, giving me a narrow-eyed stare. Mitroan slapped me on the shoulder. "Clean up in here, would you?"

I nodded, resolving to leave at the first opportunity. I'd sneak out and rescue Feldsken. I'd trade Denab the letter and what was left of the money. Insane plan. But I had to do something, anything, and that was the best I could come up with.

I washed dishes, waiting for them to fall asleep. Pink grunted and rolled sideways, covering his eyes with a grimy shirt. I crept to the stack of crates by the door. I couldn't open them without making too much noise, but with teeth and fingers, I undid the knots on the backpack.

Resonator bombs, flash powder, hand knives, and an innocuous-seeming cardboard box labeled "Squidsphere." I undid the packaging to find a glass ball about the size of a crabapple. Penciled instructions said, "Non-lethal."

I tucked the sphere in my jeans' pocket. I didn't want to kill anyone. I eased the door open and told the stumpy guide I had to visit Ogile at the Bookworm. He stared as if he could see right through me, but he stepped aside and let me pass.

The dank, garbage-filled alley seemed a sultan's palace to me, full of dawn sunlight and playful breezes. I stretched my wings and laughed, pumping my good arm and running for the sheer joy of being outside.

I waved at a taxi-carriage, and the driver stopped, scowling at me from his seat. The horse turned and snuffled at my shoulder. I flashed a handful of bills and climbed aboard, giving him the address of my school.

The driver clucked to his horse. We started with a jerk. I opened the curtain and watched the passing buildings. Smoke trickled from the smashed window of a bank. Clumps of vets stared at Queen's men across intersections. The bully boys' swagger seemed even more exaggerated than usual.

My stomach growled and the driver took pity, handing half his breakfast through a sliding door behind his seat. An hour rolled by while he talked politics, thinly veiled criticisms of the Queen. I grunted when the conversation flagged. That seemed to be enough.

We arrived, and I handed the driver a bill, a thousand times the correct amount. His eyes grew huge. I could tell he was trying to place me. It didn't matter. I felt cut loose, committed. Off the cliff and trying to fly.

I arrived at school as second lunch period ended. Ms. Kenali waved at me, canary plumage flashing yellow and white. She twittered, but I skipped through a classroom of wide-eyed first-years, dodged into an abandoned foyer, and lost her on the third floor. I poked my head through the door to the roof, startling a flock of pigeons into ungainly flight. Their wings clacked together as they wheeled around me, settling on a ridgeline of roof one building over.

The sun beat down out of a sky so hot and light it looked white. I squatted, back to a chimney, and pulled Denab's crumpled business card from my pocket. I held the stiff paper and read the text again. "Denab Ghast, Queen's Chief." Clean black font. Creamy white paper. My fingers tingled from latent spells. I rubbed my thumb across the name and muttered under my breath. "Denab, Denab, Denab."

"Hullo." Denab's voice emanated from the air above the card. "Who is this?"

I took a deep breath. "Lianne."

"Lianne." I could almost see Denab take a long, slow puff on a cigar. "Well, well, well. I'd love to talk with you in person."

"You still have Feldsken?"

"What's that?" Denab paused. "Feldsken? What do you want with him?"

"I'll trade you. Straight up. The letter and the money for Feldsken." I took a breath. "Most of the money. I had to spend some."

Puff. Puff. "We should meet. I could consider a deal along those lines."

"No. Right now. Bring Feldsken to my school. You and him. No other Queen's men. No sirens. Wait in the south playground. All alone in the center of the field. No funny business."

"Well. It'll take some time to get Feldsken. And more time to get there."

"You have an hour." I tore the card in half, and then in half again. The magic fizzled out. I was left with the sound of a flag flapping in the breeze. I tucked my knees even higher to my chest, not sure how I could stand to wait an hour, but also hoping I could stay here forever, locked in a bubble beyond time.

The quarter-hour bells rang, and a line of ants crawled around my sandal, disappearing into a crack. A ginger cat padded onto the roof and yawned, showing me its sharp, white fangs, before lying down in the sun. I squinted at the people walking the street below. My sharp eyes could pick out their features even from this far away. They seemed worn down, weary. Scared.

I stroked my mother's cup. The wind gathered around me, pulling at my hair. "Lianne."

"Mother."

"It's not safe up here."

I laughed. A short, rueful bark. "No, it's not."

The wind teased my hair, tickling my nose. "You should eat more, put on some weight."

I stuffed the teacup back in my pack. The bells rang below me, rattling the tiles. I tried to think about what I'd do with Feldsken once I rescued him, but my mind stayed a stubborn blank.

Bells rang again. Only a quarter hour to go. I scanned the streets below. Was that a Queen's man in disguise as a street sweeper? Why was the ice cream cart taking so long? Where were all the children? I bit my nails to the quick, drawing blood.

The cat sprang to its feet and darted out of sight. Two people moved through the gate to the south field. I recognized Denab's arrogant swagger and the thick cloud of smoke that swirled around his face. Bandages wrapped the other person's head. He limped behind Denab, whiskers twitching.

I got to my feet. Time to meet. A finger tapped my shoulder. I jumped, scrabbling to keep my footing on the slippery tiles. "Queen's tits," I yelped.

"Hey, babe. What you up to?" Feldsken leaned against the chimney. He looked rumpled. His feathered hat had disappeared and the silk suit hung in near tatters, but he was whole and well and next to me—not standing in a field with Denab.

"How?" I gaped, looking back and forth from Feldsken to the pair of men walking through the ankle-high grass.

Feldsken peered towards the field. "Did you offer to trade for me?" He cocked his head. "That's sweet."

"They lied." I felt like an idiot. "They never captured you?"

"You didn't think a few bully boys could catch me in your bamboo? I was awful worried for you, though, till I read the broadsheets. Ha! Still missing. But you never showed at your house."

"How did you find me?" My pulse raced, and I felt like Feldsken had stuffed my head full of gunpowder and was blowing sparks in my ear.

"Oh, that." Feldsken waved his hand. "I took to following Mr. Cigar Breath. Man alive, he can stink up a neighborhood."

"Queen's tits."

"You said that."

"Yeah." I hugged Feldsken. A solid, full-body hug. He looked surprised, and then hugged me back.

"We should scram." Feldsken's arms stayed wrapped around me. "What happened to your hand?" He stepped back and stroked the bicep of my left arm. Concern filled his face.

"It had to come off." I shrugged, playing it tough. "Long story." I knew I could tell him anything.

Denab pointed at the roof. The fake Feldsken blew a whistle. The ice cream cart flew apart, boards banging into the street. A dozen Queen's men pounded towards the school.

Feldsken's eyes bugged out. "By the Queen's malignant brain tumors. We've gotta jet." He darted to an access panel and slid inside.

I slipped right behind him, rattling down the ladder, feet inches from his head, grabbing and releasing one-handed. "Go, go, go," I panted.

Feldsken laughed. I realized he loved the chase. My heart hammered like a steam engine. I tasted bile in my throat. I preferred less excitement.

We dodged through hallways, leaping down flights of stairs so fast we hardly touched a single step. I grabbed Feldsken and pulled him towards a classroom. "Window. Courtyard. Maintenance shaft."

Feldsken nodded, eyes bright as fireworks. "Excellent idea."

We burst into Ms. Kenali's first-year civics. Sweet, young faces stared wide-eyed. Ms. Kenali pointed a yardstick towards us like a rapier, her yellow plumage lying flat on her head. "Lianne Helstrom. What is the meaning of this interruption?"

Feldsken kept moving, ducking and weaving to the windows. I faltered. Words covered the chalkboard. A list of the Queen's benevolence. "Safety. Prosperity. Glory. Happiness."

Outrage coursed through my body as if my blood had ignited. "You lie!" I shouted. I turned to the class. "Lies, all lies." Words erupted with volcanic force. "The Queen deceives us. Lord Zorahn is a murderer."

Ms. Kenali stepped forward. "Young lady. You are disturbing our lessons. Leave at once."

Feldsken swarmed up a bookshelf and opened a high window. Brick walls overshadowed the courtyard. "Come on, Lianne."

"No." I snatched the yardstick from Ms. Kenali. I pictured the crippled vets on street corners, the horse-faced woman at the diner. The thought of these children soaking up this bullshit made me want to vomit.

Ms. Kenali hissed in my face. "I have a job to do. I have a family. Don't make trouble."

"A job?" I dug in my pocket. "Here." I threw a wad of bills at her. "How about the truth for a change?" Money fluttered through the air. Children gaped. One boy snatched a bill and stuffed it in his desk. I whipped the teacup from my pack. "Mom? Tell them. Tell the children about Operation Toddler Bait."

Ms. Kenali gasped and sank into her chair. She'd heard of it. I could tell.

Wind swept through the room, swirling loose papers and money into short-lived tornadoes. "Lord Zorahn dropped toys and dolls in my village." My mother's voice throbbed with pain. I strode up and down the rows of desks while the grim story continued.

Feldsken stopped twitching and listened, gaze riveted on me as I paced. The children's faces filled with shock and confusion. Ms. Kenali put her head in her hands.

The door burst open. Denab stormed the room at the head of half a dozen bully boys, knocking a student's desk over and grabbing my left wing. "Long time, no see, Lianne."

I screamed in pain as Denab twisted, forcing me to the floor. My hand opened, and the tea cup fell, shattering into hundreds of tiny pieces. My mother's voice cut off in mid-word. Children screamed and cried.

Feldsken threw a big red dictionary, catching Denab on the side of the head. The grip on my wing slackened. I lunged away. Bone snapped. Bright white agony seared through my shoulder blade. Denab lifted half my wing over his head.

I stumbled and fell face down. Flat on the floor, retching and whimpering, I managed to yank the sphere from my pocket. I threw it at Denab. Glass shattered. Icy coldness enveloped me. Inky black smoke boiled into the room with a low rumble.

"Move it, Lianne. Please?" Feldsken dragged at my shoulders, throwing his weight into every step.

I struggled to one knee, numb from the cold, shaking with pain. I grunted and pushed upright. Smoke writhed around the Queen's men, covering their heads in dense, opaque clouds.

Denab roared with anger and charged forward, smashing into desks and grabbing at empty air. Children clutched each other, crying. The bully boys tangled and tripped. I climbed the bookshelf, pushing my body against

Feldsken and grabbing shelves with my right hand. My left arm and side pulsed in torment, useless for the task.

Ms. Kenali stared at us as we clambered out the window, and I swore she mouthed a friendly good bye. We dropped to the crooked flagstones. My breath whistled like consumption, and black spots flared in my vision.

I pointed to the maintenance shaft. Feldsken nodded. "You okay?"

Alarms sounded above us, a clamoring of bells and sirens, but I knew once we hit the tunnels underneath the school, we'd be safe. "Sure." I hitched forward, limping, but moving at a decent pace.

Half an hour later, Feldsken pushed a manhole cover aside with a solid thump. We resurfaced in an empty alley behind a dry cleaners. We jogged across bustling streets, putting more and more distance between us and the Queen's men. In between ragged breaths, I told Feldsken about Mitroan and Ogile. The setting sun tinged the Spire red.

"I want real change," I panted. I felt giddy and lightheaded, like the ground was falling away, like I was flying. I cupped Feldsken's face with my right palm and kissed him. He twitched with surprise but kissed me back.

"That's extremely nice." Feldsken raised his eyebrows. "But we gotta get you to a doctor."

I nodded. "I know. But after we fix me, we go to Ogile's. We print the letter. Use the damn money to cover the city with the truth. Shout our message to the rooftops."

Feldsken nodded, eyes bright. A hawk took off from a roof and soared over the street, circling high above us.

NOT EVEN IF I
WANTED TO

BY KODIAK JULIAN

Near twilight of the third day, I still had not found the children. Instead, I found the candy house. I recognized it from the picture book I'd read to the boy when he couldn't sleep. There had been those long nights when his father was away for work and the boy would allow me to be the one to sing him back to comfort. Perhaps he would be inside the house, still in his rocket ship pajamas, stuffed platypus clutched to his chest. But no. Of course not. I knew who lived in candy houses. I put my fingers on the sticky doorknob and opened the door, knowing it would be the end.

The witch wasn't there, and neither were the children. Hurricane lamps cast buttery light around the little room, its low ceilings, its kindergarten-sized furniture. I opened the potbellied stove's door. No bones inside, no ashes. Either the witch had already devoured the children and cleaned up the mess, or she hadn't yet found them. She might be hunting them by starlight. When she returned, I could be waiting. I could fight. I could fling boiling water at her. The children and I would race out the door, through the forest, back home where my husband must still be on the couch in his dirty jeans. For the first time in three days, he would rise. He would gather us in his arms. For the first time in three days, he would weep.

I searched the shelves for a hatchet, for matches, for a vial of poison. The closest I found to weapons were bludgeons: a frying pan, porcelain figures of milkmaids and shepherds. Wood and coal piles waited by the stove, and I used them to make a fire. I sat on the floor before its heat. For three days, I had eaten nothing but the season's last red berries, and I had grown dizzy with hunger. For two nights, I had shivered against jagged rocks, longing for sleep. Would it be wrong to eat? Would it be wrong to lay down my head, to search again in the morning? I rose to slide the lock across the door. I could find no food but the house itself. What did the witch eat when she couldn't catch a child? Perhaps the witch was long gone. Perhaps the children were safe yet undiscovered, living in a cave, rubbing sticks together to make a jolly little fire, roasting the fish they had caught in the stream. I tore off a bit of gingerbread windowsill, feeling the house's answering shift. It was soft enough to eat, yet strong enough to hold up the house. The girl and I had only managed those horrible brittle walls with burnt edges. We piled dishes in the sink and spent a winter night trying again and again to create something wonderful.

I finished the bit of windowsill, craving more. I found an old nightgown in a dresser drawer and changed from the clothes I had been wearing since the first moment we realized the children were missing. I set the frying pan beneath the bed and pulled the quilts around me. Tree branches thrashed against the roof.

I dreamed about the time when the boy's dog had messed itself and the boy wouldn't clean it.

"It's gross," he said.

"It's your dog," I said.

The girl put her hands on her hips like her mother. "You're being unfair. You're always unfair."

"Oh yeah?" I said. "When exactly am I unfair?"

"When we have to have homemade pizza instead of the real kind!" said the girl.

"So it's unfair that I try to save money so you can go to college? Is that it? If only more parents were unfair!"

"It's not your money, it's Dad's," said the girl.

"Excuse me," I said. "You don't think I work? I'm the one who makes more money. I'm saving for your college! I pay for this house!"

"No you don't!" said the boy. "Mommy said so."

"Well I do," I said.

"Are you calling Mommy a liar?" said the girl.

"As a matter of fact," I said. As a matter of fact.

I dreamed of the children's mother, all claws and cigarette voice. I dreamed of how she fed the children candy on the weekends they spent with her so they would love her more. Yet who roused them on Monday mornings, made them practice their spelling words, combed their hair for lice?

In the morning, I dressed in my dirty clothes. I pulled another piece of gingerbread from the windowsill and went outside to search.

🜊

Dawn was gray and misty. The woods had no paths. I stomped through the easy places of grasses and ferns, but the easy places never lasted. Devil's Club and fruitless blackberry brambles snared my clothes. Thorns crept into my socks, puncturing my ankles. A briar ripped open a seam in my arm. Blood rushed to fill it, a vein on the wrong side of my skin.

Leaves on trees and bushes matched the color the children and I used for school projects: the red we built by pressing the crayon hard against paper, rubbing in circles until the wax shimmered like an exoskeleton. In another week, it would be easy to see my way through the woods. In another week, half the trees would become clusters of antlers, leaving only the evergreens to block my view. In another week, the children would no longer be alive. I knew what the police avoided saying, that the first few hours were critical, that when the children hadn't been found on the first day or on the second day or on the third day, that hope slipped further and further across the horizon like the evening sun.

I came upon sudden cliff sides plummeting to soft, green meadows. I leapt over brooks, hind foot dragging through frigid water. I stopped short at the sight of a bull snake in my path. I grew hungry, hungry, with nothing to eat.

If I didn't find the children, then every day could be like the weekends they spent with their mother, except that we wouldn't have to spend our time driving into town to bring outgrown clothes to the thrift store. We wouldn't have to rush around, cleaning the mud stains and the blood stains from the floor. The children would not return on Sunday night, the girl's backpack full of homework she had not completed at her mother's house. Of course she hadn't done it there. She never did, not even when we gave her mother a clear list of what needed to be done.

"That's because my real mom is nice," the girl always said. She came home tired from having spent the night watching R-rated movies. She would talk like her mother, squinting her mean little eyes and thrusting her chin. "I guess we'll just have to suffer and die."

That would never happen again. Not unless we found them.

If my husband and I lived alone, perhaps life would be like those few weeks two years ago, when my husband touched fingertips and lips to my belly, the secret humming between us, and we intertwined our fingers and I pressed my toes against his toes and we were like an androgyne, like a child of the moon. Perhaps there would be a stillness, and we would be the only people in the world. But no: if I did not find the children, then life would be like the days that followed, the days after the blood, and I would watch him rock himself, beyond comfort. I would be a cracked and empty bottle. This time would be worse, because he had loved the children. Because I was supposed to love the children.

Late afternoon came with no north, no south. There were no paths, not even deer paths, not even scat. I followed streams. Streams are all supposed to come from somewhere, to go somewhere, to connect. One ended in a marsh. Another ended with water draining into a pool of pebbles. One narrowed into a stream's soggy memory, and then the memory, too, disappeared.

I did not want to return home to the people who would touch each other's arms when they spotted me in the grocery store. When one did not know why the sight of me filled the other with pity, the knowing one would whisper, "I'll tell you later." I did not want to return to the torrent of phone calls, and then the months of the phone's silence as no one would want to talk. No one would want to share in the sorrow. When others finally did call, they would pretend that everything was normal, and I would pretend that they were not pretending. I did not want to return as the callous one if I were actually able to sleep in my bed at night. I did not want to be awakened by my husband vomiting.

Even if I had wanted to return, there was no sign of home. I could not remember the last time I'd heard a car. I had never known the woods stretched for so many miles. They might take lifetimes to cross.

The low sun turned leaves to gold. Hares darted across my path. Perhaps the children hunted them. Perhaps they had learned to roast them on a spit, to wear their soft fur. The golden light turned to evening's thin blue. Deer grazed. Tiny insects bit my neck and hands. Trees thickened. Darkness spread.

Didn't those who were lost in the woods walk in circles? Could I have been walking in a great circle all this time? The children might be making small circles, and I might be making a circle around them. It would be a way to hold them, the way I held the little boy when a wasp stung his ankle, the way I put my arms around the girl after some boys from school said she had dirty things shoved up inside her. This walking was holding them, holding them, smoothing their hair for school pictures, laughing at the dinner table with corn sticking in our teeth.

Again, in darkness, the brambles grabbed and stung. I should have stopped earlier. I took a step and the thorns stabbed. I took a step in another direction and they stabbed again. Wasn't this the time when bears strolled in search of food? Were there mountain lions in these woods? At least a bear's steps might give warning. At least a mountain lion would kill swiftly. Then I was walking, walking fast, briars ripping at either side, then running, as though there were a hundred eyes on me, eyes I could not see.

Then I fell. I rolled and slid. I smashed against rocks, smashed my arm, my head, my leg. I crashed into a river gully: my feet in glacial melt, my body splayed against the rocks. I tried to move. I might be too broken to walk. If death came for me, I hoped it would race. Still, death might taunt me. It might leave me here all night, awake and aching. I had never known death. I did not know what it liked to do.

A light shone above me. Then a voice. "You. I thought it might be... I hoped it might be..."

The children's mother set her lantern against the rocks and offered her hand. I took it, letting her pull me up.

"Come along," she said. By lantern light, she led me up the hillside. She did not ask why I was in the woods. Each step chiseled my bones. I did not ask why she was there.

At the hilltop was the clearing with the candy house. The children's mother had left the door open when she came for me with the lantern, and a teapot screamed on the stove, hot where she had left it. She wrapped a pot holder around the teapot's handle and lifted it from the stove.

I dropped my body into a chair at the little table. I wanted to ask if she had looked to see whether anyone had nibbled the piping near the front door. I wanted to ask what kind of fat made the stove's fire spurt and hiss. I would not. After the children left, my mother asked me if I had punished them recently, if I had told them I loved them. I hung up the phone. My mother called back. "I love you, you know."

The children's mother poured two cups of tea. She sat beside me at the table and shoved a plate toward me. It had a hunk of gingerbread. I looked around and saw where this windowsill had been. I took tiny bites. It was the last windowsill.

The children's mother removed her shoes. She had a gash on one foot. She poured water from the kettle into a deep bowl. She rubbed her feet, kneading into the gash, and when no more steam rose, she lowered her feet into the water.

I pushed myself from the table, turned my back to the children's mother, and changed into the nightgown I had worn a night ago. The children's mother rose and dried her feet. She brought the bowl of dirty water to me. I sat on the edge of the bed, and put my feet in the cold water. The children's mother took another nightgown from a dresser drawer and changed. I tried not to watch, but I watched. Her body had pits and mounds. I had imagined how my husband used to touch it, how the children grew within it.

I opened the door. It hung from its hinges like a loose tooth. I dumped the water into the woods, and crawled into the narrow bed beside the children's mother. We lay still to keep from touching.

W

The next day, the children's mother returned to the woods. I did not go far from the candy house. I lay in my underwear beside the house, my skin puckered in the cold, in the cool sunlight. Violet bruises dappled my limbs. When I could no longer ignore my hunger, I broke off a bit of piping from beneath the window. I ate and dressed, then climbed into the bed and slept. When I woke, the air was dark behind the house's sugar windows. The children's mother had returned, her sweater torn. I found a deck of playing cards on a shelf above the bed. The children's mother and I sat at the table, playing rummy until the night grew too cold to stray from beneath the quilts.

The following day, neither of us left the house. We sat in front of the stove, playing cards. Snow fell. I slept on the floor and dreamed of the time we had tried to go camping, how we had huddled in the wind-battered tent. The boy had stuck the flashlight in his mouth and blown up his cheeks, his eyes wide as though he had made the light himself. The girl zipped his sleeping bag together with hers. When the wind yowled and the boy ducked his head inside their joined sleeping bags, the girl began to sing a song about the ocean, and then she sang a song about geese and then one about stinky socks. In the morning, after we rushed to pack our site, we drove through the storm to a little town. We sat in a warm diner's booth and ordered pancakes. When they came, I poured syrup all over the girl's food, and she lowered her face to her plate and licked. My husband wrestled his fork against the boy's fork. Beneath the table, my husband and I interlocked our legs.

I woke to wind shrieking through a crack in the wall. I looked at the children's mother as she squinted and shivered in the dawn. I pointed to the crack in the wall. "Why did you do it? You've ruined everything! Don't you think I might be hungry, too?" I put my fist through the wall, just above her pillowed head. I crammed gingerbread into my mouth. So sweet, but I would not savor. I would have all that I wanted, all that I wanted, all that I wanted.

Soon there would be nothing but us and the woods. At last, we might find the children: their bodies, barely human with decomposition and maggots, the hidden shack with a man's secret cellar, a lost piece, a shoe, a finger. Some hidden hook had ripped open a seam within my heart. We would wander and search until the woods were finished with us.

YES, I'M A WITCH

BY JULIE MCGALLIARD

"**S**o, the Girl Scouts used to give out merit badges for witchcraft?" My husband Alan holds up my green sash, liberated from a box in my mother's sewing room, where it has spent thirty years nestled against the mummified remains of an apple head doll.

I laugh. "What? Let me see that." I instantly see the badge he's talking about, one that depicts a large black cauldron squatting over orange and red flames. I run my fingers over the smooth machine embroidery, and try to remember. "Outdoor cooking, I think. But you're right, it looks like something they'd give out at Hogwarts."

I can't believe I never thought of that before. Because Sharyn Wakeman, my best friend when I was eleven, the last year I was in scouts, was a witch.

◈

I met Sharyn at the beginning of sixth grade, when I wanted to quit Scouting, but my mom wouldn't let me.

"Tabby, you have to go."

"But why?"

"Because Scouting is good for you."

"You mean, like broccoli is good for you?" A proto-teenage sneer crept into my voice, and my mother frowned. I continued. "Everybody hates me at Scouts just like they hate me everywhere else."

"Nobody hates you, honey." She tried to smooth my hair back from my eyes, and I brushed her hand away with irritation.

"Yes they do. You always say that. But you don't see them—they call me a brain and stuff." I self-censored, omitting the more sexually suggestive insults that were often thrown in my direction.

"Well, you see? They're just jealous because you do well in school."

"They're not jealous, Mom. You were little miss popular in school, weren't you? Like the kids who make fun of me. You don't have a clue what it's like to be a nerd."

She inhaled sharply, as if getting ready to rebuke me. But instead she sighed. "Don't call yourself names, honey. Look, you're upset right now, but I promise, if you go to the meeting, you'll feel better. It's a new school year. You might make a friend."

I prepared to spit out a retort, something along the lines of, why would I make a friend today when I didn't all last year or the year before? But instead, I was filled with the sudden and inexplicable conviction that my mother was right. If I went to the meeting, I would make a friend. But I didn't want to admit that. So I said, "All right. I'm doing this as a favor, okay? But if I don't make a friend before Christmas, I'm quitting. I don't want to sell cookies again."

She smiled. "That sounds fair."

❥

I was disappointed when I arrived at the meeting. After a six-week break, some of the girls were obviously taller, or had new haircuts, or braces. Some even appeared to be wearing training bras. But there was nobody new. Nobody who hadn't already failed to make friends with me. I took a glass of blood-red punch and settled into a chair at the edge of the room, where I sullenly watched the other girls chatter with each other. I told myself I didn't believe in premonitions, or Girl Scouts. And I hated the cloying, oddly flavorless punch. Cherry? Raspberry? I couldn't even tell. It tasted of chemicals and disappointment.

Miss Farrell, the troop leader, was a slight woman who never stopped smiling, and reminded me a bit of a chipmunk. She went around the room in a circle, pointing, after which we were supposed to give our name and describe something fun or educational that we had done during the break. Some girls had been on exotic vacations, to Hawaii or Europe. Some talked about visiting museums, or the aquarium. I was in a foul mood and didn't feel like talking, so when she got to me, I said only, "Tabitha Reynolds. Nothing."

Her perma-smile broadened. "Now, Tabby, you know that's not true. Your mother told me that the whole family took a car trip back east. You saw lots of historic sites. Why don't you tell us about one?"

"Because I don't feel like boring everyone," I snapped out. The room erupted in laughter, and I turned hot and light-headed. Laughing at me, or with me, I couldn't tell, and suddenly didn't care. I just had to get out of there, quick, before I fainted.

"Excuse me." I ran to the women's bathroom of the community center and locked myself in the larger of the two stalls, sank into a corner, and tried to catch my breath. I was embarrassed that Miss Farrell singled me out the way she did, embarrassed that I bit her head off because of it, embarrassed that everybody laughed, embarrassed that I ran out of the room. Now the rest of them were back there, either discussing me, which was embarrassing, or ignoring me, which was also embarrassing. I wondered if a person could literally explode from embarrassment.

"Hey, merit badge girl, you in there?" One of the other girls knocked on the outside of the stall.

"I don't feel well," I shouted back. Merit badge girl? Is that what they called me? Embarrassing. My sash full of badges, previously a source of quiet pride, instantly turned into shame. Just one more example of me being a hopeless nerd.

"It's Sharyn. Sorry, I forgot your regular name. Anyway, I know you're too shy to go back in there. It'll be okay. You can just say you had to barf."

I opened the stall door. "You want me to lie?" I hadn't recognized her name or her voice, but I knew Sharyn by sight. She was a skinny girl of medium height, in a uniform that was too big and slightly outdated. Lank, long hair in a shade you might call "dirty blond." Pale skin, beginning to break out in acne along her forehead. No merit badges. Arms folded, she grinned at me with crooked teeth.

"Okay, here." She handed me a small, brown bottle labeled DRINK ME.

I stared at it. "I'm supposed to drink this?"

"That's what it says."

I swallowed the whole thing in one gulp, so quickly that it was already down by the time I noticed how bad it tasted, worse than moldy bread, worse than the time I was going for my cooking merit badge and made banana bread with salt in place of sugar. The sides of my jaw began to tingle unpleasantly, mouth watering, and, just like that, I needed to throw up.

I collapsed to my knees and gagged up a disgusting mixture of bright red punch and partially digested oatmeal raisin cookies. When it was over, I turned to Sharyn angrily. "What the hell? Are you trying to kill me?"

She handed me a glass of water and a wad of paper towels. "Now it's not a lie when you say you puked."

I took the water and swished it around my mouth. "What was that stuff?"

"An herbal emetic. Emetic means it makes you throw up. I found the recipe in one of my books. I keep some handy ever since my mom tried to pull a Marilyn after Dad left." She paused, saw by my blank look that I didn't understand. "I mean, she tried to kill herself like Marilyn Monroe, by overdosing on tranquilizers and mixing it with booze." She held out her hand for the empty bottle. "Anyway, I'm glad my dad is gone. Mom kinda is too, mostly. But she's such a drama queen. I don't think she really wanted to die." She put the bottle in her backpack.

"Thanks, I guess. I'm Tabby."

Miss Farrell appeared in the door of the bathroom, her perma-smile turned slightly worried. "Are you girls all right in here?"

"I'm okay now." I wiped sweat from my forehead with a paper towel, and grimaced. The inside of my nose still smelled like punch vomit.

"Tabby just had to puke, Miss Farrell," Sharyn said. "I think it was the punch and cookies."

"What? No!"

"Or stomach flu. You should call her mom and say to come pick her up."

"Oh, I will." Miss Farrell rushed off to find a pay phone.

So, that's how I became friends with Sharyn. She made me puke, then lied to my Girl Scout troop leader about it.

A few weeks later, at my mother's urging, Sharyn spent the night at my house. Saturday afternoon, an unfamiliar car pulled up and idled, engine loud and sputtering. My mother stood in the driveway, arms folded, scowling at it, until the mismatched passenger door opened to let Sharyn out. Then Mom forced a smile. "Tell your mother she can come inside for a minute, I'd like to meet her."

"It's my sister, not my mom," Sharyn said.

"She can still come inside."

"She's on her way to work. She can't be late." She waved at the driver, who sped off.

My mother's face fell, then she gathered up her smile again, big and fake. "Well, hello there, Sharyn! My daughter has told me so much about you."

"Did she?" Sharyn gave me a sidelong look, and I tried to keep from bursting out laughing.

"She said you both like the same music?"

"Oh, yeah. Sure." She nodded. We shared a fondness for Electric Lunch, the noontime program of sixties psychedelia hosted by the local hard rock station, and we both agreed that disco sucked. It was 1981, and the seventies were barely over. Our T-shirts were close-fitting and decorated with sparkling vinyl iron-on decals. The legs of our painter pants were wide. In our back pockets, we carried plastic combs.

My mother led us into the house, where she explained the snacks, and asked Sharyn personal questions. How old was her sister? Did she have other siblings? What did her father do for a living?

"I have no idea. Nothing, probably. He's a bum." Sharyn folded her arms and met my mother's gaze, until my mother backed down.

"I'm sorry. You mean your father is—?"

"Not a part of my life anymore, and good riddance."

"Oh." A moment of unspeakable awkwardness trembled in the air, then, "Well, if he's not a good guy, I'm glad he's out of your life. I guess I'll let Tabby show you the rumpus room."

Mom went out to putter in the garden, and Sharyn and I went downstairs. "Sorry," I said. "My mom is super nosy."

"It's okay. A lot of moms are." She looked around at the space my mother called the rumpus room, taking in the pool table, the microwave. "This is a pretty big house. Are you guys rich?"

"I don't think so. I mean, my parents are always talking about how expensive stuff is like they can't afford it."

"You're rich. Rich kids never think they are."

We were supposed to have the downstairs room to ourselves all night, with no interruptions from siblings or parents. For entertainment we had comics borrowed from Sharyn's sister, broadcast television, and vinyl records. Video tapes, cable TV, and CD players existed, even mobile phones, but only yuppies had them. We danced to Beatles records, hopping up and down hard enough to make them skip. Then we collapsed, exhausted, onto the carpet, drinking cans of Coke—New Coke and Diet Coke still several years in the future—and staring at the lava lamp.

"It's too bad about Yoko Ono," she said.

"What about her?"

"Well, marrying her totally ruined John Lennon's career. She got him doing all this weird experimental noise music and stupid modern art and politics and stuff. And now he's assassinated, so his last record ever in the world is half Yoko, so I can't even listen to it."

"Hmmm." I didn't know anything about it, but I usually accepted her opinion on things like that. There was a long moment of silence. Then I asked, "Sharyn, why did you call me 'merit badge girl'?"

"What? Oh." She laughed. "That's what I always called you in my head. Before I knew your name."

"You don't like merit badges?"

"Well, don't you think they're kind of stupid? Old-fashioned, I mean. Like, for housekeeping and needlework and cooking and all that stuff. Who needs to do needlework these days? Why do you have all those merit badges anyway?"

"Because I'm a dork."

"You're not a dork. Real dorks never know they are." Another long pause. "Tabby, are you super religious?"

"Not really. My family is, but I'm not."

"You promise not to get freaked out if I tell you something?"

"I promise."

"I'm a witch."

She paused to let that sink in, while the needle of the record player reached the end of the first side of *The White Album* and began to hiss, in a weird, mechanical rhythm. I hopped up to flip the record, then sat back down again. "Seriously?"

"Seriously." She nodded. "But it's not like on TV. You can't just wiggle your finger and make anything you want happen."

"Well, of course not." On the stereo speakers, Paul McCartney began to sing about his sheepdog Martha. "So, what is it like?"

"It's hard to explain. You kind of have to do it. Do you want to?"

My heart thumped. Maybe I was more religious than I thought. "I don't know. I guess. What do we do?"

"We could try to talk to the spirits. Maybe a séance. Do you want to talk to the ghost of John Lennon?"

"We can do that?"

"Maybe. The spirits have to decide whether they want to talk to you or not."

"Is it dangerous?"

"Not just to talk. It can be dangerous to ask for stuff. Usually only if you're a jerk, though. You see, if you draw their attention, and they like you, they'll help you out. Little things. Whisper the right answers on tests, show you discarded money, help you find lost items. But if you draw their attention and don't show the proper respect, you piss them off, and they start messing with you. Make you trip on tree roots and give you zits and stuff."

Chills cascaded down the back of my spine, until I tingled all over. I knew she was telling me the truth. Or just making stuff up, but it was still true. An unseen world of mystery sat uneasily on top of our own, and maybe we could touch it.

"When do we do it?" My mouth was dry.

"Midnight. That's always when you do magic." She patted her backpack. "I've got the supplies in here."

We killed the hours until midnight with more music and television and comic books. When it was almost twelve, we began to set things up. We used a pencil and a string as a compass, and delineated a circle with masking tape. A copy of *Double Fantasy*, John Lennon's last album, went in the center of the circle. On top of the album cover she poured a small pile of sand. "The spirits can use it to write messages if they want," she explained.

We lit four black candles, and placed them around the circle at the cardinal direction points. Then the lights went off. Inside the circle, we sat cross-legged, mirroring each other. The candles gave off a heavy, musty perfume, not exactly pleasant, but it did seem mystical. Their flickering light turned Sharyn's face to shadow. She looked ominous, and older, at least seventeen.

"Now what?" I whispered.

"We chant, to get ourselves in the right frame of mind."

"What do we chant?"

She closed her eyes for a long time. Then she said, "Repeat after me. Let me take you down."

"Let me take you down."

"Nothing is real."

"Nothing is real."

"Forever."

"Forever."

At the familiar lyrics, altered, I felt a fresh wave of chills. Had they always been so strange and morbid? We repeated the words in unison, over and over, turning them into a chant, into sounds that began to lose their meaning as English words. I kept my eyes open, but my vision unfocused, candle flames turning to fuzzy points of light that receded into the distance. The world retreated, and it seemed that I stared into a long, dark tunnel, into infinity, and I could almost see something beyond, something formerly hidden, something—

A gust of wind extinguished the candles and we screamed together. "Aaaaaaa!"

My father's voice. "Tabby? Tabitha? Are you in here?"

The light flared on and I realized that, in our shock, we had knocked one of the candles over. Black wax dripped onto the carpet.

"Oh, sh-ooot!" I said, and started trying to mop it up with paper towels.

"What were you girls doing?" My father frowned at the candles, the circle, the John Lennon album with its pile of sand now scattered. (But didn't it look—a bit—as if someone had scrawled one of Lennon's self-portraits in it?)

"It was meditation, Dad," I said. "You messed it all up!"

Suddenly Mom was there, beside him. "What on earth is going on down here?" Her eyes found the wax, and widened. "TABITHA! WHAT HAVE YOU DONE TO THE CARPET!"

"I'm cleaning it! I'm cleaning it!"

But the puddle of wax had already soaked deep into the fibers, permanently it seemed. I never heard the end of it, not until I went to college and they finally ripped up the old shag and put in fake hardwood instead.

W

A few days after the sleepover, I got The Lecture. My mother sat me down at the kitchen table, wanting to Talk About the Other Night. I assumed it would be some kind of plan for working off whatever amount of money it would take to de-waxify the carpet. But, no. She wanted to talk about why the candles were there. Were we doing a séance? I admitted that yes, we had been. She said that was fine, in a tone of voice that indicated exactly the opposite. She understood that girls my age liked to experiment with such things. She had once gone to a slumber party where a Ouija board was used as entertainment.

"But we thought it was just harmless fun. We didn't know how dangerous it could be," she said.

"Dangerous how?" I thought of Sharyn's warnings, about what could happen if you pissed off the spirits. So far, I had noticed no particular increase in my clumsiness, or acne. I did sometimes imagine Beatles tunes hummed just at the edge of my hearing.

"Well, the occult," she said. She pushed a pamphlet in my direction. "We've been studying it in adult Sunday school class. There's a lot more than you know. Things like—Satanic ritual sacrifice. There's groups out there, you know? And they—they put weird things in rock music." She must have known she wasn't making much sense, because she touched the pamphlet again, scooted it toward me. "Please, just read. Okay? I want you and your friend to know that stuff—it probably isn't okay to be doing that."

Now, as an adult, I recognize my mother's incoherent and superstitious worry as the early stages of the Satanic Panic that would grow as the eighties progressed and the religious right came to dominate both politics and the Christian church. But then, as an eleven-year-old, all I knew was that my mother had apparently lost her mind.

I complained to Sharyn. We were at her place in the trailer park, and I was uncomfortable with my new class-consciousness, the knowledge that I lived in a spacious split level in a nice neighborhood, and she lived in a small manufactured home that smelled perpetually of the urine from an aging, incontinent dachshund. She did have her own room, but it was small, and the furniture inside was old and battered. She was playing records, while I worked on the final stages of my needlework badge. I can still recall the precise sensation of drawing silk through linen stretched tight across an embroidery hoop. She was right, it was a ridiculous thing for a girl to be doing in 1981. But I was doing it anyway. I don't think I've done it again in all the years since.

"Isn't it the stupidest thing you've ever seen?" I pointed to the pamphlet. "Check out the way light imagery is supposed to be Jesus, because he's the light of the world, and also Satan, because Lucifer is the light bringer. Which is it, people? Come on." I poked the needle with too much force, pricked my thumb. A tiny pain, a tiny spot of blood. "Look, I'm bleeding. Can you use that for anything witchy?"

Her smile was sad. "I can, but I won't. Not right now. How can you believe I'm a witch if you don't believe in all this other occult stuff? Isn't it the same thing?"

That stopped me short. How could I? Either spirits were real, or they weren't. Either you could summon them, or you couldn't. "No. It's not the same. Do witches believe that some spirits are inherently evil? Like, it doesn't matter what they do, they just—exist in badness?"

She thought for a moment, then shook her head. "No. Evil lies in human action, and human intent. The spirits are a force of nature. Nature is never evil."

"Okay, see. That makes a lot more sense to me."

"We do believe that evil acts tend to rebound on the one who commits them. That's why you don't want to use curses, hexes, things with an intent to harm. Everything you do, good or bad, comes back to you three times." A car drove up outside, and she paused, frowning. "That sounds like they stopped in our driveway."

We heard the car door slam, and a rumbling masculine voice, distorted words that we couldn't catch. Her face turned gray. "Oh, my God, that's my dad. I thought he was never coming back here."

I caught her fear, and formed an image of her father as a shadowy ogre. "What's he going to do?"

"I don't know. I don't know why he's here. Maybe it's nothing. Maybe he's just getting some clothes." She lifted the needle off the record player, and we sat in silence, hardly daring to breathe, like cornered teenagers in a horror movie waiting for the madman with the ax. Heavy footsteps shook the trailer like an earthquake.

"Sheila! Sheila, you bitch, where the fuck are you? It's Harry! Your god-damned husband!" Now that he was inside, I could understand the words he was saying, bellowed in a high state of outrage, and slurred. He was drunk, I realized. I could smell it all the way inside Sharyn's room.

His footsteps lurched toward us. He must have been a big man, a giant. Fee, fi, fo, fum. I tried to suppress the giggles that threatened to overwhelm me.

"Sharyn! Sharyn, are you in there? Sharyn, you come out of there! You come out of there or I'll make you come out!"

The doorknob rattled and I clutched her arm. She picked up a rock from the top of her dresser, a sparkling geode, a half sphere about four inch-es across. She held it at the ready, while both of us watched the doorknob as if it were a cobra. Her lips moved, in a spell, or a prayer. The raw opening scream from "Revolution" sounded over and over in my head.

"Sharyn! Why is this door locked? Shit!" He slammed against the door, so hard that I worried he would punch a hole in it. But he turned away again, thundered down the hallway. We continued to hold our breath, through the sounds of somebody in a rage, tossing small objects around, until he fell over. A few moments later he was passed out and snoring like a buzzsaw.

"You need to leave before he wakes up," Sharyn said.

"Don't you?"

"I'll be okay. I don't know why he couldn't get the door open. It's weird. It doesn't actually lock. He must have been turning it the wrong way the whole time and just not realized."

"Or maybe it was the spirits."

She grimaced. "Huh. Maybe. They've never protected me from him before, but…" She fell silent, as her eyes rested on the dresser, found the empty space where the geode had been. Or, what should have been empty space. But instead, both of us saw three quarters, stacked neatly, in exactly the same spot.

"Tabby, you're not messing with me, are you?"

I shook my head. "And you're not messing with me."

"No, of course not." She shook her head. "Well, that's weird."

"Understatement of the year."

Sharyn told me that her father left the next morning without further incident. I was now convinced of both the reality and benevolence of the spirits, and became Sharyn's apprentice in witchery. For cover, I told my mother that I had joined a history club that met after school. I discovered that if I went without a fuss to Girl Scouts and meetings of the church youth group, she never questioned it.

So, that became my life in sixth grade: walking through the motions of piety and scouting, while inhabiting with Sharyn a private world of Beatles records and witchcraft. We made potions and charms and gris-gris bags, wrote incantations, drew symbols. We visited haunted locations, local cemeteries, and enigmatic ruins. We shared insights supposedly gifted by the ghost of John Lennon, embraced by both of us as a kind of guardian spirit.

One day, in the spring, she wanted my help with something big.

"It's my father. He's been coming around a lot, acting really nice, taking my mom out for dinner and stuff. He even bought me new shoes."

"But isn't that good?"

"No." Her face twisted, as if she smelled something foul. "It's never real with him. He doesn't reform. He just tricks people. He's a good liar. I know because I'm a liar too. I learned it from him."

"So what do you want to do?"

"I want to curse him." She paused, noticed my jaw dropping open, and smiled. "Don't worry. I want to, but I won't. I remember the rule of threes.

I guess I don't care if anything bad happens to him, not really. I just want him to stay away."

"A warding spell," I said.

"That's right. But I think I need more power than I can get on my own. You've got kind of a knack. The spirits like you. Will you help me cast a warding?"

"Sure. What do I need to do?"

I was surprised when it was hard getting permission to spend the night at Sharyn's house. My mother didn't mention the occult, she just "didn't think it was the best idea" for me to be there overnight.

"Why? What do you think is going to happen?"

She pursed her lips. "It's just that where she lives—that sort of place— they aren't always very safe."

I tried to keep the anger out of my voice. "What do you mean, 'sort of place'? A trailer park? A home without a father?"

She sighed. "Tabitha, please. I just think—Sharyn's family isn't—" She floundered for a moment, then folded her arms and lifted her chin. "I still haven't met her mother. I have to meet her mother first."

I shrugged. "Okay."

She looked dismayed, as if she expected a different answer. "Before Saturday? But it's such a busy week."

"Just come over earlier in the day. Her mom will be home." I promised this, without knowing it would be true. Her mother worked an unpredictable schedule as a nursing assistant. But early Saturday afternoon she was home, it turned out, wearing a bathrobe and a bleary expression.

"Mrs. Wakeman? I'm Tabitha's mother, Amy Reynolds."

Sheila blinked for a moment, as if unable to process those concepts, then threw open the door. "Oh yeah? Come on in. Fran, turn that TV down! Sharyn! Your friend is here! You want some coffee or anything?"

"No thank you." I saw my mother glance around the small living room,

crowded and messy. Her nose wrinkled with the smell of stale beer, incontinent dachshund, and the red polish Sharyn's sister Fran was applying to her
toenails. "We don't drink coffee. Besides, we're not staying long."

We? Was that a Freudian slip? I started to panic. She met Sharyn's mom,
but she didn't like Sharyn's mom, so now I wouldn't be allowed to spend the
night. "Mrs. Wakeman works the night shift, Mom. At the hospital. That's
why she just got up."

"I told you to call me Sheila, kiddo. Mrs. Wakeman is my mother-in-
law." She yawned hugely, then walked over to the counter that divided the
living room from the small kitchen, and poured herself a cup of coffee. "So,
Amy, what did you want to talk about? Everybody's grades okay? Nobody's
pregnant?" She grinned and nudged me in the ribs, while inside I withered.
I was used to Sheila's somewhat crude sense of humor, but my mother—

My mother gasped. "Sharyn is pregnant?"

Sheila barked out a laugh, seemingly oblivious to my mother's horrified
expression. "Not if she knows what's good for her. Hey! Sharyn!" she called
out, then shrugged at us. "Probably got her headphones on. I was just heading outside for a smoke, you want to talk out back?"

My mother's look of horror deepened. "I'm not talking to you while
you smoke," she snapped. A moment later she seemed to notice the inap-
propriately bitchy tone in her voice, and added, "It's just that the smoke
makes me sick. Tabitha, why don't we go?" I followed her out to the car,
thinking that I was going to collect my overnight equipment. But she said,
"You can't sleep in a house with smoking."

"She smokes outside, didn't you hear?"

Her expression was tight. "Even second-hand smoke is really bad for
you, Tabby. This is serious. I won't allow it."

"Mom, you're not listening. She smokes outside. I won't be inhaling
second-hand smoke, okay?"

We went around in circles. It started to seem as if she thought smokers
were bad people, and she was attempting to make a case for the idea that
Sheila's mother was a bad person. She regressed, until I heard in her voice
the high school princess who used to make fun of awkward girls like me, or

women like Sheila, with her "tacky bleach job," "ugly bathrobe" and "dumpy figure."

"Dumpy figure." I stepped back, glaring at my mother with all my power. I was genuinely mad, but I also knew that she had given me a weapon. "You don't like fat people, do you?"

"Honey, you know that's not what I meant." But her posture was already slumping in defeat.

"Yes it is! You want to tell me I can't spend the night with my friend because her mother is too fat!" I paused dramatically. "You're trying to give me an eating disorder!" Anorexia nervosa was much in the news back then, in the women's magazines that my mother read. I read them too.

"No." Her voice was small. "I didn't mean that. Just make sure she always smokes outside, okay?"

We hugged, stiffly. Sharyn came out to help me collect my stuff, and I wondered if she had been watching us argue. My mom drove away, finally, with a promise to collect me at noon the next day. As soon as the car was out of sight, I yelled.

"My mom is such a bitch!"

"Don't do that. Don't call your own mother a bitch." She smiled slightly. "Not even when she's acting like one."

The rest of the evening at Sharyn's was strange, tense compared to the sleepover at my house. She kept twisting strands of hair around her fingers, drawing the ends between her lips, as if barely stopping herself from chewing on it. Instead of Coke we drank actual coffee, doctored with copious amounts of cream and sugar, to keep us awake until midnight. After her sister left for work, and then her mother, we went out to the living room to watch television with the sound turned off, records playing instead. I noticed an unfamiliar female vocalist and asked who it was.

She laughed nervously. "It's Yoko Ono. I think I was wrong about her. She's kinda cool sometimes. Anyway, I like this song. Yes, I'm a witch... I'm a bitch..." She sang along, then replayed it a few times until I could sing along too.

"What's wrong?" I finally asked. "Is it the spell?"

"It's just that I really, really want it to work. It's making me all stressed out. Usually when I ask the spirits for something it's no big deal. Like, who really cares about my grade on one little test, right? But this is important."

I nodded. It made sense, but I felt the lie behind it, something she wasn't telling me. I knew she was a liar. What I believed was that she wouldn't lie when it was really important. I had faith that if she was keeping secrets, it was about things that were none of my business anyway.

As midnight approached, we began to prepare the ingredients for the spell. She had hair and nail clippings from her father, and put them in a copper bowl, mixed together with crumbled charcoal. We pricked our fingers, and mingled drops of our blood in with it. Then she gave me a wooden bowl, piled high with coarse, grayish sea salt.

"You'll walk widdershins around the trailer, facing backwards, making a circle with the salt," she said. "You don't have to say anything, just think really hard about how you want my father to stay away from the circle."

"And what are you going to do?"

"I stand at the eastern point and light the contents of this bowl on fire, then I put the flame out with my spit and breath. Fire, water, air. Then I dump it into the earth."

"Okay," I said. That sounded similar to many of our rituals. But I still had that twinge of worry, that there was something she wasn't telling me. I didn't want to think it was anything dangerous.

Midnight was almost upon us, and we went outside. A spring day, it had seemed warm when the sun was up, but was chilly now. In a coat that was too light, my skin prickled from the cold, or maybe the caress of the uncanny. The sky above was clear, the moon perfectly full, lighting our way with silver brilliance.

"Oh, and don't hum. You've been humming that Yoko Ono song all night. While you draw the circle, don't make any noise except your breathing."

I felt weirdly hurt. My humming was bad? She was the one who made me listen to the same song over and over until it was going through my head. But I said, "Okay."

She had a digital watch, cheap plastic with a green display, and when it changed from 11:59 to 12:00 she nodded at me. I began a slow, careful back-wards walk, in a counterclockwise direction. I pinched the salt between the fingers of my left hand as I drizzled it out before me, letting the bowl rest on the flat of my right palm. The pale crystals and flakes were barely visible in the moonlight. Mesmerized, I watched them fall.

Sharyn dropped a lit match into her copper bowl, which began to smolder, giving off the distinct, foul odor of burning hair. She held the bowl above her head with both hands, and turned her face up to it, as if worship-ing. She chanted softly, foreign words I didn't recognize. Eventually, as I continued my circuit around the trailer, I lost sight of her.

Something odd happened when I was directly opposite her. I encoun-tered resistance as I moved, as if the air had thickened. It became strangely difficult to put one foot behind the other, and I felt a curiously powerful urge to lie down, right there, in the soil. My peripheral vision went mad, suggesting monstrous shadows flitting just out of sight all around me. Mag-ic, maybe. Or maybe I was just getting tired.

Circuit completed, I found Sharyn sunk to her knees on the ground, copper bowl overturned, face pressed to the soil. "Sharyn?"

She straightened, smiled at me. A smudge of dirt marred her forehead. "It's done."

Back inside, I dropped off to sleep right away, and had strange dreams I couldn't later recall.

The next day, I felt unaccountably worn out and dull. Eventually I started coughing, and decided I must have a cold. The cough lingered and turned into nasty bronchitis, so I ended up missing three days of school. When I went back, the school was abuzz with news: Harry Wakeman had died. He was drunk, and crashed his car into a concrete barricade. Luckily, nobody else was hurt.

I cornered Sharyn at lunch.

"You cursed him, didn't you?" I was outraged, and terrified. Superstitious dread weighed down my heart.

She sighed, wincing. "I cursed him. Not you. Your part with the salt was just what I said. A warding. To keep him away."

"But you did a curse. Right? What about the rule of threes? That's going to come back to us, Sharyn. Three times, that's what you said. Three deaths. I don't want three deaths, Sharyn. How do I make it stop?"

"There won't be three deaths. I didn't ask the spirits to kill him. That was their idea."

"You lied to me. I mean a real lie, a serious lie. And now I'm going to be cursed, it's all going to come back to me, three people I love are going to die—"

"No! If anything bad happens, it'll happen to me. I did the curse. You just did a warding."

"You used my blood too, remember? You said I had power. You said the spirits liked me."

"They do like you. They won't hurt you because of me."

"You don't know that. You used me, Sharyn. Behind my back. You used my blood."

She closed her eyes. "I knew it was wrong," she said, in a whisper. "I just wanted so badly for it to work."

"I'm through, Sharyn. No more spells, no more witchy stuff. I want the spirits to forget I exist." I paused, gathered my breath. "I'm not even sure if we can still be friends after that."

She nodded. When she opened her eyes, they were full of tears. "I know."

V

My guilt and fear were so extreme, I didn't talk to Sharyn at all for several weeks. Then sixth grade was done, and it was summer. For a brief period I threw myself into church, trying to salve my conscience, trying to make new friends. My mother was ecstatic about that, but it didn't last. I was willing to give up witchcraft, sure, but not rock and roll or critical thought.

I turned twelve, too old for junior Scouts, and had no interest in moving on to higher levels. My merit badges went into the box where they would stay for thirty years. Then middle school, and puberty. Sharyn and I were civil, when we ran into each other, but that wasn't often. We didn't have any of the same classes. Eventually we drifted apart entirely. I haven't thought of her at all for a very long time.

But, now that I do think of her, I'm sorry. I feel like I'm the one who screwed everything up. I remember the terror in her eyes the day her father tried to get into her room. When he died, he was driving a car, drunk, with a license that was already suspended for DUI. What if he hadn't been killed that night? Just a few weeks ago, a repeat drunk driver hit and killed three people in my town. One of them was a newborn baby. That's what could have happened, if Sharyn's father hadn't died when he did.

Maybe the spirits knew exactly what they were doing.

I wish I could talk to her, tell her all this. I wish I knew how her life turned out. I want to know it turned out okay. And if it didn't turn out okay, I want to try to make it better. But how could we ever find each other? Is she online? My parents have the same phone number, heck, the same phone, that they did when I was eleven. I doubt Sharyn's mother does.

I hold the Girl Scout sash in my hand, covered in badges, hand-stitched to form rows and columns, machine-embroidered with symbols that time has rendered obscure, occult. Two crossed keys, the symbol of Saint Peter, a badge in being the Pope? A doll made of red and purple straw—pretty sure that's a merit badge in voodoo. A red treasure chest, is that for piracy? A big, black cauldron—might as well be for witchcraft.

Somebody starts whistling "Strawberry Fields Forever."

I jump, but it's only my husband Alan, leaning over to drag another box out of the closet. I did end up marrying a Beatles fan. Better, a Yoko fan. "How did your mother fit so much stuff into this one little room?" He straightens, wipes sweat and dust from his forehead. "That's weird. I thought we cleaned everything off that dresser."

I follow his gaze. Three silver dollars, neatly stacked, sit in the middle of what should be empty space.

Downstairs, the phone begins to ring.

The Far Horizon

by J.H. Fleming

I felt my lover die as I slept.

James had sailed early that morning, bound for the capital. I had been dreaming of dancing. We were in the forest, away from all the whispers and glares of the town. I spun about in freedom, letting the peace of the forest fill my soul. He followed along behind, content to watch me. As I turned back to him he began to flicker in and out, as though he was a ghost trying to take form. I tried to hold him, to keep him there with me. In the end all I held was air.

I stopped where I was, let my arms fall to my side. I woke in bed, my blankets twisted around my legs and my hair sticking up in all directions. I knew he was gone.

$$\mathW$$

My abilities had manifested at a young age.

My mother had been a forest healer, and my earliest memories involved the sounds of crunching leaves, the sun breaking through the treetops to light the forest floor, the quiet solitude that came with forest life. I spent my days wandering the woods, familiarizing myself with all the strange plants and creatures that called it home. I could distinguish between the different bird calls, the sound one animal made as it walked as opposed to another, and could predict the weather based on scent and the shifting of the breeze. I knew things instinctively, so that my mother was hard pressed to keep any secrets from me. With a certainty based on more than mere observation, I knew when she was ill, or tired, or when we'd have company.

She had taught me there was no such thing as coincidence, which meant I was gifted with foresight. It manifested in other ways: dreams, sometimes waking visions, but usually it was only a feeling. The gods didn't give gifts lightly, so I accepted the ability as part of who I was.

"Above all else, be thankful, Ella," my mother used to say. "And remember that there's a reason for everything."

Because of this I simply lay in bed after the dream had faded. There was no need to cast a seeking spell, or go into town for news. I was never wrong.

I held the glass ball carefully in one hand, knowing that I probably wouldn't like what I would see. It was one of the last gifts from my mother, and could be used for any number of spells. I focused my sight now on the town, on anyone who was speaking of James. It didn't take long. Everyone seemed to be talking of him, but my search latched onto one and visualized in the glass.

"It's such a tragedy," Mrs. Winscomb was saying to the baker. She was an elderly matron of the town, distantly related to some founder or other. "Master James being so young and all, and poor Miss Daisy. What will become of her now?"

"I heard they argued before he left," the baker answered. "Miss Daisy's torn up about it now. Apparently he left in a rage, and she doesn't know where he went for all that time before the ship sailed."

Daisy. Of course they would speak of her. James's annoying, useless wife was the town's sweetheart, who could do no wrong.

Mrs. Winscomb leaned in conspiratorially and whispered, "There was a rumor he had a mistress."

I leaned in closer, as though that would help me to hear better.

"Master James? Absurd! He was an upstanding member of this community. And Miss Daisy's such a lovely girl."

"You know how young men are," Mrs. Winscomb said with a knowing tone. "Never satisfied with what they have. If that mistress knows what's right, she'll not say one word. She took him away from Miss Daisy enough when he was alive. It's only fair Miss Daisy has him in death."

I laughed aloud, the first time I'd done so since the dream. People would convince themselves of anything.

"Who do you think it is?" the baker asked. "Anyone we know?"

Mrs. Winscomb glanced around before leaning in closer to whisper again. "You didn't hear it from me. But the night watchman's mentioned seeing Master James heading toward the harbor late at night."

"No! Not the forest witch."

"The same."

"What would a man like Master James see in a woman like her? I don't believe it for a second."

"Think what you like. Seems like things have only taken a turn for the worse since she got here. Perhaps she even bewitched him."

I scowled at the vision, wishing I had walked into the bakery right at that moment just to see the old woman's flustered face. I wasn't surprised that they would blame me for James's failed marriage. The fact that it had died long before I ever arrived wasn't well known.

I set the glass carefully back in its velvet-lined box and stood to work on the morning's potions.

"Well, it will work if you're trying to poison a frog."

My failed potion sat on the table between us, and I was trying not to cry. My mother had done her best, gods bless her, but I'd been a miserable student.

"Again," she'd said, and I'd groaned and dropped my head against the table.

"Maybe I'm more suited to poisons than healing," I'd mumbled. "I've managed five perfectly good death potions so far."

My mother had ruffled my hair and crouched down beside me. "If healing were easy, Ella, more women of power would take it up. But it's not, so you have to dig in your heels and work for it."

I'd sat up and looked in her eyes. "You really believe I have what it takes to be a healer?"

"I do," she'd answered with a nod. "If I didn't I wouldn't waste my time making you practice. You'd make a pretty good living at poisons, I'll admit, but I know you can do better."

"What happens if I choose the easy way? Give up healing and sell my potions to the highest bidder?"

She'd studied my face for a moment, either preparing to rebuke me or formulating a retort that was both witty and gently scolding. I could never tell which it would be.

"You choose that path and I'll move to the village with you and open a sweet shop. At least then your customers can mask the taste."

Since that was as likely as me sprouting wings, I'd laughed and grabbed an empty container. It took me a while, but with time I finally managed to master what potions she taught me. Added to my own innate ability, I made a pretty decent healer, or so she'd said. It was enough to make a start, anyway, and that was really all I could ask for.

I couldn't weep openly for him, my James. That right belonged to Daisy. He'd told me once that he wished he'd never married her.

"My parents betrothed me as a baby," he'd said. We were tangled in my bed, the only two awake in the early hours of the morning. His house was off limits, thanks to Daisy. "I was told all the time that we were meant for each other, that not only was she a second cousin to Duchess Sofina, but she was beautiful and educated and everything a proper lady should be. It wasn't until after we were married that I even considered that I might want something different."

He'd sighed then, the frustration he must have once felt withered down to nothing more than lofty regret.

"She's nothing like you, Ella," he'd said then, turning back to me. "Daisy is like a china doll, fragile, lovely, and cold. She's nice to look at, but there's no substance."

"And me?"

He'd smiled, rubbed a hand over my bare skin and kissed my side. "You, my dear, are a woodland goddess. Wild, alluring, mysterious. I could seek you for the rest of my life and never fully attain you."

"You're just saying that."

But he'd meant it. He'd always meant every word.

Making a living as a healer is no easy thing. If I had been raised in the village, my family established for generations, there would be no problem. But although we'd occasionally get visits to our forest home, for the most part we were alone, meaning I had to start from scratch. Luckily my mother had taught me how to listen.

Women talk of things together that they won't speak of around their men folk, and after a couple overheard conversations I had my first customers. I set up shop in the small cottage I rented. It was only one room, filled with my meager belongings, but luckily that wasn't much, so I could fill the remaining space with ingredients and tools.

"Does this really work?" one woman asked me, eying the bottle she held with obvious doubts.

"Of course," I promised. "But you have to come back every week for a fresh supply."

"It smells like swamp water."

"It's supposed to. It wouldn't work properly if it didn't."

I could tell one woman was holding back, probably wanting to speak to me privately, so I ushered the others out as quickly as I could, with promises that they'd come again.

"You need something special?" I asked her when it was just the two of us.

She fidgeted with her skirt and bit her lip, finally asking softly, "Do you have anything to… to make someone sick?"

"Poison, you mean?"

My mother had never dealt in poison, though she knew it well. How better to detect its presence than by mastering its creation? And through a quirk of nature, I happened to have a talent for it.

"It's all right," I reassured her. "No word of this will pass beyond these walls. Just tell me what you need."

Although my mother had looked down on it, I saw no reason to not use every bit of knowledge and power I could. If I didn't offer this service to the woman, she would only find another, less effective way, and probably end up in a whole heap of trouble. Really, I was offering the only way that would assure the least amount of heartache.

The house was full of townsfolk, all come to pay their respects to James's widow. I hadn't been invited, but there was no way I was going to miss any gathering that had to do with James. Keeping to the shadows, careful to not draw attention to myself, I moved through the crowd until I found a safe corner to watch and listen. I could focus my hearing on any conversation I chose, blocking out all others.

Daisy was easy to find, her bright golden hair shining in the early evening light. The old gossip, Mrs. Winscomb, approached her and wrapped her in a motherly hug.

"I am so very sorry for your loss," I heard her say.

"Thank you," Daisy answered, her voice sickeningly sweet. Everyone seemed determined to speak with her face-to-face before leaving, crowding around the two of them like vultures. Daisy searched their faces a moment, but apparently didn't find what she was looking for.

"If there's anything I can do, you let me know," Mrs. Winscomb continued.

"Of course," Daisy answered absentmindedly.

What distracted her? Was she simply so bored that she couldn't focus on those in front of her? No wonder she had driven James crazy.

Mrs. Winscomb was replaced by another comforter, and another. From the way she looked around, the sooner everyone left the better.

"Deepest sympathies," the latest person was saying. "If there is anything you need—"

And then Daisy froze. I followed her gaze, finally spotting the object of her attention.

His head was just visible, moving through the group by the door, making his way toward her. He was tall, black-haired, with dark eyes and a smug smile. So. This was the one Daisy had fallen for. James had mentioned it a couple times, but it wasn't a subject he liked to dwell on.

"Excuse me," she said, not even seeing who she was talking to. They moved slowly toward one another, both of them struggling against the press of bodies, as though some power beyond their control drew them together. Her blonde curls were coming loose of their pins, spilling into her face and down her back.

"My lady," he said when he reached her. He held her hand delicately, as though she were made of glass or butterfly wings, which likely wasn't far from the truth. Then he leaned in closer, his lips touching the skin of her ear, and I had to strain to hear him whisper, "Come with me."

And then, against anything I would expect from her, she kissed him, in front of the entire town. They kissed as though they were the only two in the room, as though no one else mattered, as though James hadn't been dead for three days.

My pulse raced at the sight of it, at her blatant selfishness. It was in that moment, seeing them disrespect James's memory, that I decided what I would do.

◍

I remember our first night together. I could feel his eyes on me from across the room. It was my first time in the village, and the inn was crowded and noisy. My hair was a tangled mess falling past my shoulders, and I very likely had dirt on my face. I was used to going barefoot in the woods, and it was odd to not only hear and see so many people, but to have my feet confined by new black boots. My mother had insisted, though.

"People are different in the village, Ella," she'd said. "There are some things you'll just have to get used to."

I hadn't known that when she'd said "some things" she'd meant everything.

It had still hurt to think about her then, her body buried barely a week. I'd seen her death a few days before I was supposed to leave, and I'd insisted on staying until it came to pass. We'd argued about it, and finally she'd agreed to let me stay longer, so long as I kept my own promises.

She'd warned me that many people had negative views of forest healers. It was simple ignorance, but it could make for uncomfortable situations, or so she'd said. "Just pay attention to that ability of yours and you'll be fine," she'd said.

When he'd first come in I'd followed him with my eyes until he sat down in a remote corner. He was tall, with wavy brown hair and eyes so bright a blue that I could tell their color from a distance. I never once seriously thought he'd be interested in me.

He talked to everyone, ignoring none. I later learned this was just part of his good nature. Everyone deserved respect and attention, at least until proven otherwise. It was part of what made the people love him.

I was sure that he'd question my presence when he got to me. After all, I was a stranger, and he was obviously well known, and besides, I wasn't anyone worth noting.

But instead he'd asked, "What's your name?"

I'd considered him for a moment, wondering if he was about to have me thrown out. "Ella," I'd finally answered.

"Would you like to take a walk with me?" he'd asked, surprising me. Fear and rebuke I had been prepared for. But not that. I must have stammered a yes, for we were both soon out the door and walking along the beach. His eyes had glimmered in the moonlight and I'd had to restrain myself from reaching out and touching his hair. "Tell me about yourself," he'd said.

I'd shrugged. "What do you want to know?"

"Everything."

♦

For hours without end I'd sat in the dark, unable to sleep, unwilling to move. The sun found me sitting in the same chair by the dead fire, and the sight of my empty house ignited my fury all over again. With a cry I grabbed my empty mug and threw it at the opposite wall, where it shattered and sprinkled to the floor. Riding the momentum, I retrieved the glass from its box and called forth a vision. It was the same two gossips as before, but I wouldn't expect anything less from the old biddy.

"She has a right to move on," Mrs. Winscomb was telling the baker. "She's young, and beautiful besides. You can't expect her to stay in mourning all her life."

"Her husband's been in the ground for barely a week," said the baker. "Surely a man deserves more respect than that, especially one as upstanding as Master James."

"Well, you can't really blame her. From what I hear he hardly paid her any mind while alive. Even so, I'm sure she's heartbroken. It's understandable she'd latch on to the first handsome man she saw."

"Hmpf," said the baker.

"What's worse," Mrs. Winscomb whispered, "is that... woman... always standing on the cliffs, gazing at the sea all day long. You'd think she'd try to be a little more discreet. I mean, it's so improper."

The baker frowned. "Seems she's the only one truly in mourning. I'm just glad Master James has someone to miss him so much."

Mrs. Winscomb gasped, apparently appalled that the baker would even suggest such a thing. "It'd be better if that woman had never come here. She's the one who took Master James from Miss Daisy in the first place. If she had any decency at all she'd go back to the forest she crawled out of."

I let the glass go dark then. Mrs. Winscomb would wake the next morning with a breath that no amount of cleaning could vanquish. A foul breath for a foul heart. No one would listen to her gossip, then. The baker, though, had surprised me. I was the forest witch, the source of every toothache, upset stomach, and bad change of weather.

I couldn't make sense of it, and I couldn't bear the sight of my house anymore, so I grabbed my shawl and headed to the cliff.

◊

I had gone to their house one night, even though he'd told me not to. I was in a reckless mood, and I was in love. What did I care who saw me there? I arrived just in time to hear the end of an argument. Daisy and James were in the parlor, and I could see them through the window from outside.

"Don't act like I'm stupid," Daisy said, her voice a false calm. "If you want to sneak around with the forest witch, that's your affair, but I will not be treated like a fool."

"And what do you have to say about your own affairs?" James demanded. "You're quick to judge me, but you're not half so secretive as you imagine yourself to be."

She flushed, but she stood her ground. The fact that she thought she was justified, that her situation was different, only showed just how naïve she was.

"We came into this marriage knowing we didn't love each other," she said. "I'm not asking that you stop seeing her, because you wouldn't listen."

I wouldn't let him.

"And you're right, I'm not innocent either, and even if you begged you couldn't make me give him up."

Stupid whore.

"But there's a difference between discreetly carrying on your affairs and publicly making a fool of yourself and ruining your reputation. Just use a little common sense."

As if she had any!

"You're a fine one to talk," he said, grabbing his coat. "Don't expect me home tonight."

"At least take a bath before you come home," she called after him. "You always reek of herbs and sickness."

He left then without so much as a goodbye. I melted back into the darkness, heading home to be there when he arrived.

◆

"No one escapes death, Ella," my mother had said. "When it comes for us, the best we can do is face it with our heads held high."

I hadn't wanted to listen. I'd dreamed of my mother's death the night before, and the last thing I wanted to do was calmly accept it.

"There are ways to prevent it," I'd insisted. "You know I'm right."

"You don't know what you're talking about," she'd said, her voice cold and stern, two things she never was with me. "Now you listen well, you hear? The minute you start meddling with the dead, you lose a part of yourself, and there's no going back. The whole thing is unnatural, and more dangerous than you realize. I want you to promise me that you won't try to bring me back when I'm gone, understood?"

I'd nodded dejectedly, but I wasn't convinced by her words. If such a spell existed, it meant it had been successful before, and what did I have to lose, anyway? James had died too soon, and he deserved to live a full and happy life. I may have promised to not bring my mother back, but I had made no such promise about James.

◆

I waited until the sun began to set, then snuck to the house Daisy and her lover shared. I'd heard his name was Henry, a second son of a minor family. Not that his background was important. Only Daisy's feelings for him.

The gossips had revealed that they didn't have any servants or pets, which meant I had a good chance of catching him by surprise. The side door opened at my touch, revealing a dim, narrow hallway. I softly closed the door behind me and tiptoed to where the hall intersected with another one, also dim. The sounds of movement came from the left, so I carefully moved down the hall, passing every open door hesitantly. One revealed a library, where I saw Daisy sitting in an armchair. Her back was to me, so I quietly hurried past. I would've shut the door if I was certain it wouldn't creak, but I didn't want to take that chance. Daisy may have gone from the town sweetheart to a harlot, but the townspeople would still help her if she ran for help.

A little further down and I knew I'd found the right place. I could hear him moving around on the other side of the door. I'd brought a bag filled with various objects, and I reached into it and retrieved my dagger, along with a vial of noxious gas. After a deep breath I carefully pushed the door open and placed the vial on the floor, unstopping the lid so it could release into the room. I shut the door again and then it was only a matter of time.

I gripped the dagger's handle tighter as I waited for the poison to do its work. Down the hall Daisy hadn't moved, but I held my breath anyway, my eyes riveted to the library door. If she came out, I couldn't hesitate. Too much depended on secrecy, at least until I managed to sneak Henry away...

A loud thump sounded in the room behind me, the sign that the gas had been successful. I opened the door all the way and quickly shut it behind me. It was a dining room, the table set for two and a single violet standing as centerpiece. Henry lay sprawled on the floor face down. I hurriedly stoppered the vial and stowed it back in my bag. The smell was still strong, but as long as I got him out quickly I wouldn't need to worry about it affecting me. At least he wasn't an exceptionally large man. It was relatively easy to drag him across the room then, pulling the door open again, out into the hallway. I stopped then, just listening, and when I was certain that Daisy still hadn't moved, I dragged him further. He made little noise. Nothing to attract notice at least. Still, I went as slowly as I could and was careful to not let his limbs hit the walls.

As I passed the library again I couldn't resist glancing in, but Daisy sat in the same spot, oblivious to my presence. It looked like she was sewing, of all things, working on some shirt or blanket most likely. She was probably mending a hem, playing at being the dutiful wife. But she didn't fool me.

Another minute of breathless anticipation and I had reached the side door once more. The sun had sunk even lower, full dark only minutes away, when I escaped outside. I had a wheelbarrow waiting, and after a minute of struggle I had Henry securely nestled inside. The darkness effectively hid my retreat, and the first phase was done.

"I don't understand why you can't just leave her." James was pulling his boots on, preparing to head back to a lonely house. I was usually content to spend what little time with him I could, but after months of stolen evenings I'd longed for something more.

"It's not that easy," he'd said, not looking at me. When I'd sighed he'd turned and reached out for me, but I'd drawn away. "You know I'd do it if I could. And as much as I dislike her, she *is* my wife, and I have a duty towards her."

"Don't speak to me of duty," I'd hissed. "If you spent more time doing as you pleased and less of what the world expects of you, you'd be a lot happier."

"Like you, Ella?"

I hadn't answered, merely rose from the bed and went to stare out the window. He'd known the way the town felt about me, how they whispered behind closed doors. It wasn't that I minded the rumors. People will have their own opinions, after all. But sometimes I thought it would be nice to receive a thank you from someone and not hear the judgment beneath their words.

He'd moved across the room to where I'd stood and wrapped his arms around me. "I'm sorry," he'd said. "You know I don't care what any of them think of you. They don't matter."

I'd held onto his arms, wishing we could just stay that way forever.

One day you'll find someone to share your life with, Ella, and when you do you should hold onto him, my mother had said. *You never know how much time you'll be given.*

"I'm leaving for the capital in the morning," he'd said. "When I get back we'll talk about it, I promise."

I'd stayed silent, pretending to ponder his words. Truth was I would've forgiven him for anything, even if he'd chosen to stay with her. "Okay," I'd said.

The faint glow of sunrise was just becoming visible out across the water when I saw Daisy approach my cottage. I was on the cliff, waiting for the dawn to complete the ritual. There was something powerful about light piercing through the darkness, illuminating the secrets the shadows tried to hide.

Daisy pounded on the door over and over, even going so far as to kick it. It was almost comical, until I considered that I'd do the same thing, and more, if our roles were reversed. And then she looked toward the cliff and I knew she saw me. It was surprising that she hadn't brought the town guard with her. Did she think I would simply do whatever she demanded, hand over her lover and apologize?

Daisy's a fool, but stubborn, James had once said. *She'll persist until she gets her way.*

Which was admirable, but futile.

She struggled up the hill until she stood before me, the wind blowing our hair around our faces, as though to heighten the tension. Her eyes moved to Henry, who still lay in the wheelbarrow beside me. Questions crowded her eyes, but she couldn't decide which one to voice first.

"You shouldn't have come," I finally said.

"What did you do to him?" she demanded, her voice shaky.

"Just a simple sleeping potion, nothing more. He's not dead, if that's what you're asking."

"I knew it was you, as soon as I smelled those damn herbs. Why did you take him?" she asked. Her outer calm was starting to crack, giving way to the rage growing stronger inside her.

"I need him," I answered. "Or rather, his blood. A sacrifice must be made."

I could see the wheels turn in her mind as she processed the words, until finally something clicked and she understood. Gritting her teeth she said, "You won't have him. I'll die first."

Death is a heavy burden, Ella, my mother had said. *It weighs on you, pulls you down until you're so deep you can no longer see the light.*

But my light had died with James. There was only darkness now.

"As you wish," I said, drawing my dagger.

Daisy leapt to the side as I moved toward her. She circled the edge of the cliff, barely managing to stay out of range. Back and forth we went, again and again my blade flashing toward her, always that much closer. She wouldn't leave the cliff top, though, not with her lover left helpless here.

We began another circuit, and then Henry stirred, moaning softly as he tried to rise. Daisy's gaze turned to him, and I took that moment to strike.

For a moment it was as though she didn't realize she'd been stabbed. She looked down at the blood oozing from the wound in her side, staining her white dress, as though she couldn't understand what it was. My blade entered her flesh a second time, and a third. Her legs gave out and she fell to the ground, her gaze still on Henry.

He was opening his eyes now, squinting through the dim light to where she lay. Then I moved between them, my blade still dripping, and gladly added one more weight to my troubled mind.

◊

I'd found the spell in my mother's old grimoire. Though I'd known it would require a sacrifice, I hadn't expected how easy it would be for me to take another's life. Or two, for that matter. It was exhilarating, the power I held at my fingertips. It was better this way, of course. Now Daisy and her lover were still together, and soon James would be with me, so everyone won, really.

I had gathered the rest of the ingredients carefully. Mandrake root, bel-
ladonna, the mushrooms of a faery ring. I added them to the container of
blood I'd already filled and retrieved my dagger, which I'd had to steal from
the cave of a sea witch to complete the spell. It cut through my wrist easily,
and I let my blood spill into the top of the container, mixing with the blood
of the dead.

"James," I whispered as I raised the rim to my lips. The spell completed,
I sat down among the rocks and wrapped my arms around my legs. Sea
gulls were crying overhead as the sun rose further in the sky, and the breeze
whipped my bloody hair around my face. I sat as still as the stones I leaned
against and watched the far horizon for the hint of a sail.

THE THREE
GATEWAYS

BY EVA LANGSTON

There once was a girl named Nadine who had eyes as blue as gumballs and hair as black as pavement. She lived with her mother and wicked stepfather in a small, yellow house by the river. The river was wide and brown, and on hot days it smelled like sewage. The smell wafted through Nadine's neighborhood of old, crumbling houses and made everyone wish they had enough money to live somewhere else.

Nadine's stepfather, Roy, was a plumber, so the sewage smell in the neighborhood didn't bother him as much. He did want more money, though, so he could buy nice things like a motorcycle and a flat-screen television. He made extra money by selling marijuana, which he grew in the garage behind the house. He was very proud of his plants, and his customers said his pot was smoother and more potent than anything they'd ever smoked. They asked to know his secret, but Nadine and her mother were the only ones who knew: it was Roy's special fertilizer, made of his own feces, that made his plants so healthy.

Roy kept a small, ziploc baggie of dried pot in the freezer for an occasional smoke, but he preferred liquor, which he drank on a regular basis. One night, shortly after Nadine began the tenth grade, her stepfather stormed into her bedroom, his face flushed and his breath smelling of whiskey. "You stole some of my weed, didn't you?"

Nadine sat cross-legged on her bed, doing her math homework. She looked at him with wide eyes and shook her head. "No."

He lurched towards her. His chin was patchy with dark stubble. "Well, half my weed is gone, so where'd it go?"

Nadine stared down at the faint blue lines on her notebook paper. "I didn't take it." She was lying. She had, in fact, stolen it. She hadn't realized that Roy would be so observant.

Suddenly he was upon her, grabbing at her face with his hand. He squeezed her cheeks together between his thumb and fingers. "You're lying to me. I know you're lying."

"I don't have it," Nadine mumbled out of her pinched mouth. That much was true. The pot was gone. She and her friends had smoked it the day before.

He released his grip, only to use his open palm to smack her across the face. Nadine's cheek burned.

He reached for her arm and yanked on it, glaring at her with wild, black eyes. "That's my shit. You don't steal my shit."

"Stop it! You're hurting me." She tried to twist out of his grip.

"Yeah?" His fingers tightened. "I could hurt you worse."

"Let me go!"

"Fucking drug addict," Roy said, dropping her arm. He left her room, but the smell of his musky sweat remained.

Nadine wasn't a drug addict, not yet at least, but she and her best friend, Elizabeth, had been doing drugs recreationally since middle school— around the time when Nadine and her mother had moved in with Roy. In the sixth grade, they'd stolen a pack of Elizabeth's mother's cigarettes and ran with them to the graveyard. They'd sat next to a small angel perched at a baby's headstone and smoked skinny Virginia Slims until their heads were spinning and they felt like puking. In the seventh grade, they raided Roy's liquor cabinet and poured whiskey into a half-full bottle of Sunny Delight. The next day, Nadine brought the bottle to school in her book bag, and they drank the potion in the third floor bathroom before choir practice. When they sang, their young voices were husky and carried the scent of fire and oranges. In the eighth grade, they started meeting high school boys in the park after school and riding with them to the Chuck E. Cheese where they smoked joints in the back parking lot next to the dumpsters.

Since then, they had moved on to other things. Pink and white pills stolen from friends' medicine cabinets. Thick, red cough syrup that made them see swirling colors when they looked at the street lights. And once, at an older kid's party, they had tried a beautiful white powder, like fairy dust, which they had snorted through cut plastic straws. There was still weed, too, of course. Usually it made Nadine feel relaxed. But lately, the drugs weren't helping much. She felt anxious and frightened, always holed up in her room in the evenings, trying to avoid her stepfather's wrath.

Nadine knew better than to tell people about her problems. In her experience, nothing changed, or it made things worse. But sometimes she forgot this, and the morning after Roy had yelled at her for the stolen weed, she decided to talk to her mother.

As soon as Nadine's alarm went off Tuesday morning, she got out of bed, pulled on a sweatshirt, and walked down the hall to her mother and Roy's bedroom. Roy always left early for work, and her mother usually didn't get up until ten. She worked as a cashier at the Food Lion, but only part-time because of her back. She'd been in a terrible car accident as a teenager, and she couldn't stand for very long, even though she took a lot of pills that were supposed to ease her pain.

Nadine rapped lightly on the door to her mother's bedroom then pushed it open. The king-sized bed spanned most of the room so that the rest of the furniture had to be squeezed into the leftover spaces. A large dresser stood next to the bed, an old television on top of it. The door to the closet was open, and inside it the horizontal metal bar sagged under the weight of too many clothes.

Nadine shimmied sideways past the dresser and perched on the edge of the bed by the nightstand. Her mother was buried under a thick mountain of blankets with a pillow on top of her head. Nadine pushed at the lump underneath the covers. "He was drunk again last night, Mom. Look what he did to me."

Her mother didn't move.

"Mom." Nadine pulled the pillow off her mother's head, revealing a pile of brown, matted curls. "Mom. Wake up."

Her mother groaned and rolled over, her face emerging slowly.

"Look what he did to me." Nadine held out her arm to display thin purple bruises where Roy's fingers had clutched her.

"He said you stole from him." Her mother squinted at the light coming through the blinds behind the bed and pushed the tangles out of her face.

"Well…"

"Nadine, I can't stick up for you if you're the one who started it in the first place."

"You never stick up for me anyway!" Nadine heard her voice climbing into a whine.

"That's not true."

"It is. He *hurt* me."

Her mother struggled to pull herself up. She sighed and leaned back against the wooden headboard. "I'm sure he didn't mean to hurt you, baby. He doesn't know his own strength sometimes, you know that. Maybe if you hadn't stolen from him…"

"He *meant* to hurt me."

"Relationships are a compromise, Nadine. He provides for us. We'd be living at Nana's house eating ramen noodles every night if it wasn't for him. Is that what you want?"

"No," Nadine whispered. Her grandmother's house smelled like cat pee and Brussels sprouts. When they stayed there, Nadine had to sleep on the couch, and cat fur tickled her nose in the night, making her eyes red and swollen.

"Sometimes he gets too drunk," her mother said, sinking back down into the covers. "We just have to deal with it." She closed her eyes. "Can you do that for me?"

"I guess."

"That's my girl."

W

Nadine knew the only way to get rid of her stepfather was to take matters into her own hands. She decided that very day to go to Luci for advice.

Luci, short for Lucifer Marie, was a senior girl who openly admitted to practicing dark magic. Her real name was April, but it was said that she would put a curse on anyone who called her that. Even the teachers had consented to calling her Luci.

Rumor had it that Luci could actually perform magic, and there were several incidents to prove it. The first was her nomination and election into Homecoming Court her sophomore year. "It had to be magic," Elizabeth always said. "She must have bewitched people into voting for her." Luci had been a sophomore before Nadine and Elizabeth were even in high school, but one day they had looked through the old yearbooks at the library, and sure enough, there on the Homecoming Court page was Luci's picture with the words "Sophomore Princess" underneath it. She wore a long-sleeved black dress with a high, lacy collar, and her eyes were dark with make-up. She stood sullenly next to her date, an enormous, curly-haired boy nicknamed Ogre, who wore a black trench coat over army fatigues.

The second incident involved Ogre. Legend had it that after six months of dating, he attempted to break up with Luci. The very next day, he woke with huge pimples covering his cheeks and a bulbous cold sore developing in the corner of his mouth. Then he got lice and had to shave his head. A week later, he fell down a flight of stairs and broke his leg. He was out of school for a few days, and Luci told the teachers she could bring him his assignments. The next thing everyone knew, Luci and Ogre were back together, his acne was gone, and people said that his leg had healed much faster than normal.

The most astonishing proof of Luci's powers happened shortly after she and Ogre got back together. She was enjoying a black clove cigarette in the second floor bathroom. This was the bathroom where everyone smoked, even some of the teachers. But on this certain day, Mrs. Robins-Pratt, the assistant principal, walked in and wrote Luci a three-day suspension. The injustice of it infuriated Luci, and she swore to get even with the old hag. A few days later, Mrs. Robins-Pratt came down with a terrible illness. She was out for nearly two months with what other teachers said was mono, but then she resigned from her position and moved to Florida. Students whispered that her illness was actually insanity brought on by the nightmares that Luci was charming into her brain. The truth of this incident was what Nadine was counting on. She needed Luci to teach her how to bewitch her stepfather into leaving the state.

And so, that day at lunch, Nadine and Elizabeth went looking for the high school witch. "I'm kind of afraid of her," Elizabeth said as they walked through the quad, scanning the crowd for people wearing black.

Nadine tucked her hair behind her ears. "Well, you don't have to say anything to her. I'll do all the talking."

Luci was nowhere to be found in the quad or the cafeteria, so the girls headed to the theater because Ogre was the head of the tech department, and they'd heard that Luci hung out there with him sometimes. The theater was a large, windowless building at the very edge of campus. They entered through the side door, which led down a dark hall towards the Black Box, which was empty except for an ugly couple making out on an old couch. Next they searched the bathroom and the costume closet and the green room, but there was no sign of Luci anywhere. They walked backstage, past hulking wooden flats and through swirling black curtains until they came, suddenly, upon Ogre. He was hunched over on the stage in his army fatigues, marking x's on the floor with white tape that glowed faintly in the dimness.

"Do you know where Luci is?" Nadine asked.

Ogre turned his large head towards them. "Lighting booth." He pointed out past the rows of seats in the auditorium to the little room, high in the back of the theater, which looked out over everything. Nadine saw a flash of movement in the small window and shivered. Luci was up there, watching them.

The girls jumped off the stage and walked the sloping path to the back of the house. They opened the door and climbed a set of narrow, curving steps to find Luci sitting in front of the switchboard, eating raisins and reading the Cliff's Notes for *The Crucible*.

"Luci?" Nadine asked, hovering by the door. Luci looked up. She was wearing a long, bright blue wig, a black dress, and combat boots. Her face had been powdered to a chalky white, and her eyes and lips were lined in dark purple. She raised a penciled eyebrow at the two girls.

"Hi." Nadine took a few steps closer, but Elizabeth stayed on the last step. "Um, I'm Nadine. Can I talk to you for a minute?"

Luci picked a raisin out of the red cardboard box and held it between her long, black fingernails. From a distance it looked like a bug. She popped it into her mouth and nodded, just slightly.

"I was wondering if I could get your help. I'm sort of trying to get rid of someone."

"I'm not a hit man, you know." Luci's voice was deep and tremulous, like the vibrating of a cello.

"Yeah, I know." Nadine tugged at a piece of hair brushing her shoulder. "I just heard that you were able to do something to Mrs. Robins-Pratt last year to make her leave school, and I'm trying get my stepdad to leave town, so…"

Nadine could feel Luci's eyes upon her, noticing the puffy white scar on the back of her hand from where Roy had burned her with a cigarette last month, as well as the fresh, angry bruises on her arm. Nadine felt her face flushing under the heat of Luci's gaze.

"I can help you," the older girl said finally. "But it won't be easy." Luci motioned for Nadine to come closer. "What you need to do is tap into your stepfather's subconscious." She plucked out another raisin and ate it before continuing. "Once you have access to a person's subconscious, you can pretty much control them. You can torture them. You can plant ideas in their brains. You can find out what they're really thinking and feeling."

Nadine nodded and took a step closer. She sat down in the chair beside Luci. Elizabeth came forward slowly and stood behind Nadine.

"There are three gateways into the subconscious," Luci explained. "They aren't guaranteed access, but they are the things that can break down the barrier and create a way in. The first is drugs." She stared at Nadine for a moment, her eyes hard and judgmental. "I think you might have some experience with that."

Nadine felt herself blushing again. "So what do I do?"

"Are you sure you want to get rid of him?" Luci asked.

Nadine nodded quickly. "Yes."

The older girl paused, and her purple lips clamped closed, like two caterpillars against her pebble-white skin. Her dark eyes stared into Nadine's blue ones. "Okay," she said finally. "Drugs are the easiest gateway. We'll try that first."

The pill was small and white, as unassuming as aspirin. It would dissolve quickly in an alcoholic beverage, Luci said. Once in effect, the victim was highly susceptible to suggestion, like being hypnotized.

That night, Nadine's mother brought home a bucket of fried chicken, a container of coleslaw, and a flimsy cardboard box with four buttery biscuits. She set everything down in the middle of the kitchen table and pulled three mismatched plates from the cabinet. Unlike the other rooms, which were crowded with furniture and knick-knacks, the kitchen was bare, and when Nadine's mother opened the refrigerator to pull out a pitcher of iced tea, the inside gleamed white and empty except for a few condiment jars and bottles.

"When are you going to learn to cook?" Roy asked, dropping two ice cubes into a glass and filling it with whiskey. "It'd save us some money if you weren't always getting take-out."

Nadine's mother sank into a chair and scooped coleslaw onto her plate from the Styrofoam container. "I'm doing my best," she said. Nadine peeled the brown skin off her chicken and glanced at Roy. The pill was in her pocket.

"What was that?" Nadine asked. She jumped out of her chair and ran to the window above the sink.

"What?" Nadine's mother stood.

"I thought I saw somebody outside by the garage."

Roy slammed his glass of whiskey onto the counter. "What?" He was always paranoid about the neighbors finding out what he did in the garage.

"I don't know. I thought I did." Nadine shrugged.

He threw open the side door and marched towards the garage. Nadine's mother followed him halfway.

"Hello?" he yelled into the back yard. "Better not be nobody on my property!" Quickly, Nadine pulled the pill from her pocket and dropped it into the glass of liquor. It fizzed for a moment then disappeared.

The adults came back inside. "Don't make shit up, Nadine, it's not funny," Roy said.

"I really thought I saw something." Nadine shrank back towards her seat.

"Maybe it was a cat." Her mother sat down at the table. "I'm sure it's fine."

Nadine resumed picking at her chicken. She pulled a string of greasy meat off the bone and put it slowly into her mouth. She watched Roy as he picked up his glass and took a long swallow. His hard, pinched face softened a little. The deep lines in his forehead smoothed. Nadine waited.

Nothing happened until he was on his second glass of whiskey. Then his pupils began to grow large, and his head swayed back and forth slightly on his neck. Suddenly he slumped forward onto the table, smashing his cheek down next to his half-empty plate. "I feel fucked up," he said, his voice coming out through squashed lips.

Nadine's mother looked at him with concern. She moved a hand towards his glass of whiskey, but then stopped, her arm hovering in the air. "You feel sick?"

"No," came his garbled voice. "I feel like I just took a shitload of acid." He struggled to lift his head up and waved a palm in front of his face. "My hand looks like a piece of chicken."

"Why don't you eat it?" Nadine muttered. To her surprise, almost immediately, he crammed two thick fingers into his mouth.

"Roy!" Her mother jumped out of her chair and ran behind him, yanking his hand from his mouth. Nadine saw red teeth marks on his wet fingers. "Why don't you lay down on the couch?"

Roy pushed himself up from his chair and staggered, zombie-like, towards the living room.

"Nadine, go bring him a glass of water," her mother said. "And a trash can just in case. I'll heat him up some coffee."

Nadine filled a glass with water from the tap and grabbed the trash can before heading into the living room. At first she thought he was asleep, but he wasn't. His eyes were open; the large pupils stared at the blank television screen.

She set down the trash can and water at the end of the couch near his head and then backed away slowly. "Roy?" she said softly. She felt like she was locked in a cage with a sedated tiger that might, at any moment, shake off the effects of the drug and lunge for her throat.

"Yeah?" he mumbled. He didn't turn to look at her. His eyes stayed focused on the black screen.

Nadine had planned out her suggestions carefully. "You don't want to be trapped in a house with a nagging woman and her stupid teenage daughter, just fixing toilets all your life, do you?" she asked, her voice trembling. "Wouldn't you rather be free? Riding a motorcycle across the country to California? Doing whatever you want, and sleeping with whoever you want? You could go anywhere."

"I can do whatever I want," he said. His voice was heavy.

Nadine heard the microwave beep and glanced towards the kitchen. She had to hurry up. "You should leave town. Just pack up and go," she said. "Tomorrow you will take your savings and buy a motorcycle, just like you've always wanted. And then you will leave all this crap behind and ride off across the country to sunny California."

"California," he said. His eyelids were drooping. Nadine's mother appeared in the doorway with a microwaved mug of coffee.

"I think he's asleep," Nadine said before trotting up the stairs to her room.

∨

"It didn't work," Nadine reported to Elizabeth the next day at lunch.

"Nothing happened?" Elizabeth pulled her long hair into a messy pony-tail before picking up her sandwich.

"Oh, something happened. He was super fucked up," Nadine said. "And I made suggestions and everything. So this morning, I was expecting him to come downstairs with his bags packed, but he just said that he's going to buy a motorcycle when he gets his tax rebate, and that he wants to go on a vacation to California one day."

"So it halfway worked?"

"We need to see Luci."

The girls set off for the theater and again found Luci in the lighting booth. This time she wore a red wig, cut in a short, swinging bob. Her eyes were rimmed with red, and her lips were crimson. She sat in Ogre's lap, and when Nadine and Elizabeth arrived, she regarded them both with annoyance. "Yes?"

"It didn't exactly work," Nadine said.

"You mean you didn't give him the right suggestions." Luci narrowed her eyes at the girls.

"Should we try it again?"

"No. We'll try something else." Luci ran her sharp fingernails through Ogre's curly hair. She bent her head close and kissed him on the lips, staining them a bloody red.

"Um, should we come back later?" Nadine started to back away towards the stairs.

"No. Stay." Luci's deep voice echoed through the little room. She stood up, and Ogre excused himself with a nod of his big head. He ducked out the door and thundered down the narrow stairs.

Nadine approached Luci slowly. "What do we do now?" she asked.

"The second gateway." Luci curled herself into the chair where Ogre had been sitting. "The second gateway is dreams. Dreams are the playground of the subconscious, you know, but the gateway can be hard to find."

Nadine nodded.

"I can help you create dreams and send them into your stepfather's subconscious, but it's hard work, and I won't do it for free."

"How much?"

"A hundred bucks."

Nadine had ninety-seven dollars in her savings account, and a few dollars hidden between the pages of her old *Charlotte's Web* book at home in her room. "Okay," she agreed. It would be worth it.

"Tomorrow." Luci pointed a long, skinny finger towards the girls. "I'll need the money, plus a pillowcase, three of his hairs, and a written script for the dreams you want him to have. Leave the items at the foot of the lighting booth stairs before first period. At the end of the day, come back. You will find the pillowcase. Try not to touch it too much because it will be saturated with nightmares. If he sleeps on it, he will have terrible dreams for three nights. Dreams so real he will begin to think they are."

That afternoon, Nadine and Elizabeth stopped by the bank and withdrew all the money from Nadine's savings account. Then they walked to Elizabeth's apartment. The girls wound through the small living room where Elizabeth's mother sat in the dark, smoking a cigarette and watching daytime television.

Elizabeth closed and locked the door to her room, and Nadine sat down cross-legged on the bed with a pad of paper in her lap. "Okay, what sort of dream is going to make him want to leave?" she asked.

Elizabeth opened the bottom drawer of her dresser and pulled out a small pink jewelry box with a ballerina painted on the lid. She tossed it onto the bed where it made an indentation in the fluffy comforter. Nadine opened the box to find a small glass bowl and a little baggie of green weed. "Inspiration." Elizabeth grinned.

Nadine sprinkled the dried green crumbles into the bowl. "He makes it so that all I want to do is get fucked up and never go home again," she said quietly.

"That's why you have to think. What would make Roy want to leave?" Elizabeth sat down next to Nadine and handed her the lighter.

Nadine inhaled deeply, feeling the smoke burn inside her lungs. She blew it out and watched it stream across the room and disappear. "He always says that if he found out my mom was cheating on him, it'd be over."

Elizabeth took the bowl from Nadine's hand. "Perfect."

When Nadine got home, her mother was washing dishes and Roy was watching television, so she went upstairs and tiptoed into their bedroom. She pulled back the covers and examined the pillows, looking for hair. Her brain still felt fuzzy from the pot, and she imagined that her eyes were focusing in together like a high-powered microscope. Her vision zoomed towards something dark and thin, like the stroke of a fine-tipped pen. She picked it up, but it was too long and curly to be Roy's. She found another piece on the edge of his pillow. Short and straight. She put it in the ziploc baggie she'd taken from the kitchen. She heard Roy yelling downstairs, and her heart pounded. What if he found her? What if he knew what she was doing? But of course, he couldn't know. She found another short hair on the sheet below the pillow, and then another one, even further down. Coarse and dark. She shuddered to think where on his body it might have come from. She put the hairs in the baggie and went to the hallway closet to find a pillowcase.

The next day, Nadine left everything in a plastic grocery bag at the foot of the stairs leading to the lighting booth. At the end of seventh period, she went back to the theater and found the bag waiting for her, empty now except for the pillowcase. Nadine went straight home so she could be there before her mother or Roy got home. She went into their room and pulled the regular pillowcase off the pillow on Roy's side of the bed. She took the nightmare pillowcase out of the plastic bag with the tips of her fingers. It looked the same as it had before, except for a strange symbol stitched into one corner. Nadine looked closer at the dark thread and realized it had been stitched with her stepfather's hair. She shuddered. Very carefully, she eased the pillow into the case and left it, plump and inviting, on top of the covers. Then she went to the bathroom and washed her hands with hot, soapy water.

For the next three mornings, Nadine woke hoping to hear the scuffle of boxes or the rev of an engine, but the first two mornings there was nothing. Well, not nothing, exactly. Her stepfather looked terrible. He had purple circles under his eyes, and he staggered around the kitchen, drinking cup after cup of black coffee and complaining of a headache.

Sunday morning, after the last night of Luci-induced nightmares, they finally seemed to be taking effect. Nadine sat in the living room, pretending to read a magazine, but really listening to the conversation in the kitchen.

"I've been having the same fucked up dream," Roy said. "I'm watching you have sex with another man, and you're laughing in my face and telling me I'm stupid. It was so real. I woke up this morning, and I could've sworn it actually happened."

"Oh, baby!" Nadine's mother crooned. "It was just a dream. That would never happen."

"Well why am I dreaming it?"

"I don't know."

"If you're cheating on me…"

"I'm not cheating on you!"

"Why do you sound so defensive?"

"I'm not, Roy. It was just a dream you were having."

"Maybe I should just buy a motorcycle and fucking take off to California or something. I don't need this shit."

"Roy, I swear. I'm not cheating. Why don't you go back to bed, baby? You look tired."

"I'm going out to the garage."

All day, Nadine waited for something to trigger Roy's departure. But he didn't leave. He just spent the day in the garage, tending to his plants. Monday came, and the nightmares had stopped. Roy was better rested, and he was already forgetting about his suspicions. He didn't even complain, like he usually did, that there was nothing good to eat for breakfast. If only the nightmares had kept up for a few more days, Nadine thought on the bus ride to school, it would have been enough to really push him over the edge.

At lunch, Nadine ran to the theater by herself to find Luci. The older girl was on her back on the floor of the lighting booth, her arms folded across her chest like she was lying in a coffin.

"Luci?" Nadine asked.

"What do you want?" Luci didn't open her eyes, and her black lips barely moved.

"I'm sorry. Is this a bad time?"

Slowly, Luci raised herself up. She glared at Nadine. "Just make it fast." She was wearing a long, black wig. A pillbox hat perched on top of her head, and from it sprouted black mesh, which covered the top half of her pale face like a spider's web.

"I was wondering, the nightmares were doing really well, but I think I need a few more to do the trick. Please? Just a few more." Nadine looked down at her feet to avoid Luci's dark, angry eyes.

"You know my price."

"Well, I don't actually have any money right now, but I could get some. By next week maybe, if I baby-sit a lot over the weekend."

"Then next week I'll stitch another pillowcase."

"But I think it's got to be now! We're so close."

Luci shrugged. "I don't accept credit."

"What else can I do?"

Luci's black lips parted in a smile, and her teeth looked unnaturally white against them. "You can try the third gateway," she said. "Love."

"Love?"

"If someone or something a person loves is being threatened, the path to the subconscious can emerge."

"I doubt my stepfather knows what love is." Nadine felt her eyes prick with tears. "Isn't there anything else you can do?"

"I'm afraid not." Luci's voice was cold and metallic. "Please leave now." She sank back to the floor and closed her eyes.

Sniffing back tears, Nadine ran down the steps, through the empty theater, and out into an afternoon growing dark with heavy clouds.

$$\mathbb{V}$$

Normally after school, Nadine and Elizabeth hung out behind the library with the potheads and skaters, or they walked to Elizabeth's house to listen to music and talk about boys. But by the end of the day, it was pouring rain, so they rode the school bus to Nadine's house.

Nadine unlocked the door and led Elizabeth up the stairs to her bedroom. The rain smeared down her windows and rapped against the thin roof. The girls kicked off their shoes and sprawled out on the bed, looking up at the ceiling, which was mottled with little paint bumps, like tiny pimples.

"Luci's such a bitch," Elizabeth said. She mocked Luci's deep voice. "Love is the third gateway." She dangled her arms behind her and they trailed off the bed. "What a bunch of shit."

"I know." Nadine sighed. "What does she want me to do? Get him to fall in love with someone else? How am I supposed to do that?" Nadine stared at the naked bulb in the middle of her ceiling. She closed her eyes and saw it still, pulsing red then yellow. "He doesn't even love my mom." She opened her eyes and rolled onto her side, facing Elizabeth. "I'm serious. I don't think they love each other."

"So what does he love?"

"He loves whiskey. And his precious pot plants."

"That's sad."

"Maybe we should try the drug thing again," Nadine said. "Maybe if I give him different suggestions this time, it'll work."

"But Luci has the drug."

"Yeah, and don't know what she gave us. It could have been anything. Like meth or DXM or something." Nadine sat up. She pulled her pillow into her lap and hugged it.

"Okay. But we don't have anything like that."

"No, but…" She squeezed the pillow with growing excitement. "You know that guy Jerry from Chuck E. Cheese? He once told me how to make DXM pills with Robitussin and cornstarch."

Elizabeth sat up. "For real?"

Nadine nodded. "We have a bunch of Robitussin because my mom's always sick. And we might have cornstarch." She bounced off the bed. "Let's do it right now!"

Nadine's mother would be home from work soon, but Roy wouldn't be home until late. "We can make it in the garage. There's an old Bunsen burner in there."

"Are you sure that's a good idea?" Elizabeth was scared of Roy, too.

"It'll be fine. He won't be home for hours."

Nadine took a bottle of cough syrup from the upstairs bathroom cabinet before they headed to the kitchen to find a deep frying pan, a box of cornstarch, and a big metal spoon.

"Basically, DXM is the same as the main ingredient in Robitussin," Nadine explained as she and Elizabeth pushed open the garage door. Contrary to Roy's knowledge, Nadine knew where he kept the key. It wasn't raining as hard now, but still the bottoms of their jeans were wet from the grass, and raindrops rolled down their foreheads and into their eyes. They stepped into the garage, which smelled faintly of sewage, and pulled the door shut behind them. Inside, their faces glowed blue in the grow lights, and they stared in awe at the neat rows of clay pots, each one holding a long, leafy stalk of the forbidden plant.

Nadine found the Bunsen burner in a corner and plugged it in. She set it on top of a flimsy card table in the middle of the garage. "Jerry said all you have to do is heat up the Robitussin to burn off all the sugar, and what's left is pure, liquid DXM."

"So what's the cornstarch do?" Elizabeth asked.

"I don't know. I guess it helps it thicken into pills or something." Nadine poured the cough syrup into the pan. "We'll figure it out." She turned the knob on the burner, and a high blue flame leapt out, carrying the scent of heated metal. "I guess I'll just have to hold the pan over it," Nadine said. "I don't know how long it'll take."

"We can take turns," Elizabeth suggested. "And whoever's not holding it can be the lookout." She pushed an overturned bucket against the garage door and stood on it. The small windows were covered with black electrical tape, but the window on the end had some tape missing, so Elizabeth put her face there and peered through the dusty opening. "All clear," she reported.

Nadine held the heavy pan over the steady blue flame. She looked around the garage. She hadn't been in here in a long time. There were more plants than there had been before. The garage was crowded with regular things, too: cardboard boxes, tools, the lawnmower, a jug of gasoline. And under the card table were buckets of paint and paint thinner from two years ago when Roy said he was going to repaint the house but never did.

"Do you think things will be better once Roy's gone?" Elizabeth asked from the window.

"Are you kidding? Of course." Nadine picked up the spoon from the table and stirred the red liquid. In the eerie blue light her hand looked translucent.

"What if she just finds another shitty guy? That's what my mom does."

"No," Nadine said. "When Roy's gone, my mom will realize that she never really needed him. Plus, I'll be sixteen soon, so I'll get a job and help her out."

Elizabeth was quiet, and Nadine watched the syrup begin to move inside the pan. Thick bubbles grew slowly on the surface and popped. It began bubbling quicker. "Your mom's here," Elizabeth reported. "She's parking in the driveway."

"That's okay," Nadine said. "We just have to be out of here before Roy gets home." The liquid churned.

"Oh my God, Nadine," Elizabeth said. "Roy's getting out of the passenger side of the car."

"What?" Nadine's hand shook, and the syrup sloshed against the sides of the pan. "Are you sure?"

"Yeah. He's definitely standing right there in the driveway."

Nadine's hand began to shake. "What should we do?" she hissed.

"Oh my God!" Elizabeth jumped off the bucket. "He just looked right at me."

"Shut up," Nadine whispered. "Just be quiet."

Suddenly the garage door began to rattle open. The bucket fell and began to roll. Elizabeth shrieked. Roy stood in front of them, wet from the rain outside.

"Nadine!" he roared, coming towards her.

"Stay away from me!" Without thinking, Nadine flung the pan at him. Hot, red cough syrup flew through the air. The pan landed on the ground, but the red liquid hit his face and rolled down his cheeks. He bellowed like a wounded animal and, even though he seemed half blind from the burning syrup, he lunged for Nadine, his arms groping wildly.

Nadine ran towards the door as Roy knocked into the card table. The table collapsed, and the burner fell. Roy didn't even notice. He turned around, swatting at his face to wipe off the syrup. It oozed down his neck like blood.

The girls ran outside into the rain. Nadine's mother stood motionless in the driveway, holding an umbrella and staring at them. "What's going on?"

Roy emerged from the open garage door. "I'm gonna kill you both," he yelled. He moved towards them, but he could barely see. His eyes were red and puffy.

"Oh my god, what happened?" Nadine's mother looked at Roy's face in horror.

Just then, a familiar odor came through the damp air: the skunky smell of burning marijuana. Roy sniffed, his nostrils flaring. "What the fuck?" He turned back towards the garage. Flames licked the floor where the Bunsen burner had fallen onto some spilled paint thinner. A few of the plants had caught fire. Their leaves crumbled into glowing white ash, accompanied by thick gray smoke.

"Fucking shit." Roy ran into the garage.

"Oh my God," Nadine's mother said. "I'm calling the fire department."

"No!" Roy emerged from the garage with two of the plants. He set them down in the driveway. "Go get the hose. We can't—they'll arrest us." He ran back into the garage, which was filling quickly with the pungent smoke. Nadine's mother dropped her umbrella and ran towards the side of the house to get the hose. Nadine and Elizabeth stood in the driveway in the misting rain, not sure what to do. Roy emerged again with two more plants. He looked insane. His eyes were bloodshot, and wet hair clung to his red, sticky face. "Help me, for god's sake," he shouted at them.

Nadine looked at him carefully. "You want us to help you?" she asked.

Roy set the plants down on the driveway. "Yes, dammit!" He pressed his lips together, and his chest rose and fell. "Come on, please, Nadine," he said. There was hint of sad desperation in his voice. For a moment, Nadine thought he looked almost human.

She pursed her lips and looked him in the eye. "No. I think we'll go call 911."

The girls ran into the house, ignoring Roy's angry bellows.

In the kitchen, Nadine peered out the window. Her mother was by the side of the house, struggling to untangle the old garden hose. Roy ran from the garage with an armload of plants. Behind him, the fire grew. "Are you really calling 911?" Elizabeth asked.

"No. I don't want my mom to get in trouble or anything. I just said that to scare him."

"He's going to be so mad at you."

"I know. But it's worth it to see him like this." Nadine watched Roy deposit another load of plants and head back into the garage. It was sad in a way. He loved the plants more than anyone, more than himself.

Suddenly, there was an explosion of noise and light. The garage seemed to shudder for a split second before it burst into flames. It was both startling and beautiful, like fireworks.

The funeral was small. There was no casket—barely any remains. Two months later, Nadine and her mother moved back in with Nana because, without Roy, they couldn't afford the mortgage on the house. Nadine slept on the living room couch, hearing when her mother staggered in at three AM from various bars. Every night cat hair tickled Nadine's nose and got caught in her throat. She went to school with itchy red eyes, and her teachers recommended her for drug counseling, even though she tried to tell them it was just allergies.

One night, she dreamed of a wolverine chasing her in the school theater. She ran through the labyrinth of black curtains, twisting, and turning, until she came to a dead end. Luci, in a long, gray wig, watched from the lighting booth above as the wolverine advanced. It jumped at Nadine, its nostrils spewing pot smoke, and when it slashed at her heart with its sharp claws, cherry red cough syrup poured out. Her eyes flew open, and she was back on the couch in the dark living room, with one of Nana's cats asleep on her chest. Nadine pushed the animal onto the floor and fell back asleep.

❦

And that is how the girl with the gumdrop eyes rid herself of the evil stepfather and moved away from the yellow house by the brown river. But she did not feel contented, and she was haunted by a ghost that lurked in the gateways of her subconscious. She knew that something had to change. She stopped doing drugs and began to apply herself in school so that she could get a college scholarship and leave her pathetic little town. As it turned out, she was quite clever, and she enjoyed learning about the brain. After graduation, she moved to New York City and studied psychology, focusing on dream analysis. She obtained her PhD and married a wealthy, eccentric man she met in graduate school. Together they opened a hypnotherapy clinic in Manhattan, and that is where they are living to this very day.

For Want Of
A Unicorn

By Camille Griep

I didn't start to get suspicious of the fairy godmother until I asked her for a unicorn. The smoke rings from her unbidden arrival should have been my first clue that she was too good to be true.

"What on Frith's green earth do you want one of those lumpy nags for?"

"Oh no, godmother!" I cried. "Silken manes and glittering horns! Soft companionship and eternal devotion! Riding through the sweet dewdrops of sunrise!"

For as long as I could remember, I had wanted a unicorn. It seemed only natural to wish for one since the technicalities of maidenhood and the determined march of time had dimmed the chance of luring one to my side the old-fashioned way. More importantly, Betsy Meadowfair didn't have a unicorn, either. I'd never have her blonde locks, cobalt eyes, or heaving bosom, but I'd never be in want of a unicorn.

"Nonsense," said the fairy godmother, glowering at me as if I'd asked for a shark. An iridescent black beetle on her shoulder chirruped for emphasis. "Unicorns are ill-tempered in the morning, their teeth are sharp enough to snap the bones of small children, and they drink saltwater… preferably in the form of tears." She shook her grey curls and looked me up and down with the eye not covered by a patch. I supposed it was all a matter of perspective.

So I asked for a goat instead.

"Young people," she sighed. "You never know what you want." She rolled her eyes, inhaled, and waved her gnarled wand. From the puff of glittering smoke, a dog emerged, the end of his tail smoking slightly.

It was the second time she'd given me something other than what I'd asked for. One wish ago, when I had requested a castle on the hill, she'd conjured a white cottage by the lake.

"I'm sorry," she'd said as I complained, "but that spot's already been taken."

"By who?"

"My last client."

"Whose name is… ?"

"I don't know, child. Betsy something or other. Beautiful young woman. Just the kind you'd want to end up with your son, wouldn't you say?"

"I don't have a son."

"It's because you're more of a handsome girl, aren't you?"

"I don't have a son because—" I stammered. "Oh, never mind."

I didn't see what good it was to have a bona fide fairy godmother if she simply gave you the cut-rate version of whatever you wanted and insulted you to boot. The goat was supposed to mow the grass and make cheese. What good was another mouth to feed? My job as the local seamstress barely brought in enough to feed myself.

But the dog was ugly and earnest and friendly. He greeted me, one ear standing and the other flopping to the side, making it difficult to maintain a proper scowl. I knelt down and looked into his eyes, hoping to reveal some deep woman-to-dog connection, a friendship for the ages, a soul trapped by an evil spell. There was no hidden prince inside, just a slobbery companion.

"Let's call you Boris, shall we?" He licked my face with a sopping tongue.

"And your last wish?" asked the fairy godmother. The beetle made a sound close to laughter as the godmother straightened her back and shook out her rainbow of skirts. "The look on your face…" She put her free hand over her mouth and mirthful tears filled her visible eye.

"I don't think I like you," I said, scuffing the dirt with my pink satin slipper.

"Come, now," she said. "Don't be like that. Tell me your final wish."

"You won't grant it anyway. What's the point?"

"Indeed, what is the point?" she chuckled. The beetle hopped up and down. "Seriously, though." Her voice fell an octave. "I have a schedule to keep."

"Well, I certainly wouldn't want to keep you from disappointing anyone else today," I said. "Where are you headed next? I hear Muffy Miller wants a magic mirror."

"My, she's a pretty girl, too," said the godmother. "But I've already chosen, haven't I."

I hadn't the slightest idea what she was going on about. "Chosen what?"

"Pay that no mind, dear," she said, the "dear" sticking a bit in her throat. "Go ahead with that wish."

Boris leaned against my legs like a counterbalance, and I took a deep breath. "I wish... I wish for true love."

"Good enough," she said and folded her chubby arms over her round bosom. "It's been a pleasure doing business with you."

The godmother and her beetle disappeared in a shower of sparks. Boris cowered and shook behind me while I stamped out the small flames in the grass. Inside a burnt ring of buttercups, a jug of strawberry wine sat beside the godmother's boot prints. It figured.

That evening, Boris and I sat on the front porch of the cottage while I worked my way through the strawberry wine. The sun dipped low over the water and loons floated past with the low notes of late summer. The night was warm and Boris and I fell asleep on the swing.

The next morning we hiked up to the hill to look at Betsy Meadowfair's new castle. It was a spectacular sight. Sparkling white stone accented by crimson pennants and rows of red roses. A shining black stallion grazed the trim grass on the front lawn. I felt an arm around my shoulders and looked to see Betsy's heaving bosom encroaching mine.

"Now, don't be jealous," she said with an exaggerated wink.

"Overdoing it a little, aren't we?" I asked. Boris wagged his tail and licked her hand.

She squealed. "What is that?"

"It's a dog. Named Boris."

"Get it off me!"

"It isn't on you, it was just saying hello."

Boris's greeting had the useful result of making Betsy move a good ten paces away.

"What are you doing with that horse?" I asked. "Is that what you got when you asked for a unicorn?"

"Oh no, my unicorn's out back."

I felt my ears and throat flush. "That scheming witch…"

Betsy prattled on. "No, no, silly. The horse is for my true love."

"What, he stumbles along and says, 'A devil horse! Just what I've always wanted! And I'll take you too'?"

"Yes. Maybe? Who cares! When I wished for true love, the fairy god-mother gave it to me."

"You don't need to wish for true love. Half the village is in true love with you."

"Ah yes, but I want a true love with money. And a big codpiece."

"Of course," I said, shaking my head, "how silly of me."

"How big is your castle?"

"I didn't get a castle."

"Oh you poor thing. Homely and homeless. And you didn't get a uni-corn either?" She raised an eyebrow at Boris. "Well, you can always come for tea." She flounced off up the path, spooking the stallion and then racing to the front door as it huffed and snorted at her.

Boris let out a woof.

"I agree," I said. "Let's go home."

◈

Over the next few weeks, Boris brought home a butterfly, a cat, and a raccoon for a visit. I painted a few things for the walls and planted herbs for the sunny windowsill. The grass grew thick around the cottage and we played hide-and-seek until the fireflies began to glow. The bottle of wine replenished itself each night, and on a Friday evening, I poured myself a generous glass, retiring outside to count the stars over the water, relating each constellation to the yawning dog.

"And that one is the giant bear," I said to Boris.

"I'm sorry, but that's Orion," said a voice followed by soft hoof falls. It was finally my unicorn! A talking unicorn, at that. I wondered how much wine I'd had. I peered into the murk of the night as a tall figure resolved into view. It was no unicorn. Instead there stood a man, dark and strong, be-decked in the gear of a hunter, a great bow slung from his shoulder. "I didn't know anyone lived here now... I didn't mean to startle you."

I probably should have panicked, but instead I said, "Are you my true love, then?"

"How come everyone keeps asking me that?"

"And what are you doing with Betsy Meadowfair's horse?" I stood, suddenly flooded with the panic that should have arrived thirty seconds earlier.

"My name is Adam and I mean you no harm. Why do you think I've stolen a horse?"

"There's this fairy godmother... You know, never mind. You're not going to take my dog, are you?"

"He's a very nice dog," said the man.

"No. He snores and he slobbers and he eats like a pig. Please don't take him." I found myself kneeling in supplication as Boris licked my cheek.

Adam began to laugh. "I'm not going to abscond with your dog."

I accepted his hand to get back up. "Would you like some strawberry wine?"

"I guess I would, now that you ask." He smiled and set his bow on the porch, sat down on the steps, and scratched Boris's ears. He told me of his adventures, far and wide, dragons and elves and trolls and tempests. Born in a nearby village, he was returning to settle down.

"It's the strangest thing," he said. "I got to the top of the big hill and there's a brand-new castle there. Lo and behold, there's Pete running around the front lawn."

"Its name is Pete?" I looked at the horse whose eyes and nostrils seemed to glow red in the dark. I felt a pang of sorrow for the fence he was tethered to.

"His name is Pete and he just looks mean. He's harmless."

"Better tell that to Betsy Meadowfair."

"Is that the blonde?" He swirled his finger around his temple.

"Yes. That's her."

"She kept going on and on about the horse and a godmother and true love. In truth, I can't believe I got away from her."

"Persistent, eh?"

"She ripped my breeches!" He turned around to show me a handspan-length tear on the rear of his trousers. Evidently we'd both had enough wine to dispense with modesty.

"Take them off," I said. "I'm a seamstress by trade. I'll have you good as new in no time."

I gave him my shawl to cover up while I worked and excused myself to grab my sewing notions. When I came back, he'd refilled our glasses and Boris had fallen asleep on his feet.

"I don't know how straight I'll be sewing after all this wine," I laughed, examining my work.

"Anything helps. Thank you for doing it for me, Lady... Lady..."

"Oh, yes, of course. It's Millicent. I'm not a lady, though."

"No matter. I'm very grateful, no matter how crooked the results." He gave a little bow of his head. "Now that you mention it, though, this wine really is extraordinary. It tastes almost exactly like the vintage my mother makes."

"Merlin's arse!" I said, jamming the needle into my finger as realization pushed the warm hum of the wine from my head. "Your mother is the fairy godmother?"

"I certainly doubt it. My mother's no fairy godmother. She dabbles in spellcraft and such. I'd call it more of a hobby, really."

"Not a fairy godmother. Spellcraft. You're telling me she's a witch?"

A flash and the chirp of a cricket and the fairy godmother-witch materialized in front of us. Boris slunk behind me, tail curled protectively to his side.

"Mother?" he asked.

"This isn't what it looks like," I said. I cringed as she pointed her gnarled wand at me, taking in her tipsy, trouser-less son.

"You've ruined everything!" she said.

"I didn't. I mean... How could I?" I stammered. Before I could continue, Boris gave a bark and Betsy Meadowfair stumbled into view, muddy and tattered and wild-eyed.

"What the hell happened to you?" I asked.

"You!" she screeched.

"Me?"

"He's mine! You can't have him!" She lunged at Adam, who stood, shawl falling to the ground.

I threw his pants at him and Boris and I placed ourselves between him and our guests.

"Betsy, you're about to fall out of your corset and you have lipstick on your forehead," I said in a hushed voice. "Pull yourself together." Her hands flew to her chest where she began to rearrange things.

I turned to the witch. "Some fairy godmother you are. Who do you think you are, waltzing into the woods and meddling with the hearts of unsuspecting maidens?"

"The name is Matilda the Grand, and you're in possession of something that doesn't belong to you."

"I'm not in possession of anything that doesn't want to be here."

"Idiot girl, I set it all up, you see?"

"I understand perfectly," I said. "It's just that you don't have a willing participant."

"Look at her," Matilda said, pointing at Betsy. "You can't get more willing."

"No, I mean Adam."

"What's he got to do with it?"

"Mother!" he said.

"Everything," I said.

"Mine!" yelled Betsy.

"Adam is my son. I know exactly what he wants." Matilda lowered her wand. "Come now, Adam. We're going to Betsy's."

Betsy smirked and took a step backwards towards the fence, bumping straight into the black horse. Pete peeled back his upper lip, exposing a line of straight, white teeth. Betsy yelped and began to flail, beaning herself on the fencepost.

"You want me to marry that?" asked Adam.

"She's very pretty," said Matilda. "Just the type of real lady for you."

"For me?" asked Adam. "I didn't ask for any of this."

"Yes, but you're family, dear. You didn't have to." She looked rather pleased with herself, a smile curling her wrinkled lips. The cricket gave a hop.

"I think I've already found the real lady for me."

"Nonsense," said Matilda. "This one's just a featureless seamstress."

"Not so," Adam said. "She's my friend and confidante. And if she'll have me, I'll be more."

"Mine!" whimpered Betsy, coming round to a not-so-gentle nudging by Pete.

"Can't you do something for her?" I whispered to Matilda.

The witch twisted her wrist and a cloud of smoke fell over Betsy. Her petticoats were clean and her hair fell in uniform directions once more.

"I'd thought you'd console yourself with the wine, not entrap my son with it."

"It was a nice thought," I said.

"Do you want to come stay with me?" Betsy asked Matilda. "Perhaps you could still teach me a few things about becoming a fairy witch."

"Somehow I doubt that," sighed Matilda. "But a good soft bed wouldn't be amiss."

"Wait," I said. "How many other girls did you promise true love?"

"I didn't promise you anything," she said. "I only steered things a bit. For my son. It was a gift. Unappreciated, I might add."

"You meant well, Mother," he sighed. "You have given me a gift—albeit accidentally—and I will accept the friendship of this maiden and her dog and help to drink the strawberry wine and count the stars."

Matilda seemed to deflate in front of us. "Are you sure? I always pictured you with a blonde."

No one else saw the shining white beast moving past the hedge later that night, drinking the laughter we sent toward the stars. I excused myself and sent her back home to Betsy's courtyard.

At least she'll never be in want of a unicorn.

BLOOD OF
THE MOTHER
BY ALAINA EWING

Terra hurried under the eave to avoid getting drenched. The moment she got under cover, the rain began coming down in sheets, flooding the drains along the shop-lined street. *Blasted rain*, she thought, *it would have to ruin my night.*

She tucked her hair into a bun, pulled her navy cloak tighter around her neck, and cursed as she wandered down the sidewalk. Each time she hit a gap in the eave, she thrust a hand toward the sky and an invisible umbrella appeared above her. If only she could maintain the umbrella, then she would have stopped Starla by now.

Thunder rumbled, and a sharp flash of lightning filled the skyline. Terra couldn't do anything about a storm. Her abilities were too limited. She shook her head, frustrated.

Three blocks later, the rain still hadn't let up. Several more thunderheads rolled in above her, visible only by the darker hue they cast against the night sky. It appeared to Terra that this sudden storm was no mere storm. *Starla*, she cursed. Had getting her plans canceled not been enough? Now she had to throw a storm at her as well?

What did Starla have against her anyway? Terra wasn't the most popular gal in town. She hardly maintained the few friendships she had, let alone a boyfriend. Terra ran through the possibilities, but nothing came to her mind. Starla's rage toward her would remain a mystery.

Terra lifted her invisible umbrella again and hopped over several puddles occupying the broken brick walkway. She missed the edge of the last puddle by half an inch. The smell of wet stone made her nose wrinkle. After a slight shiver, she continued.

There were people ahead of her, about half a block away. They gathered in front of the small town theater. All huddled together as though they couldn't understand what was happening.

One particularly tall man stuck his hand into the rain, and then withdrew it with haste. His forehead creased, and he shook his hand several times above his head.

Terra picked up her pace until she reached the crowd.

"Are you okay?" she asked the tall man.

He shook his head. "That shit burns!"

"What do you mean?" Terra walked closer to observe the man's hand. It was flaming red. "Did the rain do this to you?"

"Yeah," he replied. "I know global warming sucks and all, but shit. I didn't think acid rain could do this!"

"That's not acid rain," Terra explained. "Stay under cover."

Either Starla had cursed the rain or she was creating the storm itself. But why punish everyone? Whatever the case, Terra needed to find her before anyone else got hurt. She pulled her chunk of fluorite from her pocket and held it up to her forehead.

"To all the magic people of Harrowton, someone is casting spells against the general populace and the rain is burning like acid. I believe it to be Starla Bermaine, but I cannot be certain yet. Your assistance is required," Terra whispered aloud, and in doing so, sent her message to all possessing the rest of the fluorite chunk.

Sirens rang out through the streets, alerting all the non-magicals to stay inside. Terra stopped to look in the window of Billy's shop. There were lights twinkling like stars around the countertops and tables. They looked bewitched, as they flickered more brightly the moment her eyes locked on to them. She knew he was probably asleep upstairs, as he got up before dawn, but she couldn't resist. She reached for the door and it opened without a touch.

Terra went in. The smell of jasmine, fresh lemon, rosemary, mint, and several other teas overwhelmed her senses. She tried to navigate the shop carefully to keep from knocking over any tea displays or antique cups. The stairs were toward the back.

Thunder cracked so loud above the shop that Terra jumped, knocking over a small table with daisy print napkins and some bowls of sugar cubes. *Damn*, she thought.

A light turned on upstairs, and the shadow of Billy filled Terra's view. Her heart thudded. Maybe waking him was a bad idea.

He came downstairs in nothing but boxers, sending her heart racing. The moment he caught sight of Terra, he smiled.

"I should have known," he said with a hint of tease. "This storm seems worse than the average one."

"Yeah," Terra agreed, her word heavy.

"Did you call for help?"

She nodded.

"Good. Let me just slip on some clothes. Wait here." Billy went back upstairs.

Terra felt heat rising up inside her chest. She'd known Billy since high school, but lately, he'd changed. He was no longer the gangly teen in over-sized clothing. Now, his muscles filled his shirts, his bronze hair fell just right and his smoky eyes seemed to penetrate the deepest levels of her. Terra tried to shrug off her giddiness. She needed to focus.

Billy hopped down the stairs, skipping every third step. He had on his black cloak with the gray patterns woven into it, her favorite. Before leaving the shop, he grabbed a handful of sugar cubes and popped one in his mouth.

"Ew." Terra didn't mean to come off as rude, but she'd never seen anyone eat straight sugar.

"I need to stay awake." Billy shrugged as if it were no big deal, and headed for the door. "So, what'd she do this time?"

"You mean Starla?"

"Who else would pull something like this? Of course I mean Starla." He chuckled.

"This isn't funny. She's turned the rain to acid somehow. And I think she created this storm."

"That doesn't surprise me," Billy said.

"I don't know where to find her. I was following her, but lost her when the rains came. I'm not even one hundred percent sure this is her doing."

"I can pretty much guarantee this is Starla's doing. She's been withdrawing more and more lately."

"How do you know?" Terra's words came out accusatory, her right eyebrow rose.

"I've worked with her on some things," he said.

"Like what?"

"Just stuff the elders asked me to help her with." He didn't explain further.

"I see." She straightened her shoulders.

Billy smirked playfully. "Jealous much?"

"Maybe."

He chuckled, blushing slightly.

"Ass." She punched him.

"Butt," he said with a smile. "You do know why Starla hates you. Right?"

"How would I know that?" Terra rolled her eyes.

Billy sighed, and shook his head. Clearly he didn't buy her answer. She sensed why Starla hated her, but she wanted to hear Billy say it. Something he didn't seem to want to do.

"You're stubborn," he finally said.

"A trait I got from my grandmother." She laughed. "Father always said she was quite the pain."

"And powerful," Billy added.

"Huh. Too bad I didn't inherit that." Terra finally fell silent, not wanting to think of all she could do given her grandmother's skills. Instead, she focused on the sidewalk.

The rain let up slightly now that Billy was with her. His magic naturally calmed situations when it came to Starla, though no one knew why. Terra suspected it had something to do with the crush Starla had had on Billy for most of their childhood years, but she didn't know for certain.

The streetlamps shuddered as they walked by. Their invisible shield of protection seemed to be affecting the electrical elements around them, including the lightning that struck just feet above their heads. Terra ducked instinctively as the flash of light surrounded them both.

Billy put his arm around her shoulders. "She can't hurt you. Not with both of us putting our magic together."

"I'm not so sure of that," Terra admitted.

Billy chuckled again, and urged her forward. The streets were completely empty now. Everyone seemed to have listened to the siren's warnings and gotten out of the storm. At least they would be safe.

"Do you have any idea where Starla might be?" Terra asked.

"Not really. You did check her house, right?"

"Of course," she said with a hint of sarcasm. "That's the first place I went when I found the altar room empty. The elders were supposed to be planning for Mabon, but they weren't there. I've never received an invite to assist in the planning process before this. Do you think that's why Starla is doing this? Because I won the invite, and not her?"

"That's a probability." Billy stopped before walking out into the rain. "I don't think we should go out there."

"Why?" Terra asked, but then understood.

The rain was no longer the color of water. It was glowing red. Something in the pit of her stomach twisted, and she latched onto Billy as though her life were in danger.

"I think we need help. This just went from worrisome to insane." Billy held Terra tight as he pulled out his own crystal. He held it to his forehead and whispered inside, "The rain has turned to blood. Someone died tonight."

Sirens rang out through the streets again, but this time, the bells clanged four times at the end. No one would leave their homes now. Not until the safety alarm sounded.

Terra gulped. She wanted to be brave, but this was more than she'd bargained for. Hunting down Starla no longer seemed so simple. Her heart hammered.

"Billy?"

"Yes?" His tone was low as he watched the bloody rain pool at their feet.

"Where do the elders go when they're not meeting?"

"Into the caves. Do you think we need them?"

Terra turned to face him. "I know they don't like to be disturbed, especially so close to a celebration, but they weren't in the altar room today. Why? Something doesn't feel right, Billy. Besides, I don't think they'd mind being disturbed if someone was murdered tonight."

"You're right, Terr. We should go get them."

Terra nodded, but stopped before walking out into the crimson rain. "How? We can't walk in this. What if it still burns?"

"Let's head back to my shop. If we take the long way, we can stay under the eave. We can come up with a plan once we're there." Billy smiled, his mood appearing lifted.

Terra struggled with the spell book. It was heavy, dusty, and the pages were hanging on to the binding by magic alone. She flipped to the section on binding spells. The moment her eyes found the lower section of the page, Terra's breath caught.

"What about this one?" She shoved the book at Billy.

He was silent as he surveyed the spell. His eyes opened wide when he saw the last item needed, a lock of Starla's hair.

"This won't be easy." He met Terra's eyes with concern.

"What else can we do?" she asked. "When I checked her house earlier, she wasn't home. I can find a way inside and snatch some hair from her brush. Her place isn't far, and I'm certain I can keep under the eaves until I get there."

"Even if you made it safely there, if she happened to come home and find you inside…" He shuddered. "I just can't risk that. Better her find me than you. I'll go."

"Why would it be better for her to find you?" She crossed her arms.

"She doesn't hate me."

"Oh, right. Fine. I'll prepare things while you're gone." She turned away from him, but then faced Billy again. "Be careful."

"I will." He grinned, and headed for the stairs.

She cleared Billy's altar and began gathering other items they needed. She found a ribbon, sage, five candles, matches, and a crushed velvet cloth to cover the wood altar. Too bad photos were of no use for such a spell. That would have been much easier.

Terra waited impatiently for Billy to return. His ceremony room was dark, too dark, and it made her anxious. With black walls and only candlelight illuminating the place, the chill in the air was more than she wanted to deal with. She tapped her fingers on the altar's surface while her eyes followed any hint of a shadow across the low-lit room.

Finally, the door to the shop slammed with a bang and she heard Billy coming upstairs. Her heartbeat quickened when he came around the corner of the door, a few strands of hair in his hand. He approached the altar.

"Do you think this binding spell will stop her? She'll know a way around this. She is altering the weather, you know," Terra said.

"I know. But this will prevent her from affecting us while we find the elders. They can stop her. You were right to suggest this spell. You should trust your instincts more." Billy stood tall, his black cloak hanging slightly open, betraying his muscled chest covered only by a thin shirt. The sight made Terra squirm.

Billy placed the hair on the altar and began lighting candles. Then he saged the room, blowing smoke into each corner, clearing any negative remnants Starla might have thrown at them. He approached the altar again and picked up the hair.

"Put your hands over mine and say this with me," he instructed.

Terra nodded and placed her hands over Billy's. She knew he was more successful when it came to spells, so she let him take the lead. He began wrapping Starla's hair in the ribbon as he spoke.

"Starla Bermaine, we bind you from doing harm against others or yourself." They repeated the chant three times before setting the hair down.

Then Billy headed for a drawer and retrieved some thread, scissors, and a needle.

"What's that for?" she asked.

"One more spell. This is one only I can perform, and I can only do it for others. May I take your sleeve?"

"I guess."

Terra pulled her shirtsleeve out of her cloak and thrust her arm toward Billy. His hair fell forward, just into his eyes, and he blew it out of his face. He grabbed the chunk of wrapped hair and folded it into her sleeve. Then he sewed several stitches to keep it tucked into place, while chanting something inaudible under his breath. He was focused, focused so much that had Terra screamed at him, he wouldn't have flinched. Billy's eyes rolled back as his quiet chant continued. When he finally finished, his eyes returned to normal and he looked up at her.

"This won't hold for long. Let's get going."

"What did you do?"

"I can't tell you. We have to go now."

"You just sewed that bitch's hair into my sleeve." She grimaced. "You better tell me."

"It's part of my magic. If I tell you, it may not work. Can you just trust me on this?" He caressed her cheek, and it made her insides swirl.

"For now." Terra wanted to argue, but knew she would be more successful when they were not in a hurry looking for the elders. She fastened her cloak as they hurried for the door again.

The truck sputtered and spit mud into the air as Billy tried to get through the puddle. They were almost to the caves, and Terra really didn't want to walk in the dark. After ten minutes of rocking the truck back and forth between drive and reverse, all they'd managed to do was bury the wheels deeper into the mud. Terra sighed.

"Let's just walk the rest of the way." She hopped out of the Ford Raptor and straight into a foot of muck. She cursed under her breath and flipped her hood up.

Billy came around the side of the truck and saw Terra standing in thick brown goo. She saw him trying to suppress a giggle, and she glared at him. He reached his hand out to help her from the mud.

"Sorry." He looked away from her, probably trying to keep from laughing still. "I didn't think this mud was so deep."

"Doesn't that blasted truck have four-wheel drive?" she grumbled as he helped her retrieve her shoe from the pile of muck. She put it on, despite its being cold and wet.

"Yes," he said. "But this isn't exactly a *normal* storm. I'm not sure rain made of blood is exactly what the creators of the Raptor had in mind when designing the truck. At least it's not burning us. The binding spell seems to have helped." He shrugged.

"Huh," Terra scoffed, and looked down at her mud-soaked foot. "I wouldn't say the spell worked."

"It's not hurting, is it?" His forehead wrinkled.

"No." She sighed. "I suppose it's just an annoyance." She turned away from him and faced the woods ahead. "Let's go."

She let Billy take her hand and they made their way down the road. The moment she felt his hand in hers, she shivered. Her cloak was snug around her, and her hood in place, but his warm touch against the contrast of the chilly night still made her body respond unfavorably. Hopefully he hadn't noticed.

After several minutes of walking, the road narrowed into a trail only two feet wide. The trees were thrashing so hard in the newly picked-up wind that walking into the woods didn't feel as safe to Terra, but she knew she had to go. Billy must have sensed her nerves because he held her tighter.

An owl was hooting louder than the average nocturnal bird, audible over breaking branches and flooding rains. Terra was so drenched, her once-sapphire cloak looked permanently discolored. She was sure her skin looked no better, but at least it would wash clean when this was all over with. Her cloak would never be the same.

Throughout the night, thoughts of who might have died kept passing through her mind. What if it were her parents, or Ursus—her mentor? Would she even want to continue her magical studies if one of them were gone? She couldn't allow the thought to consume her. If she did, her demeanor might waver and she could fail in her mission to stop Starla. She shoved the thought from her mind once again and focused instead on the sloshing sound coming from her shoes.

When they came to an ending in the trail, Billy reached out in front of them and waved his hand through the air several times. He chanted something under his breath again. Terra couldn't make out the words, but that didn't matter. She knew what he was doing the moment the bushes before them parted and a crude cave opening appeared.

He led her inside, and Terra followed without hesitation. The walls lining the cave had sconces every ten feet which lit instantly as they entered. There was a draft whirling through the caves that far outweighed the wind outside. This was a surreal chill. Not something created by a storm. Terra shivered again.

"We'll be okay, Terr. Trust me," Billy assured her.

Terra wasn't buying it. She nodded, but with a heaviness on her chest she'd never felt before.

The cave led down into earth, circling around and around. She had no idea just how far down they'd ventured, or when they would find the elders. So far, the only sounds she heard were the echoes of their own footsteps and breathing. Nothing more. At least they were out of the rain.

The bloody substance began to dry on her skin, making it itch and feel rough. The rust smell associated with it turned her stomach, but she couldn't let that get to her either. She scratched at her hands, trying to flake some of it off as they wandered the cave.

Billy stopped abruptly in front of her, causing her to bump into his back.

"What is it?" she asked.

"Shhh." He held up a finger and turned his head toward an opening in the cave wall.

Once they were silent, Terra heard voices coming from the hole. It was big enough for them to get through, even if they had to duck. Once they got closer, however, she faltered. The voices were raised. Some shouting. Some pleading. And above it all, she made out one voice clearer than all the rest. Starla.

Her chest tightened with realization. She felt the color leave her face as she backed away from the opening.

"Terr?" Billy looked at her. "What are you doing? They need us."

She shook her head, her hands running over one another instinctively. "Starla has the elders trapped."

"Yes." He held out his hand for her. "That's why they need us. This is worse than we thought. What if she hurt one of them?"

Terra looked deep into Billy's eyes, seeing a depth in him that made her fear lessen. He was so much stronger than she realized. So much braver. How could she not have seen it all those years? Though she really wanted to turn and run, she reached for his hand instead. He smiled, and led her into the opening.

A scream traveled up the small tunnel, making her temperature plummet. As they progressed, Terra realized it was a ventilation shaft, not a place for walking. The only visible light was at the end, shining like the sun at mid-day. The aroma of sulfur increased to nauseating proportions as they continued. They both covered their noses.

Billy had to crawl to reach the opening, and Terra crawled up beside him. It was only a foot and a half wide, way too small for Billy to fit in and she knew it. Her heart raced, but she forced herself to look around the room.

The opening was roughly six feet off the ground. She made out several elders in their brown cloaks sitting on the floor in the corner, roughly thirty feet away. She didn't know all of them, but the one on the end eased her heart. It was Ursus. She kept looking, but didn't see Starla, or the rest of the elders.

"You need to go in there, Terr." Billy took her hand in his. "I'll head back and see if I can find another way in. I know they didn't get into there through here."

"Maybe I should come with you," she pled. "It's dangerous to be alone. Plus, I don't see Starla. And I can't account for at least twenty of the elders."

"Terr…" He eyed her. "I can't get in there or I would go."

"But my magic, it's not very good. How am I going to protect myself?"

"If it's not good, how did you win against Starla?"

Terra stopped breathing heavily and stared into his eyes. How had she beaten her? She knew her magic wasn't that strong, yet she'd won. She always had to work twice as hard as the others did, sometimes four times harder. Maybe her effort was the reason for her win, and if that were the case, then maybe her effort would help her defeat Starla now.

"Okay," she surrendered. "I'll go."

"Good." His grin was gentle. "If you can distract Starla, the elders might be able to regain control of the situation."

"How do you think they lost it to begin with?" she asked.

"I don't know. If Starla called on something darker, she may not be herself. Might be more powerful. Be careful."

Terra nodded, and slipped by Billy. He reached for her before she climbed through the hole. She turned back to face him.

"If we make it out of this, will you go to dinner with me?" His cheeks reddened, visible only by the light seeping from the other room.

"We go to dinner all the time, silly."

"I mean…" He hesitated. "As a date."

"Oh." She was silent for a moment, her heart racing as Billy made his feelings toward her known. "It's a date."

He smiled, and backed out of the way. Terra faced the opening again and shoved her way through. She tried to make a soft landing and have the element of surprise, but there was no silent dropping with the distance and the soggy shoes. She landed with a thud.

Ursus looked over and began coughing, as though trying to cover the sound of her in the room. There was a wall of rock between Terra and where she assumed the others were. A suspicion confirmed when Ursus's eyes shot back and forth between her and the other side of the wall.

Terra straightened, gathered her wits, unfastened her drenched cloak and tossed it aside, and headed for Starla. She wanted her movements to be as fast as possible. The closer she got to the rock wall separating them, the more her stomach turned. It took all her control not to lose her dinner.

Starla was around the corner; she could hear her talking to someone. There was a low growl coming between her words, and Terra suspected she'd called on something dark, as Billy had said. Would it even be wise to confront her? Especially now that she couldn't tell what she was up against?

Before she could talk herself out of helping, another scream came from around the corner. But this was no scream of fright. It was a death scream, a last breath of someone in excruciating pain. Lou? Thane? She couldn't place the voice. Terra wanted to jump around the corner, try to prevent Starla from doing any more harm, but Ursus shook his head.

He turned his gaze toward Starla again and fell forward. A sob of anguish escaped his lips as he appeared to be watching someone at Starla's feet.

Starla screamed at Ursus to sit up and pay attention, but he refused. Terra could feel Starla walking toward him, so she leaned against the side of the wall as far as she could to keep out of sight.

Something began burning inside her. She felt as though she would combust. The fire blazed through her veins, into each limb, every finger and toe, and finally, to her heart. She looked down at her hands, once covered in dried blood from the earlier rains, now glowing the likeness of lava.

Flame shot from her fingers as a force much stronger than her took over her body. Starla whipped around quickly, flashing something inside her as well, the light of the moon. Both powers equally as strong.

Starla jumped, the fear evident in her glowing blue eyes. Terra's glowed as well, but she knew hers glowed the color of flame. Her heart beat so fast she thought it would leap from her chest. She forced herself to approach Starla.

"What have you done?" Terra demanded, her gaze fierce.

"What have *you* done?" Starla shot back.

"Nothing. I didn't ask for this. You made this happen with your actions." The words came from her mouth, but Terra didn't feel like herself. Things were different. She was different. The blood of the mother had risen up inside her, and she was no longer the simple witch from town.

"This isn't my fault!" Starla yelled. It sounded like a tornado thrashing through a forest. Terra heard trees uprooting themselves at her shout, snapping and breaking like mere twigs.

Terra didn't want to have that same reaction, as she wasn't altogether sure what abilities she had. So she kept her voice calm. "Let the elders go."

"Excuse me?" Starla's eyes shone brighter, her rage visible through her glow.

"Let. Them. Go."

"You bitch! How dare you demand anything of me? If it weren't for you, I'd have the position with the elders! I'd have Billy! But no! You always take everything from me! You think I'm going to let the elders go? Think again!" Starla's chest radiated with fury, sending sparks of acidic water toward Terra, but Terra didn't back away.

The acid rain bounced off Terra's own glowing chest. Hers was the color of flame, and as the water hit it, it evaporated before a single burn took place. This enraged Starla even further, and she screamed again. The surrounding rockery let off a crack as it tore open, shaking with the violence of an earthquake. But Terra compensated. Soon, the rock heated to thousands of degrees and sealed shut again. Starla cursed.

"Damn you!" She paced the area, distracted by her attempts to overpower Terra, and that seemed to be all the elders needed to regain their strength. They stood, one by one, and clasped hands together. Lou stood with Rina—Billy's mentor—and Ursus joined in at the end.

Terra walked closer to the elders. Starla was still pacing, the only thing separating Terra from the elders. From behind, she saw Billy coming through another entrance. His eyes lit up the moment he saw her. She must have been impressive.

She tried to suppress her smile. It would only make Starla angrier. She tried to distract Starla as the others surrounded her. Billy clasped hands with the elders.

"Did you really think we'd let you get away with this, Starla?" Terra kept her voice steady.

"You can't stop me from doing anything, bitch!"

"Are you sure?" Terra countered. She saw the elders and Billy chanting something silently behind Starla. The more they chanted, the less Starla glowed. Soon, she was a simple blonde with tangled hair and pale skin.

Starla looked down at her hands, realizing she no longer had the power she had wielded moments ago. Her face filled with color.

"How dare you?" She screamed again, but the elders rushed her and bound her arms. They pulled her from the cave room as more elders gathered the lifeless bodies of their fallen. Among the three deceased lay Ner, Starla's mentor. His eyes were still open, empty.

Billy approached Terra. "I need you to calm down. I can't touch you like this."

"I don't know how," she admitted. "I don't even know how this happened."

Billy smiled, his eyes wandering to the sleeve he had stitched Starla's hair into.

"You did this to me?" Terra's mouth fell open.

"No," he chuckled. "I don't have that kind of power. I merely made way for you to open your own abilities. I'm in training to assist the elders with new recruits. My ability is to help unlock those of others."

"Oh," she said. "How do I turn it off, then? So I don't burn anyone?"

"Just calm down. It will fade on its own. Why don't we go outside? The rain has stopped, I'm sure. And it's almost morning."

"Lead the way." Terra let Billy walk first. Allowing herself plenty of space so she would not get too close and set him ablaze.

By the time they reached the edge of the cave, Terra felt much calmer. She walked outside to see the sun just peeking over the horizon. The remnants of blood rain had all washed away, leaving the natural hues of green and brown to fill her sight.

Birds had returned to their homes, singing the song of the forest. A fresh breeze passed her nose, and she took in all the smells of the area. Moss, dirt, damp feathers, oily fur of a nearby black bear, and each scent carried with it awareness.

Terra looked down at her hands, and they were fading to their natural shade again. The entire forest was alive inside her. Beating like a drum along with her heart.

"Billy, what's happening?"

He rubbed her hand. "You have a different magic than others, Terra. You carry a bit of the mother inside you. I've known since childhood, but you had to reach this state on your own."

"You could have hinted, at least." She eyed him.

"I did." He laughed, and it warmed her heart. "But you're much more stubborn than the typical person. You just kept repeating how you aren't very powerful."

"And I'm not," she corrected.

"That's why only *you* can carry the blood of the mother in you. You're humble. Just as she is. Though you both can pack quite the punch when you want to."

"Huh…" was all Terra managed.

"Come on," he urged, taking her arm in his. "It's morning, and I'm hungry. I know you promised me dinner, but I think breakfast will serve us better."

"Then breakfast it is." Terra felt her heart flutter like the wings of a hummingbird as she walked the trail with him. She had changed, beyond going back, and her new awareness brought with it a comfort that trifled any fear of dating him. This time, she held him just as confidently as he held her.

DRESSES OF FUR
AND FANGS
BY REBECCA FUNG

I tried the conjuring one more time. I waved my hand, but the dark puff of smoke that eventuated was a lame, weak ball and nothing appeared as the cloud began to dissipate. Agatha looked at me, almost embarrassed for me, and waved her hand to perform the conjuring perfectly, pulling a djinni from the crack of the dark world with ease. Even Bethilda, who wasn't exactly what you'd call a bright witch, managed to get it right and pulled out a minor djinni with some effort.

I sighed and watched a red cross go against my name. Again.

"Francesca!" said Professor Brewhaha, as I tried to escape from class. "You'll have to practice at home. I expect you to concentrate and be able to get that exercise correct for next lesson. You'll fall behind at this rate. And I *know* you don't want that." Professor Brewhaha taught Psychic Powers as well as Conjurings. There was no point in arguing.

"You could start by thinking less about the wart on your hand while you're conjuring, and more about the conjuring itself," she went on icily. "Haven't we gone through this? Lesson one: focus. Lesson two: focus *correctly*. Your obsession is becoming dangerous. It's not just potentially putting you back a class. If your focus is on your hand instead of on the djinni you were supposed to be pulling, you might accidentally conjure off your own hand. Can you remember the official emergency wizardry procedure that would be needed in such an event?"

I sighed. Another quiz. "Four fully qualified emergency wizards, and back-up staff, plus carriage to the Wizardry Medical Treatment Centre for full examination whether hand is recovered or not. Each wizard and staff member charges by the minute."

"Exactly, and the fees are getting higher and higher each month," said Professor Brewhaha. "I often think I should have chosen health over education. Some of those staff charge for just turning up and standing about doing nothing. Your insurance doesn't fully cover this. So we don't encourage young girls to conjure their hands off, do you hear me? Not to mention it becomes quite impractical in later stages of witching if the hand cannot be retrieved. Now go." Her face softened for a moment. "Francesca, you had quite good grades in your past years. You were one of the better students in class. I hate to see someone as soft in the head as Bethilda get ahead of you. I know you could do well if you tried."

That's what they always tell you, teachers, oh, it's only a matter of trying. Just try, Francesca. As if I hadn't been trying. As if this burden was theirs to carry alone. Do you think I liked being shown up in class by someone like Bethilda? But I couldn't help it. Professor Brewhaha was right. I was obsessing over my wart.

Oh no. Oh no. I can see where this story is going. Witch fails at conjurings. She's not as good as the other witches at the school. She gets told off by her teacher. She needs to change her life.

Maybe, you're thinking, Francesca (that's me, if you haven't been paying attention) is going to meet a handsome wizard or soulful vampire type, or maybe both and dither dather about which one is really her type while they lust after her pathetically, and then she gets to rub it into Bethilda and Agatha's faces and who cares about conjuring—well, unfortunately that's not this story. It's not the story where Francesca finds out that she's no good at conjuring but she's really good at being good at making things like little pink heart-shaped flowers and is really an angel not a witch. Nup. I've got those stories. I don't want to re-tell them. Those, and every other story where the witch starts off failing at conjuring. The one where the witch is an orphan, the witch finds her true calling among dragons, the witch goes on to save the world, the witch has a whole series devoted to just being kind of jolly and fun, the witch travels backwards in time… It's a whole genre in the witch's library and my autobiography is joining it just because of my opening lines.

I knew I should have started my story in a different place. There isn't a genre for "Witch starts day eating her toadstool extra-fiber cereal". I could have been original just by starting there.

I was already annoyed with myself. I'd crapped up a conjuring, and I'd slipped dangerously into a witching cliché. My books started to slip from my arms, and I tried to catch them but the more I tried, the more they slipped and eventually the whole lot ended up on the floor. I cursed and started to pick them up. I examined my hand. It seemed the big wart on my right hand had got larger and darker red, or was it just my imagination? I'd have to do something about it. Both the wart *and* my imagination.

I knew what Professor Brewhaha said about conjuring off my hand, but surely, I thought, there could be some way to conjure off a wart. I walked home from school, turning my hand over and back and staring. I kept bumping into things and walking in the wrong direction but I didn't care, or at least, I couldn't help myself, and I was thinking so much about my hand that I hardly noticed as my head hit a few random trees on the way back home. The wart was like a huge red star—no, a huge red planet. It had gravity. It pulled my eyes in and made them stay and circle it. I couldn't help it, and I couldn't stop it. The wart on my hand was getting so large and fiery I could swear you could see it through the other side of my hand. I could feel it with my eyes and I hated it. Professor Brewhaha called me obsessive and Mum called me vain.

Oops, it looked like that was Mum now. I stuck my hand behind my back. The last thing I needed was another tussle with Mum.

"Francesca!" called Mum. Suddenly she appeared in front of me. I hate it when she does that. I think people should give notice when they're going to appear that close to you, but Mum doesn't obey such rules of etiquette, at least not around me. She was wearing a wide smile which faded as she looked me up and down.

"Francesca, have you been worrying about that wart again?"

Damnation.

Mum doesn't have the psychic powers of Professor Brewhaha but she notices everything. And this time she was staring at my school uniform.

"Uniforms aren't cheap, Francesca. What have you been doing in that one? Bumping into trees—too busy worrying about your wart and not where you're going?"

"I hate my wart!" I burst out.

"There's nothing wrong with a wart," said Mum. "I have eleven of them. And there's nothing wrong with me—quite the opposite, in fact! I don't know where you get some of your strange ideas, but it's not from my gene pool."

Mum does indeed have eleven warts and what's more, she's cultivating another one on her nose. She even belongs to a society called Warts and All, dedicated to the preservation and celebration of warts. They have a newsletter with large wart photographs on celebrities and how to make cupcakes shaped as warts.

"Mum," I explained, "warts are ugly."

"Francesca," she said, "you are vain. Don't tell me you idolize one of those namby-pamby perfect princess types. Please don't. I've tried to bring you up with worthwhile witching values. Don't break my heart. You're a witch, an ugly witch, love it, embrace it. Who would want to be one of those wilting princess petals whose only power is to ponce about prettily at fancy dress balls catching princes? Your powers are so much better! Do not say you want to be a princess instead of a witch!"

"I like my powers. I want to be a witch. I *am* a witch," I said. Mum looked relieved. There were some witches who were closet princess-types; they struggled with it all through puberty and when they realized they couldn't help being attracted to the wrong types (princes, not ghouls/wizards/vampires) they usually had to be exiled, before they went crazy. "I just don't like my looks," I added.

"Witching and bad looks go together," said Mum.

"I don't see why they should."

"Don't argue," said Mum. Then she vanished and reappeared by her cauldron in the next room.

I envied Mum. I sat on the couch nibbling dried frogs' legs. Mum was brewing a dark potion, a Havoc-Wreaker for her girls' club tonight. This was one of the newer recipes she wanted to show off. She had a hobbled left foot and a disfigured eye and one of her arms was significantly fatter than the other, and her nose was all crooked and warty. But these things never bothered her. She was still amazingly social; she belonged to so many clubs and she genuinely enjoyed life. They never seemed to bother anyone, except me. Why did they bother me?

There was something wrong with me. I woke up one day and I wanted my face to be symmetrical. Nobody around me had a symmetrical face, though; if a baby witch had a symmetrical face you hit her hard to make sure she got a scar or a deformity so she looked a bit twisted like everyone else. Otherwise she'd be teased. Is that weird, that I wanted the kind of face that other people would tease me for?

I looked around at the photographs in the room. There was Mum and me, on my first day at school, and there was another of my grandmother. There was the school photo, too, warts and wrinkles on us all, and Professor Brewhaha with her rough flyaway hair. Crooked faces, hunched backs, gnarled fingers, uneven limbs, dark features. "I love your greasy skin and your crooked nose, Francesca," Mum would say. "It's true witchiness." For the most of my life I thought so too. Why wouldn't I? Every witch around me looked similar. Agatha, and Cressida and even dumpy old Bethilda, all my best friends growing up.

The magazines we subscribed to as teenage witches hadn't given me any of my strange ideas. If anything, they had reinforced—or tried to—my mother's values. I had a stack of them, with bright ghoulish headlines in luminescent green or metallic gold on black or a red font like dripping blood on dark brown.

How to Get More Warts Than Your Girlfriend, The Biggest Scar You've Ever Seen, More Wrinkles More Love, The Best Cream Guaranteed to Give You Acne, Twist Your Nose Right Out of Shape, Thickest Eyebrows Ever!!!, Short, Dark, Flat, Flatulent and Fabulous…

Then why didn't I feel fabulous reading these, and noting my warts and wrinkles? Instead, I felt there was something out of place.

I felt a curious disconnect while flicking through these magazines. All my teachers told us of how these magazines risked making us just want to follow the crowd. Somehow, though, I had no desire to follow the crowd. What's more, I could not see any approval from my teachers at my daring to resist peer pressure.

Once, I had started to collect some herbs by moonlight. I had always enjoyed picking out herbs—I liked the smell of them, and being able to apprehend the brews and potions I'd mix with them. I was leaning over to pick a bunch of deadly nightshade when I became aware of how the moonlight hit its leaves.

It was truly beautiful. The light separated the leaves and speckled them and made a symmetrical pattern. I looked up at the round full moon hanging there in the sky, and I remembered thinking about the moon and the deadly nightshade, and how the evenness of the light, the perfection of the roundness of the moon, was what made them so captivating. The crookedness in my mother's face, in the faces of my friends, was so ordinary compared to the elegance of these objects.

I wanted to be like that, have smooth sides that captivated, to have curves worked in harmony with the conjurings I performed, not gnarled knuckles that jerked spasmodically over my brews to find their way to the dark side. But the more I thought about it, all that happened was I found it more difficult to connect with the dark side at all.

I let Mum continue her chanting and brewing, and I sneaked out to my witch's studio. It was a small hut a little way from the rest of the house, where Mum wasn't easily disturbed by my wild singing and chanting or the odors of what she politely called "your little experiments". I would take care of my wart.

I didn't know much about this sort of conjuring. My grades had not been bad in dark spells, though, until I'd started failing dismally more recently. Professor Brewhaha said it mainly had to do with focus. Well, if there was one thing I knew how to focus on, it was my wart, so that should not be too big a problem here.

I could practice and experiment all I liked in my studio; at least Mum believed in my own space. I pulled out my textbook and started to line up the ingredients for the conjuring. It didn't look too difficult; though I'd never worked with dried gilkinroot, I'd seen Mum do it heaps of times. I began to chop and boil. Professor Brewhaha always said the smell of a brew was important to a good conjuring, though I wasn't sure what I was smelling for here. It smelled comfortingly old with a hint of sweetness in it. I boiled and boiled, and the brew looked clean and bubbled neatly.

All right, now for the conjuring. I concentrated on the brew and began to hum and chant. I positioned my hand over the cauldron, and I could feel a tingling. That was a good sign, I hoped—wasn't something supposed to be happening to my hand? My voice grew more confident as I said the words louder and my hand moved rhythmically over the cauldron. What exactly was supposed to happen? The suspense was killing me. Should I keep going or adjust the brew?

Professor Brewhaha said it was a bad idea to adjust mid-conjure unless you were absolutely sure that an adjustment needed to be made. You should always aim to get the mixture perfect to begin with so you didn't have to, so you didn't disrupt the chanting part. An unnecessary disruption could do far more harm than good to a conjuring, no matter how virtuous the intentions.

"You will be tempted to tweak. Don't," she told us.

I tried to push away the temptation.

I kept rotating my right hand over the brew, watching my wart with fascination. The orange-colored steam from the brew was shrouding my hand and making my wart look angrier and larger and suddenly I thought it might burst altogether.

That wasn't my wart. That popping sound, that sound of the explosion was the sound of my hand—a sudden, cracking sound, and I was thrown backwards, my hand went flying into the air—did it detach itself from me? I can only remember seeing a flash of light and a vision of my outstretched fingers in the air.

Then I felt the dull thud of my head on the floor, and I heard no more and thought no more. I felt and saw only blackness.

$$\mathbb{W}$$

"You stupid, stupid girl!"

That was Professor Brewhaha and Mum, interchangeably. They took turns calling me a moron. That was what I woke up to.

When I opened my eyes I was in the shiny Wizardry Medical Treatment Centre, Emergency Wing, the place all witches avoid as much as possible but have an odd fascination with, given so few of us end up here. I felt bad for being there but I couldn't help wanting to look around as much as possible. It was an extremely bright white place and every wall was stocked with every potion imaginable, and boxes of mysterious things I couldn't imagine. There were little silver scalpels and wands of varying sizes cut from different woods and pendants of various metals hanging from little stands. There were piles of little towelettes, all neatly embroidered, and two trained cats watching me. There was also, I found out later, a camera shaped as a cat, sending the information off to a pool of interns who recorded my every movement.

It must cost a fortune if every room was like this. No wonder we were discouraged from ending up here.

Mum appeared by my side, right next to my ear. "The basic emergency procedure itself will already cost a fortune, not to mention ongoing costs and higher insurance premiums," she moaned. "How could you be so idiotic—administering a cosmetic surgery to yourself! A wart-blaster conjure—you fool! Especially on a wart that size."

"Have I lost my hand?" I asked weakly. It was all I could think about. The image of my hand and the blast of light a second before I'd been knocked out.

"There! Vanity again," said Professor Brewhaha. "She never learns. All she thinks about is whether or not she'll be symmetrical!"

"That's not fair!" I burst out. "You said yourself that a witch without a hand wasn't much use."

I just wanted my hand so I can do all the things every girl does—like conjure and brush my teeth. Why did Professor Brewhaha and Mum insist on thinking the worst of me? But I had to admit, deep in the recesses of my mind, when I thought of myself without my hand, without my arm—with only a *stump*—I grimaced. I looked grotesque. Maybe there was more vanity in it than I liked to believe. I caught Professor Brewhaha looking at me. Damned Psychic Powers.

I was fortunate, though. My hand was still there, though it felt flimsy and weak.

"You gave it a real knock and blast," said the Wizard Doctor. "We're going to recommend you stay here for two weeks for observation and rehabilitation. That is, unless you want to lose it." I could almost hear her adding up the fees and charges by the minute as she said that, but she had so much authority no one dared challenge her.

Mum berated me. But there was nothing else to be done; I couldn't go armless. Mum sniped about missing her girls' club and not getting to show off her Havoc-Wreaker, and she appeared and disappeared around the room pettily, but I could sense some relief when she confirmed with the Wizard Doctor that I would be fine. Professor Brewhaha poured scorn on me and called me some fairly choice names. I tried calling some back but I was tired. Hers were better.

Agatha, Bethilda and Cressida sent me a large bunch of poisonous fungi and Davina sent me a singing toad message. Evita baked me some rat's eye biscuits; they were a bit on the dry side, but then none of us were great at bakery. Still, I guess it was nice of them, though after a time I started to grow skeptical of the presents I received. Getting them reminded me, though, that they were probably all wondering why on Earth I was here in the first place. Professor Brewhaha no doubt forced them to send me things. She was probably even grading them on the appropriateness of their gifts; I could imagine her stalking the classes saying, "You must all send Francesca a gift and what are appropriate tokens when a person is ill? I *know* you don't want to send the incorrect symbol!"

Still, it's not to say it wasn't nice of them, but I could feel their bemusement. I'm sure none of them would be caught dead or alive trying to blast a wart off their hand. Their sympathy felt fake. They had no idea what I was feeling.

The Wizardry Medical Expert was Dr. Potenbility. She didn't get it either. She looked slightly bemused when she read my chart; she opened her mouth to ask why I tried to blast a wart off my hand—and then changed her mind. She was there to make sure I didn't lose the hand, not to worry about the vagaries of my mind. So she chirped pleasantries and wrapped the bandages dipped in potions around my hand, warned me not to make any sudden movements.

"Rest up and you'll be conjuring and flying and everything just like all the other girls, in no time," she said.

But I couldn't explain to her why I did it, either.

For the most part of the day, though, I was left alone. Dr. Potenbility had other patients to see and a thesis on stinging symptoms in right nostrils of babies caused by full moons to finish, otherwise they'd cut off funding to the medical centre. I couldn't conjure, I couldn't write, and I was getting sick of the back issues of *Coven* and *Wily Witch Weekly* they had there. I'd stared at the same pictures over a million times.

I spent a lot of time staring out the window instead, to pass the time. I tried to clear my head and think. I couldn't explain what I did to anyone else. Could I explain it to myself? If I could only sort out, in my own head, what I wanted, then maybe I would feel better.

I knew I hated my wart, there was no doubt of that, but it wasn't just the wart. And yet I didn't hate being a witch, or at least I didn't think I did. I loved collecting herbs at night. I still wanted to conjure. Did I have to do that with warts?

My room faced what looked like a garden, or at least some grass and then some trees, and some bushes and flowers. There was a pile of old rocks

and what looked like an abandoned bit of wooden rubbish—a piece of furniture that had been dismantled beyond the point of recognition, just some
planks and some nails and pieces, with bits of moss growing on it. I never
saw anyone else there, though, so maybe it wasn't your usual kind of garden.
Not any humans, anyway.

There was a line of beetles and one of ants that marched steadily up one
of the rocks all day. Every so often a small bird swooped in and swooped out
of the garden. But the inhabitants I watched the most were the dogs.

I had no idea where the dogs came from, but they prowled in the garden by late afternoon and took it by dusk, and had disappeared by morning each day. There was a pack of them, ranging from dark to a brilliant
golden-brown. It was the bright golden-brown one who caught my eye. Her
coat positively shimmered as she moved. She was a lean bitch, she walked
proudly, exalting in each movement her athletic body made and the way her
muscles rippled and her golden fur showed herself off to perfection among
her peers.

The other dogs were nice to look at, but she was clearly the queen
among them.

I fell in love.

I watched the dogs, hypnotized by their movements as they came to
the garden at dusk. They did not just walk in, four legs marching. Their
legs carried their torsos which almost swam as they moved; one side of the
dog seemed to ripple easily and then the other, a sexy shimmy, in harmony
with nature. Then the queen of the dogs leaped into the air, and I watched
that gorgeous body curve and arch, and then she landed neatly on the other
side of the boulder. Her tail wagged carelessly, signalling her disdain, and
the other dogs began to leap as she did. Her body was poetry with the
air around her, she sliced through it so easily and landed softly, without a
quiver.

How could I explain this to my mother? I did not want to be "pretty"
with all the sneer-worthy connotations it carried. I had every intention of
being the fully evil witch I had trained to be. But I was distracted with my
poor body, and its stupid warts. I wanted something I could feel proud of.

Just like these dogs, and their bodies which worked so perfectly with their environment.

That was what I wanted. It was not about having a princess outfit. I did not care for dresses of pink ruffles and lace petticoats or billowed skirts and bows. But I wanted a body like this dog's I could be proud of—sleek, fitting, showing off each of my muscles to its greatest advantage, slicing through the air and ambling through the cool dark night. I wanted a dress of fur and fangs.

I watched the bitch every day. *I'll have it*, I thought. *I'll have that dress.* I'm sure no ugly stepmother or wicked witch in history obsessed over magical slippers or rings or tiaras nearly as much as I obsessed over that bitch. But the decision was as simple and selfish as any fairy story. I saw it and I decided I would take it for my own because I wanted it, and I gave no heed to who got in the way.

No worthwhile witch would.

At each meal, I examined the implements needed. A knife, that was what I wanted, but those I was given to eat my meals with were hardly the right sort. A knife to smear jam was not a knife that I could seriously take dog-hunting. It was risky, but I needed a real knife. I eventually resorted to Freezing in Time everyone in the Wizardry Medical Centre for thirty minutes while I dashed out and bought one across the road, and hoped nobody said a word to my mother, and that the Time-Freezing spell didn't wear off early.

It was crude, but once I had that large, sharp knife in my bedside table, I felt safe. The bitch would be mine. She was not escaping now.

I needed to lure the dog closer to home, so I had somewhere I could make the dress of fur and fangs in relative peace. I knew it would not be made quickly or easily—needlework wasn't my top subject. I even found embroidering a handkerchief laborious. If I could have done this without stitching, I would have. But I swallowed and accepted that it was for the greater good.

I just needed to get out of here. It came fairly soon. Dr. Potenbility got sick of me, and presumably the Wizardry Medical Treatment Centre had squeezed enough money out of my condition. I was released.

I managed to convince Mum to let me travel home by myself—it would give her more time with her girls' club and a breath of fresh air would only do me good. As I walked back home, I sang. I sang the song to keep the dog after me.

I did not try being too experimental. It was an old-fashioned song and I sang it in the old tongue, and did not bother with attempting to modify or modernize it much. The dog followed me. Her beautiful body padded after me as I walked home.

Then I turned around. I wanted to see her just a little more in action, before she died. I brought the pitch of my voice higher, and the dog lurched and sprang high in the air, and I took in the arch of her torso as she did and shivered. I tried it several times more, and then I knew it was time to stop. I moved in.

I took the bitch. She looked up at me with those soft, weepy eyes, pleading with me. How very beautiful it would be to have such eyes, a perfect nut-brown, nothing like the empty black pools I had now! I made a mental note to keep the eyes too.

Then I plunged the knife in.

Sometimes, there is no way better than the old-fashioned way. A magic charm, a spell, a song of elves which would freeze her, a murmuring of trolls which would have exploded her—it was not that I did not know how to control a dog without the trusty silver blade. But each would have ruined her fur, or taken the genuine emotion from those perfect brown eyes. And I was determined to take her as I had seen her, in her true canine glory. She would be mine.

The dog howled and the body squirted blood. The blood was all over my hands now, and I was sitting there, soaked in the smell of dog's blood pouring from this body.

But I loved it. I loved the strong odor of dog. And oh, this dog!

The dog's body was still panting and yelping, and I could feel the last essence of dog draining out of her. I was attuned to sensing the souls of dead things; it was a class I'd always excelled in at school. Now as the dog escaped its body, I recited the ancient words of the spell quickly to enslave it, and chose a viscous, burnt orange liquid to keep the soul entrapped in. It wouldn't have to face the indignity of being forced to take on the form of a being that was ugly. It bubbled away gorgeously in its vial and I turned my attention to the cadaver.

The dog's gorgeous golden-brown body was slumped in my arms, sodden with blood. She would need cleaning, but even soaked and splattered as she was, I pondered the sleek beauty of her dress. Some creatures were so fortunate. They were born to good looks and grace. I was not, but I knew how to take them for my own.

The fur was still warm against my skin and it made me feel alive and happy. I sank my face into the wetness of her hair and inhaled. Then I picked up the body—she was still heavy, but I managed—and carried her back to my little witch's studio nearby.

Now for the skinning. I checked that my knife was perfectly sharp and I slit the dog right down the middle of the back. Then I slipped in my knife and began to skin her.

It was not easy to get a dog's skin off whole, or close to whole. I'd never had any experience skinning an animal. My knife needed to be sharp, that's what I had read, to get under the skin and separate it from the flesh cleanly, or as cleanly as possible, but it's certainly not easy. It's not like peeling a banana or even pulling the skin of an orange. The skin was tough to pull off but so easy to pierce—I was wary of that each moment. I didn't dare move my knife too quickly.

I didn't want to have to find another dog. This girl was perfect.

Every moment I stayed there, pushing my knife in deeper and trying to cut the skin away without damaging it, more blood flowed out like a river. I sat in a pool of redness, but I didn't mind that. The blood made me feel closer to her, like I knew her already. She was part of me, because that bit of her blood was being soaked into my pores and was running down my face. There was a trickle in my nostril and a bit of dog's blood flowed into the side of my mouth. I sucked it in. It was very sweet. I wondered what they ate that kept it like that.

It took a long time and a lot of concentration, but I managed to pull the skin away. The dog underneath, the red and pink flesh of her, with the bones sticking out in places, was to be discarded. It was ugly; I had no use for ugliness. It was the gorgeousness of the fur I came here for.

The fur was heavier than I thought it would be. It's amazing how dogs carry this around all day and still manage to stride and leap as gracefully as they do. I held this one up, my arms straining. *I'll get used to it.* I was rather proud of my handiwork. I'd had to slit the coat of the dog in several places to pull it off, but I kept the slits to a minimum to preserve the fur. It wasn't bad for a first go and it was all in one piece, even the head which was still dangling off one end, and the tail at the other.

Now the rough work was over. Now to make her shine.

I put the coat in a large tub of cold water and watched the blood swirl. There's a simple trick almost every woman knows, witch or non-witch. Never soak blood-stained material in hot water, not if you want it to run free. Hot water keeps the blood in; cold water washes it out. The cold water was doing its work as I mopped the floors and changed my smock. I know it doesn't seem witch-like, wielding a mop or throwing dog entrails out the window. People like to think of us brewing herbs and flying around on our broomsticks, not using them to brush up bloodied remnants from the floor.

That's what every witch loves about her job—the brewing, the chanting, and most of all, the plucking of something dark from between the real and unreal. But sometimes it's not all fun. Sometimes it's a hard slog, sometimes work is boring. The Reality of Witching They Never Tell You. Sometimes there's boring administrative stuff you have to do. Sometimes there's other boring stuff. Like now.

It took six soaks in the tub to get the coat the way I wanted it. Each time the water would get to a dark reddish brown, so dark with dirt and blood it was useless to ask it to soak up any more, so I'd throw the water out the window and start again, scrubbing the fur and watching the water fill with redness. It was amazing, how much blood and dirt one dog's coat could hold. But each wash paid off. The blood washed away and the golden brown I had so admired in this dog began to shine through. The hair remained as fine and soft and smooth as she had felt the first time I had petted her. The first time I had fallen for her looks.

When the fur was golden-brown, I dried it out. I hung it up in the moonlight and tried to sleep. Whenever I looked outside, I could see it twinkling at me in the moonlight. The bitch's head hung from the sheet of fur and smiled at me. She wanted me to be beautiful, and I would be. I promised myself that. I'd come so far. With just a bit of work, I thought, with just a little bit of work, this one would be mine.

When the fur was dried out, I took out a needle and a strong ball of thread. Thank goodness for those classes with Miss Cottonpick, who had forced us to mend all the tears in our uniforms. No one, including myself, enjoyed sewing class—it didn't have the breezy fun of Flying or the enchanting mystery of Spells and Brews. But as I had never envisaged it, it was actually coming in handy.

I got stitching.

It might seem that there was no brains to it—simply stitching the dog up along the lines I'd slit her. But sewing her back up, I wanted something different.

Now that I'd thrown out her bones and flesh, I wanted to be able to be sewn inside. I wanted to make myself my own dog dress.

Not, I emphasize, some shawl or cape made of dog fur, following the latest in witches' fashion, which meant shapeless, unflattering garb in a cut several centuries old. I could get any number of those I wanted.

I lifted my hand and stitched, thinking of the dog as it leaped across the field, its lean sleek body shown off in the moonlight, the legs accentuating each of the curves and muscles being used to its utmost strength.

That's what I wanted. I stuck in the needle. I was pretty sure I knew what to do. I pulled the thread after it. Over and over again. This was nothing like Spells and Brews. What do they say about an evil which must be done? This wasn't even an evil. It was too stinking boring to be an evil.

If you have an idea of some sweet little girly witch, or a cone-shaped black hat, or green skin or something—sitting by the night window, doing her embroidery, delicately sewing invisible little stitches—well, you've got it completely wrong. The reality was far from it. And they say I'm the deluded, romantic one.

My hands were still rubbed raw and rough from the night's work in luring and snaring the dog, and the stink of blood hadn't left my skin. My hair was as knotty and coarse as the mops in the corner which were becoming rougher and more brittle with drying canine blood. No holding a needle between forefinger and thumb: this was serious work. Sometimes I felt as if I was sweating, dragging a huge, heavy log after me in a chain gang. Sometimes I felt as if I was doing battle, launching a massive steel rod as an army against the enemy and barely making a dent through its walls. Sometimes I pierced its battalions, then I went crazy with excitement, almost dropping the sharpened weapon. Oh dog, oh skin, I had to drag that needle every day after me! Sometimes I would manage to point that needle at the right place in the fur skin and give it a good, hard hit and push it through, and I could feel the little scars and bruises developing on my hand. I wanted to cry—scars to go with my horrible wart! But I gritted my teeth. Sometimes you had to make sacrifices. When I thought of my dress, when I thought of its possibilities, I knew it was all worth it.

I slipped my arms into the dog dress, and it felt as if it was molding itself to me. That was just one arm—I hadn't even got the rest of the dress on. The sense was uncanny. I started to put the rest of the dress on and pulled on a few, heavy stitches. I could feel the dress start to mold itself to me, the insides of the dog frame adjusting themselves against my body. I tried to remember where I might have learned something about this, my mind searched frantically for names or anything to do with bodies or costumes or molding themselves—but I couldn't remember a thing.

Breathe, that's what. That's one thing to do when you're panicking. I tried to force myself to stop, and I began to enjoy it. I could concentrate on the feeling right down to the ends of my arms and the tops of my thighs, as the dress fitted itself to me perfectly, not too tightly, but made itself part of me and an asset to each movement I made. I could feel, as it began to flow around me, the power surging into my bones. I thought of the legs of the dog, and I could feel my legs becoming those elegant hound legs.

The dress is becoming me. I'm one with the dress.

I'm the dog. I'm that bitch. That beautiful, beautiful bitch.

It was one thing to have the dog's body covering my arms, legs and shoulders, but then there was the head. I picked up the dog's skull I had so neatly carved off. Her dark brown eyes were still in place and they held the gentle glow I had always admired so. Her cheekbones were so well-defined and I stroked her ears.

I'd always wanted brown eyes.

I cleared out the inside of the skull so I could slip my head inside. It was dark, but not uncomfortable. With glue, my knife and a few more stitches, I cleared a passageway to breathe through the nose and mouth, and I retained the glowing brown eyes. I could see my way through the nostrils. I tried to peep through the eyeballs, and just as the dress had molded itself to my arms and legs, I was dimly able to see through the dog's eyeballs, though the world took on a strange, tan color I wasn't used to. I could feel the eyeballs become mine—I could even feel them lose some of that gentleness and take on the hardness that defined my workings throughout the night.

They were truly me.

I gave out a low growl, and then a roar, and then I leaped in the air myself. I could feel my legs curve out and my arms move into position instinctively.

The world around me glowed a light golden-brown, and I sniffed the air. I picked up the vial of orange, viscous fluid. *I'm over here and you're in there*, I thought triumphantly. I raised a paw to my eye level. Covered in the little glove of the dress, there was no wart to be seen. This was what I lived for. And I was going to make the most of it.

I sashayed forth, enjoying the way I moved in my new dress. *Let's pay some visits.*

The night air flew by my coat and whistled by my ears.

"A doggie!" cried some small children, and I heard one of them laugh. I walked up to them and bowed my head to let them pat me. They each grew trusting of the dress of fur and fangs, and then I looked up.

The spells came easily to me. I felt confident in this body, there was no fumbling in a conjuring, no lack of focus. The first child froze to the spot and her skin turned to stone. She began to crumble away. I casually turned to the second, and a nest of giant wasps descended on him and attacked each part of his body. With the third, large boils started to emerge all over his skin and he began to scream in pain.

This was almost too easy. I leaped, and looked elsewhere in search of finer prey.

A fat man on the street burst into flames as I waved my paw. An old lady befriended me in the park and murmured how much she loved me as I whispered a dark enchantment on the loaves of bread in her shopping bag which would curse every female in her family with disappointment and sorrow for years to come.

As I completed each black charm, I smiled, and I felt the power surge through my veins.

The world was glowing golden-brown, and I felt on fire. What couldn't I do in a dress like this? I cackled. I would have to show Professor Brewhaha. She'd appreciate a demonstration. She deserved a demonstration. I should let her know that I could figure out my looks—and that I didn't need to be as ugly as she was. I already could feel I was one hell of a witch.

I went to pay Professor Brewhaha a visit. Her house is a fortress, all nettles and thorns, and no student has ever got up to the threshold, not even close, before. It's one of her sources of pride. I don't know if any human being has, except Professor Brewhaha, and she doesn't really count. But I didn't worry. In my dog-suit, that was no problem at all. Everyone was embracing me, and my weapon was the trust I invariably created. Why should Professor Brewhaha be any different?

I hung back and waited for the Professor to come out.

"What an interesting creature," she said, observing me, and she crooked her finger, allowing me past the walls into her property. She scratched my head, and then after a while she led me past the next set of barriers, and then got to digging up some roots from around her home.

I looked around. There were still further, rather nasty-looking barriers to go, and I wasn't sure how much more till we reached her home itself. But I wanted nothing less than where she ate and slept and brewed her potions.

I'd have to be patient. I wasn't exactly sure what I was going to do, but I sure wasn't going to do a thing till we had got within the threshold of the divine sanctity of her home. I'd show Professor Brewhaha I could do that much.

Then Professor Brewhaha twitched.

"What was that?" she asked aloud. She turned to me. "Was that you? I recognize… no, I must be wrong. Or…" Her brow wrinkled. I knew that look. I'd forgotten about the Psychic Powers. Was I leaking something? Could she recognize me? Now that I was thinking of her recognizing me, was I giving myself away all the more?

How could I ensure that the only signal she received from me was "dog"?

I felt for the vial in the fold of my fur dress. The burnt orange viscous liquid glared at me. *Go on*, it said. *I dare you.*

What happened if you swallowed the soul of a dog?

I watched as Professor Brewhaha began to look at me more carefully. If she suspected something wrong, would she simply release me and let me walk away, or would she be as merciless as I had been to the children? I had made it this far on to her property. It wasn't something either of us would take lightly.

What happened if you did not swallow?

I made my decision.

I turned aside and in a quick, swift motion, I downed the orange liquid. It began to burn inside of me, and the golden-brown glare I had on the world grew brighter and stronger, as the perspective of the dog burnt into my own.

I could feel something in me erupt, and I gave a little jump, in celebration of the arrival of a new persona.

I gave a low growl, and I could feel my belly roaring. I looked up at Professor Brewhaha and I saw someone with whom I had no connections, someone whose land I was on and who was staring at me suspiciously.

And I didn't like being looked at like a criminal. So I leaped forward.

Professor Brewhaha screamed, but I had her pinned down under my four glorious legs. *Look, Professor, look at what four beautiful limbs can do! Do you understand now?* She was quaking as my head bowed towards her and I bared my fangs. She struggled underneath me, and I could see real tears coming out of her eyes as she pushed and shoved on the muddy grass. Her breath turned to short pants, I watched her neck heave up and down. So bare a neck, so easy it would have been to just sink my teeth into.

But then, all I wanted to do was show her.

I leaped away and Professor Brewhaha gave a little yelp of mixed relief and surprise. I knew I looked spectacular, my golden-brown body dashing away in the silky night, bathed in moonlight. Part of me hoped she was watching as I went.

And part of me didn't care. I didn't care what Professor Brewhaha thought of me anymore. I knew I just loved being a bitch.

EDITOR BIOGRAPHY

SHANNON PAGE was born on Halloween night and spent her early years on a commune in northern California's backwoods. A childhood without television gave her a great love of books and the worlds she found in them. She has published several dozen short stories, and her first two novels are appearing within the year. As an editor for Per Aspera Press, she looks for unusual fantasy stories with complex and interesting characters. She also loves editing anthologies. Shannon is a longtime yoga practitioner, has no tattoos, and is an avid gardener at home in Portland, Oregon. Visit her at www.shannonpage.net.

AUTHOR BIOGRAPHIES

BO BALDER resides in the Netherlands, where she is a writer, counselor, painter and avid knitter. Bo has always wanted to be an SFF writer. For that reason, she practiced a series of pointless yet for a writer vital professions like dishwasher, rowing coach, computer programmer, model and management consultant. She's a graduate of Viable Paradise Writer's Workshop. More work by Bo can be found at Bewildering Stories, in the *Ancient New Anthology* by Deepwood Press, several Dutch print publications and at www.boukjebalder.nl.

STEPHANIE BISSETTE-ROARK is a writer of horror, fantasy, and poetry. Her two close encounters with death in childhood led to a lifelong fascination with the macabre. Stephanie holds a BA in History from Pacific Lutheran University, which she judiciously ignores when writing her speculative fiction. When not writing, her hobbies include gardening, thrift-store shopping, roleplaying, and adding to her ever-increasing stash of tea. She lives in Tacoma, Washington, with her husband, Matthew, and their two wrasslin' cats. This anthology features her first published story.

KATE BRANDT wanted to be a witch since she was nine years old. That was the year she began to make potions: concoctions of secret ingredients she kept in old whiskey bottles and lined up along the bookshelves in her bedroom. Older, she lives by the power of the pen. She teaches adult literacy in New York City, and writes whenever she finds the time. Her work has appeared in *Talking Writing*, *Literary Mama*, and *Tricycle: the Buddhist Review*.

BOB BROWN lives, works, and writes with his two pugs, two cats, and several dozen chickens in Washington state. He is the author of numerous short stories and the recently released children's book, *The Damsel, the Dragon, and the Knight*. He is currently working on several projects including a space opera techno thriller with Irene Radford. He is well known in the science fiction convention community as RadCon Bob, due in part to the nature of his work as a Health Physicist at the Hanford Nuclear Reservation where he supports cleanup of nuclear waste left over from the Cold War. Bob is an avid gardener and a teller of chicken jokes.

ALAINA EWING lives in the Pacific Northwest with her husband and two boys. She holds a degree in Multimedia Production and is the Assistant Director for Cascade Writers, a nonprofit Milford-style workshop. She also makes jewelry, dream catchers, and enjoys working with herbs and essential oils. Her first novel, *The Heart-Shaped Emblor*, releases in the fall of 2013 with Evil Girlfriend Media. The novel is the first in the Ewlishash Series. Read more about Alaina at www.alainayewing.com.

J. H. FLEMING received her Bachelor's in Creative Writing from the University of Central Arkansas. While attending college her play, "Cheats and Liars," was performed by Alpha Psi Omega, a theater fraternity. Her first publication was "The Lady of the Fog," which appeared in Issue 27 of *Visionary Tongue*, a dark fantasy magazine out of England. In addition to writing fantastical short stories and novels, she spends her free time reading as many books as she can get her hands on, learning piano, playing video games, and watching anime. She is currently hard at work on several short stories and novels in Northwest Arkansas, where she lives with her Yorkie and two turtles.

REBECCA FUNG is a legal editor from Sydney, Australia. By day she fiercely, mercilessly hacks up, strips down, and pieces together manuscripts, by night she shamelessly (attempts to) create them. She has previously published her short fiction in *Eclecticism Magazine* and in Strange Weird and Wonderful's anthology *The Inanimates* I. Her next stories will be released in Fringeworks' *Potatoes!* and *Grimm and Grimmer* anthologies in 2013.

CAMILLE GRIEP lives and writes north of Seattle, Washington, though she still claims her birthright as a Montanan. Her fiction has been featured in The *Lascaux Review, Bound Off, The First Line*, and *Every Day Fiction*, in addition to other fine journals and anthologies. When she's not hard at work on her first novel, she's stumbling through ballet class, muddling a sonatina on the piano, or refusing to follow the recipe. She can be found @camillethegriep on Twitter or at www.camillegriep.com.

CAREN GUSSOFF is an SF writer living in Seattle, WA. The author of *Homecoming* (2000) and *The Wave and Other Stories* (2003), first published by Serpent's Tail/High Risk Books, Gussoff's been published in anthologies by Seal Press, Prime Books, and Hadley Rille, as well as in *Abyss & Apex, Cabinet des Fées* and *Fantasy Magazine*. She received her MFA from the School of the Art Institute of Chicago, and in 2008, was the Carl Brandon Society's Octavia E. Butler Scholar at Clarion West. Her new novel, *The Birthday Problem*, will be published by Pink Narcissus Press in 2014. Find her online at @spitkitten, facebook.com/spitkitten, and at spitkitten.com.

GABRIELLE HARBOWY (gabrielle-edits.com) wears many hats: a professional editor of fantasy and science fiction, a published author of short fiction, and an award-nominated anthologist. She is Managing Editor at Dragon Moon Press, and a copyeditor for publishers including Pyr Books. Her anthologies *When the Hero Comes Home* and *When the Villain Comes Home*—co-edited with Ed Greenwood—are soon to be joined by the forthcoming *When the Hero Comes Home 2.* In her copious spare time between editing projects, Gabrielle is working on her first novel and teaching herself to play the harp.

TOM HOWARD doesn't dream, or if he does, he never recalls them in the morning. Imagine his surprise when he awoke with Mrs. Briarwood's scolding still ringing in his ears and the dream world she and her husband inhabited vivid in his memory. He had apparently let his critique group's former beta reader, Kelly, sell her beauty parlor and move to Arizona! Considering Kelly doesn't own a beauty parlor and happily resides in Little Rock, Arkansas, Tom took this dream as a sign he'd better give his friend a call. In the meantime, he jotted down the dream, ran it by the Central Arkansas Speculative Fiction Writers' Group and the Oklahoma City Dorsal Fin critique groups, and sent it to this tailor-made anthology. Enjoy!

KODIAK JULIAN is worried that she isn't a sherpa or a trapeze artist or a magician. She's angry about the trip she hasn't taken to Buenos Aires and about the friends she hasn't called. She is excited about walking as dusk lingers in her summer neighborhood. She's eager to see pea shoots climbing in her garden and a cloud of bats fluttering from their roost. Kodiak is in love with fighting for social justice in her day job. She's smitten with her husband and their little boy, with living in Yakima, Washington, with Mount Rainier. Kodiak Julian longs to live with all the colors shining.

EVA LANGSTON received her MFA from the University of New Orleans, and her fiction has been published in *The Normal School, The Sand Hill Review*, and the *GW Review*, among others. She is a frequent contributor to Burlesque Press and is trying to figure out how to make writing her full-time job. For the time being, she works as a Skype tutor for Ukrainians and a math curriculum consultant. Follow her adventures at inthegardenofeva. com.

JULIE MCGALLIARD is a writer, occasional cartoonist, and trained ghost hunter. In her day job at Seattle Children's Hospital Research Institute she is not, strictly speaking, a scientist, but she is a scientist enabler. She is a 2006 graduate of Clarion West, and lives in Seattle.

CHRISTINE MORGAN works the overnight shift in a psychiatric facility and divides her writing time among many genres. A lifelong reader, she also writes, reviews, beta-reads, occasionally edits and dabbles in self-publishing. Among her most recent novels are *Murder Girls*, about college housemates who decide to become serial killers, and *The Horned Ones*, in which a disaster traps tourists in a scenic show-cave. Her stories have appeared in more than two dozen anthologies, 'zines and e-chapbooks. She's been nominated for the Origins Award and made Honorable Mention in two volumes of Year's Best Fantasy and Horror. Her husband is a game designer, her daughter was published in a zombie anthology at fourteen and plans to major in psychology and film. A future crazy-cat-lady, Christine's other interests include gaming, history, superheroes, crafts, and cheesy disaster movies. Lately, she's discovered a love for Viking-themed horror and dark fantasy, with several such stories already written and a blood-soaked novel called *The Slaughter* in the works.

GARTH UPSHAW: When not breeding tarantulas or raising guinea pigs for food, Garth pedals his trusty bike around the soggy streets of Portland, Oregon, using his super powers for light and truth and justice. His stories have appeared in *Clarkesworld, Beneath Ceaseless Skies, Realms* *of Fantasy*, and other stellar publications. He lives in a creaky old Victorian house with crooked floors and spiderwebs in the corners. Garth shares the space with his genius wife, Katrina, two precocious children, Kami and Luken, and a basement tenant he never sees. By day, he develops Android applications that will change the world.

7556477R00165